**It's their last summer of being single!
Off duty, these three nurses, and one
midwife, are young, free and fabulous—**
for the moment...

Work hard and play hard could be flatmates
Ruby, Ellie, Jess and Tilly's motto.
By day these three trainee nurses and
one newly qualified midwife are lifesavers
at Eastern Beaches hospital, but by night
they're seeking love in Sydney—
and only sexy doctors need apply!

Together they've made it through their
first year in hospital, with shatteringly
emotional shifts, tough new bosses and
patching together broken hearts
from inappropriate crushes over a glass of wine
(or two!)

Read on to meet the drop-dead gorgeous doc
who sweeps Ruby out of her scrubs!
Tilly's story is also available this month in
SURVIVAL GUIDE TO DATING YOUR BOSS
by Fiona McArthur. And look out for Ellie and
Jess's stories, coming next month.

We can't wait!

CORT MASON—
DR DELECTABLE

BY
CAROL MARINELLI

MILLS
BOON

First published in Great Britain 2011
by Mills & Boon, an imprint of Harlequin (UK) Limited.
Large Print edition 2012
Harlequin (UK) Limited, Eton House,
18-24 Paradise Road, Richmond, Surrey TW9 1SR

© Carol Marinelli 2011

ISBN: 978 0 263 22434 4

Harlequin (UK) policy is to use papers that are natural, renewable and recyclable products and made from wood grown in sustainable forests. The logging and manufacturing process conform to the legal environmental regulations of the country of origin.

Printed and bound in Great Britain
by CPI Antony Rowe, Chippenham, Wiltshire

Carol Marinelli recently filled in a form where she was asked for her job title and was thrilled, after all these years, to be able to put down her answer as 'writer'. Then it asked what Carol did for relaxation. After chewing her pen for a moment Carol put down the truth—'writing'. The third question asked—'What are your hobbies?' Well, not wanting to look obsessed or, worse still, boring, she crossed the fingers on her free hand and answered 'swimming and tennis'. But, given that the chlorine in the pool does terrible things to her highlights, and the closest she's got to a tennis racket in the last couple of years is watching the Australian Open, I'm sure you can guess the real answer!

Also by Carol Marinelli:

Medical™ Romance
HER LITTLE SECRET
ST PIRAN'S: RESCUING PREGNANT
  CINDERELLA*
KNIGHT ON THE CHILDREN'S WARD
ONE TINY MIRACLE…

Modern™
HEART OF THE DESERT
THE DEVIL WEARS KOLOVSKY
THE LAST KOLOVSKY PLAYBOY

St Piran's Hospital

Did you know these are also available as eBooks?
Visit www.millsandboon.co.uk

If you love Carol Marinelli,
you'll fall head over heels for Carol's
sparkling, touching, witty debut
Putting Alice Back Together—
available from MIRA Books

PROLOGUE

'You need to get back out there, Cort.'

'Leave it, Elise.'

'I won't leave it,' his sister said.

'Beth's only been dead for a month—do you really think it appropriate that I start getting "back out there"?'

And on anyone else his argument would have worked, but his sister was too matter-of-fact, and had been there through it all, and would not be swayed.

'You've been grieving for her for years,' Elise said. 'You mourned Beth long, long, long before she died.'

'So now I should suddenly start partying?'

'You've never partied in your life.' Elise grinned at her rather serious older brother. 'So, no, I don't expect you to start at thirty-two.' Elise had come here not just to see how her brother was doing since Beth's death but with intention too, and she was determined to see this conversation through. 'But there is more to life than work. You need to start going out a bit, do something you haven't done before, try new things...'

Cort knew she was right—had it been Elise in his position he'd have said exactly the same, except he just didn't know how to start. Cort had moved back to Sydney three years ago and had chosen not to tell his colleagues about his *other* life in Melbourne. He had moved back to Sydney to get away from the endless questions from colleagues, and pointless platitudes that did nothing to help.

The last years had been spent working in Sydney and then travelling back to Melbourne on his days off to sit in a nursing home and watch a woman who had once been so educated, so dignified, dribble her food and strip naked at whim. He had watched endless seizures erode what had been left of her brain and, yes, Elise was right—bit by bit, over these past years he had mourned.

'Say yes.' Elise drained her glass and bade her brother goodnight.

'Say yes to what?' Cort asked.

'Just say yes next time someone suggests something.'

'Sure,' Cort said with absolutely no intention of doing so.

'For Beth,' Elise said as she headed to his apartment door. 'She'd hate both your lives to have been cut short that night.'

She was right.

Cort knew that. He crossed his apartment and could hear the ocean from the open French doors, but he closed them to shut out the roar and the noise, and the room fell silent. Not just from the sound of the ocean but from the roar and the noise in his head.

Beth was gone.

CHAPTER ONE

'ARE you free to give me a hand in the suture room?' Cort Mason, the senior emergency registrar, asked, and Ruby swung around. 'It might take a while, though.'

Ruby jumped down from the footstool she was perched on while restocking the cupboard and turned to the voice that was aimed in her direction. She decided that she'd be delighted to give him a hand.

It had nothing to do with the fact he was gorgeous.

Really, it had completely nothing to do with it.

She just wanted an empty Resus before it filled again, which it inevitably would. Sheila, the NUM, had told her to stay in there today, that this was her area, but with a senior registrar asking for her to assist with a patient, well, surely she had no choice in the matter?

None.

'I'd be happy to.' Ruby beamed, except her smile wasn't returned. In fact, he wasn't even waiting for her response. Already Cort had walked off and was heading into the suture room, rightly perhaps assuming that a student nurse wasn't likely to say no to his request for assistance.

'Mr Mason has asked if I can give him a hand.' Ruby let Connor, the RN in charge of Resus, know where she was going. 'Is that okay?'

'Sure,' Connor said. 'It's not as if we're doing anything.' He frowned at her. 'Ruby, why have you got a crepe bandage in your hair?'

'Sheila!' Ruby rolled her eyes, because the NUM was surely out to get her. Not only had she insisted that Ruby be allocated the most grisly part of Emergency, she also had a thing about Ruby's long auburn hair, which was so thick it often defied the hair ties and clips she attempted to hold it back with. This afternoon Sheila had handed her a bandage and told her to sort it once and for all.

'She's really got it in for you.'

'I remind her of her daughter apparently—I've no idea why. Anyway, Mr Mason will be wondering where I've got to. He said it might take a while.'

'You might as well go to coffee afterwards, then,' Connor said. 'And we're on first-name terms here—it's Cort.'

She'd stick with 'Mr Mason'—her dad was Chief of Surgery at another hospital and had drilled it into her over the years just how important titles were so Ruby had decided it was better to play safe than offend anyone.

She had a quick look around for Sheila and seeing she was busy up the other end darted off, more relieved than Connor could know. Sheila had been very specific in her allocation, ensuring that Ruby was working in Resus, but apart from a febrile convulsion and couple of patients who had been brought over briefly while awaiting blood results it had been delightfully quiet.

'Put some gloves on,' Cort said as she entered the suture room. 'I just need someone to hold Ted's arm while I suture it. He keeps forgetting to stay still, don't you, Ted?'

The elderly man grunted and Ruby could smell the brandy fumes that filled the small room.

'How are you, Ted?' Ruby asked, pulling on some gloves and looking at the wound, happy, though not for the patient, to see it was a huge cut that *would* hopefully take ages, and then it would be time for her coffee break and with her assessment and everything, well, she might just not have to go back out there.

She loathed Accident and Emergency, not that anyone could tell. She was always light, breezy and happy and had chosen not to tell even her closest friends just how hard this final unit of her training had been, knowing there was nothing they could do to fix it and choosing just to soldier on.

She had never expected to like it, but the loathing was so acute Ruby was seriously wondering if she would even make it through these last weeks of her training. There was no tangible reason for hating it, nothing Ruby could point to as the reason she hated it so, but walking to her shift, every ambulance that passed, every glimpse of Eastern Beaches Hospital made her want to turn tail and run for home.

Looking back, there had been a few wobbles that might have given warning that Emergency might be unsettling for her—a young man suddenly collapsing after a routine appendectomy and the crash team being called while she was on the surgical ward had stunned Ruby and made her question her decision to study nursing—but she had, for the most part, liked her training. Only liked, though—her real aim was to work as a mental health nurse, but general training was a prerequisite if she wanted to get anywhere in her future career.

'Okay?' Cort said. 'We might be here a while, so I'd make yourself comfortable.'

He took off his jacket and tied on a plastic gown, then washed his hands, dragged a stool over with his foot and settled in for the long haul.

'He's asleep,' Ruby said, stating the obvious, because Ted was snoring loudly now, and even Ruby could see that she might be better utilised elsewhere.

'I don't want to wrestle with him if he wakes up.' He gave a tight smile. 'Sorry if it's boring.'

'Oh, I'm not bored. I'm *delighted* to be here,' Ruby said, hearing a noise from outside, a relative arguing with a security guard close to the suture-room door. She gave Cort a wide smile, a smile so bright that he hesitated for a moment before returning it with a slightly bemused one, then he turned his attention back to his patient.

He cleaned the wound and injected anaesthetic as Ruby watched and only then did he offer a response, not looking at her, just concentrating on the wound as he spoke.

'It's not often you hear that in this place.'

'What?' Ruby asked, her mind elsewhere.

'People saying that they're delighted to be here.'

'I'm a happy apple,' Ruby said, and watched as his hands stopped, the first knot of the stitch neatly tied. He seemed to be waiting for her to do something.

'Are you going to cut?'

'Oh!' She picked up the scissors with her free hand. 'I feel like a real nurse. Where do I cut?' She held the scissors over the thread.

'A bit shorter.'

There was something lovely and soothing about sitting here and actually doing something, rather than just holding the patient's hand. And contrary to what she'd heard, Cort Mason was far from grumpy. One on one with him, he was really rather nice.

She'd heard his name mentioned a lot of times. He'd been on annual leave for the first four weeks of her time here and had only been back a week, but he was nothing like the man she'd imagined, the staid man her colleagues had led her to believe he was.

Nothing.

From the way she'd heard people speaking about him Ruby had expected a dour serious man in his fifties.

Instead he'd be in his thirties, with brown hair and hazel eyes, a long straight nose and, not so much dour, or sharp, just… She couldn't really sum him up in word, and she tried for a moment.

Outside the suture room, she'd never been privy to small talk with him, had never really seen him smile. He was formal with the patients, distant with the staff, and any hint of ineptness or bureaucracy seemed to irritate him.

Crabby was the best she could come up with.

Except he wasn't being crabby now.

Ruby looked at his white thick cotton shirt and lilac tie, which was an odd sort of match for his brown suit, yet it went really well and she wondered, just for a second, how it was really possible to find someone who wore a brown suit attractive—except he was.

Up close he really, really was.

There was a lovely fresh scent to him and she thought it came from his hair, which was very close to her face as he bent over to work. She looked at it, and it was lovely and glossy and very straight and neat but there was a jagged edge to the cut that she liked too.

'Cut,' Cort reminded her when her eyes wandered, and she snipped the neat stitch he'd tied. 'I need some more 4/0.'

'You're really making me earn my keep!' Ruby jumped off the stool and tried to locate what he wanted amongst box upon box of different sutures.

'Left,' Cort said, to her hand that hovered. 'Up one,' he said.

'Got it.' She opened the material and tipped it on his tray then washed her hands and again pulled on some gloves before rejoining him. Cort was having another good look at the wound so there was nothing much for her to do and her eyes roamed the room again, landing on his jacket hanging on the door.

'It's not really brown,' she said out loud, and then she blushed, because she did this far too often. Ruby had zero attention span and her mind was constantly chatting and occasionally words just slipped out.

He glanced up and saw her cheeks were bright pink.

'Your jacket,' Ruby croaked. 'It's not really brown.'

He said nothing, just carried on checking the

wound, but his lips twitched for a moment, because he'd had a similar discussion with the shop assistant.

Sick to the back teeth of dour greys and navy suits, he'd bought a couple of new ones, and some shirts and ties. He wasn't a great shopper, hated it, in fact, and had decided to put his faith in the judgement of the eager shop assistant. But when she'd held up the suit he'd baulked and said there was no way he was wearing brown.

Brown was the sort of thing his father wore, Cort had said to her.

'It's not brown,' the shop assistant had said. 'It's taupe.'

'It's taupe.' After a few minutes' silence, he glanced up to the rather surprised eyes of Ruby. 'Apparently.'

'Well, it's very nice.'

And he didn't *quite* smile, but there was just a hint as he got back to his stitches and he saw her hands were just a little bit shaky when she snipped, though he was sure they had been steady before.

He didn't look up, but he could see her in his mind's eye for a moment. She was quite a stunning little thing—tiny, with very dark brown eyes and a thick curtain of hair that he'd heard Sheila pull her up about a few times. It was held back today with a ridiculous bandage, but defiantly kept escaping. It was lovely hair, red but not...

'It's not really ginger...' Cort said, and still didn't look up.

'Absolutely not,' was Ruby's response.

'Auburn?'

'Close,' came her voice. 'But I prefer titian.'

And he gave a very brief nod and then worked on quietly. It was actually a lovely silence, just nice to sit and watch him work, especially as she could hear things starting to pick up outside. She could hear Connor calling out for assistance and feet running and though it was par for the course here, she screwed her eyes closed for just a second, but he must have looked up and noticed.

'You okay?'

'I'm fine.'

'You don't need to cut if it's making you feel sick—just hold his hand.'

'Really, I'm fine,' Ruby said, because a nasty cut and tendons and muscle and all of that didn't bother her a jot.

It was out there that did.

It wasn't a fear of seeing people sick, Ruby thought as she snipped Cort's stitches, and it wasn't a fear of death because she'd actually enjoyed some agency shifts on the palliative care ward.

It was *this*, Ruby thought as a buzzer sounded and Cort looked up.

This moment, which arrived at any given time, the intense drama that was constantly played out here, and it actually made her feel physically ill.

'Do you need me?' She heard Cort shout in

the direction of Resus, ready to drop everything at a moment's notice, and Ruby sat, staring at the hand she was holding, sweat beading on her forehead. She would hold this hand all night if only it meant that she didn't have to go out there.

'Jamelia's here,' came Sheila's voice, and because apparently Cort liked to be kept up to date with everything, her voice came closer to the open suture-room door.

'We've got a head and facial injuries. He arrested at the approach to the hospital and they're having trouble intubating.'

'I'll come.'

'There's no need,' Sheila called. 'Jamelia's got it and the anaesthetist is on his way.' But he wasn't listening. Already he'd peeled off his gloves and was pulling off his plastic apron. 'Wait here,' he called over his shoulder. Given he was halfway through stitching, and the patient couldn't be left, Ruby had no choice but to sit and wait, which she did for a full ten or fifteen minutes before Cort returned, and if she'd seen him crabby this past week, he was really angry now.

She could feel it as he tied on a new gown and washed his hands.

'What the hell was that?' Sheila was less than impressed as she swung into the room. 'I told you we had it under control.'

'No. You told me they were having trouble intubating. Jamelia gets nervous...'

'Well, she's never going to get any confidence if you keep coming in and taking over.'

'So, what?' Cort said. 'Do we just let her stumble through and kill off a few more brain cells?'

'Give her a go, would you?' Sheila responded.

'No,' Cort said, and didn't qualify further, even as Sheila waited, but when Cort remained silent, Sheila turned her frustration back to its regular recipient.

'What are you doing here, Ruby? I told you! I specifically told you not to leave Resus.'

'Mr Mason asked me to come and hold an arm.' Ruby gulped.

'Someone else could have done that. Now you've missed watching an emergency tracheotomy…'

'Oh.' Ruby wondered how she could even attempt to sound disappointed at having missed out on seeing that! 'That's a shame.'

'A shame?' Sheila replied. 'Are you being sarcastic?'

'I asked her to come in here.' Cort intervened as Ruby struggled for a better response. 'She was sorting out a cupboard, so I thought I'd give her—'

'I'll deal with my nurses, thanks, Cort.' She turned back to Ruby. 'I'm sick of this, Ruby…' She shook her head in frustration. 'I haven't got time for this right now. I'll speak to you at your assessment this evening. Bring a coffee,' she added. 'We might be there for a while.'

Sheila stormed off, and Cort carried on stitching as Ruby sat there with cheeks flaming. Cort knew that if he didn't deal with this situation now, he'd forget about it or miss out on seeing Sheila later, and with a small hiss born of frustration and anger he stood again, peeled off another pair of gloves and waded out into the department, leaving Ruby sitting there.

'It's not her fault.' Cort walked into Resus and straight up to Sheila, who was coming off the phone to ICU. 'What is a student supposed to say when a senior registrar asks her to come and do something for him? She checked with Connor...'

'Ruby finds excuses all the time, Cort,' Sheila said. 'She'd do anything to avoid work and you just gave her the perfect excuse. She searches for them...'

'She didn't, though,' Cort said. 'I approached her.'

'Fine,' Sheila said. 'I'll bear it in mind. Right now I've got more important things to deal with.' Cort looked over to the screened area where

Sheila was heading, where the team was working solidly. He caught Jamelia's eye and she came
over.

'Thanks, Cort.' Jamelia meant it. The hellish
intubation had turned into a nightmare just as
Cort had arrived and she was incredibly grateful
that Cort had taken over when he had.

'Call for help,' Cort said, 'preferably before you
really need it.'

Jamelia nodded.

'So,' Ruby said when he returned to the suture
room. 'It looks like we're both in trouble.'

'I'm not in trouble,' Cort said. 'I'm just running
out of size 9 gloves.'

He sat down and blew up his hair, because it
really was warm in the suture room and he was
still so angry he could spit. 'There's a big difference,' he said, 'between hero and ego. If you take
anything from this place—take that.'

Ruby nodded.

'I told Sheila it wasn't your fault,' he added as she snipped the last of the stitches.

'Thanks,' Ruby said. 'Though I doubt it will help.'

He wanted to ask more, wanted to find out why she was in trouble, but he didn't want to wonder more about her as well. She stayed quiet as he finished the neat row of sutures then he asked her to put on a dressing, thanked her for her help, peeled off the plastic gloves and washed his hands.

'Cort.' Jamelia came to the door and it sounded an awful lot as if she'd been crying. 'Would you mind…?' She gave a small swallow. 'Would you mind talking to the relatives for me?'

'I'll come and take a look at him first.' Cort nodded and picked up his jacket just as Sheila bustled in.

'Jamelia, the relatives really do need to be spoken to ASAP.'

'I'm going to do it,' Cort said.

'You go with Cort.' Sheila glanced over at Ruby. 'I'll finish up in here.'

Ruby would have preferred an emergency tracheotomy, even ten of them, rather than the prospect of sitting with relatives as bad news was delivered, and she fumbled for yet another excuse. 'Connor said I was to go straight to coffee after doing this.'

'You couldn't say no to the senior reg when he asked you to do something for him, I can understand that.' Sheila fixed her with a stare. 'So don't say no to the NUM.'

Ruby nodded and swallowed and glanced up to Cort.

'Come on,' he said. 'I just want to see for myself how he is first.'

They walked into Resus and the anaesthetist gave Cort a full briefing. Ruby stood quietly and looked at the young man for a moment then looked away as Cort examined his eyes and his ears and checked his reflexes for himself. She could hear all the anaesthetist was saying and it sounded a lot less than hopeful.

'Let's do this, then.'

They walked down the corridor to the little interview room and just as they got there, Ruby was quite sure that she couldn't go in.

'I don't know what to say,' she admitted, and Cort turned round briefly.

'You don't have to say anything,' Cort said. 'Come on.'

And she wanted to turn, wanted to run. For a full three seconds she seriously considered it, except he'd knocked and opened the door and there was a whole family whose eyes turned anxiously towards them. A nurse running off would only terrify them more than they were already.

It was the only reason she forced herself to go in.

CHAPTER TWO

COULD he not give them a little more hope?

Ruby sat in with the family and listened as Cort gave the grim diagnosis.

'The paramedics were unable to intubate him,' Cort reiterated.

'But he was bagged…' The young man's sister was a nurse and she was absolutely not having it, refusing to accept the grim diagnosis. 'He would have got some oxygen. And it was just a couple of minutes from the hospital when he went into respiratory arrest.'

'Yes,' Cort said. 'However, his airway was severely obstructed, so we're not sure how effective that was. His head injuries are extensive too,' he added, and the ping-pong match went on as Ruby sat there, the family demanding more hope than Cort would permit.

'We're going to move him up to ICU within the next half hour—they're just preparing for him.'

'Can we see him first?'

'Briefly,' Cort said, then he warned them all what to expect and Ruby just sat there. He told them it would be a little while till they were able to go in, but someone would be along just as soon as they could to fetch them.

And as Ruby stared at her knees, she tried not to cry as Cort finished the interview.

'I really am very sorry.'

'Don't be sorry,' the sister answered tartly. 'Just save him.'

'I see from his notes that he's Catholic,' Cort said. 'Would you like us to arrange the priest to visit him?'

Ruby thought she might stand and run out of there as the family started really sobbing, but at that point Cort stood.

'Someone will be in shortly.'

'Could you not have been a bit gentler with them?' Ruby asked when they were outside.

'Why?' Cort asked. 'Soon they're going to be approached to consider organ donation...'

'Excuse me.'

He watched as she walked quickly to the patient toilet and he thought of waiting till she came out, but it wasn't his problem. Instead he went and spoke to Connor then gave ICU a ring. He then found Jamelia in tears in his office and dealt with her as kindly as he could. Vomiting nurses and emergency doctors who couldn't deal with emergencies really weren't his problem.

He actually felt sorry for Jamelia.

A temporary locum, she had worked mainly in the country and simply wasn't used to the volume of patients that came through Eastern Beaches' doors. She was filling big shoes too—Nick, a popular locum, was on his honeymoon, and though their paths had never crossed, Cort knew the energy and fun he had brought to this difficult place. Jamelia told him that after Nick, and with Cort now back, she felt as though she was a disappointment to everyone. So after a long chat with Jamelia he headed to the kitchen, where someone had made a pot of tea. He poured himself a cup, then frowned at the watery fluid and opened the lid of the pot, only to see a pile of leaves and herbs. He made a mug of coffee instead and headed for the staffroom.

'Why is there a garden growing in the teapot?' he asked, and sat down.

'Ruby's herbs!' Siobhan, another nurse on duty, rolled her eyes. 'Just in case your immune system needs boosting.'

'I'll stick with caffeine, thanks.'

He glanced over to where Ruby sat, reading a book on her coffee break, her complexion a touch whiter than it had been in the suture room.

'Where's Jamelia?' Doug, the consultant, popped his head in. 'Hiding in the office again?'

'Go easy,' Cort sighed.

'Someone has to say something,' Doug said.

'I just have.'

'Okay.' Doug nodded. 'I'll leave her for now.'

'You know what they say...' Siobhan yawned and stretched out her legs. 'If you can't stand the heat...'

And Ruby couldn't stand this place.

They just spoke about everything and anyone wherever they wanted, just bitched and dissected people, and didn't care who heard. She couldn't stand Siobhan and her snide comments, and she really thought she might say something, just might stand up and tell her what an absolute bitch she was, that any normal person would be sitting in an office sobbing when a twenty-three-year-old was going to die. That laughing and joking and eating chocolate and watching television as the priest walked past the staffroom was bizarre behaviour.

'Ruby.' It was Sheila who popped her head

round the door now. 'Are you finished your break?'

'Yes.' She closed the book she had seemed so focused on, except she had never turned a page, Cort realised as she stood up.

'Come into my office then—bring a drink if you want to.'

'Sure.'

He could see two spots of red on the apple of her cheeks, could see the effort behind her bright smile as a couple of staff offered their best wishes as she headed out of the room, then Siobhan called out to her as she reached the door.

'Ruby, can you empty out the teapot when you use it?' Siobhan said.

'Sure.'

'Only it's annoying,' Siobhan said. 'Perhaps you could bring in your own teapot?'

Cort watched the set of her shoulders, saw her turn and look over at Siobhan, and for a second she looked as if she was about to say something less than pleasant, but instead she gave that wide smile. 'Fine,' Ruby said, and headed off for her assessment.

'Love to be a fly on the wall!' Siobhan smirked. 'Sheila's going to rip her in two.'

Someone else sniggered and Cort just sat there.

'What is it with her bloody herbs?' Siobhan just would not let up and Cort was about to tell her to do just that, but he knew what would happen if he did—there'd be rumours then that he was sticking up for a certain nurse, that he fancied her.

But Siobhan was still banging on and his mood was less than pleasant.

'Her immune system probably needs all the help it can get in this place,' Cort said as he stood up and headed out of the staffroom. 'Given how toxic this place can be at times.'

CHAPTER THREE

THEY could fail her.

Ruby tried not to think about it as she stalled the car coming out of the staff car park. There were new boom gates and the car was so low that, as she leant out of the window to swipe her ID card, it stalled and, grinding the gears in the shiny silver sports car all the way home she wished, not for the first time, that her brother had bought an automatic.

Normally she walked or took the bus to work, but it was Saturday and she'd promised her housemates to get home as soon as she could and meet them at the Stat Bar, so had taken the car. But as she pulled into Hill Street, the temptation to change her mind and forgo the rapid change of clothes and mad dash out was almost overwhelming—a noisy bar was the last place she wanted to be tonight.

Far preferable would it be to curl up on the sofa and just hide, but she'd had two excited texts from Tilly already, urging her to get there ASAP because she had some wonderful news.

Ruby let herself into the house and could smell the perfume her housemates had left behind on their way out. There was a bottle of wine opened on the kitchen table and a box of chocolates too. How much nicer it would be to pour a glass of wine and sit in the darkness alone with chocolate than head out there, but then they'd ring her, Ruby realised, and as if to prove the point her mobile shrilled.

'Where are you?' Tilly demanded.

She was about to say that she was going to give it a miss, but could not face the barrage of questions. 'I'm just getting changed.'

'Well, hurry. I'll look out for you.'

Ruby trudged up the stairs, had a rapid shower

then tried to work out what to wear—nothing in her wardrobe, or over the chair, or on the floor, matched her mood.

And it wasn't just what Sheila had said that was upsetting her. As she'd headed away from her hellish shift and a very prolonged assessment, she'd passed the young man's family, comforting each other outside the hospital—and worse, far worse, the daughter had come over and thanked her.

For what? Ruby had wanted to ask, because she'd done absolutely nothing.

'You were lovely with Mum,' the daughter had said, and only then had Ruby recalled that when Cort had asked them about the priest she'd found herself holding the woman's hand.

Their grief was so palpable, so thick and real that it seemed to have followed her home, and despite the shower it felt as if it had seeped into her skin.

'Come on, Ruby,' she told herself. She turned

on some music and danced around the room for a moment, doing all she could to raise her spirits.

And it worked a bit because she selected a nice cream skirt and a backless halter-neck top, pulled on all her silver bangles and put big silver earrings on. Looking in the mirror, Ruby decided that with a nice dash of lipstick she could pass as happy.

She didn't feel quite so brave, though, as she walked down Hill Street, turned the corner and walked past the New-Age shop she had worked in for two years after finishing school. She'd been happy then, if a little restless. Her desk had been stuffed with nursing brochures and forms and she had tried to pluck up the courage to apply to study nursing, telling herself she could do it, that even if didn't appeal, she could get through her general training and then go on to work in mental health.

It would seem she'd been wrong.

She could hear the noise and laughter from

the beer garden, knew her friends were wondering where she had got to, and she stood outside for a moment and pretended to read a text on her phone. She looked out at Coogee Beach and longed to walk there in the darkness and gather her thoughts.

'Ruby!' Tilly, her housemate, caught her just as her decision to wander was made. 'Finally you're here!' Tilly said, and then frowned. 'Are you okay?' Tilly always looked out for her, for all the girls really. Ruby wondered whether she should just come out and say that Sheila had warned her that unless things improved she was going to have to repeat her Emergency rotation, except Ruby remembered that Tilly had news of her own and was desperate to tell her friend.

'I'm fine. So what's your news?'

Tilly's face spread into a smile. She was a redhead too, but there the similarities ended. Her hair was lighter and much curlier than Ruby's and Tilly was taller and a calmer, more centred person. Also unlike Ruby, she was totally in love with her work. 'I delivered an unexpected breech today. Ruby, it was brilliant, the best feeling ever.' Tilly was a newly qualified midwife and babies, mothers, bonding, skin to skin were absolutely her passion. Even if Ruby could think of nothing more terrifying than delivering a breech baby, she knew this was food for Tilly's soul.

'That's brilliant.' Ruby didn't force her smile and hug. She was genuinely thrilled for Tilly.

'I just saw this little bottom…' Tilly gushed. 'I called for help but as quickly as that he just unfolded, his little legs and hips came out and he just hung there. Mum was amazing. I mean just amazing…'

Ruby stood and listened as Tilly gave her the first of no doubt many detailed accounts of how the senior midwife had let her finish the job, how the doctor had arrived just as the delivery was complete.

'I'm talking too much,' Tilly said.

'You're not!'

'Come on,' Tilly said. 'Your mob are here too.'

'My mob?' Ruby asked as they walked in. 'You're my mob!'

'There are loads from Emergency here.'

God, that was all she needed. Half of Ruby's problem with Emergency was that she didn't like the staff. Okay, it was probably an eighth of her problem, but they were just so confident, so cliquey, and so bloody bitchy as well, and close proximity to them was so not needed tonight.

Ruby walked in and straight over to her friends, deliberately pretending not to even see the rowdy Emergency crowd and hoping that they wouldn't see her. Not that there was much chance of that. With her long auburn hair she always stood out, but they'd hardly be wanting a student nurse to join them, she consoled herself.

'Here she is!' Jess, another housemate, had already bought her a beer and Ruby took a sip as Jess asked how her shift had gone.

'Long,' Ruby said, and she did what she always did and smiled, because she was a happy person, a positive, outgoing, slightly flaky person—it was just Emergency that affected her so much. 'Where's Ellie?'

'Chatting up "the one".' Jess grinned and nodded over to the bar, where Ellie was sitting on some guy's lap, the pair earnestly talking, utterly engrossed and oblivious to everyone around them. Ruby laughed, because for the next few weeks he would be all they heard about. Ellie, determined to find her life partner and get the family she craved, drifted happily from boyfriend to boyfriend in her quest for 'the one', but as Ruby turned back to Jess and Tilly, her eyes drifted to the emergency table, and inadvertently she caught Connor's eye.

'Ruby!' Connor waved for her to come over and she was about to pretend she hadn't noticed but knew it would be rude, so she beamed in his direction and gave a wave. 'I'll just be two minutes,' she said to her friends. 'Any longer and you *have* to come and rescue me.'

'Where did you get to at work?' Connor asked as she came over. 'I never saw you after supper. I thought you were down to work with me in Resus?'

'My assessment took a bit longer than expected,' Ruby answered.

'Yeah,' Connor joked, 'you've always got an excuse.' He was just chatting and joking, he certainly wasn't there to talk about work, or tell her off, except inadvertently he had echoed Sheila's words. It seemed to have been noticed that any patient that needed to be taken to the ward, Ruby put her hand up. Any stores or laundry that needed to be put away, Ruby was already onto it and, yes, people had noticed.

'So?' Connor asked. 'How was it?'

'How was what?' Ruby said, biting into her lemon.

'Your assessment?'

'Oh, you know…' She forced a smile and rolled her eyes. 'Must try harder.'

Her face was burning, but she certainly wasn't going to share with Connor all that had been said and stupidly she felt as if she was going to start crying. God, Ruby thought, she should have had that walk on the beach before she'd come in. Her eyes darted for escape, for a reason to excuse herself, and suddenly there he was. Cort Mason was back in her line of vision. This time, though, his tie was loosened and he was sitting next to a doctor she vaguely recognised. He gave her a very brief nod, or did he? Ruby couldn't be sure, and then he turned back to his conversation but, not that she could have known it, his mind was on her.

It had been since she'd walked into the bar and perhaps, Cort admitted to himself, for a while before that.

'Hey, Ruby!' He pretended not to be looking, except his eyes roamed the bar and his ears were certainly not on Geoff's conversation as Ruby's friend came over. 'We're supposed to be celebrating with Tilly...'

'Sorry, Jess!' Ruby smiled, glad they'd remembered to rescue her! 'Just coming... See you, Connor.' She glanced over to the table but everyone was busy with conversations of their own, but she did, Cort noticed, make an effort. 'Catch you guys.' She gave a brief unreturned wave that had the light reflecting off all her silver bracelets and then as she drifted off he saw her back and there was a lot of back because she was wearing a halter neck that showed her white shoulders and way down her spine. She was also wearing a small skirt and flat sandals and for the fist time in a very long time Cort noticed everything. Then he glanced across the table and saw Siobhan's eyes on him, watching him watching Ruby, and Cort knew to be more careful than that. So very deliberately he didn't look out for her again after that. Instead, he chatted to Geoff and the rest of the table, yet she was there in the background, laughing and happy, a blaze of colour in the middle of the bar.Though he tried not to notice, he still did, so much so that he was aware the minute she left.

'Leaving?' Siobhan asked as he drained his drink.

'No,' Cort said, even though it had been his intention. 'Just getting another.'

And he headed for the bar rather than for home, but though still packed, the Stat Bar felt empty now. Well, not empty, Cort thought as he squeezed his way back to the table, it just felt pointless, he decided as he sat down to wait it out.

'We're going to Adam's,' Geoff said a little while later, when Cort really was about to head for home. 'Are you coming?'

'Adam?' Cort asked.

'Adam Carmichael.'

'Oh!' He'd worked with Adam in the past and

even if they kept only loosely in touch as Cort commuted between Melbourne and Sydney and Adam roamed the globe, working for Operation New Faces, Cort considered him a friend. 'Is he back?'

Geoff didn't answer. Everyone was drifting off and Cort was about to do the same, but that morning, before he'd pulled on the brown suit and chosen a lighter tie, he'd walked along a beach just a couple of suburbs from here and he'd made a promise, not to his sister, but to Beth, to say yes.

To live this life.

Except, now that he was starting to, Cort so did not want to be doing this.

One drink and he'd be out of there, Cort decided as they turned into Hill Street.

It was a nice house, Cort thought as Geoff opened the creaking gate. Sure, it needed a bit of work, but it was a lovely older building and just a two-minute walk from the beach. Who cared if it was in need of a little TLC?

There was a small decked area and the front door was open. Suddenly the music was turned on and wafted out to greet them, and as he walked in through the hall Cort wanted to turn around and walk back out, because there was a danger-ous vision walking towards him.

She looked the same from the waist up as she had in the pub, though instead of a beer she was holding a glass of milk and a bag of pistachio nuts and her auburn, or rather *titian*, hair was now loosely clipped up.

He noticed, he really noticed, because if he didn't then his eyes would flick down and he really didn't want to notice that her sandals and skirt were off, that she was wearing lilac boy pants and that there was a gap between the top of them and her top, which showed a soft, pale stomach.

She'd been crying—her eyes were red and the tip of her nose was too.

'Are you okay?' her friend asked.

'I'm fine, Tilly, just watching a sad movie. I didn't realise there'd be a home invasion to-night—I'll go and get dressed.'

She slipped past him and up the stairs and Cort headed through to the lounge—a large area with lots of sofas and magazines and a little pile of tis-sues. Emergency registrars sometimes made good detectives, because for reasons that shouldn't matter to him, as someone handed him a beer, Cort put his hand on the turned-off television and confirmed what he suspected—it was cold.

And why should it even matter to him that Ruby was sitting at home crying Cort would rather not explore, he had more than enough troubles of his own to be dealing with.

No, he didn't, Cort told himself, at least, not any more.

'Where's Adam?' Cort asked Ruby's friend.

'He's away.' She smiled. 'He's hardly ever here...' She must have seen him frown, and she took a moment to explain. 'I'm Tilly, there's Jess.' She pointed to a blonde and then to another one. 'And that's Ellie.'

'And...' Cort started and then stopped, because what business of his was it if there had been a redhead in her underwear in their lounge just a few moments ago?

'Oh.' Tilly smiled. 'There's also Ruby—she's the one who's just gone to get changed. We rent the house from Adam.'

He was at a student nurses' party.

He so did not need this.

Okay, they weren't all students. Tilly was telling him now that she was a graduate midwife and that she'd had her first breech today, and as he tried to stop his eyes from glazing over as she went into detail, Cort decided to excuse himself and leave just the second that he could—he'd done enough 'must get out more' for one night.

He was just about to slip away unnoticed when Ruby came downstairs.

Whatever had been upsetting her had clearly been taken care of because there was no evidence of tears and she was back to happy now. She turned up the music and started dancing, and Cort was determined to leave, except she really was lovely to watch, all sort of loose limbed and free, and what's more she was dancing her way over to him.

'You look how I feel,' Ruby said, because if ever someone didn't want to be there it was Cort Mason. He belonged in that suit, Ruby had decided before their encounter today. He belonged behind a stethoscope, or peering down his nose at minions, except he hadn't been like that today and she'd revised her judgement. Though she loathed Emergency and most of the staff that came with it, Cort wasn't like the others, he was just aloof.

'You look like I never would,' Cort said in

return, and he wasn't sure if that made sense, but even without the hellish last five years, even a decade ago, when he had belonged at student parties, he'd been the boring one. He would never stand in a room and dance alone with others watching, had never been as free as she appeared tonight. She must have caught his words because she smiled up at him.

'Takes practice,' Ruby said, and she picked up one of the many little bowls that Tilly was dotting about the place and offered it to him. He should have just said no, should have made no comment, or just taken a handful, but he screwed his nose up at the Bombay mix, and maybe her attitude was somehow catching because a teeny, tiny corner of it seemed to have worked its way over to him.

'I'd rather have some pistachios,' Cort said, which told her he'd noticed her when he'd walked in.

'Ah, no.' Ruby shook her head. 'They're not

to be put out for the general public, you get the Bombay mix. I've hidden *my* pistachios.'

'Sensible girl,' Cort said, and he wanted to pause time for a moment, have a little conversation with himself to ask himself if he was flirting. But he wasn't, he quickly told himself, because, well, he just didn't do that and certainly not with student nurses.

'Not generally.'

'Sorry?' He was too busy thinking to keep track of the conversation.

'I'm not generally considered sensible.'

'So why?' Cort asked, when really he shouldn't, when really he should just leave. 'Do you feel how I look?'

'You first,' Ruby said. 'Why do you look like you're about to head off?'

Cort didn't answer.

'Why should I tell you what's upsetting me, only to have you leave five minutes later?'

'Fair enough,' Cort said, because what right did

he have to ask her what was on her mind when soon he'd be out of there? Anyway, he knew she was in trouble with work, but would that really matter to a flighty little thing like her?

'How was your holiday?' It was Ruby's turn to probe, but she'd been in Emergency for four weeks now and he'd just been there for only one of them.

'It wasn't really a holiday,' Cort said.

'Oh.'

'Family.' Cort certainly wasn't about to tell her the truth. Hardly anyone at work knew, just his direct boss and a couple of people in Admin, but he had always been private and in this he was intensely so, not just for his sake but for Beth's.

There really wasn't that much to talk about anyway. It didn't feel quite right that he was even here, except he was and he asked her something now about her family, if she was local, but didn't quite catch her answer and had to lower his head a bit to hear.

'At Whale Beach,' Ruby said. 'About an hour or so from here.'

And he could have lifted his head then—after all, he'd heard now what she had said—except he was terribly aware of the sensation of her face close to his, just as he had been in the suture room.

Something tightened inside Ruby as she inhaled the scent of his hair again, and she was sure, quite, quite sure that if she just stayed still, if she did not move, if she could somehow now not breathe, whatever was in the air between them would turn his mouth those few inches to hers—and she wanted it to.

'I think I should go.' Strange that he didn't lift his head, strange that still he lingered.

'Hey, Cort...' He heard his name and turned to see that another mob from Emergency was arriving and he couldn't believe how close he'd come, how very careless he had almost been, especially as there was motor-mouth Siobhan too, so for

Ruby's sake he was relieved when she quickly excused herself and slipped away.

Ruby, too, had seen them arriving and a busman's holiday she did not need, so as they blocked the stairs, talking, Ruby stepped out onto the veranda, her heart hammering just a little bit harder than normal, her lips regretting the absence of Cort's, and her problems, which she'd momentarily escaped from, caught up with her all over again. She could hear the noise and the throb of the party and decided she would pop over next door tomorrow morning just to check that Mrs. Bennett wasn't upset about the party. The old lady insisted she didn't mind a bit, but it was always nice to have a reason to pop over.

Maybe she could talk to her a little, Ruby mused. Mrs. Bennett was so lovely and wise, except…Ruby closed her eyes…nothing any one might say could actually change things. Quite simply, she was terrified to go back to work and terrified of failing too. Sheila's ominous warning replayed in her mind for perhaps the two hundred and fifty-second time that night.

'It's a pass or fail unit, Ruby.' Sheila was immutable. 'If you don't pass, you'll have to repeat.'

Six more weeks of Emergency was something she could not do. Six more shifts, six more hours, six more minutes was bad enough, but six more weeks was nigh on impossible.

She thought about telling her friends, but she was so embarrassed. They all seemed to be breezing through. Tilly just loved midwifery and Ellie and Jess were loving their studies and placements too. How could she explain that she could very easily chuck it in this minute rather than face going back there tomorrow, let alone having to repeat?

She glanced down towards the beach and thought of the little shop she had worked in for a couple of years, selling jewellery and crystals and candles, and how much safer that had been, yet it hadn't been quite enough.

She wanted so desperately to do mental health, wanted just to scrape through her emergency rotation so she could go on and study what she truly loved.

And then she saw it.

Hope hung in the sky in the shape of a new moon and Ruby smiled in relief.

'Please.' She made her wish. 'Please get me through A and E. Please find a way for me to get through it.'

Cort walked out and found her standing talking to the sky and not remotely embarrassed at being caught.

'I was just making my new-moon wishes.'

'As you do,' was Cort's rather dry response, because it would never even have entered his head that as he'd walked along his own beach, just that very morning, he'd made, if not a wish, a promise. ''Night, then. I'm off.'

He walked down the path and opened a squeaking gate and had every intention of heading down

Hill Street and seeing if there was a taxi—it was his absolute intention, but he found himself turning around. 'What did you wish for?'

'You're not supposed to tell anyone,' Ruby explained, 'or it won't happen…' She saw his brief nod, knew he would turn to go again, but she also knew that she didn't want him to. 'It was a sensible wish, though.'

'Glad to hear it.'

Keep walking, he told himself, and his legs obeyed, just not in the direction he had intended because he was walking towards her.

'Why were you crying when we came in?'

'I wasn't.' Instantly she was defensive.

'Ruby?'

'Okay—why wouldn't I be crying? A twenty-three-year-old is almost certainly going to lose his life…he's my age.'

Cort nodded, because he knew how confronting that could be. Ruby was right, she had every reason to be sitting alone in tears over a patient.

'Talk to people at work,' Cort suggested. 'We've got a good team—let them know...' He saw her eyes shutter, saw her close off, so he decided there was nothing further to be said. She had given him a reason, he'd in turn given advice, except something told him there was more to it than just that.

'What about Sheila?' He saw her shrug. 'Your assessment?'

All he got was silence and he was determined not to break it, just stood till after perhaps a full minute finally she responded.

'She wants to see an improvement.'

'In what area?' Cort asked, and this time he gave in and broke the ensuing silence. 'How much longer have you got in A and E?'

'Two weeks. Well, just tomorrow and Monday, then I'm off for a while and back for three nights the following Monday.'

'And then?'

'Then I'm finished,' Ruby said. 'Then I start, I

suppose— I want to be a mental health nurse.' As he opened his mouth, she got in first. 'I know, I know, the staff are as mad as the patients—' she smiled as she said it '—so I'll fit right in. Really, I'm just biding my time…'

'Biding your time doesn't work in A and E,' Cort said. 'And Sheila's tough, but she's good— listen to her.'

'I will.'

'Are you going back in?' He didn't like leaving her, didn't understand why she would rather stand alone in the dark than join her friends.

'I might just stay out here for a while.' She thought of Siobhan and Connor and thought of going back in and doing the happy-clappy but she really couldn't face it. 'I might just go to bed.'

'You're not going to get much sleep with that noise.'

'It's not the noise that'll disturb me. I'll have Tilly coming up to find out what's wrong, then

Ellie then Jess. It's just easier to...' She gave another shrug. 'I might go for a walk on the beach.'

'Now, that really would be stupid—walking alone...'

'Come with me, then.' He could see the white of her teeth as she spoke, could hear the waves in the background, and for a moment he actually considered it, a bizarre moment because Cort didn't do midnight walks. Well, he did, but not with company, except he did like talking to her.

'I don't think that's a very good idea.'

'I think it's a very good idea,' Ruby said, because he'd stepped a little bit closer and she didn't want him to go. Cort had been the only solace in a day that had been horrible, and even if a while ago she had wanted to be alone, it was far, far nicer being here with him. 'I like walking on the beach.'

'I meant...' Cort hesitated, 'I meant you and me...' He tried to change what he'd said, but only made matters worse. 'Us,' he attempted, and Ruby smiled.

'As I said...' She looked at his tie which was grey in the darkness, but which she knew was really a lovely lilac, and she did what she had wanted to do in the suture room—she put her hand up and felt the cool silk. She wanted him to go with her, wanted a little more of the peace she had found with him today. 'I think it's a very good idea.'

Cort wanted to go with her too, though not necessarily to the beach.

He didn't do this type of thing.

He didn't find himself at student nurse parties, neither did he find himself in situations such as this one because he didn't put himself there.

He liked it now that he was, though.

Liked it a lot because the next thing he knew he was kissing her.

It was the nicest thing. It really was a lovely kiss. He sort of bent down and caught her, not completely by surprise because she'd felt his presence all night, or had it been before that? Ruby thought as his mouth roamed hers.

She'd never kissed anyone in a suit.

Never kissed anyone as lovely before, come to think of it.

She couldn't hear the music from the house now, wasn't aware of anything except the lovely circle his arms created around them and what was happening in the centre. He had a hand on the wall and one in her hair over her neck, and his kiss was measured and deep like its owner, but as his tongue met hers, as she tasted his breath, there was more passion in his kiss than she'd ever anticipated, more passion than she'd ever tasted, and that it came from Cort made it all the more wild, like a secret only she was privy to. He pulled her head closer just a fraction and his mouth welcomed her a whole lot more and Ruby wanted to climb up his chest to wrap herself around him. She wanted his tie off, she wanted his shirt off, she wanted the party to disappear... she wanted more.

He pulled back just a fraction, and if their mouths weren't touching any more, they still thrummed. He looked down, not at a student nurse and a whole set of problems but into velvet-brown eyes and felt rare intimacy. It wasn't just lust or a sudden urge. It was, quite simply, just nice to *feel*, and he hadn't felt anything for so very long now—yet he was able to with her.

'Do you want a nut?' He could taste her words, could feel them because as she spoke her lips dusted his.

And in turn Ruby felt rather than saw him smile, felt his lips spread, and, yes, she would kiss them again in a moment, just not here. He was like her beloved pistachios, she decided, all brittle and hard but so readily cracked and such a reward to get to the delicious centre.

Cort was used to making rapid decisions—it was what he did for a living after all—but always

his decisions were measured, tempered by out-
comes and responsibilities. They just weren't tonight.

'I want you,' Cort said.

Which he did.

It was as simple as that.

CHAPTER FOUR

SHE went in first and checked that the coast was clear. It was, well, sort of. There was a couple necking in the hall, but the rest were all gathered in the lounge room, so she waved him in and up the stairs and they bolted along the hall.

'Won't they all come up?' Cort asked as they stepped into her bedroom. 'To see how you are?'

'No,' Ruby said, and grabbed a scarf and tied it onto the handle. 'That means don't disturb…'

He wanted to kiss her again, wanted to see her, but as his hand groped for the light switch she stopped him.

'Don't,' Ruby said. 'Don't break it.'

'Break what?'

'Just…whatever it is that we've got.'

He stood a touch unsure as she lit a candle in

the corner and then another and another till the room was bathed in dancing fingers of orange and white. Then she hauled over a chair and, just to be sure, wedged it against the door handle.

It was a room called Ruby. There were drapes, curtains, cushions, candles and crystals, all things that usually did not interest him.

There was the beat of the music and noises from downstairs and he was too old, too jaded, too bitter for someone so light and so lovely, but she'd been crying, he reminded himself as she turned to him.

He was going to leave, Ruby knew that. He was going to change his mind, but he could change it in the morning, because she wanted him tonight.

She wanted him in a way she had never wanted someone before. It was an imperative, a knowledge that this was their only chance, and she was incredibly bold in a way she wasn't usually. She took him by the hand and to a bed that was really rather small. She felt his hesitation and tension and she wanted it gone so she kissed him, and in that moment she welcomed him back in an instant, because out went trouble as he kissed her onto the bed and they tumbled into paradise.

Tongues and taste and the lovely wedge of his body blew cares away as he lay sort of over and beside her—backed into a corner in possibly the nicest of ways. She could feel the belt of his suit against her stomach, feel the roaming of his hands over her waist then sliding to her bottom then almost apologetically heading back to her waist. She could feel him holding back when he didn't want to.

When she didn't want him to.

She kissed his chin and up his cheek, moved his hand back to her bottom and heard the sigh of his breath, and she pressed just a little into him and kissed his eyes and his ears, and it was like tripping a switch, because suddenly he was on top of her, his mouth hungry and urgent. He kissed her throat and then up to her mouth and her body pressed into him some more, and then she could climb up and wrap herself around him as she had wanted to before, but she pulled back his head, wanted to see him again, to hear him again, before she kissed him again.

'Why,' she whispered, 'are you always so crabby?'

'Because I'm miserable?' He stopped and smiled down at her.

'But you're not.'

'I am,' he insisted. 'I really am.'

'You're not tonight,' Ruby said, and he had to agree with her.

'No. I'm not tonight.'

He wanted her skirt off, wanted to see her as she had been when he'd walked into the house, but it would seem Ruby had rules.

'I'm not making love to a man in a suit—in a brown suit.'

'Taupe.' Cort smiled, not even a little smile but a full, wide smile that she had never before seen, and Ruby caught her breath because it completely changed him. She went for his tie, then changed her mind.

'You do it,' she said.

She wriggled from under him and climbed off the bed and left him lying there. She looked down at him and he undid his tie, but that was as far as he went.

'You want it off...' Cort said. 'Come and get it.' So she did, pulling it off before she went for his jacket next.

'Shoes,' he said, and she took off one. 'Both of them.'

'You've got more clothes than me.'

Wasn't he supposed to be riddled with guilt, or aching with regret? Not sitting up just to get her to remove another sandal, which she did.

'Shirt,' Ruby said, and he obliged.

'Skirt,' Cort said, and so too did she.

She wanted to go over to the bed and climb onto him, she couldn't have ever guessed just how wanton she could be, but he rewarded her not with this game but with his smile, with a Cort Mason she would never have guessed was there beneath the austere exterior. She liked standing before him, drunk on lust and shivering with want, teasing each other and making each other wait.

'Belt,' said Ruby.

'Hardly fair on you,' Cort said, because she was down to her halter and panties and he still had socks and shoes and trousers and belt, but Ruby didn't seem to mind. In fact, she stopped him when he magnanimously went to undo his zipper.

'Just the belt will do,' Ruby said, and as with his tie he merely loosened it.

'Take it off, then.'

Which meant she got to touch him. Slowly, very slowly she pulled loose the belt and she wanted to dive onto him then, but Cort reminded her it was her turn. She slid her top up slowly and she had to close her eyes at one point because, so close to him, she wanted to bend towards his mouth, wanted to climb into bed and be with him, but instead she took off her top and it was bizarre but she didn't feel shy or stupid. Instead, with Cort she felt free.

She stared down and saw the lust and approval in the eyes that caressed her skin. Then she stared down at herself and saw two very small breasts that she now rather liked, because how could she not when Cort craved them so much that he reached out his hand and stroked one slowly, till she blew out a held breath and thought she'd sink to her knees.

'I'll help with your shoes.'

She bent over him and as he stroked her breast she took off his shoes and socks, and then she kissed his toes.

And he lay there about to pull away because how could he let her? Except her tongue was so sure.

Would he regret this?

He asked himself once as she stood again and then he answered, never, because this wasn't sad or guilt ridden. There was no one else in his head but Ruby, nothing else but him and her.

He could never have thought it would be so magical.

That it could ever be so pure and good again.

That they would have their own rules and their own ways.

He watched her kneel and rummage in a drawer and come out with pistachios.

'Trousers,' Ruby said.

'It's your turn.'

'Only if you catch this with your mouth.'

She was mad, he decided as he lay in the bed, trying to catch a pistachio. Then he didn't want to play that game, so he stood and Ruby stood maybe just a little bit embarrassed because she had never been so free before, never felt so able to be herself with another person. He was so, so slow and tender as he knelt down and slid down her pants. She squirmed just a little, but then he stroked the little hairs and he blew onto her and then she felt his lips press there and she thought her knees might give way.

She held onto his head, her thighs closed tight and shaking as his tongue slid in. His hands pushed at her bottom and his mouth worked to part her some more and she could hear a moan and it came from her.

He laid her down and parted her knees and it was so close to heaven that she felt like crying. All the tears that weren't ever allowed to fall seemed to whoosh up as his mouth found her.

It was as if he'd found her.

The real Ruby, who she couldn't be, who he mustn't see, because then he'd leave. She stopped him, rolled a little way and found a condom, which was just as well, Cort thought, because it had been a long time since he'd carried any on him.

He slid the condom on even though he didn't want it.

Didn't want a one-night stand, though this surely was what it was.

And he wanted to get back what he'd had a moment ago. He had felt her collapse beneath his mouth, had felt her about to give in, but then she'd regrouped and held back. He would have it, Cort decided, he would find her again.

She wanted him. She wanted him as he kissed her, she wanted all of him, and as his thick thigh parted her legs there was nothing more she wanted than him inside her.

Nothing else surrounded them now, no one else present, no chance of interruption, and he was so deep inside her now, and she wanted him to come so that she could too.

Just a little bit.

She didn't want the tears that had been close, and perhaps still were, to impinge on this moment; she didn't want to give in completely.

She pushed up a little, her clitoris swollen from his attention, and pressed in harder, and she felt the pulse of her body that would signal him to join her.

'Cort.' She said his name, and lifted her body to his, because she wanted him with her, but still he pushed on.

'Cort.' She heard the demand in her voice, because she was coming and now so could he and it would be done, but still his arms were not beneath her, he was on his elbows and looking down at her.

'Come on,' he said as if he knew there was more. 'It's okay,' he said as if he knew that this scared her.

Not him.

This.

Because sex was okay and all that had gone on beforehand too.

But this, lying naked beneath him, eyes open

and watching, and him knowing there was more to give.

She wanted a one-night stand, not for him to know her. She wanted him to climb off and get dressed and be out of there.

She wanted chocolate or pizza, not to expose her soul.

She didn't want to cry, but all evening it had been building.

She could feel her tears and then his tongue, feel the sob in her mouth and then his over hers, and he didn't stifle it, he took it, kissed it, accepted it, and he was so deep inside her, not just her body but her mind.

'Help me.' She didn't know what she was saying, but he seemed to get it. He smothered her with his body, just scooped her right in and she pressed her face to his lovely hot chest and screamed into it, like a pillow. She clutched at his back and wrapped her legs around him, feeling the jolt of her body, and it was more than she

could deal with so she let him absorb all the tension as it shot through her, let his body smother
her as he released too.

Oh, God, she was crying, she really was crying,
but he didn't seem to mind.

She was spent and it was over, but she didn't
want it to be. She could feel the last throes of him
and inside her still flickered a tiny, magical beat.

They could hear the party and the music and
the voices coming back into their consciousness,
could feel control seeping in where there had just
been none, and she felt as if she'd been on holiday
and had now returned, her world the same as
when she had left it but richer for the experience,
for the glimpse into another world. One she could
surely never belong in.

'You're going to hate yourself in the morning,'
Ruby said, but he just smiled.

'Probably,' Cort said. 'But not you.' It seemed
imperative that she know that and she nodded.

'No regrets, then,' Ruby said, because they both

knew it was impossible for it to be anything more than this.

'None,' Cort said. All the candles had died now and the room was in darkness as he lay on his back with her curled up beside him and tried to find a hint of regret, but right now there was none.

They slept with the window open, because Ruby loved to fall asleep to the sound of the ocean, but the slam of the front door and the sound of the last revellers leaving woke her in the small hours and for a moment she struggled to orientate herself. She looked at a sky that was all stars and hardly any moon and remembered she had to go back into work tomorrow, panicked more than a little as she recalled all that Sheila had said, and then Cort pulled her more into him. He mumbled something, that it would all be okay, and she closed her eyes and let her mind agree.

It had to be okay, Ruby told herself.

It had to be.

CHAPTER FIVE

IT WAS Ruby who woke with regret.

Well, not regret so much, she thought as she wrapped herself in a green and gold sarong and headed downstairs. More embarrassment. She'd never let herself go like that—never been so free with another. Deciding she needed more than herbal tea this morning, Ruby made two coffees and involuntarily recalled her impromptu striptease and nut-throwing act and she closed her eyes for a moment. She remembered she'd been crying, but closing your eyes while holding a kettle wasn't the most sensible of moves, and she poured scalding water onto the bench.

'Are you okay?' Tilly asked as Ruby yelped and jumped back.

'Of course,' Ruby said, but her face was burning, not because there was a man in her room but because of how she'd been with him last night.

'Is that the A and E registrar you're making coffee for?' Tilly asked as Ruby headed to her own little fridge for milk. 'Maybe he'd like normal milk?' Tilly suggested, and Ruby gave a worried nod and headed to the main fridge because, yes, most people didn't drink rice milk. 'So is it?' Tilly grinned as Ruby added milk to the coffees.

'Can't you just pretend not to have noticed?' Ruby glanced over her shoulder and looked at her friend. 'Did anyone see us?'

'No one said anything. I don't think anyone saw, I was just keeping an eye out because I was worried about you—you seemed a bit off at the pub.'

'Was I drunk?' Ruby asked hopefully, because then she'd have an excuse for her tears and her stupidity. She closed her eyes in horror as she remembered flinging nuts and swore never to eat another pistachio again.

'Were you?' Tilly asked. 'You seemed fine to me. Did you have a lot?'

'Two beers.' Ruby sighed.

'What's the problem?' Tilly asked, because she'd never seen Ruby like this. Ruby was always happy-go-lucky, but the smile seemed a bit more strained these days, and though it was hardly a nunnery they were running, Ruby really wasn't one for hauling guys off to her room.

'What was I thinking?' Ruby muttered. 'I've got to work with him. I'm in enough trouble there as it is.'

'Trouble?' Tilly checked as Jess wandered in.

'Not trouble.' Quickly she tried to backtrack. 'I had my assessment yesterday and Sheila doesn't seem to think I'm pulling my weight.'

'You—not pulling your weight?' Jess asked, her voice more than a little incredulous, because that sounded nothing like Ruby. They'd worked together last year on the children's ward, and Jess knew that couldn't be right. 'What exactly did she say?'

'It's no big deal.' Ruby waved Jess's concerns away. 'I'll be fine. I'll be fine. I've just got to get rid of the registrar in my bed.' And she did as she always did, made herself smile, even made the others laugh as she rolled her eyes and picked up the mugs of coffee. 'Wish me luck.'

Cort wasn't faring too well either.

At twenty past seven he jolted awake and the room that had last night looked so sensual, such a haven, was just a rather chaotic jumble now and a riot of colour that made him want to close his eyes again, except when he did he could smell the musk and the sex and a scent he couldn't quite decipher. He opened his eyes and saw what must be a joint lying on her bedside table and he picked it up and smelt it and wondered if that was what had possessed him, if somehow it had permeated his brain and made him act as he had last night?

'It's a smudge stick.' Ruby walked in, determinedly all smiles but absolutely unable to meet his eyes. 'It's just sage.'

'Sage?'

'You light it…' She put a mug of coffee into his hands. 'It's supposed to clear the room of negative energy…'

Why didn't he think of that?

'And these?' He picked up some tiny little figures, no bigger than her fingernails.

'They're my worry dolls,' Ruby said. 'You tell them your problems at night and then put them in a little bag under your pillow and they take care of them while you sleep…'

This was so not him.

This hadn't even been him ten years ago when it had been okay to wake up with a student nurse with a joint by her bedside.

He could hear wind chimes outside her window and they grated on his nerves.

'What time do you have to be in?' Ruby asked as he glanced again at his watch.

'I'm off today. You?' Cort asked.

'I'm on a late shift.' She was grateful of the temporary reprieve, that now she wouldn't have to face him at work till tomorrow and then she was off for almost a week before she did her stint of nights.

His phone rang then and he looked at it and grimaced.

'Cort Mason.' He took a drink of coffee, perhaps sensing that would be all he had for a long time. 'What do you mean, she's not coming in?' He shook his head. 'No it's fine to call. What's the problem?' He listened for a moment, taking in more coffee. 'Okay, tell him to leave it. Just put on a saline soak and I'll be in as soon as I can. Make sure he's got analgesia.'

'Okay?' Ruby checked.

'I've got to go in after all. Jamelia…' He didn't elaborate. 'They need me in.' He was cursing himself because he just hadn't been thinking, had not been thinking last night. He just wanted to go home and clear his head, but now he had to go into work.

'I'd better go.' Cort grimaced as his phone rang again, because now he'd said he was coming in, he was public property. Ruby felt a bit sorry for whoever was on the end of the line because he was more than a bit crabby as he took the call while at the same time retrieving his discarded, crumpled shirt. 'I said I'll be there as soon as I can,' Cort snapped, and then hung up. 'I need to get there, but I can't go in yesterday's suit.'

'You can have a shower here,' she offered. 'Maybe wear some scrubs.'

She didn't get it, but it wasn't her fault. 'I can't look as if I've been out all night,' Cort said, because, well, he couldn't. 'You know what they're like.'

'God, yes.' Because she did—the whole clique of them, with their noses in everybody's business—and she could understand why he wouldn't want them in his, especially if it involved her.

'I can get you something to wear from Adam's room,' Ruby offered, and Cort closed his eyes. God, had it really come to this? But reluctantly he nodded and then headed down the hall to a very cluttered bathroom, brimming with straighteners and make-up and tampons spilling out of a box and beach towels instead of towels. He was too bloody staid and sensible to be doing this.

Ruby had to go back downstairs, because that was where Adam's room was.

'Poor Adam.' Jess grinned as Ruby came out with a black casual shirt that looked the sort of thing a registrar might wear on a Sunday. 'No wonder he's always moaning he can't find his things when he gets back.'

Ruby met Cort in the bedroom, wrapped in

a beach towel, and she averted her eyes as he dropped it and pulled on his clothes.

'Thanks for this,' he said as he pulled on Adam's shirt.

'No problem.'

He picked up his jacket and was obviously wondering what to do with it.

'You can pick it up later,' Ruby said, and because she knew he didn't want that awkward moment where he had to face her later, she added kindly, 'I'm on a late shift so I won't be here. I'll leave it on the porch.'

'It's just…'

'I know.'

She did.

'It's not just for me,' Cort said. 'I don't want it to be difficult for you at work—and, believe me, it would be.'

'It won't be,' Ruby said, 'because no-one will find out.'

He could hear the chatter from the kitchen, the

little gaggle he'd have to walk past on the way out, but she must have read his thoughts. 'It's just my housemates, they won't say anything.'

'Ruby…'

She shook her head, because she didn't want the big speech or promises that wouldn't be kept and she really didn't want to examine last night with him.

In fact, confused as to her own part in this, her own behaviour with him, Ruby didn't want to examine last night at all.

'Go on,' she said. 'Get back to being crabby.'

And he'd do that.

He had no choice but to do that, but it would be a hard ask to forget last night.

He went to go, but he couldn't quite yet.

Couldn't just leave it at that, as if it had been nothing.

He walked over and took her into his arms and she let him hold her, and she knew he would soon be back to crabby, knew at work he had to ignore her and that was a blessing because she felt as if he had exposed her last night, but it was nice that it ended with a cuddle.

Okay, a kiss, Ruby thought as he searched for her lips.

Why couldn't he be a bastard? Ruby thought as his lips roamed hers.

Bastards were gone when you woke up, or chatted up your friend on the way out, or 'borrowed' twenty dollars for a taxi. Every girl knew that. There was even a coded list on the fridge downstairs, and now that he was kissing her, and so very nicely too, she couldn't even add him to it.

It really was a lovely kiss that tasted different from last night. It was slow and tender and laced with regret because she'd be back at work this afternoon and so would he and last night wouldn't have happened.

Except, Ruby realised as he let her go and walked out her bedroom door, it had.

CHAPTER SIX

'RUBY...' He did not look up as the nurses did their handover and Sheila did the allocations. He'd deliberately avoided the staffroom as the late staff arrived, but Cort knew there really was no avoiding her. 'You're with me in Resus.'

'Sure,' came her voice and *still* he didn't look up.

Just this awkward first bit to get through, he told himself, but really he knew that for as long as she was there, awkward was how it was going to feel.

Still, no one would notice if he ignored her. He wasn't exactly known for his small talk, or for flirting with the nurses.

'Where did you disappear to last night, Cort?'

Siobhan wasted no time in asking. 'One minute you were there…'

'I wasn't aware…' Ruby found she was holding her breath as Cort stood up and ended Siobhan's fishing with a very frosty response '…I needed to hand you a sick note.'

Sheila's eyes widened as Cort stalked off. Siobhan's face reddened and Connor let out a low whistle.

'Someone got out of the wrong side of bed,' Connor explained. 'He's been like that all morning.'

Or just the wrong bed perhaps, Ruby thought. As the afternoon wore on, crabby was actually a very good description that she'd come up with, because he growled at any member of staff who approached, whether on foot or by phone, although he was very nice to the patients, not that they had many in.

Resus, to Sheila's clear annoyance, was quiet. One chest pain came in and Ruby attached him to the monitors and ran off a trace, her hands shaking as Cort came over and she handed over to him.

'ST elevation...' Cort spoke to her just as he would any student, pointed out the abnormalities in the tracing and took bloods as an X-ray was performed, but the cardiologists were quiet too, and the patient was soon taken up to the catherisation lab, leaving Ruby just to clean up and then mooch around, checking and double-checking everything.

'The ward's ready for Justin.' Hannah came off the phone and Ruby saw her chance to escape.

'I'll take him,' Ruby offered, because it wasn't Resus she wanted to avoid now but Cort, who was sitting nearby.

'Hannah can take him,' Sheila said. 'I want you to stay in Resus.'

'There are no patients, though,' Ruby pointed out.

'There will be,' Sheila said. 'For now you can check all the equipment.'

'I just have,' Ruby said.

'Double-check,' Sheila said, 'and then you can re-check the crash drug trolley.'

It was possibly the longest, most excruciating shift of her life. Sheila was determined that Ruby was not going to get caught up, as she so often managed to, in other things, and Cort watched, while trying not to, and simply couldn't make her out.

Ruby was competent and certainly not lazy. If anything, she was looking for jobs to do, and she was smiling and happy with all the patients, more than happy to stand and talk to them. He didn't get why she annoyed Sheila so much.

'God, it's quiet,' Sheila moaned, and Cort looked up, because in Emergency you can *think* it's quiet, you can *know* it's quiet, you just never ever say that it *is*—and in response to Sheila's foolishness the emergency phone shrilled.

'You've jinxed us now.' He gave a half-smile and calmly picked up the phone, before a leaping Sheila could answer it, but he wasn't smiling at all when he hung up.

'House fire. Mum's out—she's coming to us with smoke inhalation, they're going in for the children. Seems that there are two.'

'Okay.' Sheila snapped into action, and so too did Cort, calling down the anaesthetist and paediatric team as Sheila allocated her staff. 'Ruby, come with me and set up for number one, Hannah and Siobhan take number two...'

Mum arrived and though distraught was physically well enough to go to the trolleys, but Ruby could smell smoke as she was rushed past and she could smell it on a firefighter who was brought in too, as well as a paramedic who came and gave them more information as he received it on his radio, before it made it to the emergency phone.

'They're out, both in full arrest.'

Happy now? Ruby wanted to say to Sheila

as her stomach churned in dread. Is this *busy* enough for you?

But of course Ruby didn't say anything. Instead, she did everything she was told and everything she possibly could to save the little girl in front of them. And she would have given anything she could if only it might work.

She watched Cort work and work and work on the child and she stood there when she really wanted to run. She saw her hands shaking so much she actually stabbed herself with a needle and had to discard the drug and put a sticky plaster on as Sheila snatched up a new vial and swiftly pulled up the drug.

She could feel her body soaked with adrenaline, every instinct begging her to flee as, when hope had long since left the building, Cort made the decision to stop.

And if that wasn't bad enough, the whole team then moved and helped work on the other little doll that had been brought in behind her sister.

She was bright red from the carbon monoxide, and absolutely and completely perfect, on the outside at least. Again Ruby just stood there as Siobhan and a horde of people moved her up to ICU, with her little sister forever left behind.

'I'll go and speak to the parents,' Cort said.

'Dad's just arrived,' Hannah said. 'He's in with Mum.'

'Okay.' Cort's eyes flicked to Ruby, but he wasn't that cruel. 'Hannah, could you come with me?'

'Ruby,' Sheila said. 'Come and help me get Violet ready.'

'Sorry?'

'Her parents will want to see her.'

She stared at the curtain and what was behind it.

'I can't,' Ruby said.

'You need to.' Sheila was insistent. 'We still need to look after Violet and her family.'

'I can't,' Ruby said, and it was final. She could

not be in the department for even a second longer. She could smell the smoke and hear the mother's screams, and she wasn't leaving them short because as a student she was supernumerary anyway and, Ruby realised as she headed to her locker and took her bag, they didn't need a nurse who couldn't cope.

'You can't just walk out mid-shift,' Sheila said as Ruby walked back with her bag.

'I'm sorry, Sheila.' She just had to get out of there. She wasn't being a drama queen, she knew Sheila was far too busy to beg or to follow her, and her warning was brusque and firm when it came. 'Ruby, do you realise what you're doing?' Sheila checked.

'Absolutely,' Ruby answered. Siobhan had just returned from ICU and actually smirked as Ruby walked past. 'I'm getting out of the kitchen.'

CHAPTER SEVEN

'THAT was too much, Sheila.' Cort looked at the NUM as Ruby walked out.

'We can't choose our patients,' Sheila responded. 'I can't hand-pick what comes through the doors so that it doesn't upset Ruby Carmichael.'

Cort hesitated, but just for a moment. Her surname was not the point, or the fact he might have slept with a good friend's little sister last night.

The point was, if he said anything, he'd say way too much, and right now he had a grieving family to deal with.

'Later,' he said. 'I'll talk to you later.'

He did.

Perhaps Sunday afternoon wasn't the best time to do it, especially not with the day that they'd had, but by that time he should have been home hours ago. Cort was seething—not that anyone would really notice, he wasn't the most sunny person at the best of times, but when his office door closed on Sheila there was no doubting his dark mood.

'The students are not your concern, Cort.' Sheila did not want to discuss this.

'The morale in this place is my concern, though,' Cort said. 'I'm a day away from speaking to Doug about it. There's a student nurse running out in the middle of her shift, and a doctor not turning up because she doesn't want to be here on her own because she feels the nurses have no respect for her.'

'It's not my fault Jamelia can't cope.'

He looked at Sheila, whom he liked and respected and was the leader of a good team. Yet, as happened at times, the team was splintering. Emergency was the toughest of places to work and in an effort to survive the things they saw, people hardened. Black humour darkened and sometimes it needed reeling in.

'We're supposed to be a team.'

'Really?' Sheila gave him a wide-eyed look. 'Since when, Cort? You've been hell since you got back from your holidays. You do nothing to be a part of this so-called team. Look at yesterday with Jamelia—you just swanned in and took over...' Her voice trailed off, because it wasn't the best of examples. After all, without him the patient wouldn't have even made it to ICU, so she tried a different tack instead. 'I don't see you at any of the staff functions—you didn't come on the team-building exercise. I've worked with you for years and I don't know anything more about you than I did on the first day we met.'

'I'm talking about work,' Cort said. 'We don't need to be in every aspect of each other's lives to function as a team.'

'Then I'll try to ensure we *function* better.' Sheila spat his chosen word back at him, and

Cort knew she was right, knew he was asking more than he was prepared to give.

'Okay,' Cort said. 'Point taken. I am trying to make more of an effort...' He just hated the touchy-feely stuff, and a day shooting paint balls in a team-building exercise simply wasn't him. 'And I'll work the roster and see if I can shadow Jamelia for a couple of weeks—maybe build up her confidence. What about you?' Cort said, demanding compromise.

'Fine,' Sheila snapped. 'I'll have a word, keep an eye open...' She gave a weary nod. 'I was actually going to speak to Siobhan anyway. I know how she can come across at times, but her heart is in the right place. I'll talk to them,' Sheila offered.

'Good,' Cort said, and really he should have left it there, except as he turned, he couldn't.

'What about the student?'

'Ruby.' Sheila didn't play games. 'I think we both know her name.'

Cort chose not to dwell on whatever point Sheila was making. Instead, he tried to act as he always did. 'As you said, the nursing staff are your concern.'

But weren't they supposed to be changing how they did things around here? Cort thought as he went to walk out. Hadn't Sheila demanded that he didn't act as he always had, that instead he get more involved? For the second time he turned. 'Maybe you could give her—'

'I'll think about it,' Sheila said, without Cort having the chance to speak, because despite an exchange of words she respected him far too much to make him ask what he possibly shouldn't. 'I'll ring Ruby later—I just hope she's in the right frame of mind to listen.'

He hoped so too.

He *really* hoped so, as he walked to his car, which had been parked overnight in the hospital. Cort ached, not just for a bed that was a bit bigger than the small one he'd shared last night but space and a shower and clean socks and underwear and some beans on toast and some lovely silence.

He'd done all he could, Cort told himself, turning on the radio, because silence actually sent his mind back to her.

It was up to her now, Cort insisted.

So why on earth was he indicating to turn left?

Ruby had walked along the beach, backwards and forwards, backwards and forwards, looking at the waves that kept rolling in. A little child was gone and there was no point regretting her decision to flee from Emergency because absolutely she could not have gone in to her, could not have laid a little child out.

And if that made her a bad nurse, then she was one.

If this meant she had failed, so be it.

And now she'd head home to her friends who loved her and who would try to talk her out of it, who would do everything they could to encour-

age her to go back, which they might have succeeded in doing had she told them everything.

'What are you doing here?' Jess looked up as
Ruby walked in. 'I thought you were on a late.'

'I had to come home.' Ruby saw them all care-
free and smiling and hated what her work would
do to their evening. 'There was a house fire...'

'I heard about it on the radio,' Ellie groaned. 'I
never even thought... Did they come in to you?
Oh, Ruby...' Ellie stood, but Ruby didn't want
to hear it and shrugged off Ellie's words and her
waiting hug and just headed to her room.

'Leave her,' Ruby heard Tilly say, and was
grateful for it as she went to her room. The scarf
was still on her door, but she knew Tilly would
ignore it and felt the indentation of the bed a little
while later when Tilly came in and sat down.

'I don't want to go back,' Ruby said.

'I know.' Tilly did her best to be understanding.
'Remember when I helped deliver that stillbirth?'
Tilly said gently. 'I knew the mum was coming

in for induction the next day and I honestly didn't know if I was up to it, but you told me the mum would be better off for having me there.'

'It's not the same,' Ruby said. 'Because you're good at what you do, whereas all I did today was stab myself with a needle when I was pulling up the drugs and yesterday, when I sat with the relatives, I couldn't say even one single word. I'm useless…'

'You'll be a wonderful psych nurse.'

'I'll only be a wonderful psych nurse so long as the patients don't go collapsing or fainting or getting sick.' She closed her eyes. 'And psych patients die too… Just leave me, Tilly,' Ruby said.

'I'm not leaving you.'

'Aren't you all going to the beach for a barbecue?'

'I don't want to leave you—I'm going to stay home.'

'Please don't,' Ruby begged. 'I just want to be on my own.'

She heard her friends leaving and lay there quietly. Her room was warm and she pushed the window wide open then pulled the drape and stripped down to her pants. She turned on the fan and lay on the bed and tried to work out what to do, if there even was something she could do now that she'd burnt all her bridges with Sheila.

She heard the doorbell and ignored it, just not up to speaking to anyone.

She turned on her soothing music and lay there but it didn't soothe. Then there was a knock at her door.

'Tilly, please.' She just wanted to be alone with her thoughts. 'Go out with them…' Her voice trailed off, as standing there was a man who shouldn't be back in her bedroom again. 'What are you doing here?'

'God knows,' Cort said, because she was lying on top of her bed in just her knickers with a fan blowing. She'd been crying, her eyelids were swollen, her nose and lips too, and there was a jumble of used tissues by the bed. But there were two other things he noticed as well and he couldn't have this conversation with them there. 'Don't you cover up when your friends come in?'

'My friends don't come in when there's a scarf on the door,' Ruby said with her eyes closed again. 'And, no, Tilly, probably sees a hundred boobs a day in her job.'

'Please,' he said, and she opened her eyes and with a sigh leant over to a pile of clutter beside the bed and pulled out a very little top, but at least it covered her. She lay back and closed her eyes again and Cort opened the little purple sack on her bedside and tipped out her worry dolls.

'What are you doing?'

'Checking on them,' Cort said. 'And they're looking a lot more frazzled than they did last time I was here.'

She almost smiled.

'I'm a happy person usually,' she said. 'At least I was till I worked there. I'm not going back.'

'Up to you,' he said.

'Anyway—I'm not your responsibility.'

And given twelve hours or so ago they'd been in this bed together, somehow he felt that she was.

'I spoke to Sheila.'

'Oh, that's really going to stop the gossip.'

'Not just about you,' Cort said. 'Emergency is a difficult place to work and sometimes the atmosphere and the people can turn nasty. It's how they deal with it,' Cort explained. 'You see so much, you get hard, you get tough, and sometimes it just gets like that. People forget to support one another and they just need a little bit of nudging. It can be a very nice place. We're a great team usually,' Cort said.

'I don't care if they're all singing and smiling and holding hands,' Ruby said, 'I'm not going back. It's not just the staff, it's the patients and the relatives...' She closed her eyes and tried to explain it. 'It's the violence of the place.'

'It's not exactly a walk in the park on the psych ward,' Cort pointed out. 'If you're talking violence...'

'They're sick, though,' Ruby flared in passionate response. 'In Emergency they're just plain drunk or angry.'

'You're a good nurse.'

'No, I'm not.' She hated being placated. How did he know she was a good nurse? He'd seen her hold one arm. He didn't have much to base it on.

'You're going to be a great psych nurse, but part of that means you need good general training.'

She knew he was right.

'And that also means that you can be appalled and devastated by what happened at work this afternoon. That was a shift from hell.'

Finally she looked at him.

'Are you upset?'

He just sat there, because he tried so hard not to examine it, he really tried to just get on with the job, but she made him do so and finally he answered.

'I'm gutted,' Cort said, realising just how much he was, and he closed his eyes for a moment and blew out a breath. 'I guarantee everyone on that shift today is.' He heard her snort a disbelieving sigh, and even if he didn't go on paint-ball excursions, he always supported his team, everyone, at any time, even here in her bedroom.

'Everyone hurt today—whether or not they show it as you might expect. The thing is, Ruby, you'll be gone from there in a couple of weeks, but they are there, day in, day out, doing their very best not to burn out.'

Her phone rang and Ruby frowned at it.

'It's work.' She swallowed then answered it, and opened her mouth to speak and then listened, said goodbye and hung up.

'That was Sheila. She wants me back in for my early tomorrow, and she says if I do that she won't say anything about what happened today.'

Ruby gave a tight shrug. 'She sounds like my mother.'

To Cort it didn't sound like Sheila, because she always had plenty to say on everything, but he chose to keep quiet, because at least Ruby seemed to be thinking about going back.

'I shouldn't have run out.' She closed her eyes and all she could see was Violet, just a sweet little angel, and she wanted to weep at the horror, to fold up into a ball and sob, but she wouldn't. She couldn't while he was there.

'Just go,' she said.

'No,' he said. 'I'm not leaving you on your own.'

'I'm not your problem. Why would you want to help me?'

'You were very helpful to me last night.' He said it so awkwardly that she actually laughed.

'You make it sound like I cured your erectile dysfunction or something.'

'Er, no.'

'Helpful?' She wouldn't drop it, she really was the strangest person he had ever met. 'What do you mean, I was helpful?'

'Nice, then,' Cort said. 'When I didn't know I even needed someone to be. So now it's my turn to be nice to you. Come on, I'll take you out for dinner.'

'I don't want dinner.'

'Okay, you sit with your tissues and I'll fetch you a bottle of wine, shall I? How about a tragic movie? I'll just sit in the lounge and read a magazine till your friends get home, but I'm not leaving you on your own. Is there anything to eat in this place?'

'Okay, okay!' Ruby said.

He looked at the floor that seemed to be her wardrobe, and after a huff and a puff she stood and went to the real one and selected a skirt that Cort thought a little too short and a top not much bigger than the bra thing she was wearing, then she did something he wasn't expecting.

She turned and gave him a smile, a big, bright, Ruby smile, and he didn't return it because he knew it was false.

'You don't go that fast to happy.'

'I do,' Ruby said. 'Don't worry, I won't mope about.'

'I don't need entertaining,' came Cort's response.

He took her to a place near his flat, which was a suburb further than hers from the hospital, and, yes, he hoped no one from work would see them and, yes, it felt strange to be out with a woman who wasn't his wife.

'Just water for me.' She beamed when the waiter handed him the wine menu. 'You go ahead, though.'

'Just water, thanks,' Cort said, because he needed all his wits about him tonight. As he stared at the menu he told himself he was being stupid. He'd been out with friends, with his sister, with colleagues, but that had been different. Then he looked over his menu to where she sat and knew why. He hadn't been out in a very long time with a woman he'd made love to and he was clearly rubbish at one-night stands because as much as she insisted she wasn't, she felt a whole lot like his problem.

He just couldn't read her.

He knew she was bleeding inside yet those brown eyes smiled up at the waiter.

'Mushroom tortellini, and I'll have some herb bread, please.'

'I'll have a steak.' Cort glanced through the cuts available.

'Actually,' Ruby said, 'I'm a vegetarian.'

'Well, I'm not,' Cort said. He glanced up and was about to select his choice and add 'Rare' to the waiter, but in an entirely one-off gesture, because there would be no more dinners, because this wouldn't happen again, because, after all, she hadn't even wanted to come, he revised his choice. 'I'll have the tortellini, too, thanks.'

He waited for her to interrupt, to say no, go ahead, it didn't bother her, he should have what he wanted, but she didn't, and as he handed back the menu she smiled again.

'Thanks.'

'What do your friends say about it?'

'Well, we don't go out for dinner much, but if they bring home lamb curry or something I just tend to...'

'I meant about today.' He would not let her divert him and he saw the tensing of her jaw, felt her reluctance to talk about it. 'What did they say when you told them about today?'

'That it's understandable—I mean, anyone would be upset about a child...'

'About you running off?' Only then did it dawn on him that she was being deliberately evasive. 'You haven't told them?' Cort frowned as she blushed. 'I thought you were close.'

'We are!' Ruby leapt to the defence of her housemates. They were together in everything, there for each other through thick and thin... Except Cort was right, she hadn't told anyone how she was feeling. She lifted her eyes and looked at the one person that she had told and couldn't fathom why she'd chosen to reveal it to him.

'I hate it, Cort,' Ruby admitted. 'I feel sick walking to work.' She waited for his reaction, for his eyebrows to rise, for him to frown or dismiss her, but he just sat there, his lack of reaction somehow encouraging. 'I spend the whole time I'm there dreading that buzzer going off or the emergency phone ringing... I was going to run off yesterday before we spoke to the relatives...'

'But you didn't.' Cort tried to lift her up.

'I wish I had.' Ruby was adamant. 'I wish I had, because then I wouldn't have gone back, then I'd never have seen what I did today.'

'What do you think your friends would say?' Cort asked. 'If they knew just how much you're struggling right now?'

'They'd be devastated,' Ruby said, and that was why she felt she couldn't do it to them. 'I don't want to burden them, I don't want…' She didn't want to talk about it and luckily the waiter came with their tortellini and did the cheese and pepper thing, and by the time he'd gone, thankfully for Ruby, Cort had changed the subject.

'Are you Adam's sister?'

Ruby nodded and saw his slight grimace. 'He bought the house and I guess I'm the landlady.' She grinned at the thought. 'I rent it out for him, drive his car now and then, he comes back once in a while and…' Her voice trailed off. She'd been about to make a light-hearted comment about how every time Adam returned and didn't notice Jess he broke her heart all over again, but that would be betraying a confidence, a sort of in-house secret, and she looked over at the man who had taken her out for dinner on the worst of nights, and wondered how he made it so very easy to reveal things she normally never would.

'What's he doing now?'

'He's doing aid work.'

'Still for Operation New Faces?'

Ruby nodded. 'He's in South America, I think. Don't worry, I'm not going to say anything to him about what happened.' She smiled at his shuttered features. 'Anyway, you've treated me very well. We've been out for dinner and everything...' There was almost a smile now on his lips. 'He's hardly an angel himself.'

'Still,' Cort said, and then looked at her lovely red hair and remembered something else. 'I worked once with your dad.'

She winced for him.

'Before I moved to Melbourne I did a surgical rotation. I worked with him in plastics—he was Chief.'

'He's Chief at home too.'

It was a shame he didn't have a steak because he'd have loved to stick his knife into it, because he could suddenly well remember the great

Gregory Carmichael, holding court in the theatre, throwing instruments if a nurse was a beat too late in anticipating his needs. He remembered too how he had regaled his audience as he'd worked with the dramas in his home life, the wild teenager who answered back and did everything, it would seem, any normal teenager would, just not a teenager of Gregory's, because, as he told his colleagues, he was once and for all going to sort her out.

'What does he say about you doing nursing?'

'He doesn't like it, especially that I want to go into mental health. I used to work in a little shop on the beach, selling New-Age stuff...'

'He'd have hated that.'

'Not really,' Ruby said. 'They had no problem with me working at the shop, they gave me an allowance as well.'

'It's nice that they can.'

'It's all or nothing with them. I had to follow in his grand footsteps or have a little job while

I waited for a suitable Mr Right. A psychiatric nurse isn't something he wants me doing.'

'Are you talking?'

'Of course,' Ruby said. 'We didn't fall out or anything. We talk, just not about what I do.'

'So I'm guessing you can't discuss with him the problems you're having.'

She gave a tight shake of her head.

'What about your mum?'

'She'll just say I should have listened to my father in the first place.'

'What if I keep an eye out for you.'

'How?' Ruby said, because she knew it was impossible. 'Can you imagine Siobhan if she gets so much as a sniff…?'

'Why don't you tell your friends?' Cort suggested. 'And you've got Sheila having a think… Don't give it up, Ruby.'

They didn't talk about it again, not till his car was approaching the turn for Hill Street.

'Drive me down to the beach.'

'It's time to go home, Ruby.'

'It's two hundred metres,' Ruby said, but she knew it wasn't going to happen. He was a senior registrar and didn't park his car by the beach like some newly licensed teenager, so he took her home instead.

'Are you going to come in?'

'No,' Cort said, and his face was the same but had she looked at his hands she would have seen that they were clenched around the wheel.

'Please,' Ruby said, because, well, she wanted him to.

'I'm not going into work in these trousers again,' Cort said, because he knew she wasn't asking him in for coffee. He thought of her room and the little slice of heaven they'd shared there last night, and then he told the truth, because aside from work, aside from the age difference, a relationship between them was the last thing he could consider now. There was so much hurt, so much blackness in his soul, he couldn't darken such a lovely young thing with it. 'We'd never work.' He turned to her.

'I know,' Ruby said, because, well, they couldn't. 'You're going to stop for a burger on the way home, aren't you?'

'Probably.' Still he looked at her. 'Are you going to go in tomorrow?'

'I don't know,' Ruby admitted.

'Try talking to your friends,' Cort said. 'You don't always have to be the happy one.' He saw her rapid blink. 'If they're real friends—'

'They are,' she interrupted.

'Then you can turn to them. Go on in,' he said.

'Don't I get a kiss?'

'Ruby, please…'

'One kiss,' Ruby said. 'Just one…' And she made him smile. Not a big grin, but there was lightness where there had been none. 'Then you can go back to ignoring me.'

'I'm ignoring you now,' Cort said, and went to turn on the engine.

'Just a kiss on the cheek.' Ruby's hand stopped him. 'End it as friends.'

He leant over and went to give her a peck, just to shut her up perhaps, but his lips had less control than he did and they lingered there. He felt her skin and her breath and she felt his, felt the press of his mouth on her cheek and then his lips part and he kissed her skin, traced her cheek with his mouth and traced it again. He held her hair and then removed his mouth and kissed her other cheek till she was trembling inside and her mouth was searching his cheek. If her friends were kneeling up on the sofa, watching, they might wonder why they were licking cheeks like two cats, but it was their kiss and their magic and she wanted his mouth so badly that torture was bliss.

''Night, then,' Ruby breathed, and she turned to go then heard the delicious clunk of four locking car doors. She turned to him, to the reward of his mouth and a proper goodnight kiss.

And as it ended, he did the strangest, nicest thing. He pulled down her top just a little, and kissed the top of her chest, just above her breast but not on it, he really kissed that little area, so hard and so deep that as she pressed into the seat, as her hands buried themselves in his hair, she thought she might come, and then he lifted his head to hers.

'I missed that bit last time,' Cort said, and it would be so easy to accept the invitation in her eyes, to follow every instinct and step inside, except their one night together would turn into two and that was more than Cort was ready for.

'Now, you really had better go.'

'I had,' Ruby said, because getting involved with the senior registrar of the department she was struggling so much in wasn't the most sensible mix.

Sensible.

'It wasn't supposed to be like this,' Ruby mused. 'I mean, it wasn't supposed to be this good.'

Cort gave a very wry smile. 'You make a terrible one-night stand,' he said, and it was very much a compliment, because she was more in his head than she was supposed to be.

'So do you,' Ruby said.

And that was that.

It had to be.

CHAPTER EIGHT

'WHAT time do you call this?'

They were all sitting at the kitchen table, three witches around a cauldron, three mothers to answer to, but Ruby loved them all.

'I just went out for dinner.'

'With?' Jess demanded.

'Cort,' Ruby said, 'but it *was* just dinner.'

'This morning it was supposed to be just one night.' Ellie beamed. 'And now dinner. It sounds like…' Ellie always did this, an eternal Pollyanna. Cort could have simply been giving her a lift home and she'd have them walking down the aisle in a matter of weeks, but Ruby halted her there.

'He's a nice man,' Ruby said. 'But it's not going to turn into anything.'

'Why not?' Ellie asked.

'Because it can't,' Ruby said.

'You look happier,' Tilly said, and Ruby smiled and nodded just as she always did. She really didn't need to trouble them with it, because she'd made her mind up that she was going back to do her shift tomorrow, but Ruby took a deep breath because as much as Cort was on her mind, he wasn't the only thing, and maybe her friends did have a right to know. After all, she'd expect it from them.

'There was a problem at work today. That's why he took me out. I didn't just come home because I was upset. I ran off in the middle of my shift.'

'Because of Cort?' Ellie asked.

'No! I ran off because I hate it there. I mean, I *really* hate it there and they're talking about making me repeat it…' She was close to tears as she said it, more than close to tears because she had to keep sniffing them back. Stupidly she kept saying sorry and trying to smile and apologise for how she felt, but there were arms around her, and the shocked voice of Tilly.

'Ruby, why on earth haven't you said?'

'I just...' Because she was the positive one, the one who told them all over and over that they could lift their mood and change their energy. Yet it wasn't that, it was more that she didn't want to trouble them with this, didn't want to burden them with her problems.

'I couldn't face another day like today, and who's to say it won't happen again? Or worse,' Ruby said, though she couldn't really think of anything that could be worse. 'Sheila's going to fail me if I don't pick up. Then I'll have to repeat the placement and I can't.' Ruby shook her head. 'I cannot repeat it.'

'Then you can't fail.' Jess was firm. 'How long have you got left there?' She went over to the calendar and checked Ruby's shifts. 'You've only got tomorrow left on days, the rest of your shifts are agency on the psych ward…'

'Then I've got nights.' Ruby crumpled. 'It's bad enough during the day.'

'I'm on nights that week,' Tilly said. 'I'll make sure we have our breaks together.'

'I'm on an early tomorrow,' Ellie offered. 'And if I can get away, we can meet in the canteen on your break. If I can't then Jess will. We'll get you through this, Ruby.'

'I know.' Ruby smiled, because that was what they wanted, to cheer her up, to reassure her it would all be okay, but as they said goodnight it was a relief to get to her bedroom and drop the facade because, yes, they'd be there in the mornings and evenings and even there on her breaks, but nobody could do the hard bit for her. No one could take away her very real fear of that place.

Cort had.

She undressed and ran her fingers over the

mark his mouth had made, and tonight, with him, for a while she had honestly forgotten.

So too had he.

She didn't know what, but as she climbed into bed and looked at her *frazzled* worry dolls, they reminded her of him, taking all her cares and carrying them for a while, and somehow she did the same for him. He was a different Cort when it was just them together, a lighter, funnier, terribly sexy man that sometimes he allowed her to glimpse.

And despite fighting words, despite telling her friends that it couldn't go further, there was this little question mark burning inside her, a tiny flame of hope that she dared not fan in case she blew it out completely.

Hopefully, in a couple of weeks she'd be finished with Emergency for good—and then it wouldn't be a problem.

Unless she failed.

Unless she had to go back.

It was a very good reason for closing her eyes and willing sleep to come.

She had work to do tomorrow.

And she had to do it well.

CHAPTER NINE

WALKING out had been tough, but walking back was so much harder.

Tilly walked with her to work and even if Ruby felt she couldn't tell her the full extent of how difficult it was, she was grateful for her friend's support.

'Just get through today!' Tilly said, and Ruby nodded, putting on her brightest smile and walking in through the department.

'Morning,' Ruby offered to Hannah in the locker room.

'Morning,' Hannah answered, though her voice was flat. 'Hopefully today will be better.'

Ruby suddenly got a little of what Cort had been saying—that Hannah, even though she was one of the most senior nurses, even though she was so much older and wiser, would have had a rough night processing yesterday's events too.

Ruby had timed it so that she wouldn't have to face the staffroom, so she headed straight to handover, where the early shift were starting to gather.

There was Cort, talking to an intern, but thankfully he didn't look over as she joined the group and neither did he later when Sheila did the allocations.

'Connor, take Ruby through with you to the obs ward.'

She wasn't sure if she was relieved as she headed round there—the obs ward was the easiest place to be. There were a few patients to be assessed and either discharged or admitted to the main wards, and there was the hand clinic to be held there later. But there was also plenty of time for gossip and chatter and Connor seized on it the second the night nurse had handed over and left.

'What happened?' Connor was the biggest gossip in the world and loathed missing out on anything. 'I heard that you walked out in the middle of your shift.'

'Yes,' Ruby said because she had.

'Was Siobhan giving you a hard time?' Connor rolled his eyes. 'She can be a right bitch.' But Ruby refused to say any more about it, she just wanted it forgotten, and she did her best to just chat and be her usual happy self with the patients. She even managed not to blush, well, maybe just a little bit, when Cort came in to discharge the patients or have them moved to a ward.

He sat writing at the desk as Ruby stripped some beds and, really, they had no need to worry about gossip.For all the attention he paid her, no one could have known that just a couple of nights ago…

'Ruby.' Sheila's voice came over the intercom and Ruby went over, expecting another admission. 'Can you come to my office?'

'She said she wouldn't say anything about it.' She forgot for a moment where they were.

'What's the problem?' Sensing gossip, Connor bounded over.

'Sheila wants to see me. I think it's about my dummy spit yesterday.'

'Then you'd better get there.' Connor grinned. 'I'll have a nice coffee waiting for you afterwards.'

Ruby wanted it forgotten, wanted to get back to happy, not sit in an office and go over things.

'I thought we'd agreed that you wouldn't say anything.' Ruby was shaky as she sat down.

'I meant officially,' Sheila said.

'Oh.'

'I meant if you were back at work this morning then I wasn't going to have to go through all the official channels.' She peered at her student. 'Ruby, you gave no indication you were unhappy, or that the place was distressing you so much. I just thought you were avoiding work.'

'No,' Ruby said, because she'd take a mop now and clean the whole length of the hospital and every toilet in between rather than go through yesterday again.

'You had every opportunity to tell me at your assessment how you were feeling. You coped marvellously with the resuscitation yesterday...'

'I was devastated.'

'We all were,' Sheila said. 'But we all got on with the job—as did you.' Sheila paused for a moment. 'But then suddenly you're running off.'

'I honestly couldn't have gone in there.'

'And I honestly couldn't have known how distressed you were.' Sheila gave an exasperated shrug. 'There has to be communication. How can we help you if we don't even know you're having problems?'

'Well, you know now,' Ruby said.

'Which is why I've given you a gentle day today. You can stay in Obs and run the clinics

and I'll bring you out to observe anything interesting…is that what you want?'

'No,' Ruby said. 'Yes.'

'You're supposed to be on nights next week.'

'Is it possible to stay on days?'

'No, Ruby.' Sheila shook her head. She glanced
at the roster. 'I don't just give out passes—you
chose a busy teaching hospital for your placements, and that means there are certain things
that are expected from you. A pass from Eastern
Beaches means a lot.' She did, though, relent a
touch. 'What if I change your shifts so you're
with Connor, Siobhan and I? We're doing nights
next week, but we're on over the weekend. It's
even crazier then.'

'I don't know,' Ruby said, because night duty
with Siobhan wasn't particularly enticing, but
Connor was nice and now that Sheila knew…
She hesitated too long with her answer.

'Ruby…' Sheila was not going to spoonfeed her.
'We're not going to ask you to deal with things

single-handed, we'll be there with you, but you have to fulfil your placement. I'll put you down for Wednesday, Thursday and Friday. I'm on Saturday night as well but I think you might want to miss that one—there's a festival on in the city and the place will be steaming. Do you want me to change you?'

Ruby nodded. 'Thanks, Sheila. I'm sorry to have caused so much trouble, and I really am sorry for walking out yesterday.'

'We've all done it,' Sheila said, and when Ruby shot her a look of disbelief, Sheila smiled. 'Okay, I don't head for home, but I've handed over the keys more than a few times and headed to my office or just out to the car park. And,' Sheila added, 'there is some tentative good news on little Victoria, Violet's sister—it's looking more promising than it did yesterday. They're talking about extubating her later on this afternoon.'

It was good news, far, far better than Ruby had

hoped, except it didn't take away the pain—it just didn't.

'How was it?' Cort asked a little later as she took the discharge book through to the main section and asked him to write up some discharge meds. She gave a tight shrug.

'Ruby?'

'I *have* to do nights.'

'You'll be fine.'

'I don't think I can do it, Cort.'

'Did you speak to your housemates?'

She couldn't really talk much more because Siobhan came over, and what could Cort really have to say to a student apart from discussing the patients? He took the folder from her and skimmed through it.

'Is everything quiet around there?' Siobhan asked.

'Fine,' Ruby said. 'One's just waiting for a lift home. I'm just asking Mr Mason to write up some analgesia.'

He didn't get another chance to talk to her.

At about half past three the day staff left, including Ruby, and that was that.

Some one-night stand!

For the rest of the week Cort thought about her. Once when Connor rang Psych to see if they were ready for a patient that was being admitted, Cort almost wanted to rip the phone out of his hand when he realised Connor was talking to Ruby.

'I might just bring the patient up myself!' Connor said, and then laughed at something Ruby had said. 'Well, enjoy it while you can. We'll run you ragged next week.' And then he told her he was on a lunch break soon and then added, 'Two sugars!' Cort felt his jaw tighten, not jealous so much, because Connor would never be interested in Ruby in that way but, yes, jealous, because why did he get to have a drink with Ruby, why did he get to chat to her in his lunch break, why did he get to see her in an environment she loved?

'Because,' Elise said, when, desperate for some female insight, finally Cort cracked and told his sister just a little of what had taken place, 'you're not friends with her.'

'Oh, so just because we've slept together we can't be friends?'

'Cort,' Elise said. 'Do you want to be just friends?'

'No.'

'Friends with benefits?'

'No!' God, no! Cort thought in horror—he really wasn't ready for all this. 'I'm just worried about her. She's got a lot to deal with at the moment. I don't know who, if anyone, she's talking about it with. I guess I just want to be around for her and I don't want to make things more complicated for her either.' He was more confused about a woman than he had ever been in his life.

Ever.

'She's nothing like you'd expect, Elise.'

'You mean she's nothing like Beth.'

And did his sister always have to be so forthright? But she was on to something.

'I thought that was what it would be,' Cort said, because feelings for another woman, if ever they arrived again, were supposed to enter slowly. Another Beth, or close, or similar.

'What do you want, Cort?'

Not this, he thought, but didn't say it.

Not this, Cort thought, because surely he wasn't ready.

'Just leave it,' Cort said, and decided that he would too.

CHAPTER TEN

HE TRIED to leave it.

Cort really did.

But when he was called in late on Monday night, he sensed the second he arrived that Ruby wasn't there.

There was no one he could ask without making things obvious, which was what he was hoping to avoid.

He couldn't even ring her, because they hadn't even swapped phone numbers, which, Cort told himself, was a pretty good indicator as to what they had both wanted from each other that night.

It just felt like something more now.

'I'm going to lie down in the on-call room for a couple of hours.' Cort yawned around seven a.m., because he was officially on duty at nine a.m. and two hours' sleep was too good to pass up.

'No, you're not.' Hannah grinned as she walked over. 'We've got a mum who's not going to make it up to Maternity.'

'Oh, God,' Cort groaned, because this was happening rather too often. The car park for Maternity was currently closed so that new boom gates could be erected, which meant mums-to-be were currently having to walk a considerable distance further, and on more than a couple of occasions they landed in Emergency.

'We've rung Maternity, they're sending some-one down.' Hannah smiled 'Come on, Cort—let's go and have a baby!'

'I'm not responsible enough,' Cort said, and Hannah grinned back, but it was Cort who checked himself, because normally he'd have said nothing. Normally, he didn't joke along with the staff, not even a little bit. Usually he just rolled up his sleeves and got on with whatever job presented itself. Ruby had changed him, Cort realised. Ruby really was infectious.

'Hi, there…' Cort smiled at the mother who was groaning in pain but, unlike the last couple of maternity patients who had landed in Emergency, Cort wasn't quite sure if she was at that toe-curling, holding-it-in stage. He put a hand on her stomach and asked a couple of questions, but to save her from two examinations, as Maternity was sending someone down, he decided to hold off for a moment.

'Can you believe it?' Hannah was looking more than a little boot-faced when Cort stepped outside. 'Maternity sent a grad midwife—she's just washing her hands.' Hannah rolled her eyes. 'She looks about twelve!'

Cort said nothing. Hannah was clearly offended that, on her summons, the entire obstetric team wasn't running down the corridors now, but privately he thought it was a little wishful thinking on Hannah's part that an emergency room birth was imminent.

'Hi, there!' Cort deliberately didn't react when it was Tilly who walked towards them and was also quietly grateful that she introduced herself as if they had never met. 'I'm Matilda. Tilly. We're incredibly busy in Maternity at the moment, so they asked me to dash down and see if I could help.'

'She's through there,' Cort said, and told her a little of his findings, adding, 'Though I haven't done an internal yet.'

'I'll come in with you,' Hannah said.

'I'll be fine,' Tilly politely declined.

She was very calm and unruffled and thanked both Cort and Hannah then disappeared into the cubicle as Hannah sat brooding at the nurses' station, staring at the curtains like a cat put out in a storm. 'If we say we need help,' Hannah said, 'surely they should send—'

'They're busy,' Cort interrupted. 'And I guess

they figured the patient can't come to much harm as there are doctors and nurses here.' He would normally have left it there, but Ruby must still be in the air for him, because he looked over and continued the conversation with Hannah. 'Have you thought about doing midwifery?'

'Me?' Hannah scoffed, then rolled her eyes and added a little sheepishly, 'Every day for the last six months or so. I'm just not sure it's worth trying—I'm nearly fifty. I've been in Emergency for ever.'

'Maybe if you're nicer to Tilly you could see if you could spend a few hours up there. It might help you make up your mind.' He looked over as Tilly came towards them.

'She's fine.' Tilly smiled. 'Still a while to go, I think. I'll take her up to Maternity—how do I arrange a porter?'

'The porters are just having a coffee. I'll take her up with you if you like,' Hannah offered. 'I'll just go and grab my cardigan.'

And there was a moment, just a moment where he could have asked Tilly why Ruby hadn't come in—to check if she was okay or had, in fact, just not shown up. A moment to acknowledge Tilly and to step down from the safe higher ground of Senior Reg and just talk as you would to someone you knew casually, who was a friend of someone you cared about.

He chose not to take it.

Hannah returned with her cardigan and a marked shift in attitude towards the *grad* midwife and Cort pushed through the morning, but it all felt wrong. The busy department felt strangely quiet without that blaze of red to silently ponder, and at lunchtime, unable to face the staffroom, Cort headed up to the canteen.

'It's good to get away from there, even for a little while.' Sheila joined him in the canteen queue and Cort gave her a smile, though his own company was really all that he wanted. It had been a long night, followed by a very long morning.

'I thought you were on nights this week.'

'I'm supposed to be in for a management day,' Sheila said as they shuffled down the queue and rather dispiritedly checked out the food on offer. 'Which is a bit of a joke—I haven't even seen my office.'

The queue slowed down and Cort yawned and asked for another shot to be added to his coffee. Instead of the chicken salad he was half considering, or the cream-cheese bagel that was curling at the edges, he decided to push his luck with the canteen lady.

'Can I have a bacon sandwich?'

'Then they'll all want one,' she said, because most of the meals were wrapped in plastic and pre-made now, except on very rare occasions.

'He's been here eighteen hours straight.' Sheila put in a word for him and as Cort turned to thank her, a normal day, a normal shuffle along the queue in the canteen suddenly somehow brightened.

She was like a butterfly.

Swooping in on a gloomy canteen, which was wall to wall navy and white uniforms and dark green scrubs or sensible suits, Ruby gave it colour.

Her hair was down and she was wearing denim shorts that showed slim, pale legs and a sort of mesh shirt that was reds and golds and swirls of white, and she had on leather strappy sandals and was just so light and breezy that apart from the lanyard round her neck and the anxious-looking woman by her side, you'd never have known she was working.

The queue passed him as he stood waiting for his order and he listened as she stood and helped her patient with her food selection, encouraging her and gently suggesting alternatives, and she made him notice things that he never had before. Like how kind the staff were with the patient, and how other staff behind in the queue didn't huff and puff and moan about how long she was taking, but with a nod from the cashier moved subtly past.

He saw Ruby's calm presence, and he saw something else too—that just as she felt she couldn't do Emergency, couldn't stand what he did, he realised that he couldn't readily do her job either. He could not stand with endless patience as the woman struggled with a seemingly simple decision, pasta or potato salad, but, Cort knew, what a vital job it was.

'Maybe rice?' the patient said, and Cort felt his jaw clench, but Ruby just nodded.

'That sounds good.'

And Ruby waited and waited for her patient's decision, except she didn't seem to be waiting, just pausing, and Cort found himself wanting to know what the woman would choose, to prod her in the back and say, 'Just have the rice, for

God's sake.' Because, yes, there were some jobs that not everyone could do.

'Here we are, Cort.' The largest bacon sandwich ever came over the counter and for the first time since he'd been a teenager, Cort thought he might blush as he took the plate, headed over to Sheila and sat down.

'I've had a word with some of the staff,' Sheila said, because it was easier to talk away from the ward. 'As you know, I'm going to do a stint on nights and see how it's all going on there.'

Cort took a sip of his coffee and nodded.

'How's Jamelia?'

'She's doing better,' Cort admitted, though his eyes kept wandering to where Ruby was warming her patient's meal in the microwave. 'She just needs someone to shadow her and I've spoken with Doug about it—we'll get there,' he said, because they would.

'I've got a good team, Cort,' Sheila said. 'I

know they can go a bit far at times, but they have to deal with a lot.'

'I'm aware of that.' He was *more* than aware of that.

'We just need to remember we are a team,' Sheila said. 'And that sometimes we struggle. All of us do, Cort.' He glanced up at her, because for a moment there he thought she was referring to him. 'It's good to hear you went out last week.'

Cort rolled his eyes and took a large bite of his sandwich.

'It really is,' Sheila said. 'You want teamwork, Cort, well, you have to be a part of it.'

And his eyes roamed the canteen as he went to take another bite and then he saw where she was sitting and Ruby looked over at him and somehow the sandwich didn't taste quite so nice. Part of him wanted to take another bite, a really big one, but instead he put the sandwich down and then he was rewarded with a very private smile, and that did it.

He *would* go there tonight, Cort decided.

He would go over, because he knew that she was struggling and he didn't know if she'd told her friends, and, he admitted to himself, if he was going to be there at any point in the future, then he ought to be there for her now.

'Not hungry?' Sheila frowned at his discarded sandwich.

'Not as much as I thought I was.'

'Is that Ruby?' Sheila asked, knowing full well that it was. 'Doing an agency shift?'

Cort said nothing, just as he usually would.

'She finishes soon,' Sheila said, which she never usually would either. 'I'm having a lot of trouble getting that one through.' She picked up the untouched half of Cort's sandwich and took a bite. 'She's like Lila…'

'Your daughter?'

'Both vegetarians, both live on another planet.' Cort drained his coffee and still said nothing, but for the second time in fifteen minutes or so he was blushing.

'I still don't know if she'll turn up for her shift. What is it with these girls? My daughter just dropped out of maths—two years of study gone, just like that.'

'Sheila,' Cort asked, 'what if your pager went and they asked you to go and work on Ophthalmology?'

'They wouldn't.' Sheila flushed, because she could not stand eyes—they were her thing, the one thing she ran from—she didn't even like putting in eyedrops.

'If they did, though?' Cort said. 'If they told you that you had to spend six weeks there—and in the ophthalmic theatre too.'

'I'd say no,' Sheila said. 'Because I'm allowed to. Emergency is an essential part of her course. Anyway…' Sheila met him with a firm gaze '…let's hope she turns up and that we can keep things uneventful for her.' And that was all she did say, but he took the warning, because in three years he'd never so much as looked at anyone and, yep, Emergency could be a horrible place to work at times and he didn't want any more of the spotlight falling on Ruby.

'Cort?' Sheila checked, and he nodded. Nothing more was said, but both fully understood.

As he headed back to work, deliberately he avoided Ruby's table, and deliberately he didn't glance back.

It hurt not to be acknowledged, though Ruby did her best not to let it show, just concentrated on her patient, the aim to keep things light and un-eventful, because Louise hated eating in public.

'Can we go now?' Louise said, for perhaps the fiftieth time.

'Soon,' Ruby said, gently but firmly, delib-erately eating her salad as slowly as she could. 'I want to finish my lunch, I won't get another break.' Though as Sheila walked directly towards them, Ruby was rather tempted to take the easy option and tell Louise they were heading back to the unit.

'Hi, there, Ruby.' She gave a brief smile to Louise too.

'Hi, Sheila.' Ruby wasn't too embarrassed to be seen working. As a third-year student, she was able to practise as a division-two nurse and a lot of the students crammed in as many shifts as they could. Still, it was just a little awkward given she was due to be on night shift tomorrow.

'Are you doing some agency?'

'Hospital bank.' Ruby gave a sweet smile and then pointedly turned her attention back to her patient. When Sheila continued to hover, Ruby extended the conversation a touch. 'It's my last one for this week.'

'Good,' Sheila said, 'because you'll need all your wits about you for night duty. I'll see you tomorrow.'

'Looking forward to it,' Ruby said as Sheila finally left.

'Who was that?' Louise asked.

'The A and E NUM.' Ruby rolled her eyes. 'She's not too bad really, but she runs a tight ship.'

'She reminds me of my mother.' Louise gave a wry smile and Ruby was delighted to see that now the conversation was rather more normal, without thinking, Louise took another mouthful of food.

'Funny you say that!' Ruby grinned. 'I remind her of her daughter apparently.'

It was a slow walk back to the unit, deliberately so, because Louise would have happily run all the way back, just to burn up a few extra calories, but Ruby deliberately ambled, and never in a million years would Sheila, or even Jess, Ellie or Tilly, realise that as she stopped by the guest shop and chatted about some flowers, her mind really was on the patient, that this was, in fact, a deliberate action and part of her job.

Doing this, she was happy, Ruby realised, then tried to push away that thought, although it was occurring all too frequently lately. She could stay a div two if she didn't complete Emergency, or Sheila insisted that she repeat, but Ruby didn't have to—she could still work in her beloved psych. Okay, she might not be able to go as far in her career as she would like, but she could still do the job she loved.

As she swiped her ID card and they entered the unit that actually felt like home, Ruby had no intention of not showing up tomorrow.

It was just nice to have options, that was all.

CHAPTER ELEVEN

HE SAW her again, walking down the hill towards her home, and, yes, he had guessed at the time she might finish and had taken a different route home, because though he had heeded Sheila's warning he did need to see her—away from the hospital and house—just to check in with her, to find out if she was okay and, Cort admitted, tell her how much he was thinking of her.

'Hey.' He felt like a kerb-crawler as he pulled in beside her, but she gave him a very nice smile. 'Do you want a lift?'

'I'm five minutes away,' Ruby said, but she climbed into the car anyway.

'How come you're not on nights?'

'Sheila swapped them round so that I'd be on

with her so I'm doing a couple of shifts on Psych.
I can work as a div two,' Ruby explained.

'And you're liking it?'

'Loving it.'

'Not long now till you'll be studying again.'
He glanced at her. 'For your mental-health nursing...'

She stayed silent.

'A few nights and you'll be done.'

'Yep.'

He turned and looked at her again and she
smiled back at him but he was quite sure it didn't
reach her eyes.

'Ruby?'

'It wouldn't be the end of the world if I don't
pass,' Ruby said, and instead of looking at him
she looked out of the window. 'I can work as a
div two—I've loved my shifts.'

'For three nights' work you can be Div One.'

Ruby shrugged. 'If she passes me. If not, maybe
I can speak to the uni...'

Cort knew he should just drop her home, should go back to his own and sort out his head instead of her, because he didn't know how he was feeling. Elise was right, as always—if love came again, he'd expected more of the same. With Beth, passion had been a slower-building thing, colleagues first, then friendship, dinner, a steady incline to a higher place, but with Ruby it was like a rapid descent, this jump into the unknown.

'Do you want to come in?' As they sat at the traffic lights he just said it and he saw her frown, because they were two minutes from her home. 'My place,' Cort said.

'Careful,' Ruby warned. 'You'll be giving Ellie ideas.'

'I'm always careful,' Cort said, just not where Ruby was concerned.

It was the most stunning flat she had ever seen—not the interior, more the view.

Cort fetched her a drink and flicked through his post but didn't open it. It was from lawyers who were tying up Beth's estate and one from the nursing home too, no doubt with the final bill. He thought for a moment about telling her, but despite her smile she was dealing with so much already. He knew that, though he longed to share it, it might be better to wait just a little while longer, because this evening was about Ruby and getting her through the next week— his grief, his past, would still be there, waiting. Ruby's future was the only thing that he might be able to change.

'They pay registrars too much.' She looked out at the view and swirled her drink. 'It's gorgeous.'

He couldn't embarrass her or make her feel awkward—couldn't tell her about insurance pay-outs and the guilt of buying a place that his wife would have loved. So deep was the pain of his past, he just didn't know how to share it.

He knew, though, how to remove it for a while.

And if that sounded selfish, Cort didn't care

because he knew he helped her too. Knew that somehow she confided in him.

'You need colour.' She looked at his surroundings. 'This is brown, Cort, not taupe.'

'I've got colour.'

And that made her blush because his eyes were on hers, and her cheeks turned up the colour a little bit more.

'Look,' he said, because he was worried for her, 'about nights—'

'Am I here for a lecture or sex?' Ruby interrupted, 'and if it's both, can we skip the lecture? I'll be fine on nights. I'm just going to...' she gave an impatient shrug '...not think about it.'

'I'm shadowing Jamelia,' Cort said, 'so I'll be around, but...' he hesitated, 'I don't know how she could know anything, but I think Sheila warned me today, about you, about us. I certainly haven't said anything.'

Of that she had no doubt.

'Sheila's a witch,' Ruby said. 'She'd just have

to look into her crystal ball.' But Cort just stood there, not impressed with her theory.

'I don't think we've done anything at work that's been obvious, but there were a lot of people at the party and your housemates...'

'They would never say anything.' She had no doubt there either. 'Siobhan was at the party. I don't think she likes me...'

And that made sense to Cort, because Siobhan had made it clear on a number of occasions that she liked him.

'Maybe they just...' Cort tried for the right word and came up with a very simple one. 'Noticed.' Even if he played it down, even if he'd pretended not to notice, from his first day back at work he'd noticed Ruby, had found himself watching her when he hadn't intended to.

And now he told her just how much he had... noticed.

'I didn't need help with that arm,' Cort said, and he watched her blink as his words hit home.

'Ted was completely zonked, I could have done it without local anaesthetic and he wouldn't have felt a thing, wouldn't have moved a muscle.'

Ruby started to laugh. 'So you got me into trouble.'

'You were already in trouble,' Cort pointed out. 'I do feel bad, though.'

'For what?' Ruby asked, and she felt a sort of warmness spread through her that this guarded man, one she'd thought she'd hauled to her room and randomly seduced, had been attracted to her all along.

Had, in fact, instigated it.

She'd never have guessed, not for a moment, not if she looked back and replayed every minute before that night over and over, because all he'd been was crabby.

'I'm glad you told me.'

'And you?' Cort asked, not for ego but he was curious. Had the attraction that had hit been as instant for her?

'I thought you were good looking,' Ruby breathed. 'I guess I didn't think further. You were just...' And she looked at him and told him exactly what he was. 'Gorgeous.'

'We have to be careful,' Cort said, 'till you're done.'

And the warmness that spread through her turned to fire as she realised what he was saying.

'I shouldn't have picked you up today, but I was worried about you,' Cort admitted. 'I thought you hadn't shown up for your nights. You told me you were on nights on Monday.'

'Sheila changed them,' Ruby explained again. 'I have to do three, and she suggested I do them with her. I'm on tomorrow.' He could hear the dread in her voice even though she tried to veil it, and he didn't really understand. There were so many things he loathed. Every step he had walked along the corridor in Beth's nursing home he had dreaded and her funeral hadn't exactly been something he'd looked forward to, but he'd just put one foot in front of the other and got on with it. It had never entered his head to walk away.

'You're going to be fine. I'll be at work, though I'll have to—'

'I know, I know,' Ruby interrupted. 'You'll just ignore me like you ignore everyone.'

'I don't.'

Ruby just shrugged.

'And I won't come to the house…'

'They really wouldn't say anything.'

'It's a few nights, Ruby.' Which sounded easy, except he'd driven around looking for her when he shouldn't have and even a few nights seemed impossible from here. 'Once it's over…' He left the rest to her imagination and, boy, did it soar.

She had been scared to even glimpse at a future, hadn't thought that her blissful night with this incredible man could be anything other than a cherished memory. That a man like Cort might really want to get to know her more.

That, as brilliant as it was, it wasn't just sex.

'You'll get through these nights.' He saw her eyes briefly shutter, knew there was so much more going on behind that smile. 'Ruby...'

'I don't want to talk about it.'

Maybe it was better left, Cort decided. Maybe by talking about it, he would build it up to something bigger than it was for her.

'Can I have a tour?' Quickly she changed the subject.

'I've just got to ring work.'

'You just left there.'

'I said I'd check back.' Which was true, but even though there was no real need to take the call in the bedroom, he did so.

There was only one photo of Beth.

And even that made him feel guilty—that the one he kept was one taken before the accident. He hated the Christmas and birthday photos that the staff had taken of what had been left of his wife afterwards and the guilt that came that he loved the woman she had been.

He chatted to his boss, made sure his messages had been relayed and put the Beth of yesteryear into a drawer for now, because it wasn't the time to share it with Ruby. He wondered how it was even possible that somehow his heart was actually moving on.

Then he turned and he didn't have to wonder how he was moving on because somehow, so easily, Ruby made it possible.

'That is not taupe,' she said of his bedspread when he turned off his phone. 'That's completely brown.'

'We'll go shopping soon,' Cort said, and the thought both thrilled and terrified—not sheets, or whatever, but that she was being asked into his life.Then he gave a slight grimace. 'Actually, I might have to go shopping now...'

'I'm on the Pill,' Ruby said, and she looked

at him, 'which is something I've never said to anyone before...'

And he nodded, because he got it, got the enormity of what they were both saying, the confirmation they were home.

It was different here, in his bedroom, Ruby thought. More special, somehow, to be here in his home. There was no urgency, just purpose in their kiss. And there was no chance of regret tomorrow, because it was still daytime.

She could hear sirens whizzing past and traffic outside as he undressed her, and that it was afternoon mattered, because the world was going on, it was they two that very deliberately chose to stop.

There was no music or booze or party, just each other, and she wasn't scared that the light might break the moment because naked before him the light let this be real.

It was bliss to climb into his bed and watch

as he undressed and climbed in beside her. She heard his phone bleep and he checked it.

'I'm going to hate that phone, aren't I?'

'You are,' Cort promised.

'Do you ever get to turn it off?'

'Holidays…' Cort started, and then changed his mind, because he wanted the future to be different, he wanted a part of him to be solely devoted to her. And Doug was there, Cort told himself, and Jamelia was there too, and the world could carry on without him, would just have to carry on without him sometimes. He reached over and turned it off, and it felt like a holiday, felt like freedom, felt like life as he let go of the reins and reached for her.

'What would Sheila say?' Ruby asked as he lay beside her and started kissing her.

'I don't want to think about it.'

'And Siobhan?' Ruby laughed.

And then she wasn't joking any more, she was just next to him and he felt lovely, they felt lovely, in a great big bed with them at the centre and nothing to disturb their kiss except the bleep of her phone. She said a rude word in his mouth and happily chose to ignore it.

'You'd better get it,' Cort said.

'I don't get urgent calls,' Ruby said. 'I'm not important enough.'

'You are to me,' Cort said, and she got back to being kissed, got back to the passionate man that no one but her knew existed. She'd been told that you couldn't faint lying down but that's what his kiss made her feel like. She felt the dizzy sensation of removal as his tongue captured hers, she felt the world slide away as his body met hers, and wondered how she had got so lucky, how the place she hated so much could give her something so sublime.

'You're my new-moon wish,' Ruby said as he kissed her, his hand stroking her slippery warmth. Her mouth moved to his neck and she kissed it, then deeper, as his hand worked on, and she tried to resist her body's demands. She was mindful of him and lifted her head because she didn't want to leave a mark, but his thigh hooked over her and still his fingers worked their magic and still she moved her mouth lower and kissed his taut shoulder and then let herself kiss deeper, sucked on his skin as he brought her so close, and then she worked her head down, kissed him as intimately as he had once kissed her, tasted every lovely inch of him till she breathed and blew on him and kissed him again, and told him her truth. 'You got me through.'

'I haven't finished yet,' Cort said, and then she heard his wry laugh, because if she didn't stop now, he might rue his own words. 'Come here,' he said, and slid her up to face him. There were no sheets now, they had fallen somewhere on the floor, so side by side they kissed and then side by side they watched, no barriers, no protection, because they were already safe, and the moment of merging was overwhelming. Cort slid into her and her body shivered and tightened and wrapped right around him.He pushed deeper into her again then he stilled for a moment but she didn't want that, because he couldn't come soon enough for Ruby, so ready was her body to join his.

'Come with me,' she said.

'Soon,' Cort said, because he wanted to enjoy her longer, he wanted the impossible, because as he drove into her, Ruby's hips moved towards him and then towards him again, and it was Ruby who couldn't wait a moment longer. There was such passion in him, such a rare match of want, that she could let go and feel him, feel the friction they made and the taste of his skin, could drown in their scent and call out his name. She felt the rip of tension run through him, felt the shudder of his release and the lovely spill of him inside her, and the absence of fear and the amazing knowledge that she could do anything if this was her reward at the end of each day.

'You're bad for me.' Cort grinned.

'You're so good for me?' Ruby smiled. 'Can I tell you something?'

'Anything,' Cort said.

'I'm starving,' Ruby admitted. 'I only had a salad at the canteen—I didn't want to freak my patient out.'

'What did she have in the end?' Cort asked, because, amazingly he was curious.

'A jacket potato.'

'I don't know how you do it.'

'That was an easy one,' Ruby said. 'Believe me!'

'I do—and I'm starving too,' Cort admitted. 'A certain someone put me off my sandwich...' He did a quick mental run of what was in the kitchen. 'I can ring out for something. I don't think I've got anything...er...suitable.'

Ruby rolled her eyes. 'We don't just eat vegetables.' She climbed out of bed and headed off to the kitchen. By the time he got there, she was already flinging open his cupboards and raiding his rather pathetic fridge contents. 'It's like when you're on a plane and order vegetarian—we get a stupid apple for dessert and everyone else gets chocolate pudding. Why?' she demanded.

'I have no idea.'

Cort had never considered having anyone back at the flat, let alone the possibility of someone moving in, but now she was here, he wondered how he could stand her to leave.

She was colour.

A lively, vivid colour that was neither blinding nor irritating, but just by her presence she brightened the place. The television was on, not on the news as it normally would be early evening, but she'd commandeered the remote and had flicked to a soap Cort hadn't seen in more than a decade.

'He forgave her!' Ruby was disgusted. 'I can't believe he forgave her.'

'Again!' Cort said, eating beans on toast on the sofa and amazed that even after a decade it was so easy to catch up. 'She was at it last time I watched.'

What was it with Ruby? Cort tried to fathom. It couldn't just be sex, Cort reasoned, even though beneath his towel, things were stirring again—what was it with her that made him want to dive right back into living?

He needed to tell her about Beth.

Cort knew that and sat there wondering what her reaction would be, but she was laughing and she hadn't done that for ages, relaxed for once, which she needed to be.

'Once your nights are finished,' Cort said, 'if it's okay with you, maybe we could go away for a couple of days...' Away from here, he decided. Away from a photo she'd demand instantly to see. To a place that was neither his nor hers—where they could talk properly, and if she was upset, they could work through it. The last thing he wanted was to trouble her now.

Her phone bleeped and, checking her messages, Ruby saw that there had been a couple.

Should I be worried?

'Oh.' Ruby winced. 'It's Tilly. I texted her about...' she glanced at her watch '...oh, a few hours or so ago to tell her to put the kettle on.' She texted back a quick message.

'What did you say?'

'Just that I was fine, and sorry.' She could read his expression. 'They wouldn't say anything. I know you might find it impossible to believe...'

'Not impossible,' Cort said, and realised he'd be wasting his time telling her not to say anything about them. Clearly she trusted them, but reluctantly he stood. 'Come on, I'll take you home.'

'Now?' Ruby grumbled.

'Now,' Cort said, or he'd take her back to bed and then they'd both fall asleep and they'd have all her housemates to answer to. 'Let's just get through the next week—ignoring each other.'

CHAPTER TWELVE

'TELL me again!' Ellie said.

'I've told you four times.' Ruby laughed. Jess and Ellie were home when she tumbled into the house, though Tilly, who was working that night, had left early to help with an antenatal class. 'Once I'm finished in Emergency, once I've got through nights, well, it's not written in stone, but I think we'll be more open, able to show our faces together in public. I don't know...' she admitted, because at the time it had seemed obvious what the other was saying—that once they'd got through this bit, they had a future, but under the scrutiny of her friends, she wondered if she was clutching at straws, and she certainly wasn't about to discuss the absence of condoms.

So she played it down instead, toned it down,

tried to calm things down in her heart, and after a good gossip she wished her friends goodnight and headed for bed. Except despite a tired body her mind wouldn't quieten down and Ruby found herself staring out of the window, knowing she had work tomorrow and wishing she could sleep. She eventually did, but only for a little while, she was quite sure of it, when at eight a.m. she staggered into the kitchen.

'What are you doing up?' Tilly was nursing a huge mug of tea. 'I thought you'd have a lie-in.'

'I heard the kettle.' Ruby smiled. 'I'm going back to bed soon.'

'So where did you get to yesterday?' Tilly asked, and Ruby told her, well, some of it, but even though she sounded upbeat and happy she could see the worry in her friend's eyes.

'You haven't known him very long,' Tilly gently pointed out.

'I know.' Ruby ran a hand through her hair and tried to apply logic to a heart that had made up its mind. 'I'm not doing an Ellie—I'm not convincing myself this is "the one". I just can't believe how he makes me feel and I know he feels the same.' She could see Tilly wasn't completely mollified. 'What?' Ruby demanded, because she could do that with her best friend. 'What aren't you telling me?'

'Nothing.' Tilly was honest. 'I don't know a single thing about him. I remember him when I did my emergency rotation and I don't think I said two words to him in the time I was there. He was just "Call Paeds. Organise a social worker…"'

'He's actually not like that at all,' Ruby said, 'once you know him.'

'Good,' Tilly said, and she would never meddle, but she was concerned about Ruby, knew she was struggling at work and knew that her friend didn't give her heart away easily.

'Oh, I got your payslip…you said you were worried…'

Ruby peeled it open and groaned as she scanned the little slip.

'I knew they'd paid me too much. I was hoping it was back pay or something.' But instead they'd put her down as working on a night that her shift had been cancelled. 'I'll ring them later,' Ruby said. 'Right now I'm going back to bed.' But she still couldn't sleep. Tilly's unvoiced concern had her thinking—what did she know about him? She knew that he had family in Melbourne, that he had worked with her brother, there hadn't exactly been time to take a history. Still, as the morning stretched on, and sleep remained elusive, and as a couple of hundred dollars extra in her bank account niggled, a walk into work to clear her conscience seemed like a good idea. Though she'd held little hope of bumping into Cort, as the lift doors opened on the admin floor and she saw him standing there, it was certainly an added bonus.

'Hi.' She smiled and he remembered Sheila's warning.

'Hi.' He stepped aside to let her out, as was the polite thing to do, but Ruby just stood there, temptation beckoning, and he stepped into the lift. 'Shouldn't you be in bed?'

'I wish I was.'

So did Cort. He glanced to the lift panel, wished he knew how to stop the lift, but one push of the button and he'd no doubt get it wrong and they'd come up for air, to find half of security gathered and watching.

'You okay?' Cort checked, and she nodded, but then she changed her mind.

'Cort…' She wanted quiet for her mind, she wanted the assurance only he gave, she wanted supper at his place and the quiet confidence he imbued in her. Maybe if he came for dinner, or she went there… 'Can we…?' But she didn't get to ask. The busy lift was soon in demand and instead she stepped out. But, still, she was all the better for seeing him, because when he was there, there was no doubt in her mind that they would work.

'I think I've been overpaid.' Still high from seeing him, Ruby spoke to one of the girls at the pay office.

'People don't normally complain about that. Let's have a look.' The woman whose name badge said 'Ruth' took Ruby's slip and read through it.

'I didn't work that Saturday,' Ruby explained. 'I was down to work, but my shift got cancelled. You have to take it off me today…' Ruby smiled '…or I'll spend it.'

It was one of those messy problems. Ruby had signed her time sheet apparently, which she hadn't, of course, and Ruby accepted Ruth's offer to take a seat while she located the time sheet to see what had happened.

'Marie?' Ruth called to a colleague. 'Can you take a look at this?'

'One moment,' came the response as Ruby sat

reading through a pamphlet on superannuation and not really listening as the women chatted on.

'So what part is annual leave?'

'He had five weeks of annual leave owing,' Ruth said, 'then ten days' paid carer's leave, plus two days paid compassionate from the date his wife died.'

'Do we need to see the death certificate?'

'That's what he just brought in,' Ruth said. 'I've taken a copy.'

They never said his name, and had she not seen him in the lift she would never have known. Even sitting there, Ruby couldn't be absolutely sure.

She just was.

This was the family stuff he had been dealing with.

His wife had just died and he'd been in bed with her.

'I have to go.' Ruby stood.

'I've just found your timesheet,' Ruth said. Ruby wanted to run, but she was trying not to do that any more, so she waited and it was worked out that someone had used her sheet but signed their name and that it would be amended at the next pay cycle. She smiled and thanked them and then she left. Finally free, she didn't take the bus but walked down the hill to her house. There was Mrs Bennett in her garden and she smiled and waved as Ruby went past and Ruby somehow managed to smile and wave back, but she couldn't even force a smile as she saw Tilly on the stairs.

'What on earth's wrong?'

'Nothing.' Ruby brushed past.

'Ruby...' Tilly's feet followed her.

'I've got the worst headache,' Ruby attempted. 'I can't sleep and I have to get to sleep—I'm working tonight.'

'You've got hours till your shift starts,' Tilly soothed, but the hours slipped away and all Ruby could think was that he hadn't told her. She had slept with a man, glimpsed a future with a man she really knew very little about. She was embarrassed too, ashamed to share her problem with her friends. His wife had been dead just over a month after all.

She wasn't sure whether it was nerves, exhaustion or humiliation, but when Tilly heard her retching in the toilet a few hours later, she knew her housemate's plight was genuine.

'I can't go in,' Ruby said. 'I've hardly slept since …' She tried to work it out. 'In ages.' It would, in fact, be irresponsible to go in with no sleep, but how could she not?

'It's okay,' Tilly said. 'You go back to bed. I'll ring in for you.' Ruby lay there and closed her eyes as she heard her friend on the landline.

'Who did you speak to?'

'The ward clerk,' Tilly said. 'She said she'd pass it on.'

'Sheila's going to be furious.'

'You can't help being sick,' Tilly pointed out,

and then she looked at her friend, saw the real trouble in her eyes and wasn't sure what was going on. 'Do you want me to go down tonight?' Tilly offered. 'I can explain to Sheila that you really are sick—ask if you can make it up over the weekend…'

'I'll speak to her myself,' Ruby broke in. 'Go on, you get ready for work.'

'Ruby…'

'Please, Tilly…' Ruby said, because that was the good and the bad of sharing a house—there was always someone there when you needed them to be, but there was always someone there too when perhaps you just needed to be alone. 'You've got to get ready for work.'

Cort found himself lingering in the staffroom as the night staff started to drift in.

'We're short tonight,' Siobhan said. 'We've got two from the bank.'

'We don't have a student either,' Sheila said. 'Ruby rang in sick.'

'What a surprise!' Siobhan smirked. 'She must be worn out from all the agency shifts that she's doing.'

Cort kept his face impassive, but he would have loved to tell Siobhan to shut up.

'I've swapped her around so she can come in to do Thursday, Friday and Saturday.'

Which were the worst nights.

He couldn't believe she'd throw it all in—then he thought about Ruby and actually he could. He thought back to the canteen where he'd seen her confident in her own environment, and she *was* like a butterfly, one who'd found herself fluttering around the coals of hell. This place was damaged and wounded.

Cort walked across the ambulance bay towards the car park, unsure what he could do. He could hardly turn up there, and then what? Insist that she go in?

'Hi, there.' It was Tilly who greeted him, walking towards Maternity.

'Hi.' Cort gave a brief nod, which was more than he usually did. 'On nights?' he asked, and she smiled and stopped.

'Yep.'

Normally he'd have nodded and walked on, refused to acknowledge what they both knew.

'How's Ruby?' Cort cleared his throat. 'I heard she'd rung in sick.'

'I don't know how she is,' Tilly said. 'She's not really talking to anyone.'

'If she doesn't do her nights, she's going to have to repeat.'

'I can't see that happening.' He was surprised at the thick sound to her voice, and it dawned on him that Tilly had been crying. 'If she can't do three nights, she's hardly going to do another six weeks. I don't know what to say to her.'

'I'll talk to her.'

'Her phone's off.'

'I'll go round,' Cort said, because if she wasn't going in again, there was nothing to keep things quiet for anyway.

'Door for you,' Ellie called up the stairs to Ruby. As Ellie was on her way out and left it wide open, it gave Ruby no choice but to haul herself out of bed, pull on a sarong and answer it.

'Is everything okay?'

She looked at him.

'Only I wondered…'

She blinked.

'I heard you were sick. I bumped into Tilly. Is everything okay?' Cort checked.

'You tell me?'

'I'm here to find out about you. Ruby, you know you have to do these nights.'

'I don't have to do anything.'

'I know you're having a difficult time. I know this week—'

'How's your week been, Cort?' she interrupted.

'I thought it was going well.'

'How's your month been? Anything happen that you might want to talk about?'

And then he got it—she knew.

She wanted to hop she was so angry. She wanted to shake him as she gave him every opportunity to explain things, to tell her, but he just stood there.

'You bang on about support, about backing each other, helping each other through...being open.'

'How do you know?' Cort said, because to him it mattered. 'Adam?'

'Adam?' Ruby's voice was incredulous. 'Of course it wasn't Adam. Adam doesn't talk about things that matter. I can see now why the two of you are friends.'

'Then how do you know?'

'It doesn't matter how I know,' Ruby said. 'Actually, it does. Do you not think it should have been you who told me? Do you not think...?' She was close to crying, just disgusted with herself and angry with him. 'Six weeks?' Ruby croaked. 'She's been dead six weeks.'

'You don't understand.'

'I'll never understand.' She wouldn't. 'If it had been just that night...' Ruby said. 'But you came back, you took me out, we sat in the car...' She jabbed her finger at the pavement behind. 'And you took me to your home and you still didn't tell me.'

'I don't talk about it with anyone,' Cort said. 'She suffered a brain injury, and for years she was in a home...'

'So you were embarrassed by her?' Ruby said. Sometimes she said things; the thoughts in her head popped out and this was one of those times.

That he didn't deny it really did make her want to cry. 'Maybe you're right, maybe there is no point talking about it. As you said, we can never work.'

'We might.'

'No.' Ruby shook her head. 'We're at different stages.' There was so much against them. 'You're too closed off.'

'That's rich, coming from you.' He looked at her and did the most bizarre thing—stood on her doorstep in his suit, threw his arms in the air and did a brief dance that looked a lot like the one Ruby had done the night of the party. 'The life and soul…' Cort said. 'Happy Ruby…' He turned away. 'You're the one closed off, Ruby, you can't even tell your best friends how you're really feeling.' He walked down to the gate. 'You do your happy-clappy dance rather than admit your true feelings. You just avoid everything—like you're avoiding tonight, like you're refusing to listen about Beth…'

'You want true feelings…' She could not stand that she had a name, that Beth was real and he hadn't told her. 'You're too boring for me, Cort, too old and too staid…' She pushed him away with words, because he was getting too close, not physically, just too close to the real her, and she didn't want anyone to see that.

'Well, at least I see things through,' Cort said. 'Just don't blame me for not showing up.' He tossed the comment over his shoulder. 'To anything.'

CHAPTER THIRTEEN

IT WAS a row. Her first row in more than a decade. It was the one thing she tried to avoid and there was no one home so she fled to her room because that was what she did, Ruby realised.

Avoided.

Hid like a wounded cat and licked her wounds till she was ready to come out.

Except she didn't want to come out to the wreckage she was surely creating.

To repeating A and E or to have thrown it in.

But how could she go back there now, after the way she had spoken to Cort?

He wasn't or ever had been boring.

'Men!' Ellie stood at the door, already back from her date. Clearly the latest love of her life had been relegated to history, but unlike Ruby she wasn't curled up on the bed because Ellie just moved on, determined to find the true love of her life.

Ruby had just lost it.

'What happened with Cort?'

'I said the most awful things...' She told her friend some but not all of them.

'It's called a row,' Ellie said, but it was far more than that.

'I found out...' But she couldn't tell her, couldn't reveal the part of Cort that he clearly didn't want anyone to know, and round and round things went in her head, even after Ellie had gone to bed. When Jess came home, she tried talking to her too, but it was hard when she couldn't tell her Cort's truth.

'I'm going to ring Adam.' Giddy from way too little sleep, Ruby stood up.

Jess, of course, should have suggested she check the time difference, but Jess had an agenda of her own and gave a nod of encouragement, even went and got her the phone. Ruby dialled her brother's number but, of course, got a recorded message.

'You didn't leave a message.'

'What's the point?' Ruby said. 'Adam won't tell me anything. I'm going to bed.'

But ten minutes later she heard the phone ring and Jess laughing and talking, and because it was the landline that had rung she knew who it was.

'It's Adam,' Jess said as she knocked on her door. 'And he's not best pleased—it's four a.m. in South America apparently!'

'Thanks,' Ruby said when Jess hovered and rather reluctantly handed the phone then dragged herself out the door.

'Do you ever look at the clock, Ruby?' Adam asked, because she did this all the time.

'No. Anyway, I never know where you are to work out the time difference.'

'What's wrong?' Adam asked, because he could tell by her voice that something was.

'Nothing,' Ruby said. 'I just need to ask you something. It's just a friend of mine, well, she's got mixed up with Cort Mason. Apparently you know him.'

'And this friend wants to know more?' Adam asked.

'Yes.'

'Nice guy,' Adam said.

'That's it?' Ruby said, and when Adam was less than forthcoming she pushed a little harder. 'My friend knows about his wife.'

'Really?' Adam said. 'I'm surprised he told her.'

'He didn't,' Ruby said. 'She found out.'

There was a long pause.

'Adam, please.'

'Is this for you, Ruby, or your friend?'

She paused, because Adam didn't gossip, even to his sister. 'Me,' she finally said, and waited through the longest pause.

'You and Cort?' She heard the incredulity in his voice.

'Please,' Ruby said.

'Okay, but there's not much to tell. He took a job in Melbourne some years back. I think he worked at the Children's Hospital and she was a paediatrician. I don't know much, we just emailed now and then, just that there was an accident in Queensland on their honeymoon. Beth got a nasty head injury, it would be four or more years ago now. She ended up in a nursing home.'

'And he moved to Sydney?' She couldn't believe he'd just leave her.

'After a year or so—he's always back there, visiting. Like I said, we don't go out when I'm back, because if Cort's on days off then he's down in Melbourne. I offered to go once when I was down in Melbourne, but he didn't want me to see her like that.'

'And?'

'And what?'

'What he did he say? About her, I mean?'

'I don't know...' Adam wasn't the type to replay conversations in his head, let alone to anyone else. 'We just play golf… Look, Ruby, there's no hope with Beth. I mean, I'm glad Cort's trying to move on, because I do know there's completely no hope…'

'Beth died,' Ruby said, and closed her eyes as Adam went quiet. 'Didn't he tell you?'

'Ruby, I'm in the middle of the jungle. Like I said, we're not that close—I don't think anyone is with Cort.'

She put down the phone and padded out to put it back in its charger, and there, of course, waiting, was Jess.

'How's Adam?' She didn't await Ruby's response. 'Did he say when he was coming home?'

'When does Adam ever really say anything about anything? Honestly…' She looked up at her friend, who carried a torch for her brother, and even if Ruby loved him, she felt it only fair to warn her, properly this time. 'I can see why Caroline broke up with him.'

'Caroline?'

'His fiancée,' Ruby said, and saw Jess's jaw tighten. 'She really thought she'd change him, that somehow Adam would open up. She just didn't get that he's...' She closed her eyes, because Adam was a whole lot like Cort. 'He's an emotional desert. He is!' Ruby said, when Jess refused to buy it. 'He was in bed with the next one a week after Caroline...and the next and the next... There is no deeper Adam,' Ruby reiterated, because there wasn't. Nice clothes, nice car, lots of women—they were all there waiting for him whenever he returned. It really was just as simple as that with her brother, and she didn't want him breaking her best friend's heart. Except Jess refused to hear it.

'Just because someone doesn't spill out their heart, Ruby, it doesn't mean they don't still have feelings.' Jess would not be swayed. 'We all hurt, Ruby.' Jess huffed off to bed, no doubt to stick pins in a little doll she'd name Caroline. 'We just all have different ways of showing it.'

CHAPTER FOURTEEN

RUBY leapt on the phone when it rang the next evening. Dressed for her shift, her heart leapt in hope that it might be Cort, that he might want to clear the air before she commenced her shifts, but the voice on the other end brought no relief. 'I just wanted to check that you're coming to church on Sunday.' Ruby closed her eyes at the sound of her mother's voice on the phone.

'I'm on nights,' Ruby said, because even if it killed her, she'd at least have died trying.

'You just said you were working Thursday, Friday, Saturday.'

'Which means I'll be home in bed on Sunday,' Ruby explained as patiently as she could.

'Your dad does whole weekends without sleep, and he's doing a reading this Sunday. It would be nice if his family was there,' her mum said. 'It's the nine a.m. service. If you take Adam's car to work, you'll get there in time. I'll do a nice lamb roast.'

And that was it.

There was just no point arguing.

'How's your mum?' Tilly asked when she hung up the phone.

'Still keeping the peace,' Ruby said. She was in her navy shorts and white shirt and her hair was tied tight. If you didn't know how much she was shaking inside, she could almost have passed for a nurse. 'Still keeping the chief happy!'

'Come on,' Tilly said. 'I'll walk with you.'

They walked up the hill under the lovely moon that had once held so much promise and Ruby was so glad to have her friend beside her.

'Cort was widowed recently,' Ruby said. Was it breaking a confidence to confide in her best friend when her heart was breaking? Probably, but she knew it would never be repeated by Tilly, not even to the others, and she was very grateful when Tilly said nothing for a little while and just walked on.

'How recently?' Tilly asked.

'A month,' Ruby said. 'Well, it was a month when we...' It still made her stomach churn to think of it. 'She was in a car accident a few years ago—she had a head injury.'

'It sounds like he lost her a long time ago,' Tilly said gently.

'Still...'

'We had a couple the other week,' Tilly said, 'they were just so happy, so excited to be having this baby, and I found out halfway through labour that the baby wasn't actually his—she'd lost her partner right at the start of the pregnancy.' And they walked up the hill and Ruby listened. 'It's none of my business,' Tilly said, 'but I couldn't get it at first, how she could move on so quickly. And then I saw the love, and I saw how happy they were and how he was with the baby...' Tilly was the kindest person Ruby knew. 'Don't judge him, Ruby.'

'He should have told me.'

'When?' Tilly asked. 'You wanted him out the next morning...'

'He hasn't told anyone about her,' Ruby said. 'Even his colleagues don't know or most of his friends.' Tilly turned then and looked at her.

'Hurts, doesn't it? When someone you care about can't confide in you?' But Tilly didn't hold grudges and she gave her friend a hug as the lights of Emergency came into view. 'Maybe he had his reasons.'

'I think I was supposed to be his get back out there fling.'

'And what was he supposed to be?'

'I don't know,' Ruby admitted. 'If I'd even thought about it for a moment it would never have happened. I've just made things a whole lot more complicated—not only do I have to face

Emergency, I have to work alongside him, after all the terrible things that I said.'

'Then say sorry.'

'What if he won't accept it?'

'Then at least you'll have said it.' Which wasn't the answer Ruby wanted, but it was, she knew, the right one.

'You'll be fine,' Tilly said. 'No running away.'

'I won't.'

At night the side door wasn't open so she had to walk through the waiting room and already it was steaming, two people asking her on her way through how much longer they would have to wait. Already her temples were pounding, but she went to the staffroom, took out a little white teapot she had painted her name on in red nail varnish, made a big pot of herbal tea and told herself she could do this.

'Evening, Ruby!' Sheila gave a tight smile as she walked into the staffroom and Cort deliberately didn't turn his head from the television. 'Ready for some action?'

'Bring it on!' Ruby smiled.

Cort had been unable to comprehend that she, that anyone, could throw so much away for the sake of three nights, but as the weekend progressed, he started to see it.

See what he never really had before.

It was like finding out about sex when he had been younger. Suddenly it was there glaring at him at every turn—how on earth had he not noticed? Now, though, it was the dark side of A and E that was illuminated. All the stuff he usually just ignored or shrugged off or put up with was blazingly obvious, and there was this part of him that wanted to shield her from it. There were fights breaking out in the waiting room, angry relatives, abusive patients and the drama of sudden illness. He watched her face become pinched, even though she smiled; he saw her eyes shutter regularly as if another knife had been stabbed in her back; and he started to see that for some, the emergency room was damaging.

Not that he could do anything about it.

Once she tried to talk to him, but Cort was still too churned up, and he blanked her, then regretted it all through the next day when he couldn't sleep, wondering if she'd be back.

She was.

To a place that was twice as busy and twice as angry as before, and he noticed it—all of it—even the little things he would never have seen before.

'I'll eat my supper here.' Siobhan peeled off the lid of her container. Ruby had made it through Thursday and was back for round two—a busy Friday night and the patients were particularly feral.

Siobhan was in the grumpiest of moods because she'd been brought back from the staffroom as the numbers were too low for her to take a proper break. They had a young overdose in cubicle six and they couldn't identify the tablets she'd taken, despite poring through books and the internet, and Sheila had asked Siobhan to make a phone call. Now Siobhan sat, stuck on hold to Poisons Information, as Cort tried to work out a drug dose. He watched Ruby's shoulders tense as Siobhan's bored eyes fell on the student nurse.

'What are you doing, Ruby?' she asked. Ruby was holding a newborn baby and screaming toddler, who'd cut his forehead falling against his toybox and had blood all down his pyjamas.

'Mum's just gone to the toilet,' Ruby answered.

'Well, can't she take them with her?' Siobhan asked. 'We're not a child-minding service.'

'It's no problem.'

'Actually,' Siobhan answered, 'if another emergency comes in, or someone goes off and you're holding a baby, it becomes one!'

'Ooh, that smells nice!' Sheila's only comment was about the smell wafting over as Siobhan stirred her supper. 'What is it?'

'Veal and noodles,' Siobhan said, and just for a second, so small no one, not even Ruby, noticed, there was a shadow of a smile on Cort's mouth as Ruby rolled her eyes and muttered under her breath.

'That'd be right.'

She hated it, Cort fully realised. Behind the smile she was in torture, and given what had gone on, he'd made it much worse for her.

'Thanks so much.' A tearful mum came and took her baby and tried to scoop up the toddler, who was on the floor.

'I know I keep asking, but have you any idea how much longer?'

'We'll get to him as soon as we can,' Siobhan answered before Ruby had a chance. 'Only there are still a couple of patients before him and it will take two staff to hold him down and we just can't spare them at the moment.'

'But you've time to sit and eat,' the mum snapped.

'I'm eating my supper at the desk because I'm on hold to Poisons Information and I expect to be for the next half-hour,' came Siobhan's tart response. 'I'm actually supposed to be on my break, but I'm here to hopefully free up a colleague.'

Yes, she was right, but it could have been handled so much better, because the mum promptly burst into tears. 'There are drunks down in the waiting room. I can't sit and breastfeed…'

And Ruby truly didn't know what to do. There was literally nowhere to put them. Every cubicle was full, all the interview rooms were taken, and though, had it been up to her, she'd have popped Mum into the staffroom, the reality was it was needed for staff to get a break from the perpetual craziness.

'Bring him through.' Cort stood up. He didn't have time, but he'd just have to make it.

'Suture room's not cleaned from the last one.'

'I'll do it,' Ruby said, and glanced at Siobhan. 'And I can hold him by myself.'

Ruby scuttled off and did the quickest clean-up she could, then washed her hands and set up a trolley for Cort.

'You'll need a drawer sheet to wrap him in.' Cort came in, but didn't look at her. 'Mum won't be able to help with holding him.'

'I know.'

He pulled up the anaesthetic so that the little boy wouldn't see the needle, opened up the sutures then told Ruby to bring him in.

'What's his name?'

'Adam,' Ruby said, and flushed, and it was stupid and so, so irrelevant that it was the same name as her brother's, but it just made a point, a stupid point, that they knew more about the other than they ought to officially. 'I'll go and get him.'

'You don't have to come in,' Ruby offered, but his mum was sure that she'd rather.

'Well, if it gets too much,' Ruby said, just as she'd seen the others do, 'just slip out.'

'He's going to struggle and scream,' Cort explained, 'and it will sting for a bit when I put the anaesthetic in, but after that he won't feel a thing.' He explained a little further as Ruby tightly wrapped the little boy. 'It's not fair to settle him down only to stick him with a needle, so once the anaesthetic is in, we'll try and calm him.'

The only way one person could hold him was to practically use the weight of her body over the swaddled child and hold his face with two gloved hands as he screamed loudly in Ruby's ear.

'It will be finished soon, Adam,' Ruby said, and she swore she felt the needle go in as he shrieked even louder.

'That's it.' Cort's voice was loud and deep and caught Adam by surprise. He paused his screaming for just a second. 'All the horrible

bit's finished with,' Cort said to the little boy,
and then spoke to Ruby. 'Loosen up on him
while it takes effect.'

'It's okay.' His mum tried to soothe him, but
the baby was crying now too and she was about
to as well—either that or pass out. 'I think I'll
go out...'

'We'll take good care of him,' Cort said, and
then he looked down at the toddler. 'I'm going to
make it better in a moment and then you can go
home.' He spoke to him in a matter-of-fact voice
and maybe all the fight had left him, but the little
boy did stop screaming. 'It's not going to hurt
now.' He turned to Ruby. 'Go round the other
side.' She did so and Cort changed his gloves and
put a little green drape over his head, and they
were back to where they started, away from the
bedlam and shut in the suture room, but there
was a whole lot more between them than a patient
now. 'You just look at Ruby,' Cort said, which

Adam did, and though he did whimper a few times, he was much calmer as Cort worked on quietly.

'Could it have been glued?' Ruby asked, because it would have been much easier.

'It needs a couple of dissolvable sutures—it's a pretty deep cut,' Cort explained. 'And it needed a good clean.' He turned and smiled as a much calmer mum stepped into the room. 'Just wait there,' Cort said, but very nicely. 'He's in the zone. If he sees you he'll think it's over. We shan't be long.' There was one more snip and then as he went to clean it, Ruby could see what he meant by in the zone, because the second Adam sensed it was over, he shot up, saw his mum and not a tightly wrapped drawer sheet or Ruby could have kept him still a second longer.

'Mum!' He burst into tears all over again.

'We're finished!' Cort said. 'You get to choose your plaster now.' And he would have left it to

Ruby, but he didn't, took just that one moment to help the little boy select.

'Thanks so much. I'm sorry about before...' the mum said.

'We're sorry you've had to wait,' Ruby said.

'That nurse...' she explained. 'I know she should get her proper break. I had no right to say anything.'

'It's fine,' Cort said.

'I don't know how you do it.' She looked at Ruby, who smiled back at her. 'I don't know how you can work in this place.'

'You get used to it,' Ruby said, because it was either that or fall into the woman's arms like Adam and beg her to take her away from here.

'Take him home to bed and let him sleep, but you need to check him regularly.'

'I'll have him in with me.'

'Good. Stitches out in five days at your GP.' He went through all the head-injury instructions as Ruby found a leaflet then started to clean up.

'Cort,' Ruby said, because it was the only chance she had to do so, 'about—'

'Leave it, Ruby.' Because he just couldn't do this.

'I am sorry.'

So that made it fine, then. Mature he may be, but still it hurt and he just didn't have it in him to accept her apology as easily as that.

'You just concentrate on getting through your work.'

'And that's it?'

'What do you want, Ruby?' He glanced to the door to check no one could hear. 'You've made your feelings perfectly clear.' When she opened her mouth to dispute, Cort overrode her. 'You're right, things would never have worked out between us. I was looking for a diversion, missing Beth. We should have left it at one night.'

And he might just as well have taken a fist and pushed it into her stomach, but somehow she stayed standing.

'I don't believe you.'

'Yeah, well, given the stuff you believe in you might need to take a reality check.'

Yes he was harsh, and perhaps a bit mean, but he couldn't just stand there and accept her apology. It was far easier to push her away.

He didn't want to forgive her, because then he might have to love her, and Cort just wasn't ready for that.

CHAPTER FIFTEEN

'HERE'S to Ruby's last night!' They were all made up, sipping wine, doing each other's hair and getting ready to head down to the Stat Bar. Ruby would have given anything to be joining them and told her friends so.

'We'll take you out tomorrow,' Jess said. 'We'll have a little celebration. Just think—you'll be done!'

She would, Ruby realised.

Somehow she'd got through, not just the work but being alongside Cort. She didn't blame him for not accepting her apology, but she was beginning to realise that it had probably been her only chance to offer one. She was back at uni in a couple of weeks, then exams. There was little chance of seeing him and realisation was dawning that it wasn't just her time in Emergency that would be finally over with by morning.

'Good luck.' Tilly gave her a hug at the door.

'What about...?' Ruby's voice trailed off. She'd been over and over it with Tilly, had been over and over it with herself, and no matter what positive spin she tried to put on it, she and Cort had only known one another for two weeks, which meant not a lot of history to fight for—an elongated one-night stand that didn't stand up to the scrutiny of day.

The full moon was rising as she drove the short distance to Eastern Beaches—the same moon she'd wished on to get her through her time in Emergency, and somehow she knew that it would do its job. Come what may, she'd make it through tonight and then never have to set foot in the place again.

Strange that it made her feel like crying.

God, she hated Adam's car—no matter how she judged it, the seats were so low and she was so short that as she pulled up at boom gates, she couldn't reach to swipe her ID and had to put it in neutral, pull on the handbrake, take off her seat belt and hang out of the open car door to get it to beep. As she turned and gave the queue of cars behind her an apologetic wave, it had to be Cort's car behind hers. Cheeks burning, she promptly stalled and then jerked her way through the gates, but thankfully she found a space easily, cursing quietly to herself as she delved into the tiny boot for her massive bag that contained clothes, shoes and toiletry bag, so she could speedily change for church in the morning. Cort pulled up in the space beside her and she would have dashed off but it was Adam's car, which meant even as she turned to walk, Ruby had to turn back and check *again* that it was locked and that the handbrake was on.

For Cort, it was impossible to ignore her—aside from all that had happened, she intrigued him.

What was it with the bag on her shoulder and why had she parked here?

'This is the doctors' area.' Cort saw her tense as his words reached her. 'Senior doctors.'

Ruby spun round, unsure if she was being told off. 'There's hierarchy even in the car park?'

'Especially in the car park,' Cort replied, and Ruby glanced over to see a line of cars all battling for a few spots. 'I think night staff are Area D.'

She drove so rarely it had never entered her head but, come to think of it, she vaguely remembered being given a map when she'd had her security photo taken for Emergency.

'Are you going to move it?' Cort couldn't care less whether she did or not, it was just conversation as he fell into step beside her.

'God, no,' Ruby replied. 'I'd rather face wheel clamps than Sheila's wrath if I'm late. And,' she added, 'it's not for emergencies, just to save your poor legs.'

Cort almost smiled, but falling into step with

her, with anyone, came not too readily to him, but he was determined to try, to not just nod and walk on as he so often did. Cort almost admitted to himself that he missed her and if it had to end, he didn't want it to end on the sour note that had played out last night. 'How have you found the nights?'

'Awful,' Ruby admitted. 'But this is the last.'

'Oy! Wait!' Connor half ran to catch up with them and Cort deliberately chose not to make excuses as to why he was walking with Ruby, but to his surprise it was Ruby who offered a reason.

'Mr Mason was telling me I'd parked in the doctors' area.'

'You'll be shot at dawn,' Connor warned. 'Or wheel clamped.'

'Fantastic,' Ruby breathed. 'Then I'll miss out on church and Sunday dinner with my family— it's a win-win.'

'How was the traffic?' Cort asked Connor, when really he wanted to ask Ruby much more.

'Hell,' Connor said. 'All the traffic's diverted for the festival, we're going to have a shocking night—brace yourself, young Ruby,' he warned as they reached the emergency entrance.

'Already braced.' Ruby smiled, but Cort could hear the high note to her voice, could feel, even though he didn't turn his head to look, her back straighten as they walked through the waiting room. As they entered they saw two sets of police officers alongside two soon-to-be patients, and a pumping waiting room. For her last night, Emergency had turned it on and there was a temptation, a strange urge, a protectiveness almost to take her by the hand and walk her out, tell her she didn't actually need to be there.

It was the busiest she'd ever seen it. Inebriated patients lay on mattresses on the floor, every trolley was full and for once Sheila didn't seem to mind Ruby's willingness to trudge up and down to the wards to hand over patients if it freed up a cubicle. Still, when a stabbing came in, Sheila hauled her into Resus to watch as Jamelia inserted a chest drain.

'Excellent.' Cort was encouraging. Ruby could see Jamelia's confidence growing and wished hers would too.

'Can I grab Ruby to do some obs?' For once, Ruby was glad to hear Siobhan's voice, especially when Sheila agreed to release her student. 'He's bipolar, hypermanic, we're just waiting for Psych to come and admit him. Jamelia, can you come and take another look when you've got a moment?'

'Go.' Cort nodded. 'I'll stitch this.'

'Bill!' Ruby recognised the patient as soon as she opened the curtain.

'You know him?' Jamelia asked.

'I do some bank work on the psychiatric ward,' Ruby explained. 'He was in a few weeks ago.'

'How are you, Bill?' Ruby asked. 'How have you been?'

'Not good, not good, not good.' He gripped

Ruby's hand as she went to wrap the blood-pressure cuff. 'This isn't, isn't, isn't...' he said. 'I'm not...' Ruby frowned as Bill struggled to explain himself. 'I'm not manic.'

'It's okay, Bill,' Ruby said, carefully checking his obs. She spoke to him some more. 'We'll take good care of you.' She turned to Jamelia. 'His blood pressure's high.'

'I know,' Jamelia said, 'but he's extremely agitated. I've just given him some diazepam. Psych shouldn't be too long.'

'Doctor, doctor, doctor,' Bill begged, but Jamelia didn't understand what he was saying.

'I'm a doctor, Bill,' Jamelia said. 'And you're going to be fine. You just need to calm down.'

'Bill's a doctor,' Ruby explained. 'That's what he's trying to tell you—and he's not normally like this.' She'd been with him just a few weeks ago during a manic episode, and again during her psych rotation, and he'd been nothing like this. She tried to speak with Jamelia, but Jamelia didn't want a student nurse's opinion and headed off to Resus, where Cort was finishing up suturing in her chest drain.

'Have you done those obs?' Sheila called out to her slippery student. 'You should be back in here.'

'I'll be there in a moment,' Ruby said, torn with indecision, because she had told Jamelia her concerns yet Jamelia didn't seem worried.

But Ruby was.

She went back in to Bill, saw the fear in his eyes and held his hand for a moment.

'Not,' he said once, blowing out air and trying to gather the strength to say it again, spittle at the sides of his mouth and just too ill and too exhausted to state his case further. Ruby knew she had to do it for him.

It was the most nerve-racking thing she had done. Sheila was clearly busy, Connor was in with a patient, so reluctantly Ruby went to Siobhan and explained her concerns, but unfortunately Jamelia came over just as Ruby said that she wasn't sure Bill was manic.

'I've seen him during two acute episodes,' Ruby explained. 'And I really think that there's more to it.'

'Of course he's manic,' Jamelia snapped. 'He's climbing off the gurney, he thinks he's a doctor, he's clanging…'

'He's not clanging,' Ruby responded. 'And he *is* a doctor.'

Jamelia gave an eye roll and went back into Resus, having clearly decided that Ruby had no idea what she was talking about, and Ruby waited for a shrug from Siobhan as Jamelia headed off. Instead, Siobhan was reading through his obs and calling Reception to ask them to hurry up with Bill's history.

'What's clanging?' Siobhan asked, and saw Ruby blink. 'I don't claim to know everything,' Siobhan said, and maybe Ruby was seeing things, but for a second there she thought Siobhan smiled. 'Just most things.'

'When they're manic, sometimes they do things with words, and it makes no real sense—like not, hot, cot, dot, or…just vague association. He's not doing that now, he just can't get his words out, but they're lucid words. He's trying to tell us that there's something very wrong.'

'Well, bring him over if you're worried,' Siobhan said, and she gave a sigh when Ruby just stood there. 'Ruby? Do you want to bring a patient over to Resus?'

'Yes,' Ruby finally said.

'Then I'll give you a hand.'

And Ruby got it a little bit then. It was indecision that was the enemy in this place, because even if she wasn't sure if it was the right one, as soon as she made the call, whether she turned out to be right or wrong, Siobhan, it would seem, supported her.

So they took off the brakes and wheeled Bill

over. Cort was probing an abdominal wound and looked up as they came in.

'Ruby's worried about this patient,' Siobhan explained. 'He's waiting on Psych, but she's looked after him before and says this presentation is unusual for him.' Which was a far more efficient way than Ruby would have described it!

'I'll take a look in a moment,' Cort said, and frowned as he glanced at Bill, who was breathing more rapidly and was much more sweaty now. As Ruby attached him to the monitors the alarm went off loudly as the cuff inflated and blew up higher to get an accurate reading.

'Has he had bloods taken?' Cort checked, and Siobhan nodded.

'He's hypertensive. Jamelia gave him some diazepam earlier as well.'

'I'm not, not, not, not...' Bill begged, and Ruby tried to reassure him.

'We know you're not well, Bill. The doctors are sorting out what's wrong.'

'Ring the lab,' Cort called, 'and ask them to push his bloods as urgent.'

Ruby did so, only to find out that they hadn't got them yet. She looked and there they were, still sitting in the chute basket, so Ruby hurriedly sent them.

'Get Jamelia to come and take another look,' Cort called, but just as Ruby was about to, Bill let out a strange cry and before it had properly registered, she knew, just knew, that he was going to start seizing. Ruby moved quickly, lowering the head of the bed and pulling out the pillow, while Siobhan put oxygen on him as Sheila came speeding over with the cart and a worried Jamelia running in too.

'He's stopped,' Sheila said, but within seconds, even as she pulled up some medication, he was seizing again, and Cort finished up what he was doing, ripped off his gloves and came over.

'He was fine…' Jamelia said, but Cort just ignored her, giving Bill some sedatives. When he continued to seize, he told Sheila to urgently page the medical team.

Bill's blood pressure was becoming elevated and each seizure was running into the next. All Ruby could think was that he didn't deserve this.

'He said this wasn't normal for him.' Ruby heard her own voice, but apparently from the lack of response, she was the only one who did.

'Ring the lab,' Cort said. 'Tell them we need those bloods.' Ruby did so, waiting on the line as they ran some rapid blood tests and delivered the news that Bill's sodium was dangerously low.

'At least we know what we're dealing with.'

They hung some saline, and the medical team worked on him till finally his seizures were halted. But Bill was clearly very sick, and instead of the psychiatric ward he was transferred to ICU. Ruby even went with Siobhan to take him up and hand him over.

'Nice call,' Siobhan said, and gave a compliment in her own backhanded way. 'You have to go with your gut sometimes, even if you have no idea what you're basing it on...'

Though it was nice of Siobhan to say so, Ruby was incensed on her patient's behalf, annoyed at how he had been dismissed, and that anger simmered inside her all night, especially when Jamelia carried on as if nothing had happened.

It was just a horrible, busy, chaotic night, though there was order to the chaos and, Ruby realised, even if she didn't like the bubbling anger inside her, even if resentment didn't generally suit her, it helped to be carrying some in a place like this. When a group of revellers noisily crossed all boundaries and spilled into Resus, where behind a curtain Ruby had just finished inserting a catheter, to demand when they'd be seen, it was actually Ruby who dealt with them—all five and a bit feet of her. She covered her patient, the poor woman clearly distressed by the intrusion, and Ruby ripped off her gloves and strode over to the three angry men and shooed them out. Sheila, who had been about to summon Security from the waiting room, smothered a smile and replaced the phone.

'You do not come in here!' Ruby was enraged. 'Go back down to the waiting room and when it's your turn you'll be called.'

'Ah, come on, darling…' They made a few comments about her temper and her hair and Ruby just stood her ground, told them that if they took one step further, she'd have them removed, and she meant it. Absolutely, she meant it.

'They're gone.' She went back in and reassured her patient. 'I'll go and get you some water. The doctor wants you to drink a lot.'

'You did well,' Cort said as he made himself a drink, while Ruby banged about in the kitchen where she was getting a jug of water for her patient. For a second there she thought she was about to get to say her piece, that finally the way Bill had been treated was about to be acknowledged, except Cort was talking about something else. With the drunks bursting into Resus.

'It's good to assert yourself,' Cort pushed, but still she said nothing, this mini red tornado in the kitchen, and he wanted her to talk to him, to open up to him, to treat him as she did others, so he pushed a little further. 'You're angry?'

'Yes,' Ruby said. 'I'm angry.'

'Which is fine—'

'Well, I don't like it,' Ruby said. 'I prefer enjoying my work to walking around…' She couldn't say it, couldn't let rip without criticising Jamelia and she didn't want to do that, so she just ignored him, because they'd used up all the free tokens that had come with their first night together. But Cort wouldn't let it slide, Cort wanted the ten minutes of Ruby that her friends and colleagues seemed to get.

'Walking around?' Cort continued. 'Walking around, what?'

'Angry,' Ruby said. 'Is that what it takes to survive this place?'

'For some,' Cort admitted. 'Ruby, it's okay to be angry.'

'That's a joke, coming from you.' She blasted a jug of ice with water. 'I got hurt and the one time I was angry, the one time I let it show...' She turned off the tap. 'Look what it cost me.' She turned on a smile because that was all anyone really wanted from her. '*You* carry on with crabby Cort. As soon as I'm out of here, I'll get back to being happy.'

Except she couldn't quite get there.

The place incensed her, especially when it turned out that no one had bothered to ring Psych and let them know what had happened with Bill. Imran, a psych doctor Ruby knew quite well, came down at two a.m. to admit him.

'Oh, he had a seizure,' Jamelia said. 'Hyponatraemic. He's under ICU for now.'

'Well, thanks so much for advising me,' Imran

said. 'I'll get back to bed, then.' But his sarcasm was wasted on Jamelia who just moved on to her next patient.

'Busy?' Ruby asked.

'Full moon,' Imran answered, and Cort, who was on the phone, felt his jaw snap down. 'Have you got time for a drink before I head back up there?'

'I doubt we'll be getting breaks tonight.'

'I don't know how you stand the place,' Imran said, and then he saw a flash of tears in Ruby's eyes. She muttered something about not knowing how she stood it either.

'Can I steal Ruby for a drink?' Imran clearly knew Sheila. 'To compensate for my wasted journey?'

'Ten minutes,' Sheila called over, because no one would be getting a proper break tonight and Ruby clearly needed a short one. Her cheeks were burning with colour, she was tense and angry, and Sheila didn't blame her a bit—she just didn't have time to address it.

As Ruby and Imran headed off to the staff-room, Cort found something out about himself—occasionally he ground his teeth.

Ruby did feel a bit better for talking to Imran. 'What if he'd been still stuck in a cubicle when he'd had the seizure?' Ruby asked as they broke open a bar of chocolate.

'They'd have heard him,' Imran said. 'Bill's going to be fine. They'll sort him out and then he'll be back with us.'

'He's not manic.'

'Of course he's manic.' Imran laughed. 'He does this all the time.'

She closed her eyes, because it was almost impossible. There was just so much to learn, so much to take in, and three years just didn't cut it.

'You'll get there,' Imran said as they headed

out to the unit. 'This sort of thing happens all the time.'

'Well, it shouldn't.'

'You'll be back with us soon,' Imran said as they walked passed Cort.

'Thank God,' Ruby muttered, and Cort rather agreed. He needed his mind to get back to work.

CHAPTER SIXTEEN

THERE was a lull about five.

The suture room had a list of patients waiting and there were some still waiting to be taken to the ward, but for a moment they sat at the nurses' station, because a break, Sheila said, was vital. Ruby glanced at the clock. Two and a half hours and her time in Emergency would be over—it couldn't come soon enough for her. Sheila had even said that given she hadn't had her dinner break, if the place was quiet, she could shower and change and be out by seven-thirty.

'Here.' Siobhan waddled in with a laden tray and though Ruby had fully intended to have a strong black coffee with three sugars, she was so touched that Siobhan had filled her little white teapot, it seemed churlish not to drink it, so though she yearned for a hit of caffeine, Ruby sipped on dandelion leaves and chamomile instead.

'He's doing better.' Jamelia came off the phone and smiled over at Ruby, who had no idea who she was talking about. 'Bill,' Jamelia said. 'They're transferring him to a medical ward now.' Then Ruby blinked as Jamelia continued. 'It's good you knew him. I listened too much to his family,' Jamelia admitted. 'They said this is how he got when he came off his medication…'

'He still needed a proper work-up before he was referred to Psych,' Cort broke in, neither judgmental nor angry, just matter-of-fact. 'When a patient's manic, they don't always think to eat and drink properly,' Cort said, 'or they get grandiose and think they can survive on nothing, or, like Bill, start training for a marathon. You don't just label someone as psych till you've done a full work-up.'

He didn't labour the point, in fact no one did,

they just spoke about it for a little while, and Sheila regaled them with a few stories from the past. For Ruby it was a revelation and she started to get the place a bit better. Saw that no one was blaming—instead they were teaching and learning.

'Have you heard of clanging, Sheila?' Siobhan said, adding about four sugars to her coffee. Ruby would have killed for a taste. It turned out Sheila hadn't heard the term and they had a bit of fun explaining. Ruby started to see that you were allowed to not know things, you just had to be honest enough to admit it, and it wasn't about scoring points or pulling rank, it was about a group of minds that, when pooled, were formidable.

And finally, when the emergency phone shrilled, whether it was the chamomile or she was just numb from the experience of Emergency, Ruby didn't jolt on her stool when it went off.

If anyone seemed stressed, it was Sheila.

'Yuk!' Sheila put down the phone and pulled a face. 'We've got a penetrating eye injury coming in...' She gave a shudder. 'Siobhan, you'll have to deal with it.' She glanced at Ruby, who couldn't hide her surprise at Sheila's reaction. 'We've all got our things—even me,' Sheila said. 'Mine's eyes. Can't go near them.'

'What's yours, Siobhan?' Sheila asked.

'Dunno.' Siobhan shrugged. 'I guess old people.'

'What?' Sheila grinned. 'You can't go near them?'

'No, they just get to me. Like that woman the other day, moaning about her child not being seen while I was sitting eating—she moaned loudly enough and got straight to the top of the queue and there was poor old Tom who'd been waiting to be stitched since we came on duty and because he's old...' She gave a shrug. 'It just gets to me, I guess.'

Ruby blinked because, even if it had been handled, in Ruby's eyes, poorly, there was a reason—

a side to the hard-nosed Siobhan she had never seen. Even Cort looked up in surprise.

'What about you, Cort?' Siobhan asked. 'And don't say kids, because everyone has a thing when a sick kid's brought in.'

He was about to shrug, to say nothing, to get up and walk outside and get some fresh air while they awaited the arrival of the ambulance, but then Cort realised that was what he always did. He closed up and walked off and just dealt with it in his own way, and it wasn't perhaps the best way. He wanted to be part of the solution, wanted more of a team, and he realised that meant taking part on a level that he never had.

'Prolonged resuscitations,' he said. 'I can't stand them!'

'You can't, can you?' Sheila did a double-take as realisation hit. 'You get all worked up…come-jack booting in and taking over.'

'Yeah, well, I'm working on it,' Cort said. 'My wife was in a car accident, they worked on her for way too long, and she was left with an acquired brain injury…'

'Your wife?' Sheila's face paled and Ruby just sat there quietly and could not have been more proud of him.

'My late wife,' Cort said, and then stood. 'So, yes, I get a bit tense around them, but now you know why.' He saw the flash of blue light come in through the dark window and although he'd missed his chance for fresh air, he was quietly relieved that he'd cleared the air inside a touch, 'Let's see how this guy is.'

It turned out eyes weren't one of Ruby's *things*. Which meant she didn't mind them.

She was able to talk to the patient and reassure him as Cort carefully assessed, and it was a too serious injury for a general hospital so Ruby sat and monitored him, because he was heavily sedated, as they waited for an ambulance to transfer him to the eye hospital. 'Where did you slip off to?' Ruby grinned, walking back from the ambulance foyer as Sheila returned from taking the last patient to the ward. Connor had agreed to do the escort as Ruby had to get away on time and, anyway, as a student she wasn't able to provide escort.

'Has he gone?' Sheila asked, and Ruby nodded.

'Why don't you go now?' Sheila said. 'It's nearly seven—have your shower and you can be out of here on time.'

'Are you sure?'

'I think you've earned it.'

She smiled all the way to the locker rooms and chatted for a moment to some of the day staff that were dribbling in, but only when she tucked her hair into a shower cap and turned on the taps full blast did she let the tears flow, because that, Ruby had realised, was what this place did to her. It brought every carefully checked emotion right up to the surface, made her confront things, think of things, see things she'd really rather not— and even if the staff did annoy her, even if they were cliquey and rude, now she understood why. And she loved them, every bitchy, horrible one of them.

And now she had to go out there and say goodbye to them, and say goodbye to Cort too—so she cried, where no one could hear her, because it was certainly better out than in, especially as she had to go now and see her family, and heaven forbid she go there all knotty and tense.

Because then she might just say something, speak a little of her mind.

And, as she'd recently found out, that didn't go down well.

Ruby dried and dressed in neutral clothes and brushed her hair till it was straight and shiny. She put on some neutral make-up and instead of putting on bangles and earrings she put her smile back on and headed back out there.

'Where are you off to all dolled up?' Sheila asked, and then looked again. 'Or rather all dolled down?'

'Church.'

Cort glanced up and though, of course, it was Ruby, it wasn't.

She was in a neat brown skirt, with flat brown closed-toe sandals and a neat cream top. Her hair was down and brushed and she was neither prim nor plain. In fact, she looked gorgeous. The only way he could explain it was as if she'd been de-Ruby'd. And he could tell too, just as he had on the first night, that she'd been crying. It was almost indecipherable, she'd put on make-up and her glassy eyes could be from exhaustion, but he knew there was more to it than that.

'At seven-thirty in the morning?' Sheila frowned.

'I'm going with my parents.' Ruby grinned. 'They live out at Whale Beach, which is a good hour away. I said I'd meet them there.'

'You've been working all night,' Sheila pointed out. 'Are you sure you're okay to drive?'

'I'm fine.' Ruby gave a large eye roll as she

took a seat on a stool. 'I haven't been to see them for a few weeks. I didn't want to make excuses again.'

'Well, enjoy your Sunday off.'

'I doubt it.' Ruby grimaced. 'A lovely lamb roast...' She put two fingers to her mouth. 'I can't wait!'

'You can't police the world.' Sheila laughed, because she had a daughter who was almost as flaky as this student. 'Let them enjoy their dinner without judging them.'

'Let them?' Ruby swung down her legs from the stool. 'I wish they'd let me. I have to eat the thing. They don't get that if they just let me have vegetables, I'd go and visit them more...'

'You eat it?' Cort frowned, because she had her own fridge, for goodness' sake. She'd guilt-tripped him out of steak and a bacon sandwich, and yet when it suited her, away went her principles.

'They make you eat it?' Sheila was intrigued.

'I'd have to tie Lila down.' Her voice trailed off because she could see Ruby was blushing and a bit uncomfortable.

'They don't make me,' Ruby said. 'It's just...' she gave a tight shrug '...easier. Anyway, I just wanted to say thank you for everything, Sheila.'

'Thank you,' Sheila said. 'We've enjoyed having you. We have!' Sheila smiled when Ruby gave her a disbelieving look. 'I love a challenge. We might see you back here when you're qualified,' Sheila teased.

'Not a chance.' Ruby grinned. 'But I have learnt a lot,' she admitted. 'I really have.'

'I'll see you on...Tuesday, is it? For your final assessment. But don't lose any sleep worrying about it.'

'Don't mention sleep!' Ruby said, and waved. She wanted to say something to Cort but he didn't look up because, as per his instruction, she was just another student.

* * *

Easier.

He sat there long after he'd finished writing, blankly staring at his notes, and that word re-played over and over in his head.

Easier to drive for an hour and do family duty after three consecutive nights working.

Easier to dress not as herself.

Easier to eat a roast when it went against every principle she had.

Easier to be happy than to create any waves.

Just stuff down your emotions so *they* don't have to deal with them.

He could see her father in front of him ten years ago—forceps hurled across Theatre and the angry, bullying ways that all the staff toler-ated because it was Gregory Carmichael's way.

And he remembered, too, finding a nurse in floods of tears in the coffee room, then blowing her nose and heading back out there, because, well, that's what they all did.

He got her then, got what it might have been like to be the one Gregory was going to sort out.

There was nothing easy about sitting there thinking of her driving that sleek sports car with no sleep and a bellyful of anger, and he wanted to speak to her, to accept her apology and to apologise himself.

'Well, we'll have the next lot of students on Monday,' Sheila said. 'That's it, though, for that lot.'

Was that Sheila's way of letting him know that the rules didn't apply now?

He should go home to bed, Cort decided, not give in to feelings that could probably be put down to lack of sleep. He should wait and see how he felt in a few hours, with a much clearer head.

Yes, indecision was the enemy in this place, and Cort was filled with it now, because he should leave it there, just let things lie, because there was no casual with Ruby, no hope of one night, or two or three—he was thinking of a future and it was way too soon after Beth to be thinking like that.

Anyway, he didn't even know her number to ring her.

He went round to the kitchen and there was her teapot with 'Ruby' written in red and he thought of all she'd put up with, all she'd got through, and he wished he could have had the guts to have been there for her more.

'She's forgotten her teapot.' Sheila walked in and followed where Cort's gaze lingered. 'She'd forget her head, that one. I'll ring her and remind her to pick it up on Tuesday—we've got enough clutter in here as it is.' She opened the off-duty book and pulled out her phone, but Siobhan came in yawning and asking for someone to check drugs, and Sheila did what she never did and left the off-duty book lying there open. It couldn't have been deliberate but Cort, like a guilty schoolboy, wrote a student nurse's number down and actually didn't give too much thought to what would happen if he was caught, or what others would say or think.

All he cared about was Ruby.

He tried her mobile, but if she was driving it was sensible that she didn't pick up, and later when he arrived home and still it went straight to voicemail, he told himself she was in church, so naturally it would be switched off, but there was this terrible dread that woke him around lunchtime—a horrible feeling that he'd left it too late.

He looked over at the picture of Beth, which had been reinstated, and told himself that God wouldn't be that cruel, that two women he loved wouldn't be lost in that way.

Guilt swept right through him, because he was looking at Beth and admitting he loved Ruby as well.

Then you'd better do something about it, Beth's eyes said, because, unlike Ruby, Beth was practical.

It's too soon, Cort implored, but Beth just stared back from a place where time had a different meaning.

He rang again and then again when it was after five, and there was still no answer. And then, even if her phone was off because she was asleep, he just had to know for sure, so he gave in and drove to Hill Street and parked a little way down from the house and waited for the car that was too big and too fast to come round the corner or down the hill, so that he could drive off reassured and could go back to bed and stop worrying. Except it didn't appear.

He could not stand it if anything had happened to her.

Could not go through it again.

Except he was.

He was going through it this very moment, imagining all sorts of things, when she might well be in bed, sleeping, Cort thought. One of her friends might have taken the car out, but he simply had to know—so out onto the street he went, waved to the old lady in the next house when she waved at him, opened the squeaking gate, walked up the garden path and stood on the veranda where he had first kissed Ruby and then, because he had to, he knocked on the door.

'Is Ruby here?' He tried to sound casual.

'No,' Tilly said.

'Do you know when she'll be back?'

'I'm not sure…' And he realised that she was worried too. 'I thought she'd be back a while ago, we were going to throw her a little party… for finishing.'

'She said she was going for lunch at her parents'.' Cort attempted rational. 'Maybe she stayed on there, or she just fell asleep.'

'I just rang her mum and she left ages ago. Her mum sounded upset. I think they might have had a row.' Tilly held open the door. 'Come in if you want.'

'It's okay…' He was about to decline and what?

Sit in his car or go home and pace. But he wanted to be with them because they loved her too. For a second Cort closed his eyes, because it was the second time today he'd said it to himself and he said it again for a third time. It was love, that was what it was—too soon, too fast, too much perhaps, but that it was love he was completely certain. 'Thanks,' he said, and stepped into the house that was becoming familiar, and there they all were at the table, the people who loved and cared for her. Feeling a little bit awkward, Cort sat down and joined them.

'We really should know better by now than to worry about her,' Jess said by way of greeting. 'She's always wandering off.' She pointed to a large calendar. 'She's the red one. We know her shifts better than Ruby does. We're always having to dash down to the beach to remind her she's on a late or got a lecture...'

'I might go down to the beach,' Cort offered. 'Take a look.'

'I just went,' Ellie said.

It was a very strange three hours—lots of idle small talk, all pretending not to be sick with worry, and Cort sitting there as if he just happened to have stopped by. Eventually, Cort cracked and rang work to see if they needed him and, oh, so casually asked to go through the admission list, just to see what had come in.

'Nope.'

'Told you,' Ellie said, just back from the beach for the third time.

'There are loads of hospitals,' Tilly snapped, which Cort guessed was unusual for her. 'I'll make a drink.'

'I'll make this one,' Cort offered, because they must have made him twenty. He found the tea bags and mugs and sugar okay, but when he went to the fridge to get some milk, they stopped him.

'Not that one,' Ellie said. 'That's Ruby's fridge.'

'Unless you want rice milk with your tea.' Jess rolled her eyes. 'She has her own fridge so she doesn't get depressed seeing our sausages and things. You do know what you're taking on?'

'Not really,' Cort admitted, but he hoped he'd get to find out.

He was about to suggest that they ring the police, but what could they say? That a twenty-three-year old wasn't home by nine? And then there was the slam of the front door and everyone looked at each other as a cheery call came from the hall.

'I need wine!'

They all just looked at Ruby as she burst into the kitchen. 'What?'

'Where have you been?' Tilly asked in a voice that was just a little bit shaky and not, Cort guess, just from relief.

'At the beach.'

'I looked on the beach,' Ellie said. 'I've been three times and you weren't there.'

'I went to one near my parents' and fell asleep. We had a bit of an argument,' Ruby admitted.

'We've been ringing and ringing you,' Tilly said.

'We've all been worried, Ruby.' It was the first time Cort had spoken, the first words he could manage because the relief that had flooded him was so physical, it had taken a while to find a shade of a normal voice.

'Why are you here?' Ruby blinked in surprise.

'Because I was worried about you.'

Ruby looked at the table, saw the cards and the congratulations cake and the sparkling wine surrounded by mug after mug of tea, and realised she'd missed her own little party. 'I'm sorry, guys. I never even thought.' She went into her bag for her phone. 'It's dead… I just…I didn't want to come home in the mood I was in. I was…' Still she didn't say it and he truly saw then just how guarded she was with her emotions. Happy Ruby was the one she chose to show to the world. 'I just wanted some space. I'm fine now.'

'Fair enough,' Tilly said.

'What was the row about?' Jess asked, but Ruby just shrugged.

'Nothing.'

'Nothing?' Jess frowned.

'It was about something so unbelievably tiny…' Ruby shook her head. 'I haven't got the energy to go into it.'

'Well, we're going down to the Stat Bar—we're the ones who need wine. Are you two coming?'

Ruby glanced at Cort. 'No.' She shook her head. 'Maybe later…' As her housemates walked out, she apologised again. 'I really am sorry. I had no idea you'd all be so worried.'

'It's us overeating.' Tilly hugged her. 'But ring next time you go walkabout.'

She guessed she hadn't got away with it that easily because once alone she looked at Cort and his face was white. She knew that she'd scared him and people didn't get scared if they didn't care.

'I was about to go and get the worry dolls!' He

was trying to make a joke, but he didn't have to try with Ruby. 'Don't ever do that again.'

'Why are you here?'

'You left your teapot at work.'

'Cort?'

'Because I was worried about you, because you were upset and angry when you left.'

'I wasn't.'

'Yes, Ruby, you were. And you shouldn't have been driving.'

She opened her mouth to argue then closed it because, yes, he was right, she really shouldn't have been driving. Halfway there the tears had started again and halfway home she'd nearly rear-ended someone, which was why she'd pulled over.

'I had no choice but to go. You don't know what they're like.'

'You could have come back here—got one of your friends to drive and come with you.'

'I didn't want to rot up their day.'

'Well, you did,' Cort said. 'You worried them sick. What was the row about? And don't say nothing.'

Ruby shrugged. 'It was stupid.'

'Tell me.'

'I don't want to talk about it.'

'Why?'

'Because it just winds me up.'

'So,' Cort said, and opened the bubbles that her friends had had waiting. 'Get wound up.' He poured himself a glass and took a seat and Ruby took a mouthful of wine and felt her face burn, not from the wine or lack of sleep but from the stupid row that had hurt so much, from the wave her tiny ripple had made.

'Mum always does a massive lunch. I had cauliflower cheese, pumpkin, roast potatoes and peas, and I thought about what Sheila said about her daughter, and I guess I'd just had a busy night and dealt with all those things, and…' It was beyond pathetic, embarrassing really to repeat it, but he just sat there patiently as she squirmed in her seat and then she came out and said it. 'I didn't have any meat or gravy...' She closed her eyes. 'It doesn't matter.'

'It does.'

It did.

'I just got sick of pretending! It doesn't make him happy anyway. Even if I'd eaten the whole thing, he'd still have something to complain about. I was just trying to be myself...' She shook her head in frustration. 'Now poor Mum's in tears, he's in a filthy mood.... I should have just eaten it...'

'And smiled?' Cort asked, and after a moment Ruby nodded.

'I just want to be myself,' Ruby said, 'except they don't seem to like her very much.'

'Then they don't know what they're missing,' Cort said. And he meant it, because even if he didn't agree with everything, there was nothing about her he would change.

'I try so hard to just blend in, to just…'

'Maybe stop trying.'

'I can't,' Ruby said.

'Okay,' Cort said, and wondered how he'd go, sitting beside her, watching her gag at dinner, and not be able to step in, but he would, if it made things easier, if she ever let him be there for him, if she could ever get past what he'd done.

'I'm sorry that I didn't tell you about Beth,' Cort said. 'You had every right to be angry—to be furious, in fact.'

'No I didn't—I had no right to judge, about how soon… I shouldn't have rushed in. I know everyone is different.'

'Ruby, you had every right,' Cort said, 'because I should have told you that night when I brought you back to my home. I just didn't want to burden you with it all, not till you were through with Emergency. Beth was sick for years and in all that time I couldn't look at anyone else. Every day off was spent at the nursing home. I was married,'

Cort said. 'Even if Beth didn't recognise me, I still wanted to do the right thing by her.'

Ruby nodded.

'And I wasn't embarrassed by her. I didn't want visitors or people to see her because I was embarrassed *for* her,' Cort said. 'I didn't want anyone to remember her like that and I still try not to. She was the cleverest, smartest person I've ever met, and there was hardly any of that left. She would have loathed to be seen like that.

'A month after she died, I end up in a bar, and, yep, you were supposed to be a one-night stand. It just never felt like that at the time, or after...'

It hadn't.

Not once had she felt like a temporary solution.

'You're stuck with me, Ruby,' Cort said, and she smiled. 'Even if I am too old and staid...'

She winced at her own words. 'I didn't mean those things.'

'They're all true. I just don't want it to rub off on you.'

'It won't,' Ruby promised.

'I want you to be you.'

'I will be,' Ruby said. 'And you're not boring. You could never be boring.'

'Oh I am—and happily so,' Cort said, thinking about his wardrobe of dark suits and shoes and lack of tattoos or body piercings and smudge sticks and a complete absence of alternative thinking.

'I think we should keep things quiet, though.' She felt him tense. 'We know how serious we are, I just don't think it would be fair to Beth. Let's just lie low together for a year or so...'

He was more grateful than she could ever know.

Part of him wanted to shout it from the rooftops and to hell with everyone, to tell the world about them, and yet there was loyalty there to Beth that she recognised, promoted, and it only confirmed that loving her was right.

'Someone might come in,' Cort said. As always with Ruby, their kiss was growing out of hand.

'They'll be gone for ages,' Ruby breathed. 'Hang your tie on the door.'

And, boring or not, he was not going to risk an impromptu party descending on Hill Street.

'Get dressed,' Cort said, because he wanted to be completely alone with her.

'I am dressed,' Ruby grumbled, but he took her to her bedroom and she put on her jewels and the clothes that were her, put back all the things that were Ruby, just so he could have the pleasure of taking them off later.

'Text Tilly,' Cort said as they drove past the Stat Bar towards his flat, the bay lit up by a huge moon, music pumping from the bars, and everything right with the world.

'She'll know where I am,' Ruby started, but, yes, given the worry she'd caused today, it would be only fair.

So she texted her friend, told her not to worry if she wasn't home till late tomorrow, that she was at Cort's. Two minutes later her phone bleeped and Ruby glanced at it and gave a smile.

'What did she say?'

'I'm not telling.'

'What did she say?' Cort grinned.

'That she wants all the details on my return.'

'She'd better not get them,' Cort said, and they drove along the bay and once at his flat he turned off his phone, because that was what he would do now, and Ruby duly switched off hers.

'It's like the start of an exam,' Ruby said, 'when they tell you to switch off your mobiles.'

'Let's find out what you've learnt.' Cort smiled and she was about to make a joke, to smile and dance for him, but she was suddenly serious, because with Cort she could be.

'That you love me.' She couldn't believe she'd be so bold, just to say it.

'Correct.'

'That I love you.' Nor could she believe that

she could say that so readily either, but Cort just nodded.

'Correct,' Cort said, and pulled her to him. 'Which, come what may, that we love each other is all we really need to know.'

EPILOGUE

IF YOU were lucky, life went on.

Sheila walked into the changing room before her late shift a few weeks later and tried not to roll her eyes at the sight of a new set of nursing students, some nervous, some arrogant, all about to step right into the front line for the very first time, all naïve about how they would cope.

'Lucky thing!' a loud one said. 'I wouldn't mind being in Bali.'

'I've asked her to bring me back a sarong,' another loud one said. 'But knowing Ruby she'll forget.'

Sheila smiled quietly as she headed to the staffroom, because Bali was so Ruby. She could see her now, drifting along the beach in a sarong or at the markets choosing jewellery, or just lying by

a pool, soaking in the sun, knowing she'd qualified and could now follow her heart and study
her beloved mental health.

'Postcard from Cort,' Doug said, and handed it
to Sheila for a quick read, but her eyes lingered
on the words for just a moment longer than they
would normally.

Now that they all knew what he'd been through,
Doug hadn't hesitated when Cort had asked for
a couple of weeks' unpaid leave—he needed a
holiday, he'd explained.

A *real* holiday, for the first time in many, many
years. Maybe Fiji, perhaps Bali. And on real holidays, a postcard was expected in a place like
Emergency, completely necessary, in fact, because it brought a little bit of sun to the workers, and a little smile to the sender when they
glanced up at the cork board in the staffroom
weeks and months later. A nice postcard of a
stunning view from a stunning luxury hotel in
Bali because, Sheila had a feeling, Cort had used

the supplied hotel postcards, rather than exert himself by shopping for one.

Cort, Sheila was sure, was rather too busy.

Thinking of you all as little as I can.
Clear the board for me ☺
Cort

And she couldn't be sure, but she almost was. Of course half the students were whooping it up in Bali now, it was a rite of passage almost, and just because Cort Mason happened to be there too…

'Good for him.' Sheila smiled. 'He needed a break.'

It was more than a break, it was a completely new start.

He could hear the click-clack of her hair beads as Ruby, on the second-last day of their holiday, finally wrote her postcards—Cort's had long since been posted.

She'd had her hair beaded the first day they'd arrived and her feet and hands were adorned with henna tattoos and her pale skin was now golden brown. And every day he knew her a little bit more.

'What can I put?' Ruby asked as Cort lay on a sunbed, reading the English papers.

'Who's this one for?'

'Mum and Dad.' Ruby sighed. 'I've said the weather's nice, that the hotel is lovely...' And Cort only wished they could see how much they were missing out on, by censoring their relationship with her. 'And I've written really big...' She added something else then scribbled her name, then got on with the next one, to her housemates, which would be easy.

Except Cort was right. When it was 'the one', the 'real one', you didn't share the details quite so much. He wasn't on the list on the fridge and there were things that only they two knew.

See you when I'm looking at you x

She wrote that because they were real friends and, as she was working out, she didn't have to pretend to them, didn't have to write about the beach or food or weather. She'd tell them all her news in her own good time.

'I need a rest,' Ruby said, because writing post-cards was exhausting work. She turned her head to where Cort now dozed beside her on the sump-tuous white lounger. They were a million miles away from drama and she was so relaxed it was an effort to put out a hand and lift a straw to her mouth. 'I'm exhausted, Cort. I haven't even got the energy to put on some more sun block.'

'I'll put some on for you.' Cort said without opening his eyes, but even if his face didn't twitch, inside he was smiling, because that was how she made him feel.

For Ruby it was different, because this morning when her mother had rung, instead of shrugging her shoulders and smiling and carrying on, she'd actually told him just how knotted up she felt inside, how she could feel the disapproval behind every word, and the world hadn't stopped when she'd voiced her feelings. Cort hadn't crumpled in a heap or accused her of ruining their holiday. Instead, he'd just rubbed her knotted shoulders and let her brood for a little while, because Ruby was finding out she was allowed to be miserable at times.

'Here...' He played the game, sat up and opened the tube.

'I'm too tired to sunbathe,' Ruby grumbled. 'I need a *proper* rest.'

'In bed?' Cort solemnly checked.

'I think so.' Ruby nodded.

She was so tired that he had to peel off her

bikini and pull back the sheets and turn on the fan, but she soon perked up.

'I'm feeling better already,' Ruby said, in the cool, dark room with Cort stretched out beside her.

'I thought you might be.'

'How did I get so lucky?' Ruby asked, when Cort was just thinking the same thing.

And then it was just about the two of them, and the lovely click clack of her beads as they made love, followed by the sinking feeling that in one more sleep their holiday would be over, but excitement too at the thought of the real world, with the other one there.

They had dinner on their deck the last night— Cort finally relenting and wearing 'just this once' the sarong Ruby had bought him, and finding it was surprisingly comfortable. Or was it just the company? Sitting there drinking cocktails and eating seafood, while Ruby ate from a huge selection of fruit kebabs. The waiters were waiting, the candles were hissing as one by one they fizzled out, and she didn't want her holiday to end, though she was excited about starting her mental health nurse course and seeing her friends.

'It's been wonderful,' Ruby said, when the sun had long since dipped down over the horizon and the only red glow was from her shoulders.

The waiters took the trays and said goodnight and if she and Cort went to bed then it would be morning and she didn't want it to be, didn't want the magic they'd found to end, quietly wondering every now and then if their relationship would still stand up when they were back in the real world.

'How was your seafood?' Ruby asked.

'Fantastic,' Cort said, then added, 'I won't give up meat.' Because he'd be himself too.

'I'll never ask you to.'

'I'll be eating a lot at work and stopping off—'

'Fine.' Now the waiters were gone she moved

onto his lap, kissed his mouth. 'You can do what you like.'

'What about kids?'

'What about them?' Ruby asked, kissing his mouth and running her hands over his lovely brown shoulders. Then she paused because she wasn't sure she was hearing things right.

'Our kids.'

'They'll be beautiful…'

'I meant about food.'

'They can have meat any time you buy it,' Ruby was magnanimous given it was a fantasy. 'And cook it and feed them and wash up afterwards—every night if you want.'

He got up and walked to their villa and Ruby sat and watched as he walked back. He was carrying a thick velvet box and she knew then it wasn't a fantasy, that this was their future they were discussing, and that it was real and would last the scrutiny of day.

'It's white gold,' Cort said, when she opened it. 'I thought it would blend in...'

It would never blend in to Ruby, it was completely and utterly exquisite—a heavy necklace she could wear every day, and only the knowing would see that it wasn't glass in the centre but a deep red ruby, with purple hues when she held it up to the moon, and that the jumble of knots that held it was actually an *R* and a *C* and, yes, if asked, she could say the C was for her surname, but as she slipped it on, it was Cort who rested just above her heart.

'There's a matching ring to follow.' He kissed the back of her neck as her body adjusted to the necklace's new weight, as the cool metal blended till it matched the temperature of her skin, but still she could feel it, their names set in stone, or rather a stone set in their names, and Ruby knew that together was their future.

'There's an M there too,' Cort said, and Ruby traced it with her fingers. 'It stands for Mason—

one day when you're ready—that's if marriage isn't too conventional for you?'

'I could think of nothing nicer,' Ruby said, and took his hand when he asked her to dance, even though there was no music.

It didn't matter.

Both of them could hear it.

* * * * *

A TABLE IN TUSCANY

To my friend ANDREW THOMAS
for putting up with me,
To LORRAINE, PENNY & KATI
for keeping me to the (fairly) straight & narrow,
To everyone at the LOCANDA dell'AMOROSA
for showing me what the joys of a
table in Tuscany really are,
To GUISEPPE, MAURIZIO, PAULA de FERRARI CORRADI,
GIOVANELLA STIANTI & the PANERAIS for
teaching me about Tuscan wine,
and to CARLO,
EMILIANA & everyone at PONTI di SASSO, ANGELA,
LETIZIA, MARIELLA, EBE & RENZO & FIAMETTA,
LEONARDO, JILL & everyone at IL FEDINO, FRANCA &
BEPPE near Fiesole, CLAUDI & ELIZABETHA & Signora PIRAS
on Elba, MARY at Tiglio, ANNA at the Castello di Spaltenna,
CESARE at Vipore, and my Mum, whose years of very
inspired cooking were the inspiration
for this book.

A TABLE IN TUSCANY

CLASSIC RECIPES ·from the· HEART of ITALY COLLECTED and ILLUSTRATED by LESLIE FORBES

Webb&Bower
EXETER, ENGLAND

First published in Great Britain by
Webb & Bower (Publishers) Limited
9 Colleton Crescent, Exeter, Devon EX2 4BY

Copyright © Leslie Forbes 1985

Produced by Johnson Editions Limited
30 Ingham Road, London NW6 1DE

Art editor Lorraine Johnson
Editor Penny Clarke

British Library Cataloguing in Publication Data
Forbes, Leslie
    Table in Tuscany
    1. Cookery, Tuscan
    I. Title
    641.5945'5   TX723

ISBN 0-86350-069-2

Printed and Bound in
Great Britain by
Hazell, Watson and Viney Ltd.

· CONTENTS ·

Introduction	6
The Vale of Florence	9
The Chianti Hills	39
Medieval Cities	59
Vines and Vineyards	83
The Etruscan Maremma	97
By the Sea	111
Olives and Chestnuts	141
Index	158

· INTRODUCTION ·

A kitchen table on a farm near Mont Amiata, strewn with wild asparagus and giant porcini mush-rooms, freshly gathered. A cafe table in Siena with slices of rich panforte and frothy cappucini for two. A table in a crowded Florentine trattoria, its checked cloth covered in plates of steaming spin-ach pasta. A pine table laden with pens, pencils and sketchpads in an olive grove north of Lucca. These are some of the many tables at which I ate, talked, drank and learned about Tuscany's culture and people as well her food and wine; and finally at which I distilled what I had learned into this book, more a sketchbook that grew than a traditional cookbook.

It started as a series of drawings and cooking notes on a trip to Tuscany five years ago. From that first trip my interest in the region developed over subsequent visits into a passion. I was hooked. For me Tuscany was, and still is, an irresistable com-bination of practical little family run restaurants casually serving up Italian sausages and beans next to grand Renaissance churches, of colourful food mar-kets sprawling uninhibitedly across cobbled medieval piazzas and especially of people, some raucous and crafty, some gentle and reserved, all of them passionately and understandably proud of their region and its food & wine.

Tuscany was relatively poor until the recent onslaught of mass tourism, and as a result most of its cooking trad-itions are firmly rooted in what Italians call 'la cucina povera', the poor kitchen. A good Tuscan restaurant conforms to the principles of economical home cooking, using fresh local prod-ucts rather than expensive imports. Chestnuts gathered from giant trees are used for sweet chestnut flour, the basis for many desserts. Pigs living outside for most of the year graze on

ASPARAGO

FUSILLI

BORAGINE

PENNE

FAGIOLI

6

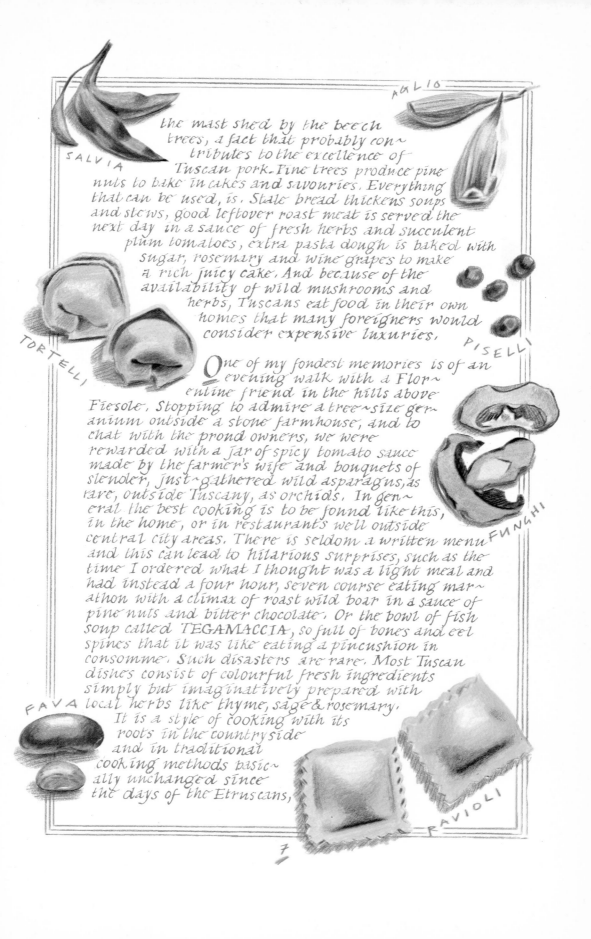

SALVIA

AGLIO

the mast shed by the beech trees, a fact that probably con~ tributes to the excellence of Tuscan pork. Pine trees produce pine nuts to bake in cakes and savouries. Everything that can be used, is. Stale bread thickens soups and stews, good leftover roast meat is served the next day in a sauce of fresh herbs and succulent plum tomatoes, extra pasta dough is baked with sugar, rosemary and wine grapes to make a rich juicy cake. And because of the availability of wild mushrooms and herbs, Tuscans eat food in their own homes that many foreigners would consider expensive luxuries.

TORTELLI

PISELLI

One of my fondest memories is of an evening walk with a Flor~ entine friend in the hills above Fiesole. Stopping to admire a tree~size ger~ anium outside a stone farmhouse, and to chat with the proud owners, we were rewarded with a jar of spicy tomato sauce made by the farmer's wife and bouquets of slender, just~gathered wild asparagus, as rare, outside Tuscany, as orchids. In gen~ eral the best cooking is to be found like this, in the home, or in restaurants well outside central city areas. There is seldom a written menu and this can lead to hilarious surprises, such as the time I ordered what I thought was a light meal and had instead a four hour, seven course eating mar~ athon with a climax of roast wild boar in a sauce of pine nuts and bitter chocolate. Or the bowl of fish soup called TEGAMACCIA, so full of bones and eel spines that it was like eating a pincushion in consomme. Such disasters are rare. Most Tuscan dishes consist of colourful fresh ingredients simply but imaginatively prepared with local herbs like thyme, sage & rosemary. It is a style of cooking with its roots in the countryside and in traditional cooking methods basic~ ally unchanged since the days of the Etruscans,

FUNGHI

FAVA

RAVIOLI

the ancient Italian tribe that first brought civil-
isation to Tuscany over 2000 years.

During the Renaissance, Tuscan cooking, like its art,
underwent a drastic change. This was the era when
one enthusiastic gourmet recommended stuffing a
wild boar with a goose, the goose with a pheasant, the
pheasant with a partridge, etc. on down the line to
finish with an olive. Florentine chefs took their skills
to barbaric France (where that very Italian device, the
fork, was still a rarity) and changed history. Recently
some of the dishes from those more exotic times have
been reintroduced by chefs anxious to bring more soph-
istication to Tuscan restaurants. But for me the best moments are still the simple & unsophisticated ones - those spent
learning from a cook the exact moment when eggs have
absorbed enough flour to give a firm but not tough pasta
dough. Or listening, in a tiny cramped Florentine trattoria,
while a chef describes how to make the perfect artichoke
omelette. Or sniffing the aroma of the chestnut cake 'cas-
tagnaccia' baking in a friend's kitchen, & burning my
fingers & tongue on deep-fried, sugary cenci, hot from a pan.

Each recipe in this book evokes a strong memory for me.
They were collected in extremely pleasant circumstances
from both professional & amateur cooks all over Tuscany.
Some are the inventions of individuals I met casually -
like the dandelion soup made by a Montalcino grandmother or the recipe for hunter's sauce given by a travelling porchetta vendor in San Gimignano.

Not all the recipes come word for word from the restaurants mentioned. Some I have had to adapt from
notes scribbled while a harassed chef continued to cook
the daily speciality. Most of the recipes can be adapted
to suit personal taste & some are just quick ideas for
giving a particularly Tuscan flavour to a standard recipe,
such as the rosemary-flavoured oil that, added to basic
bread dough, instantly conjures up a steamy Florence
bakeshop at Easter.

I hope that, when cooked in some distant kitchen,
these recipes will bring at least a few of the pleasures of a table in Tuscany. And that everyone who
shares my nostalgia for such pleasures will find something in this book to stir fond memories.

THE VALE OF FLORENCE

- PRATO ·
- The MUGELLO
- POGGIO a CAIANO ·
- CARMIGNANO ·
- VIA BOLOGNESE
- FIESOLE · Villa I Tatti
- A R N O
- FLORENCE ·
- AUTOSTRADA DEL SOLE ·
- S. ANDREA in PERCUSSINA ·
- SAN CASCIANO VAL di PESA ·

· RESTAURANTS ·
· FLORENCE · Borgo Antico · Coco Lez~ zone · La Carabaccia · Ginino's · Sostanza · FIESOLE · Le Cave di Maiano · Il Lordo · S. ANDREA Percussina · Taverna Macchiavelli

· SIGHTS ·
· CARMIGNANO · wine · Villa Artimino · FIESOLE · Roman ruins · villas · caves · POGGIO A CAIANO · Villa Medicea · PRATO · Duomo · frescoes · THE MUGELLO · villas of Cafaggiolo & Trebbio

· INTRODUCTION ·

'Fiorentin mangia fagioli
Lecca piatti e tova glioli.'
The Florentine who eats beans
Licks the plates and tablecloths
(OLD TUSCAN SAYING)

Aldous Huxley called Florence a 'third rate provincial town' which is unfair. But certainly in spite of its wealth of art and culture the city sometimes seems designed to annoy the uninformed visitor. From six in the morning when the huge covered central market rings with the shouts of what sounds like the entire Florentine population, the noise of traffic and people fills the streets. VIVOLI, the best and most famous ice cream shop in Florence is busier at midnight than any other time. Museums are open only in the mornings, shop hours alter with a bewildering frequency and just when you think you have cracked the system, everything shuts at one o'clock for lunch. Grey steel shutters clang down abruptly to cover all the tempting displays of goodies, leaving formerly lively shopping streets bare and bleak. For four hours nothing moves except the occasional fly and in the summer heat of Florence (one of the hottest and most humid cities in Italy) even the flies can be a little sluggish.

The only solution is to follow the Florentine example. Rise early to shop and see the staggering variety of museums and churches and save the afternoon for a long, lazy lunch in a cool restaurant. Or picnic and siesta in the huge formal Boboli gardens behind the Pitti Palace. If you can cope with the heat explore the narrow streets lined with medieval and Renaissance palaces in the precious quiet hours between one and five o'clock. During the rest of the day whining mopeds are a constant hazard, whizzing merrily down so-called 'pedestrian only' thoroughfares and missing tourists and Florentines alike only by centimetres.

The city is not now and never has been a restful place to visit. Exhilarating, yes. Restful, no. Its centuries-long participation in a conflict between the Guelfs, who supported the Pope, and the Ghibellines, who supported the Emperor, divided the whole of Tuscany. And although by 1266 the Guelfs were the main faction in

Florence, the internal politics were still so unstable that
Dante (1265~1321) compared his hometown to a sick woman,
twisting and turning on her bed to ease her pain. It took
Cosimo de'Medici in 1434 to initiate a period of relative
stability, and it was during the rule of the Medici family,
the height of the Renaissance, that Tuscan artists, sculptors
and architects shaped Florence into the tightly~packed
urban treasure house that it is today.

E. M. Forster called the Renaissance'...all fighting
and beauty'and the fighting was not limited to politics. Pietro Torrigiano broke Michelangelo's nose in a
fistfight on the steps of the Carmine church. They were
arguing about the stunning frescoes by Masaccio in the
Brancacci chapel. And Brunelleschi, after losing the
commission to Ghiberti to sculpt the doors of Florence's
Baptistry, left the city in a huff, returning only to design
the famous cupola of the Duomo. His advanced ideas
caused an uproar in the city but were finally realised
in 1436. The raising of the massive red dome was the
outstanding engineering feat of the Renaissance period.
Visible for miles in all directions, its size was unmatched
even by Michelangelo's dome of St. Peter's in Rome, a
generation later.

11

To Florentine food lovers the 'bistecca fiorentina' is as much a masterpiece as Brunelleschi's dome is to architects. Sit in a crowded trattoria near Florence's huge central market and you will hear arguments as passionate about grilling the perfect steak as those about politics or art. Whether the 'fiorentina' (a steak of truly monumental proportions) should be first brushed with oil and then grilled, or never see oil at all, is an argument that can last as long as the parties involved are willing to continue. But Tuscans, and especially Florentines, will argue about anything. Preferably with the benefit of a meal and some good wine for stimulation.

The best arguments and the best food are to be found not in hyperelegant hotel restaurants with elaborately served international food but in local Florentine trattorias. Eat perhaps just a plate of the white beans of which the Florentines are notoriously so fond, simmered to a creamy smoothness in sage & garlic and then drenched in fine fruity olive oil. Or ask for a slice of roast pork off the spit, its skin crackling with rosemary and black pepper. These simple dishes served in unpretentious surroundings are the real flavour of Florence, nowhere better than in one of the little neighbourhood restaurants like LA CARABACCIA, GANINO'S or SOSTANZA, sitting elbow to elbow with your fellow diners at long communal tables.

It is hard to decide the best way to enter Florence for the first time. Arriving in the main railway station of Santa Maria Novella one senses only the presence of the modern city with all its attendant modern problems: noise, traffic, smell and heat. The city of Dante & Michelangelo is as distant as the blue Appennine mountains. But drive in from the north, down the old Via Bolognese (the SS65 from Bologna) and the Florence & Tuscany of the Renaissance come to life. From the dramatic Futa Pass the road runs through the gentle Mugello valley, birthplace of Ghiotto & Fra Angelico, past some of the grandest of the Renaissance villas. First there is Michelozzi's Cafaggiolo, then Trebbio and the medieval castle of Salviati where, in the 17th century, Jacopo Salviati received the severed head of his mistress as a New Year's gift from his wife. The road then leads past Sir Harold Acton's Villa La Pietra, with one of the most beautiful formal Italian gardens in Tuscany. And along the Via Bolognese for the last stretch Roman Fiesole rises on its villa & cypress covered hill to the east. Finally Brunelleschi's famous red dome comes into view, dwarfing every building for miles around, and you are in Florence.

SOUPS

S is for soup, or in Tuscany Z is for zuppa ~ any soup served over bread, as most are. They can vary widely from the simplest clear broth with fresh herbs used to boil a chicken, to zuppa di agnello in which there is only enough 'zuppa' left to soak the bread under a rich stew of lamb and tomatoes. The key to ordering or cooking a good Tuscan soup is the season ~ check the market for best buys and choose your recipe accordingly. In Tuscany it is stale bread that thickens soups, not flour or pasta and usually a jug of olive oil is served as dressing.

Each day at La Carabaccia in Florence, Luciano Ghimassi serves different, carefully researched Florentine dishes, largely based on ingredients produced by himself and his family. His intimate little restaurant is always packed with locals and booking is essen~ tial unless you are the friend of a regular customer.

· LA CARABACCIA ·
Onion soup (4)

This dish is just one of many Tuscan dishes that form part of a centuries~old debate. In 1533 Catherine de' Medici went to France to marry the future Henry II, taking with her a retinue of chefs and so starting the debate about the origin of certain dishes. Some are internationally iden~ tified with French cuisine but the Tuscans claim them for their own. Who now knows whether Catherine and her chefs changed the course of French cooking with dishes such as anitra all'arancia (canard à l'orange) or whether the inspir~ ation came from the French and filtered back to Italy with lonely Tuscan chefs returning home? Perhaps Catherine's chefs, homesick for their Tuscan cypresses, cooked dishes like carabaccia, which later evolved into the ubiquitous soup à l'oignon of every French bistro. This first recipe is certainly of Renaissance origin, with the characteristic thickening of crushed almonds.

· RENAISSANCE VERSION ·

2 LB 2 OZ / 1 KG ONIONS, FINELY SLICED
4 OZ / 100 G ALMONDS, SKINNED &
    POUNDED TO A PASTE IN A MORTAR
1 TBSP CASTER SUGAR
4 TBSP OLIVE OIL
WHITE WINE VINEGAR
CINNAMON STICK
1 3/4 PT / 1 LTR STOCK
PINCH WHITE PEPPER
PINCH SALT
POWDERED CINNAMON (OPTIONAL)
4 SLICES BREAD

Put the crushed almonds and the cinnamon stick in enough vinegar to cover, leave about 1 hour, heat the oil in a medium~sized pan, saute the onions in it until soft, using more oil if necessary. Rinse the almond paste in a sieve and add to the onions a tablespoon at a time until they are well blended. When the mixture is smooth add the sugar, pow~ dered cinnamon if liked, white pepper, salt and stock. Cook for a further 30 minutes. Put a slice of bread that has been grilled crisp and brown into each bowl, pour the soup over.

LA CARABACCIA
MODERN VERSION

The second version of Carabaccia makes a much less extravagant soup, more acceptable to modern palates.

2 LB 2 OZ/1 KG ONIONS, FINELY SLICED
SEVERAL LEAVES BASIL, TORN
   IN SMALL PIECES
2 3/4 PT/1½ LTR CHICKEN STOCK
4 OZ/100 G GARDEN VEGETABLES
   (PEAS, BROAD BEANS ETC)
WHITE WINE
PECORINO OR PARMESAN CHEESE,
   GRATED
SALT & PEPPER
4 SLICES BREAD

Heat the oil in a large pan. Cook the carrots, celery and basil in it for 5 minutes. Add the onions, cover and cook gently for at least an hour, adding about a third

of the stock as necessary to keep the mixture moist. After an hour raise the heat and add a couple of splashes of white wine. When it has evaporated add the fresh vegetables. After about a minute pour in the remaining stock, reduce the heat and cook until the vegetables are just soft. Before serving sprinkle a few tablespoons of cheese into the soup, stir well, put a slice of bread in each bowl and pour the soup over.

food never reflected the con~
flict, unless perhaps it had
an extra zest.

·TRIPPA alla FIORENTINA·
—Florentine Tripe (4)—

You, too, may be wary of tripe,
but the Florentines have an
undeniable way with it. Try it,
you might be converted.

1 ¾ LB /800 G TRIPE, READY COOKED
1 LB 2 OZ /500 G TOMATOES, PEELED
    & ROUGHLY CHOPPED
1 ½ TSP MARJORAM
1 ¼ OZ /30 G PANCETTA (OR FATTY HAM)
3 ~4 TBSP OLIVE OIL
2 CELERY STICKS
1 CARROT
SALT & PEPPER
1 ONION

The Trattoria Sostanza op~
ened in 1869 and is still
one of the best-known
working~men's cafes in Florence.
Go there to eat the huge bistec~
ca fiorentina & sit at long com~
munal tables where it is un~
possible not to share your
conversation with half the
restaurant. According to one
customer who had been eat~
ing there regularly for 40
years, the two owners who had
the cafe previously once had a
terrible row & for years never
spoke to each other. One
worked in the front of the
restaurant, the other at the
back. Communication was
only through waiters like
Mario, who has himself been
there for 50 years. But the

Put the tripe in a big saucepan
with half the onion and a
celery stick. Cover with water
and boil for 10~15 minutes.
Meanwhile finely chop the re~
maining onion and celery &
the carrot and pancetta and
cook gently in the oil in a
flame~proof casserole. Drain
and slice the tripe into small,
fine strips about 2 in/2.5 cm
long. When the onion is slightly
coloured, add the tomatoes,
tripe and seasoning. Cover &
continue to cook over a low heat.
After 30 minutes remove the
lid, turn up the heat and
cook until the sauce thickens
(about 10 minutes), stirring
occasionally to ensure that the
tripe does not stick & burn. Serve
with plenty of grated parmesan.

· TORTINO di CARCIOFI ·
Artichoke omelette

'Carciofi' is Italian for arti~
chokes, and if there is one
way to eat them that is bet~
ter than just boiling them
and dipping them in good
oil, this is it. The artichokes
should be young, preferably
Italian, the leaves closely
packed at the end of long
thin stems.

2 EGGS PER PERSON
2 ~ 3 ARTICHOKES PER PERSON,
    DEPENDING ON SIZE
¼ PT / 150 ML GOOD OLIVE OIL
CLOVE GARLIC
2 ~ 3 TBSP. FRESH PARSLEY,
    FINELY CHOPPED
SALT & PEPPER
   JUICE OF 1 LEMON

Peel off any tough outer
leaves on the artichokes and,
if using non~Italian ones,
trim away the chokes. Slice
the 'flowers' thinly from the
top down through the stem,
and soak for 15 minutes in
water and lemon juice. Heat
the oil in a frying pan with
the garlic. Drain the arti~
choke slices and pat dry.
Put them in the pan with
the oil, cover and leave
the artichokes to simmer
over a low heat, turning once
or twice. When they are gol~
den brown add the eggs,
beaten with the salt, pepper
and parsley. Continue cooking
over a medium heat until
the eggs are set, stirring
all the time to prevent
burning. At the Trattoria
Sostanza they serve their
tortinos with a squeeze
of fresh lemon juice and
plenty of crusty bread to
mop up the delicious juice.

When using non~Italian
artichokes be sure they are
very young and small and
use only the most tender
inner leaves.

18

· GANINO'S ·

Ganino's is the place where poets rub shoulders with film stars, and are served by the entire Bernadoni family (most of whom could pass for film stars themselves). In spring the tagliatelle with wild asparagus is worth dieting for, and all year round the crostini di fegatini are the best in Tuscany.

CROSTINI di FEGATINI
Chicken livers on toast (6)

Crostini probably appear on every antipasto menu in every Tuscan trattoria, but all too often they arrive as gritty grey paste on soggy bread. At Ganino's the bread is first grilled over an open wood fire, then brushed with good green olive oil and at the last minute annointed with this hot creamy mixture of chicken livers, sharpened with capers and anchovy.

6 CHICKEN LIVERS, CLEANED
1 ANCHOVY, FINELY CHOPPED
1 TSP TOMATO PUREE
WINEGLASS WHITE WINE
BUTTER
2 TBSP CAPERS, CRUSHED IN A
    MORTAR
10 OR MORE SLICES FRENCH
    BAGUETTE BREAD
1 MEDIUM ONION, FINELY
    CHOPPED
CHICKEN STOCK
GRATED PARMESAN

Melt some butter in a small saucepan and sauté the onion in it until transparent. Add the chicken livers and break them up with a fork as they begin to colour. After a few minutes pour in the wine and allow to evaporate slowly. When evaporated add the anchovy and capers, and the tomato puree mixed in a little hot stock. Continue to cook for about 15 minutes, adding more stock when necessary to keep the mixture very creamy. Just before serving beat the livers well (or whisk in a food processor) and serve very hot on toasted bread with a generous sprinkling of freshly grated parmesan or pecorino cheese over the top.

In their minute kitchen off an equally tiny white~tiled restaurant, the Paoli family manage to produce some of the best traditional Tuscan cooking in Florence.

· FARFALLINE con PISELLI ·
Pasta butterflies with fresh peas (4)

Theoretically, this is not a difficult dish to make. Stand next to a field of fresh peas with a frying pan in your hand in which is simmering gently a generous handful of pale pink prosciutto and perhaps a few finely chopped green spring onions. Wait until the peas are barely ripe ~ still tiny and bright green in their pods. At that precise moment start shelling them straight into the pan, toss them quickly in the sauce, pour onto a bowl of freshly cooked farfalline (butterfly~shaped pasta) and run with them to the nearest table. If you do this and they were good peas to start with, they might, perhaps, taste as good as the peas and pasta served at Coco Lezzone. Failing a field of peas, take:

Cocolezzone

· Farfalline con Piselli
May '84

20 PASTA 'BUTTERFLIES' PER
   PERSON
2 LB/900 G FRESHLY SHELLED
   PEAS ~ TRY ONE RAW, IF IT IS
   NOT SWEET, ADD A GENEROUS
   PINCH OF SUGAR WHEN COOKING
4 OZ/100 G PROSCIUTTO OR GOOD
   COOKED HAM SLICED IN THIN STRIPS
2 SPRING ONIONS, FINELY CHOPPED
1 TBSP OLIVE OIL
SALT & PEPPER

Put the pasta to cook in a large
pan of boiling salted water. Heat
the oil in a frying pan. Saute
the onions gently in the oil
until soft but not brown. Add
the peas (and sugar if neces~
sary) and a tablespoon or two
of water. Cook them as quickly
as possible, about 10~15 min~
utes (less if they are small &
very tender). About 5 minutes
before they are ready add
the ham and allow to heat
through. Pour over the pasta
which should be cooked and
drained ready for serving.
Serve immediately

• FAGIOLI al FIASCO •
Beans in a Chianti bottle (6)

This must be one of the oldest
and simplest of Tuscan dishes.
       It is excellent
barbecue food but first
drink your Chianti...

12 OZ/350 G FRESH WHITE TUSCAN,
   HARICOT OR CANNELLINI BEANS
4 TBSP GOOD OLIVE OIL
5~6 SAGE LEAVES
2 CLOVES GARLIC, CRUSHED

Having drunk the Chianti, cut
the straw wrapping off the
bottle (capacity should be about
3 pints/1½ ltr) but keep it to use
as a stopper. Rinse out the
bottle and fill it about ½ to
2/3 full with beans (the beans
need room to swell). Add the
oil, sage leaves, garlic and
about 1½ cups of water. Stuff the
straw loosely in the top of the
flask so that the water can ev~
aporate ~ to achieve their char~
acteristic creamy taste, the
beans must absorb oil, not
water. Put the bottle beside
or above the embers of the fire for
3~5 hours. Failing a campfire
put the bottle in a warm place,
such as an airing cupboard,
the warm place on a stove, or
beside the boiler or a solid fuel
cooker. Leave until the water
has evaporated and the beans
have absorbed the oil. Serve
hot or cold with plenty of salt
& freshly ground black pepper
and a jug of good fruity
olive oil to pour over.

·LETIZIA·

Letizia Volpi is an artist living and working in Florence, and a passionate collector of old recipes for Tuscan sweets. Perhaps one day she will write her own book on the subject. In the meantime she is content to delight all her friends and family by cooking six times the usual quantity for recipes such as this one. And there is an added bonus. One evening of cooking crunchy CENCI is enough to fill the house for days with the delicious smell of vanilla and icing sugar.

· CENCI ·
— Fried pastry twists —

'Cenci' means 'stuff' or scraps of fabric used for dusting and cleaning. Like its fabric counter-

part, the pastry comes in all shapes and sizes, from huge pastry handkerchiefs and long strips tied in bows and lover's knots, to the heart-shaped dolce d'amore made by Letizia Volpi. They are generally popular at carnival time, just after Christmas.

9 oz/250 G PLAIN WHITE FLOUR
1 oz/25 G BUTTER, JUST MELTED
1 oz/25 G GRANULATED SUGAR
1 EGG
3 TBSP VIN SANTO ~ VIN SANTO IS
   AN ITALIAN SHERRY~LIKE WINE
   BUT YOU CAN USE SHERRY OR RUM
1 TSP VANILLA POWDER
PINCH SALT
OIL FOR DEEP FRYING

Make a little volcano of sifted flour with a crater in the middle. Into this put the egg, salt, sugar, vanilla and butter. Gently work this into a dough with your hands. When the dough begins to get stiff, moisten with a little vin santo, as the dough should always be quite pliable. Knead well, cover with a cloth and leave in a cool place to rest. After about an hour, roll the dough out very thinly and cut into whatever shapes you like. Probably the most trad-itional is a strip about 8 in/20.5 cm long and ½ in/3 cm wide tied in a bow or knot.

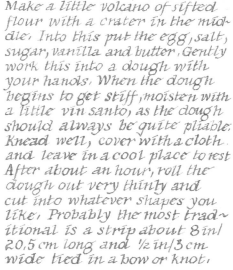

Deep fry these pieces, 2 or 3 at a time, in hot oil until they puff up & turn golden brown. Drain on paper towels and sift icing sugar over the tops. They can be eaten hot or cold and keep well in an airtight container.

The famous grey stone 'PIETRA SERENA' from which half the buildings in Florence are constructed, comes from the quarries near Fiesole, le Cave di Maiano. The trattoria of the same name is no longer the haven for workers from the nearby quarries that it once was. A more international crowd comes now for the stunning views of cypresses and villas in the Fiesolan hills, rather than for their essential evening meal. But there are still some very good traditional dishes to be found on the menu if you know your traditions and are willing (and able) to ask about them.

· PAPPA al POMODORO ·
Tomato and bread soup (8)

This thick, richly tomato-tasting soup that was once almost the porridge of Tuscany is one such traditional dish. If you make sure the tomatoes and basil are fresh, the bread stale and the garlic lavish, you cannot go far wrong. It can be, and is, served hot or cold, tepid or, less authentically, with ice cubes and topped with a generous handful of fresh chopped basil. (Failing basil, other fresh herbs can be almost as good ~ try thyme, rosemary or parsley.)

8 FL OZ/225 ML VERY GOOD OLIVE OIL
3~4 CLOVES GARLIC, CRUSHED
8 LEAVES BASIL, OR MORE IF YOU LIKE
1 LB 2 OZ/500 G TOMATOES, PEELED & CHOPPED
1 LB 2 OZ/500 G WHOLE WHEAT BREAD
1 MEDIUM LEEK, FINELY CHOPPED
2¼ PT/1.4 LTR STOCK
SALT & PEPPER
(½ TSP CRUSHED CHILI PEPPER ~ OPTIONAL)

Heat the oil in a deep pan & sauté the leek, garlic (& chili if using). When they are soft, add the tomatoes & basil & boil for 5~10 minutes. Then add the stock, salt & pepper. When the soup is boiling add the stale bread torn into small pieces. Cook for 2 minutes, cover & let stand for an hour. Then mix well, pour on some fresh oil and serve with parmesan.

· MASHA · INNOCENTI ·

Masha Innocenti runs a cookery school in Florence for foreigners pining to learn the secrets of Italian cooking. She comes from a whole family of Tuscan cooks and her culinary inspiration is as much from a Lucchesan mother as from a cordon bleu chef's course.

CONIGLIO con OLIVE NERE
— Tuscan rabbit — with black olives (6)

This recipe for rabbit with black olives is especially typical of the region around Lucca where both rabbits & excellent olives are plentiful.

3 LB/1.4 KG RABBIT WASHED & CUT INTO PIECES
2 CLOVES GARLIC
8 FL OZ/225 ML OLIVE OIL
2 OZ/60G BUTTER
4 FL OZ/110 ML WHITE WINE
1 TBSP TOMATO PASTE
6 TBSP BLACK OLIVES
8 FL OZ/225 ML STOCK
SALT & BLACK PEPPER

Remove skin from the garlic cloves and slash each clove halfway through. Heat the oil and butter or margarine in a large saucepan or fireproof casserole. Add the garlic and rabbit & brown on all sides over a medium heat. When brown add the wine, turn up the heat & let it evaporate. Then lower the heat, add the tomato paste and stock, cover and cook over a medium heat for 15 minutes. Season to taste, add the black olives & cook for another 25~30 minutes until the meat is tender & has turned a light pink. Add more stock if the stew appears to be in danger of drying out.

• POLLO in FRICASSEA •
Chicken in lemon sauce (6)

This classic method of cooking chicken in
lemon sauce is equally good with loin
of veal cut into pieces.

3 LB / 1.4 KG CHICKEN, CLEANED,
DRIED AND CUT IN PIECES
2 OZ / 60 G BUTTER
4 FL OZ / 110 ML OLIVE OIL
SMALL WHITE ONION, CHOPPED
JUICE OF 1 LEMON
2 TBSP FLOUR
3 EGG YOLKS
SALT & WHITE PEPPER
2 TBSP CHOPPED PARSLEY
6 FL OZ / 165 ML ~8 FL OZ / 220 ML STOCK

Heat the oil and butter in a shallow heat-proof
casserole, add the onion and saute gently until
transparent. Add the chicken pieces and brown
well all over. Pour in about 4 fl oz / 110 ml of
stock, cover and cook gently for 15~20 minutes,
adding more stock if necessary to prevent drying
out or burning. Mix the flour to a paste in 2 fl oz /
50 ml of stock & stir slowly into the liquid in
the casserole to thicken it. Season to taste. Beat the yolks
& lemon juice together. When the chicken is cooked,
in approximately 40 minutes, remove casserole from
the heat & add the yolks & lemon juice mixture,
blending in well. Add parsley & serve.

· TORTA della NONNA ·
Grandmother's cake (8)

Grandmothers all over Tuscany make this cake, and so do many restaurants, cafes and pastry~shops. Basically it is a del~iciously rich and creamy flan filled with confectioner's cus~tard and covered with a mixture of pastry, toasted al~monds, pine nuts and icing sugar, but there are dozens of variations on the same theme.

FOR THE CREAM:
2 EGG YOLKS
1¼ OZ / 35 G PLAIN
   WHITE FLOUR
1 PT / 575 ML MILK
2¼ OZ / 75 G CASTER
   SUGAR
SLIVERED ALMONDS
  & PINE NUTS
  FOR TOPPING
FOR PASTRY:
12½ OZ / 350 G
  PLAIN WHITE FLOUR
1 EGG & 1 EGG YOLK
2¾ OZ / 75 G CASTER
  SUGAR
4 OZ / 100 G BUTTER
1½ TSP BAKING POWDER

First make the cream. Heat the milk until it starts to boil, remove from the heat. Beat the yolks and sugar together until they form a ribbon. Stir in the flour, blending well. Add one tbsp of the hot milk to the yolk~sugar mixture and blend in well with a wooden spoon. Add the mixture to the milk and return to the heat, stirring until the cream thickens. When thickened, pour into a clean bowl and brush the surface with some melted butter to stop a skin forming. Allow to cool.

In the meantime toast a gen~erous handful of almonds and pine nuts on a baking sheet until they are slightly browned.

To make the pastry sift the flour and baking powder into a mound on a pastry-board or work surface, make a well in the middle and put all the other ingredients into it. Work every~thing into a dough with your hands. Form into a ball and chill in the refrigerator for 30 minutes. When ready to use, cut the dough in half, roll out one half into a circle ⅛ in/ 3 mm thick and place on an 8 in/20.5 cm greased pie plate, making sure that there is about ½ in/1 cm hanging over the plate's edge. Pour the cream onto the pastry base, making sure that the middle is some~what higher than the edges. Fold the pastry rim inwards and brush with some water. Roll the remaining piece of dough out to fit and place gently on top of the cream. Press well onto the pastry border & trim off any excess. Top with the almonds and pine nuts and bake in a preheated oven at 350°F/180°C/Gas 4 for 25~30 minutes until golden brown. Cool and sift with plenty of icing sugar before serving.

> *They serve a very good ver~sion of this sweet at the little, crowded trattoria 'Il Lordo' off the main square in Fiesole.

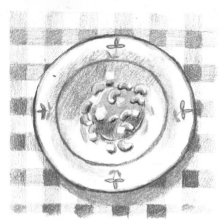

At the Borgo Antico in Florence they serve a delicious salad of freshly shelled 'baccelli' (broad beans) and equal parts pec~ orino cheese & slivers of prosciutto. Everything is then tossed in lots of good olive oil and served with fresh ground pepper.

At Il Cibreo in Flo~ rence, a trattoria near the Santa Am~ brogio market behind Santa Croce, they mix fresh ricotta cheese with marjoram, grate pecorino cheese on top & grill until golden brown.

~4~
Simple Dishes
Some of the best food in Tuscany is also the ea~ siest to prepare.

The traditional ending to a Tuscan country meal is a bowl of pears, peeled & served with pec~ orino cheese. Eaten young pecorino can be rubbery, but ask for piccante & you will get a cheese a bit like parmes~ an that goes well with ripe pears.

Fettunta is toast (usually grilled ov~ er an open fire) that is rubbed with garlic & dranched in olive oil & sea salt. It is called Brus~ chetta when topped with a mix~ ture of raw tomatoes & fresh basil.

· LEONARDO · MACCHIAVELLI ·

Niccolo Macchiavelli is one of the least liked and most misunderstood personalities in Tuscan history, probably because he made the mistake of telling the truth in his book, The Prince. His name is synonymous with treachery & deviousness. The Albergaccio Macchiavelli just outside Florence is doing much to rectify that. Directly opposite the villa (open to the public) where the original Machiavelli spent his 15-year exile from Florence, this little trattoria serves good wine, good garlic bread and good Fagioli all'uccelletto.

· FAGIOLI all'UCCELLETTO ·
Beans cooked like small birds (4)

This famous Tuscan dish is perhaps called 'all'uccelletto' because an uccelletto is a small bird and these beans are cooked in the same way that small birds are cooked during the hunting season. The recipe comes from another Machiavelli, Leonardo claims to be one of the last surviving members of the family and is himself a political thinker, although more usually the maker of vin santo and fine CARMIGNANO wines. The excellent Carmignano wines are made in a small area near the Medici villa of Poggio a Caiano north of Florence. They are not widely available outside Italy, but there is a wide selection at the little enoteca (wine store) in the centre of Poggio a Caiano, among them Leonardo's gold-medal winning Vino Carmignano from the Fattoria Ambra that he manages.

2 LB 2OZ / 1 KG FRESH WHITE TOSCANELLI BEANS OR

14 OZ / 400 G DRIED WHITE BEANS

14 OZ / 400 G PEELED TOMATOES

2~3 CLOVES GARLIC

OLIVE OIL

5 OR MORE FRESH SAGE LEAVES

SALT & FRESHLY GROUND BLACK PEPPER

Soak the dried beans overnight & then rinse, or if using fresh beans shell & wash. Boil in slightly salted water for 30~40 minutes. Heat several tablespoons of olive oil in a medium-sized heat-proof casserole. Brown the garlic, sage & pepper in the oil and then add the beans, stirring for a few minutes to allow the flavours to blend. Add the tomatoes, chopped roughly, salt to taste & continue cooking covered for about 15 minutes.

NB. These beans can be turned into a Tuscan version of wieners or bangers & beans if you sauté 2 spicy sausages per person over a low heat until browned, remove from pan and continue recipe as above, using the sausage fat instead of olive oil. About 15 minutes before the end of cooking, return the sausages to the pan and add four tablespoons of red wine.

31

ABOVE : Grapes for VIN SANTO drying on straw mats in the attic of Leonardo's farmhouse near Poggio a Caiano.

· ANITRA con VIN SANTO · Duck with vin santo (4)

Each Tuscan winemaker makes his own version of vin santo or 'holy wine', but because of the painstaking and lengthy pro~duction it is extremely difficult to buy outside Tuscany. Made from semi·dried grapes, it must be aged for a minimum of 3 years before emerging in~to the sunlight as vin santo. At its best it has a wonderfully smoky aromatic flavour rather like fine old sherry or Madeira and is traditionally served as a dessert wine with Biscotti di Prato (page 36).

1 4 lb / 1.8 KG DUCK WITH GIBLETS
2 WINE GLASSES VIN SANTO (OR GOOD MEDIUM DRY SHERRY)
1 ONION
1 STICK CELERY
5 OZ / 150 G CHOPPED PROSCIUTTO OR FATTY HAM
1 CARROT
4 SAGE LEAVES
OLIVE OIL
SALT
WHITE PEPPER
14 OZ / 400 ML CHICKEN OR BEEF STOCK

Chop the onion, celery, carrot, sage and prosciutto and put in a heat~proof casserole with the oil

32

over a medium heat.
When transparent and
soft add the duck, cut in
pieces, and brown on all
sides. Season with salt and white
pepper and pour in the vin santo.
Cover and cook for several minutes over a low heat. Then add ½
the stock and the finely chopped
duck liver. Cover again and continue to cook for about an hour,
adding a few tablespoons of stock
from time to time. The resulting
sauce should not be too liquid.
It is best to let the dish cool and
then skim off the fat, as duck
tends to give off a lot of fat.
Reheat after skimming and serve
the sauce over plain flat maccheroni, the pieces of duck to follow
as a separate course perhaps
with fagioli all'uccelletto or,
for a less heavy meal, this dish
of spinach and swiss chard.

One of the most outstanding
vin santos in Tuscany is from
the AVIGNONESI estate. They
sell only 1000 bottles a year
but also serve it in their splendid restaurant 'LA CASANUOVA'
near Chianciano.

BIETOLE e SPINACI
• con PINOLI •
—— Spinach & swiss chard ——
with pine nuts (4)

1 LB 4 OZ / ½ KG SPINACH, TRIMMED
  OR EQUIVALENT BEETTOPS
1 LB 4 OZ / ½ KG SWISS CHARD,
  TRIMMED
1 GARLIC CLOVE
SMALL HANDFUL PINE NUTS
SMALL HANDFUL RAISINS
SALT & PEPPER
OLIVE OIL

Boil the spinach and swiss chard
in separate pans of salted water
until just tender (about 15 minutes). Drain both vegetables well
and squeeze into a ball. Chop
them coarsely and put them in
a frying pan in which the oil,
garlic, pine nuts and raisins have
been gently simmering. Sauté
for several minutes to blend the
flavours, and serve hot with
freshly ground black pepper.

33

VILLA · I · TATTI

34

At the end of the last century when the art historian Bernard Berenson was a young man, he rode out on his bicycle every morning from his Florence pensione, his pockets filled with candles to light the obscure corners of unknown churches all over Tuscany, returning in the dusk to write up discoveries that would one day make him famous. In later, more prosperous years, his charming villa, I TATTI, just outside Florence, became the focal point for all the visiting members of the literary and artistic set. Now it is a Renaissance study centre (visits for ordinary tourists can be arranged through the Italian Tourist Board in Florence) and lucky Harvard University students can freely prowl the formal gardens. And equally freely supply a Renaissance recipe like this one. It is good served with a selection of other Tuscan antipasti such as crostini, prosciutto and olives, or a salad of beans & cheese.

· INVOLTINI di SALVIA ·
Sage Leaf Rolls

It is difficult to gauge quantities for these little hors d'oeuvres as it depends on the greed of the people eating them. Essentially the recipe is this: for each sage roll take two large sage leaves & one anchovy (the anchovy should be soaked in milk for 30 minutes to remove salt). Make these into a 'sandwich' with the anchovy in the middle, roll them up & secure with a toothpick. Each of these is then dipped first in beaten egg, then in flour, & finally deep fried in hot oil until crisp & puffed up.

35

· BISCOTTI di PRATO ·
Prato biscuits (1 lb)

1 LB 2 OZ / 500G CASTER SUGAR
1 LB 2 OZ / 500G WHITE FLOUR
7 OZ / 200 G PEELED ALMONDS
5 OZ / 150G PINENUTS
4 EGGS, BEATEN

1 TSP GRATED
ORANGE PEEL
½ TSP VANILLA
EXTRACT
½ TSP BAKING
POWDER
SALT
BUTTER

Probably the most common conclusion to a dinner in Tuscany is the arrival of a plate of these curiously hard, oval biscuits. Dunked liberally in a glass of vin santo, they are magically transformed into a surprisingly moreish dessert. They should be hard and dry to start with (and will keep for months in a tightly closed container) and in fact the bakers in Prato put ammonium bicarbonate, an old-fashioned leavening agent, into their biscuits to ensure an extra long hard life. In Italy Prato biscuits are seldom served without vin santo to accompany them. However if vin santo is unavailable you can use a good sweet sherry instead.

* Biscotti di Prato are also available commercially in packages, but lack the flavour & consistency of these home-made biscuits.

Preheat oven to 375°F/190°C/ Gas 5. Toast the almonds in the oven for a couple of minutes and chop roughly with the pinenuts. Sift the flour onto a pastry board or work surface. Make a well in the middle and pour in eggs, baking powder, sugar and a pinch of salt. Work to a smooth consistency with your hands and then mix in nuts. Roll pieces of the dough into long 'fingers'. Place on a greased, floured baking sheet & bake in the oven for about 15 minutes. Remove & slice dough fingers on the diagonal, about ½ in/1cm thick, and bake for another 25 minutes until brown.

· BORGO · ANTICO ·

The little birreria, Borgo Antico, in Florence's Piazza Santa Spirito serves a modern version of an authentic Renaissance Tuscan dish & definitely without the original's near disastrous consequences.

CIBREO

Cibreo was one of Catherine de'Medici's favourite dishes. There is a story that one day after eating too many heaped platefuls she nearly died of indigestion. Considering that Cibreo was once made with the livers, kidneys, testicles & crests of cockerels, this seems hardly surprising!

1 LB 2 OZ / 500 G CHICKEN
   LIVER, ROUGHLY CHOPPED
1 SMALL ONION OR LEEK
   VERY FINELY CHOPPED
2 OZ / 50 G BUTTER
2 EGG YOLKS
JUICE OF ½ LEMON
FLOUR
SALT & PEPPER
A LITTLE CHICKEN STOCK

Melt the butter in a medium-sized pan, saute the onion in it until soft but not brown. Roll the liver in flour, add to the pan with salt & pepper and cook over a low heat, adding a few tablespoons of stock as necessary to keep the mixture moist and creamy. Meanwhile lightly beat the yolks & lemon juice together. When the liver is just cooked through, take from the heat and stir in the egg mixture. Leave for two minutes and serve with toast as a light first course or luncheon dish.

· PAN di RAMERINO ·
— Rosemary buns —

The fragrant and sticky 'pan di Ramerino' is a famous sweet bun popular with Florentine children during the Easter holidays. To make these buns add 3 oz/75 g of sugar to the bread ingredients on page 67. Work into a dough and leave to rise in a warm place until doubled in size. Then put the dough on a table and mix into it 1½ wine glasses of olive oil in which 2 sprigs of fresh rosemary have been slowly heated for 10~15 minutes. Add 4 oz/100 g of raisins and 2 tbsp of finely chopped rosemary leaves to the dough and form into buns of 3 in/7.5 cm in diameter. Make a cross on the top with a pair of scissors, brush with beaten egg and bake until golden (20~30 mins) in an oven preheated to 400°F/200°C/Gas 6.

THE CHIANTI HILLS

CONSORZIO VINO CHIANTI CLASSICO · CHIANTI CLASSICO

FLORENCE

CHIANTI

San Casciano Val di Pesa

GREVE
PANZANO · Montagliari
Volpaia · Badia a Coltibuono
castellare · CASTELLINA · RADDA · Castello di Spaltenna · GAIOLE
Fonterutoli · Brolio
Autostrada del Sole

SIENA

· RESTAURANTS ·
GAIOLE · Castello di Spaltenna · GREVE · Locanda Giovanni da Verrazzano · PANZANO · Trattoria Montagliari · SAN CASCIANO · Il Fedino ·

· SIGHTS ·
BADIA A COLTIBUONO · Monastery · wine · BROLIO castle · wine · GREVE Enoteca market · VOLPAIA · walled hill village & wine estate ·

39

· INTRODUCTION ·

The Chianti wine district of Tuscany stretches from north of Florence, west to Pisa, south as far as Chiusi and east to Arezzo. But the soul of Chianti is the area of pine~clad hills rambling for 30~40 miles between Florence and Siena. This is the domain of the Chianti 'League' founded by feudal barons in the thirteenth century to protect their interests, one of the earliest regions to put controls on wine and an area almost constantly at war during the middle ages.

There is little evidence now of Chianti's turbulent past. The splendid views of vineyards and castles made famous in Renaissance paintings are more likely to be disturbed by the buzz of mopeds and Fiats than battles. Even the Castello di Volpaia, a medieval hill castle that was the scene of many violent clashes between Florence and Siena is now better known for its excellent Chianti and for the art exhibitions put on in the twelfth~century church.

The Castello di Volpaia is one of the prettiest of the walled hill villages, with a reputation for good wine dating back to the fifteenth century, but throughout the region there are castles and villages unchanged since medieval times, most selling their own wines, delicate olive oils and local products like the soaps and colognes made from olive oil and local lavender (called 'spigo' in the Chianti region), at the hill town of Fonterutoli. Tiny dusty roads link vineyards to yellow~ochre farmhouses; farms to walled villages and villages eventually to bigger wine towns. Originally the only red 'Chianti'

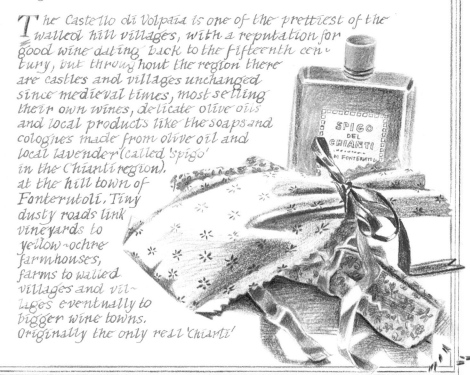

towns were Radda, Castellina and Gaiole. Now the main market town of Greve, on the stunning Via Chiantigiana (the SS222), is also included. A lively wine festival is held every September in Greve's charming seventeenth-century Piazza Matteoti and the town's Enoteca di Gallo Nero sells a complete selection of Chianti Classico, the DOC-registered wine identified by a black cockerel on the label. The Gallo Nero 'Classico' wines are not the only good Chiantis however. The black cockerel guarantees only that the wine has met the standards set by the DOC, Denominazione di Origine Controllata, originally set up by a group of Chianti producers, the Italian equivalent of the French Appellation Contrôle system.

The history of Chianti wine is almost as long as that of the district itself. By the time the straw-covered flask became famous (around 1860) it had been made for at least six centuries. It is possible that monks were the first Chianti producers. Certainly the monks at the beautiful abbey of Badia a Coltibuono (now a wine estate) were making wine at least as early as the twelfth century and continued to do so for hundreds of years. At the Castellare estate of Castellina grapes were grown for wine long before Lorenzo de' Medici ruled Florence in the fifteenth century. Monks from the nearby San Niccolo monastery worked the hard, stoney terrain with hoes in vineyards that are still producing good wine.

Chianti has evolved and changed considerably over the centuries. In the nineteenth century Baron Ricasoli of the Castello di Brolio established a basic 'recipe' for the blend of white and red grapes that would give modern Chianti its characteristic taste. Today it is one of the most famous wines in the world but not without certain problems. Disagreements on quality control amongst its producers and in some cases a lack of interest in modern techniques and an overuse of easy-to-grow white grapes have made a few Chiantis pale and insipid. This has damaged the wine's overall reputation. Fortunately Chianti is still popular thanks to the constant efforts of young wine-makers to improve and refine the taste of their wine while still maintaining its original rich quality.

There is the same diversity in the food and cooking of the Chianti region. A good meal can be as simple as a slice of creamy fresh ricotta and a handful of tiny jewel-

·FOUR·CHIANTI·TOWNS·

GAIOLE

RADDA

CASTELLINA

GREVE

42

red wild strawberries picked and eaten still warm on a steep hillside. A village trattoria may serve its own salty pecorino cheese and rough young Chianti with a dish of fresh olives from local trees, or a plate of home-made pasta with just a chunk of crusty bread to mop up the plain sauce of oil and sage leaves. Or elaborate Renaissance dishes fit for a Medici banquet may be elegantly served with a mellow, aged Chianti 'riserva' in a castle's cool vaulted dining hall. This is the country where a whole roast wild boar is not an uncommon feast during the autumn hunting season. In fact the name 'Chianti' is popularly believed to stem from the Latin 'clangor', a word for the loud blast a trumpet makes on a baronial hunting party.

More than any other part of Tuscany, wine in the Chianti region is an inescapable part of life. The people there eat, drink, talk and sleep it. They serve food to complement wine rather than the reverse. Despite this enthusiasm and such a good end product, there is little formal wine tourism in the district. However most wine estates welcome visitors and more frequently now have a trattoria or even more rustic osteria on the premises where both local wine and good simple food are served beside views of vineyards, cypresses and medieval castles.

44

Next to an eleventh~century village church on one of the vine~covered hills above Gaiole in Chianti is the Castello di Spaltenna, a beautiful and serene hotel cum restaurant. If you are lucky and go on the right day, Anna, the local cook might be there. She comes up regularly from Gaiole and in season cooks local dishes at the Castello that are seldom found outside Tuscany. She also has the Italian knack of making gnocchi & fresh pasta seem easy ~ make a pile of flour, put 5 eggs in the middle, work it a bit with enough water and there's your pasta…

· PANZANELLA ·
Bread & tomato salad (6)

This is the kind of recipe, if you can call it a recipe, that sounds awful and tastes delicious. Like many of Tuscany's deceptively simple dishes, it relies on perfectly fresh ingredients (apart, of course, from the stale bread!) and the idiosyncracies of individual cooks. Some less generous cooks use mostly onions and bread for panzanella, but it is best made with masses of very red and juicy tomatoes when they are at their ripest from June until the end of August. Don't be put off by the idea of stale bread in a salad, but do wring it out very well

8 ~ 10 PIECES HARD STALE BREAD
6 VERY RIPE TOMATOES, ROUGHLY CHOPPED
2 LARGE ONIONS, PREFERABLY RED ONIONS, SLICED THINLY
2 STICKS CELERY AND LEAVES, DICED
1 CUCUMBER CUT IN CHUNKS
8 OR MORE FRESH BASIL LEAVES, BRUISED IN A MORTAR
GOOD OLIVE OIL
SALT & PEPPER
RED WINE VINEGAR

Soak the bread in cold water for 15~20 minutes. Squeeze it out very well and crumble into a salad bowl. Add the vegetables, oil, basil, salt and pepper. Chill in the refrigerator for 2~3 hours. Just before serving toss with wine vinegar and some more basil if you have it.

SCHIACCIATA con L'UVA
Traditional flat cake
• with grapes •

Schiacciata means 'squashed flat' and this is a very ancient flat cake that has been made at the time of the vendemmia (grape harvest) in Tuscany since Etruscan times over 2000 years ago. It was devised, like so many dishes, as a method for using existing materials; left-over bread dough for the base and quantities of black wine grapes for the topping. If you are bothered by the seeds in Schiacciata you can make it with seedless grapes, or de-pip the grapes you are using, but it will not be as authentic, or as much fun ~ there won't be any pips to spit out, although a polite crunching sound is more usual in restaurants.

FOR THE BASE
1 LB 2 OZ/500 G PLAIN WHITE
    FLOUR, SIFTED
1 OZ/25 G FRESH YEAST
PINCH SALT
2½ OZ/60 G GRANULATED SUGAR
½ OZ/15 G ANISE SEED
    (SWEET CUMIN)
3/4 CUP WATER

FOR THE TOPPING
2 LB 2 OZ/1 KG LARGE JUICY
    BLACK GRAPES, WASHED
4 OZ/100 G CASTER SUGAR
SEVERAL SPRIGS FRESH ROSEMARY
6 ~ 8 TBSP OLIVE OIL

Warm the water and add the yeast, blend until smooth. On a pastry board or work~ surface make a mound of the flour, salt and granulated sugar. Make a well in the middle and slowly pour in the yeast mixture, blending with a wooden spoon or spatula until smooth. When the yeast has been incorporated, knead the dough for 5~10 minutes as you would for bread. When it is smooth and elastic, cover and put in a warm room. When it has doubled in size, grease a rectangular baking tray (about 20" × 12"/51 × 30.5cm) with oil. Roll out the dough so that it is no more than 1/2"/1cm thick and 2"/5cm bigger all around than the tray. Place the dough on the tray and cover completely with the grapes. Sprinkle with the sugar and pour oil (in which you have heated the rosemary for several minutes) over the top. Fold up the sides of the dough and pinch at the corners to make a rectangular shape. Bake for 30 minutes in an oven pre-heated to 350°F/175°C/Gas 4. It is best to put another pan underneath the Schiacciata as the juice from the grapes may overflow. Use these juices to baste the top of the cake. Chill in the refrigerator and just before serving drizzle it with honey.

There is another method for making Schiacciata con l'uva. At Spaltenna Anna makes the dough as above and then mixes into it the grapes and oil in which she has heated the rosemary and a cup of walnuts. She then rolls it out to no more than 1"/2.5cm and bakes it like a crusty flat bread or scone (at the same temperature). When the grapes are really lush, their juice stains the cake a deep crimson.

·FATTORIA · DI · MONTAGLIARI·

Giovanni Cappelli, the owner of the Fattoria di Montagliari, an excellent trattoria & vineyard near Panzano, is a faithful patron of the Antica Macelleria in Greve, (pages 50~51).

His cook specialises in local Chiantigiana cuisine and Signor Cappelli himself is quite a culinary expert. These recipes are from his own handwritten collection. The Fattoria di Montagliari also has one of the largest vin santeries in Tuscany and produces one of the best vin santos. The Riserva 1968 is particularly fine.

the rest of the ingredients (except for the French bread) and pound to a rough paste. Chill and serve on toasted French bread or deep fried polenta (see recipe opposite)

· CECINA ·
Chickpea savoury bread (4)

9 OZ / 250 G CHICKPEA FLOUR
1 ¾ PT / 1 LITRE WATER
½ GLASS OLIVE OIL
SALT

Sift the flour into a bowl, make a well in the middle and slowly add the water, beating well to avoid lumps forming. Add the oil and salt and blend in. Pour into a greased shallow baking tin to a depth of not more than ½ in/1 cm. Bake in an oven pre-heated to 450°F/ 230°C / Gas 8 until golden brown. Serve cut in wedges with plenty of freshly ground black pepper.

· CROSTINI ROSSI ·
Piquant tomato crostini(4)

1 PIECE WHOLEWHEAT BREAD
1 CLOVE GARLIC
1 TBSP CAPERS
3 TBSP OLIVE OIL
COARSE SALT
FRESHLY GROUND BLACK PEPPER
WINE VINEGAR
3 TBSP FRESH PARSLEY
2 TBSP FRESH THYME
2 LARGE RIPE TOMATOES, PEELED
8 PIECES FRENCH BREAD OR
  DEEP FRIED POLENTA

Soak the wholewheat bread in vinegar and wring out well. Put in a mortar with

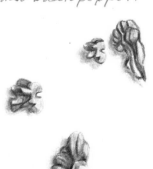

· SALSA di NOCI ·
Walnut sauce for pasta (6)

A recipe for pasta sauce that
Giovanni Cappelli believes
dates from at least the 1400s
in Siena. He serves it in his
restaurant with tortelli but
it is also very good with a
flat pasta like tagliatelle

7 oz / 200 g WALNUTS
2 oz / 50 g PINE NUTS
2 CLOVES GARLIC
3 BASIL LEAVES OR MORE
   ACCORDING TO TASTE
2 TBSP BREADCRUMBS
½ PT / 300 ML MILK
   OR MORE ~ ENOUGH
   TO MAKE A SAUCE
   THE CONSISTENCY OF
   THICK CREAM
3 TBSP OLIVE OIL
SALT
PEPPER

If you want to feel authentically quattrocentoish, you
could pound all the above
ingredients together in a
mortar to make the sauce. A
food processor is faster, if
less romantic. Serve the sauce
over the pasta and then sprinkle
with whole walnuts and more
basil to make the dish especially good.

· POLENTA FRITTA ·
Deep fried polenta (4~6)

Polenta is a corn meal porridge
more popular in the north
than in Tuscany. Tuscan cooks
tend to prefer it first chilled
and then crisply deep-fried in
small golden wedges under
rich game sauces; or to replace
toast in antipasti.

7 oz / 200 g COARSE ~ GRAINED
   CORN MEAL
SALT
OIL FOR DEEP FRYING

Boil 2 pints of water in a
large saucepan, add salt and
lower heat. When
water is just sim-
mering begin to
add cornmeal,
pouring in a thin
stream, stirring
constantly with a
wooden spoon to
prevent lumps
forming. Continue
stirring for about
15~20 minutes after
all the cornmeal has been
added. The polenta is
cooked as soon as it begins to
stand away from the side of
the pan. Pour immediately
into a shallow baking tray
to a thickness of not more
than ½ in / 1 cm. Smooth out
any lumps and chill. When
cool enough to slice, cut into
diamond shapes that are
approximately 2½ in / 5 cm
long by 2 in / 4 cm wide and
deep fry in hot oil a few at a
time. They are cooked when
transparent yellow and crusty
on both sides.

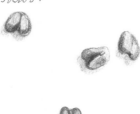

· ANTICA · MACELLERIA · FALORNI ·

Just off the main square in Greve is the Antica Macelleria Falorni, a butcher's shop that every harassed dinner~party giver would like to live next to. This business, established in the 1840s, has become justifiably famous all over Italy for the quality of its meat. The proprietors, Lorenzo and Stefano Bencistà, proudly claim that every morning on opening there are at least 60 different cuts of meat for sale, as well as roasts, meatballs and Tuscan shishkebabs prepared to their mother's recipes with fresh herbs, juniper berries, tomatoes & red peppers. Their acclaimed FINOCCHIONA sausage is made not with the usual cultivated fennel, but with feathery wild fennel gathered locally in the Chianti hills. And most astonishing of all, they still make, to an antique and ridiculously non~commercial recipe, prosciutto casalingo sotto cenere, now completely unavaible anywhere else. The ham is first stamped with the date, and then buried under wood ashes for up to two years. Originally the Tuscan peasants preserved their pork in this way throughout the summer months to have it, pink and tender, to eat during the long cold winter. Lorenzo does it now, he says, not to make money, because its impossible to do on a large scale, but 'purely for the satisfaction of it, to keep the old traditions alive'. The Antica Macelleria Falorni also exports wild boar sausages and prosciutto all over Europe.

50

ARISTA di MAIALE
· ARROSTO ·
Roast loin of Pork (5~6)

If bistecca fiorentina is Tus~
cany's most famous meat
dish, this recipe comes a
close second. 'ARISTA' is the
Tuscan word for loin of pork,
and at the Falorni Macelleria
they cut the loin to keep long
bones on the chops. These are
then used as a kind of
natural grilling rack.
In some restaurants
Arista is made
with boned
pork with
not such a
tasty result
as this one.

4 ½ LB / 2 KG
  LOIN OF
  PORK
2 CLOVES OF
  GARLIC
OLIVE OIL
2 SPRIGS FRESH ROSEMARY
1 WINEGLASS WHITE WINE
SEA SALT
BLACK PEPPER, COARSELY GROUND

Finely chop the garlic and
rosemary together. With a sharp
knife make several cuts in the
pork near the bone and stuff
with the herbs. Lightly score
the outside of the meat and
rub plenty of salt, oil and
pepper into it to give a crispy
skin. Put the wine in a roast~
ing pan and then place the
meat resting on its bones in
the roasting pan (see drawing).
Cook in a moderate oven pre~
heated to 350°F/180°C/
Gas 4 for 1½~2 hours,
basting occasionally
with the
juices. Serve
with plain
boiled
canne~
lini beans
and a jug
of olive oil
to pour
over accor~
ding to taste. Or skim the fat
off the pan juices, simmer for
a few minutes with some
more wine and herbs and
pour the resulting sauce over
the beans instead of using
olive oil.

NORCINERIA

PANCETTA NOSTRALE

· STUFATINO di VITELLO ·
Tuscan veal stew (4~6)

1½ LB / 700 G LEAN VEAL, CUT
   IN CUBES
1 WINE GLASS WHITE WINE (APPROX)
OLIVE OIL
SALT
PEPPER
¼ CHILI PEPPER, FINELY CHOPPED
1~2 LARGE RIPE TOMATOES,
   PEELED, SEEDED & CHOPPED
   OR 3 TBSP TOMATO PUREE IF
   TOMATOES ARE NOT TASTY
2 CLOVES GARLIC, CRUSHED
3 TBSP CHOPPED PARSLEY
FLOUR

Brown the garlic and chili
pepper in oil in a heavy casserole. Add the veal, well dusted
with flour, and let it brown.
Pour in the wine and when
nearly evaporated, add the

tomatoes or the tomato
puree. Season to taste, lower
the heat and cook covered
until the meat is tender,
about 1 hour. Stir in the
parsley just before serving. It
is delicious served with deep-
fried polenta and fagioli
all'uccelletto. A thinly
sliced fennel bulb added 10
minutes before the end of
cooking makes an excellent
addition to the classic version
of the dish.

· POLPETTINI ·
Tuscan meatballs (6)

Every country has its version
of the meatball. In Tuscany
they're called POLPETTINI if
they're small. When, as often
happens, they are almost the
size of a meat loaf, they are

called POLPETTONE. At the
Locanda dell'Amorosa near
Siena they serve tiny spicy
polpettini, crunchily deep~
fried, as a hot appetizer in the
winter months.

1 LB 2 OZ/500G COOKED PORK OR
  BEEF, CUT IN CUBES
3 OZ/75G GRATED PARMESAN OR
  PECORINO
4 OZ/100G PROSCIUTTO (OR HAM)
2 POTATOES, PEELED AND COOKED
2 EGGS, BEATEN
2 CLOVES GARLIC, CRUSHED
HANDFUL PARSLEY, CHOPPED
4 SAGE LEAVES, CHOPPED
JUICE OF 1 LEMON
SALT
PEPPER
½ TSP NUTMEG
(OPTIONAL ¼ TSP CINNAMON)
OIL FOR DEEP FRYING

Put the meat and potatoes
through a fine grinder, mincer
or food processor and then mix
well with other ingredients.
Form tiny round meatballs of
a maximum 1 in/2.5 cm diameter and roll in cornmeal or,
better still, breadcrumbs.
Deep fry a few at a time in
oil until crunchy and golden
brown. Drain well and serve
hot with a selection of other
antipasti.

53

· LOCANDA · GIOVANNI ·

Go into the Antica Macelleria first thing in the morning and you are likely to run into half the cooks and restaurant~owners in the area. Rossella Rossi, proprietress of the Locanda Giovanni da Verrazzano in Greve does her shopping there and, with the Bencista brothers' excellent lean veal, makes this unusual version of a classic Tuscan dish. This recipe for Stracotto, meaning overcooked, comes from an old Florentine cookbook and supposedly dates from the sixteenth century.

STRACOTTO al CHIANTI CLASSICO
· Beef with red wine (6) ·

4 ½ LB / 2 KG BONED FILLET OF
   VEAL OR BONED TOP RUMP
   OF BEEF.
3 OZ / 75 G PINE NUTS
3 OZ / 75 G RAISINS
3 OZ / 75 G PEELED TOASTED ALMONDS
½ HOT CHILI PEPPER, CHOPPED
1 ONION, FINELY CHOPPED
1 CARROT, FINELY CHOPPED
1 BOTTLE CHIANTI CLASSICO
2 CLOVES GARLIC
HANDFUL FRESH PARSLEY
1 PINT GOOD BEEF STOCK
SALT & PEPPER

DA · VERRAZZANO ·

Soften the onion, chili pepper & carrot in oil in a deep casserole. Meanwhile chop the nuts, raisins, garlic and parsley roughly. With a small sharp knife make cuts in several places all over the meat and stuff with half the nut mixture. Tie into a neat shape with string and brown on all sides in the casserole. Pour in the wine, add remaining nut mixture and top up with stock so the meat is just covered. Simmer covered for at least 2 1/4 hours, or until meat is tender, adding more stock to keep the meat cov~ ered. Remove the string, slice meat thinly and keep warm. Reduce the sauce and serve over meat, making sure some of the nuts and raisins are included. This is a wonderfully rich tasting dish that is best served with something simple such as plain buttered pasta or crisp greens.

In the busy town of San Casciano in Val di Pesa, the locals have their own special gathering place ~ the Ristorante Il Fedino, a 15th-century villa on the road to Florence. The proprietor serves essentially rustic dishes in the cool wine cellars below the family home.

CONIGLIO RIPIENO
· Stuffed Rabbit (6) ·

This way of cooking rabbit is the speciality at Il Fedino. You can use frozen rabbit from the supermarket, but the flavour will not be as good as when wild rabbit is used.

1	LARGE RABBIT, CLEANED, BONED AND FLATTENED
2	EGGS
6	TBSP GRATED PECORINO OR PARMESAN CHEESE
1/2	TSP GRATED NUTMEG
	SEVERAL SPRIGS FRESH THYME
	8 FL OZ/225 ML BEEF STOCK
	OLIVE OIL
	BUTTER
	COARSE SEA SALT
	PEPPER

Get your butcher or game dealer to clean and bone the rabbit ~ it is not an easy task for the unskilled. Beat the eggs with the salt and pepper and cook in butter to make a thin omelette. Lay the rabbit out flat and put the omelette on it. Dot with butter and sprinkle on the pecorino, nutmeg & thyme. Roll the rabbit up and tie it carefully, having tucked the ends in.

Rub plenty of pepper and coarse sea salt into the rabbit. Heat a few tablespoons of olive oil in a shallow flame-proof casserole and brown the rabbit on all sides in it. Reduce the heat & add the stock, cover. Continue cooking for 1½ hours, adding more stock if necessary. When tender, remove the string and serve sliced very thinly in the pan juices with more fresh thyme snipped over the top.

FEGATELLI di MAIALE

Tuscan pork liver
• bruschettes (4) •

A classic Tuscan dish cooked either in a frying pan or grilled, as in these two recipes, over charcoal. At Pedino's they vary the recipe slightly by chop~ ~ping & pre~cooking the liver before gril~ ling, which guar~ antees its tenderness ~ this is given as the second version of the recipe.

4 AROMATIC TWIGS (IE: BAY, ROSEMARY ETC.) FROM WHICH THE LEAVES HAVE BEEN STRIPPED

1 LB 2 OZ /500 G PORK LIVER

1 TBSP FENNEL SEEDS

4 TBSP BREADCRUMBS OR 4 PIECES BREAD, CUT IN CHUNKS

OLIVE OIL

ABOUT 1 LB /450 G CAUL FAT *
OR BACON

HANDFUL FRESH SAGE OR BAY LEAVES

SALT & PEPPER

• METHOD I •

Crush the fennel seeds in a mortar with the salt & pepper. Soak the caul fat in water to soften. Cut into squares approx~ imately 4 x 4 in /10 x 10 cm. Cut the liver into bite size chunks and roll in the fennel. Then wrap each piece in caul and skewer on a twig, alternating the liver with a sage or bay leaf and a chunk of bread dipped in olive oil. Cook over fire for 15 ~ 20 minutes or until caul fat is crisp.

• METHOD II •

Crush the fennel seeds with the salt and pepper, breadcrumbs and 3 sage leaves. Chop liver into small pieces and cook until slight~ ly browned. Mix with other ingre~ dients, wrap in fat and then in a sage or bay leaf. (If using dried bay leaves soak them well first.) Skewer & grill for 10 minutes or until caul fat is crisp.

*CAUL FAT or PORK NET (obtainable from butchers in ethnic neighbourhoods) is a lacy fat from the pig's intestines. If you cannot get it or are squeam~ ish, wrap the liver in bacon instead. The fat, however, does add a remarkably flavourful juice to the liver and keeps it very moist.

· PINZIMINIO ·
Olive~oil dip

At the CASTELLARE estate near Castellina in Chianti, the olive oil is sold in
lovely square glass decanters and the
wines and olive oils are distinguished by
painted labels of local Chiantigiana birds.

The best way to test the flavour of a
good olive oil is to make Pinziminio, nothing
more than oil into which generous amounts
of coarse sea salt and black pepper have
been ground. Tuscans use it as a dip for
fresh or briefly scalded vegetables such
as fennel root, artichokes, red peppers
and asparagus.

MEDIEVAL CITIES

·SAN GIMIGNANO·

·RADDA·

C H I A N T I

·CASTELLINA·

·GAIOLE·

AREZZO

·MONTERIGGIONI·

·SIENA·

San Galgano

AUTOSTRADA DEL SOLE

·SINALUNGA·

Locanda
dell'Amorosa

Monte Oliveto Maggiore

MONTALCINO

· RESTAURANTS ·
·AREZZO· Buca di San
Francesco·MONTERIGGIONE·
Il Pozzo·SAN GIMIGNANO·
·Ponte a Rondolino·
·SINALUNGA·Locanda
dell'Amorosa·

· SIGHTS ·
AREZZO· Piero della
Francesco frescoes·M.
OLIVETO· 14c abbey·
MONTERIGGIONI·walled
hill village·SAN GAL-
GANO· abbey·SAN
GIMIGNANO·medieval
towers·SIENA city·

59

· INTRODUCTION ·

The story goes that Senius and Aschio, sons of Remus, fled Rome in search of peace and founded a castle in Tuscany that became Siena. There is little remaining Roman influence today apart from the wolf symbol that is prominent in the city's emblems. Siena is a city of Gothic art and architecture, built of red~gold 'burnt siena' bricks and surrounded by what Virginia Woolf called 'the loveliest of all land~ scapes'. It is famous for the beauty and clarity of its language, for its rich oriental~tasting sweets like panforte and ricciarelli and for the Palio, a bare~ backed horse race of medieval origins that provides a year~long undercurrent of tension to an other~ wise gentle, dreamy city.

The city's past is not a peaceful one. For hundreds of years Ghibelline Siena was the sworn and violent enemy of Guelf Florence. In nearby medieval and Renaissance towns like San Gimignano, Monteriggioni, Montepulciano and Montalcino constant battles were fought between the two city~states. Siena's greatest victory came in 1260 with the defeat of Florence at the battle of Montaperti. Still celebrated today as a glorious event, the battle is less significant than the overwhelming Florentine victory nine years later. This victory, although galling for the Sienese, and in the long run destroying their prosperity, was initially the start of a 'Golden Age' for Siena.

In 1287 'Nine Good Men' chosen from the mid~ dle classes to rule the city were responsible for a seventy~year period of great prosperity and art~ istic achievement. Most of the work on Siena's magnificent Duomo, begun in the late twelfth century, was completed during this time, including the astonishing black and white striped mosque~like interior. Even more successful was the development of Siena's central square, the Campo, into one of the most magical city centres in Italy. Entered through narrow, covered archways, the square slopes inwards like the hub of a giant wheel. The mellow brick paving is divided into nine spokes symbolizing the Nine Good Men responsible and at the centre is the elegant and much~copied Palazzo Pubblico, Its graceful bell~tower of 503 steps soars into the air over the Campo's fourteenth~ century palaces, During the build~up to the Palio, the bell rings methodically and rythmically like the city's heart~beat until minutes before the race begins,

It could be said that the Palio itself is the city's heartbeat, and to understand the Palio is to understand Siena, Briefly it is this: a race three times around the Campo in which ten jockeys ride bareback horses representing the ten contrade (city wards) competing in the race, There are seven~ teen wards in all, each one a sworn enemy of the other, but for safety's sake not all compete, The only official prize is a silk banner called the 'Palio', and the race for it lasts roughly a minute, But this min~ ute is the culmination of a whole year's hopes and preparation, of a final three day's feasting, parades and sometimes violent fights between rival contrade, At the end of this minute the winning contrada will go, quite

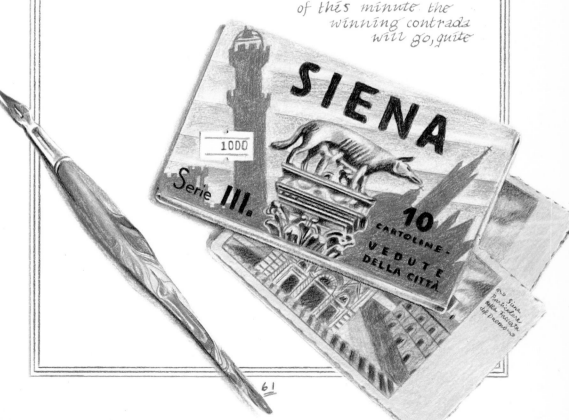

61

62

simply, mad with joy; laughing, crying, singing and marching the streets of Siena all night carrying the Palio banner. It is entirely medieval, unlike any other spectacle in the world. People faint from heat and excitement. Jockeys are thrown into the barriers and killed. Horses, drugged before the race, roll over, crash into one another, break legs and are shot. It has been criticized for its barbarity and it is barbaric without a doubt. But no one who has seen it, who has stood inside a church before the race and watched a priest bless a horse, listened to his strange cry 'Vai cavallino e torna vincatore!' (Go little horse and return a winner!) and to the haunting accompanying canto of the surrounding people; who has watched the two hour medieval parade through the streets or the river of people that floods the race square up to the last possible minute; who has seen the old and wily horse Panezio, winner of an astonishing eight Palios, thread his nimble way through the pack of careening jockeys and riderless horses, around the virtually right-angled corner of the Campo that is the most dangerous, or who has heard the spine-tingling cry 'Daccelo' (Give it to us!) after the victory, can fail to be moved by the Palio. To say that it is just a horserace is like saying that Everest is just a mountain. The Palio is not an event that occurs twice a year at Siena. It _is_ Siena.

The only place to eat in Siena is in the street the night before the Palio. Each of the city's wards has a traditional dinner, with tables a quarter of a mile long laid for 200 and 300 people. The jockeys are there, feted and kissed by beautiful girls. Siena's nobility sit next to the local barbers. There are speeches and songs, and somehow miraculously in the middle of all this the food arrives, hot and good, for those who are not too excited to eat it. If you cannot beg, borrow or steal a ticket to one of these meals, there are still plenty of restaurants that push their tables into the street and serve up the Palio atmosphere as well as food.

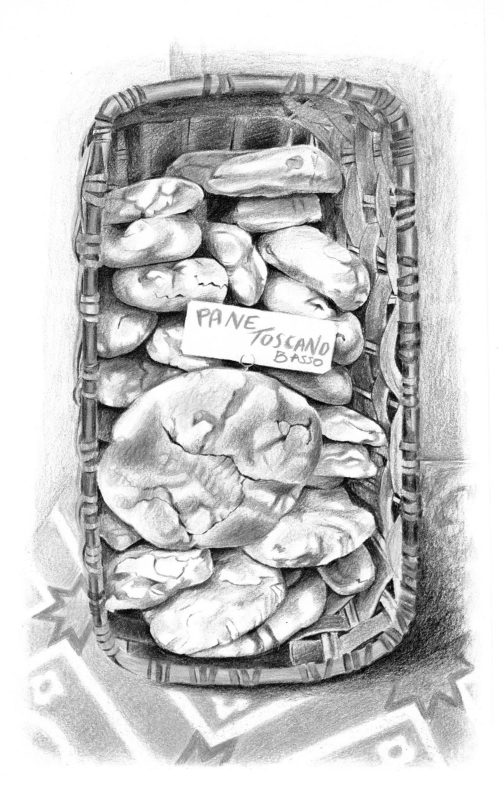

Bread is the pasta of Tuscany. It is used far more than flour or pasta to thicken soups & stews & give textures to sauces. A good Tuscan 'pan basso' loaf has almost no salt & when stale it tends to go hard & dry rather than moldy, thus remaining useful for cooking. At A. Sclavi's Panificio Moderno the bread variations are endless, all displayed in old wicker baskets around the shop. And the fresh pasta is so good that the Locanda dell'Amorosa restaurant near Sinalunga used to send a bus to Siena every weekend to collect a fresh batch.

· PANE BASSO ·
Tuscan country bread (2 loaves)

At the Panificio Moderno the baker uses brewer's yeast in the bread but this recipe using fresh yeast gives a similar result. You can make Pane integrale, the closest the Tuscans get to wholewheat bread, by substituting 1/4 lb/100g bran for the same quantity of white flour in the following recipe.

2 OZ /50G FRESH YEAST
1 PT / 500 CIL WARM WATER (LUKEWARM)
2 LB /900 G STRONG WHITE FLOUR

Dissolve the yeast in 3 fl oz/175 ml of the warm water in a small bowl. Sift in enough of the flour to make a soft dough, mixing with the hands. Cover & put in a warm place to rise. When the yeast dough has at least doubled in size, begin making the rest of the dough. Sift the remaining flour onto a wood or marble surface. Make a well in the middle; pour a little water into it & begin working the flour towards this with your hands. When the dough has absorbed enough water to bind together, add the yeast dough and work in. Knead for 5~10 minutes, occasionally lifting the dough & smacking it on the table. Continue until it no longer sticks to your hands. Sprinkle a large bowl with water and put the dough in it. Cover with a cloth & let rise in a warm place until doubled in size (about 30 minutes). Knead again 5~10 minutes and form into 2 balls. Let stand another 20 minutes and then bake on a greased, floured baking tin until crusty (about 30 minutes) in an oven preheated to 350°F/180°C Gas 4.

PAN CO SANTI

PANE francese CASALINGO

PANFORTE di SIENA
• Traditional Siena •
spice cake

5 oz/150 g SUGAR (GRANULATED)
7 oz/200 g ALMONDS, PEELED
7 oz/200 g WALNUTS, CLEANED
11 oz/300 g MIXED CANDIED
 FRUIT, CHOPPED
4 oz/100 g HONEY
4 oz/100 g DRIED FIGS
2½ oz/60 g COCOA
 POWDER
¼ TSP POWDERED
 CORIANDER
¼ TSP POWDERED
 CLOVES
½ TSP POWDERED
 NUTMEG
¼ TSP WHITE PEPPER
¾ TSP CINNAMON
2 oz/50 g FLOUR
10 LARGE BAKING WAFERS OR
 RICE PAPER

The history of Panforte or 'strong bread' dates back as far as, or further, than Siena itself and there are many recipes for it, some of which seem almost too spicey for modern palates. When panforte was first made this over-spicing probably served to preserve, as well as to cover the unwelcome taste of mold. Today the brightly-wrapped Panforte cakes in Siena are as much a part of the city as the Palio. Made before Christmas and stored in an air-tight container, the cake will keep for about a month. Served in thin slices with strong black coffee it makes an interesting alternative to christmas cake. In Siena it is often topped with melted dark chocolate instead of the icing sugar used in this recipe.

Toast the nuts in a hot oven and chop roughly. Put in a bowl with all the dried fruit, spices and cocoa. Sift in the flour and mix well. In a double saucepan or a basin over a pan of boiling water, boil the honey carefully & melt in the sugar. Stir constantly until it will form a soft ball between your fingers (remember to dip your fingers in cold water before testing for this). Immediately pour onto the fruit and blend in well with your hands. Form the dough into a flat round cake about 1 in/2.5 cm

QUARESIMALI
L 2500 l'etto

PANFORTE a taglio L 2000 l'etto

66

thick. Lay
the wafers on a buttered baking
sheet and place the cake on top.
Bake for 40 minutes, until dry,
in an oven preheated to 350°F/
180°C/Gas 4. When cool trim
wafers to fit the cake and dust
the top of the cake with a mixture
of icing sugar and cinnamon.

· RICCIARELLI ·
Sweet almond biscuits (2 dozen)

These sweet and wickedly rich
macaroons are almost as famous in Siena as panforte. They
have the taste of oriental
sweetmeats about them and
are costly to make and buy,
even in Siena. If you buy your
ricciarelli at A. Sclavi's they
will wrap them, however few,
with ribbon and pretty paper,
as if they were precious
Christmas gifts!

12 ¼ oz/360 G PEELED ALMONDS
6 oz/180 G ICING SUGAR,
    SIFTED
8 ¾ oz/240 G CASTER SUGAR,
    SIFTED
1 TBSP GRATED
    ORANGE PEEL
2 EGG WHITES
2 DOZEN ROUNDS RICE PAPER

Crush the almonds to a powder
in a mortar, or put through
a nut-grinder, making sure
you don't lose any of the oil.
Mix well with the caster sugar
and rub through a sieve into
a large bowl. Whip the egg
whites to form soft peaks.
Fold into the almond/
caster sugar mixture
together with the
icing sugar and orange
peel. It should make a
soft, smooth paste. Form into
diamond-shaped lozenges,
each lozenge about ½ in/1cm
thick, 2 in/4.5 cm long and
1½ in/3.5 cm wide. Dust heavily with more icing sugar,
place each lozenge on a piece
of rice paper and leave for 12
hours. Bake in an oven so low
that it is just warm (275°F/140°C/
Gas 1) for about 15 minutes.
Cool on a wire rack and serve
with more icing sugar sifted
on top. It is always a good idea
to use vanilla sugar for this (sugar stored with
a vanilla
pod).

68

· SAN·GIMIGNANO ·

Seen from the valley below, San Gimignano lives up to its reputation as a medieval Manhattan. Fifteen stone towers rise above the ochre~coloured walls, the last reminders of how all towns in Tuscany looked 600 years ago. In 1300, when Dante visited San Gimignano as ambassador, there were 72 towers, all built as keeps during the struggles between two warring families, the Ardinghelli and the Salvucci. Over centuries of feuding the towers were destroyed one by one until today only the fifteen remain, their crevices rootholds for straggling wild capers.

Politics may be less violent and towers may have fallen, but San Gimignano has kept its medieval appearance and apart from the growing collection of tourist shops, is virtually unchanged since the fourteenth century. In the Piazza della Cisterna, water flows from a thirteenth~century cistern and the cobbled square is sur~ rounded by houses built in the golden limestone of that region. One of the towers dominates the Piazza del Poppolo and once a week the timeless bustle of a street market fills the Piazza del Duomo.

· SALSA ·
per la CACCIA-GIONE
Hunter's Sauce

In San Gimignano's market you can find everything from the local hand~painted blue and white china to ravioli rolling pins and homemade pasta. Or buy a hot courgette flower fritter and a fresh bread roll filled with roast wild boar that has been basted in a sauce such as this.

2 CLOVES GARLIC, CRUSHED
OLIVE OIL
1 TBSP CAPERS
7~8 SAGE LEAVES, CHOPPED
LEAVES FROM 1 STALK ROSEMARY,
    CHOPPED FINELY
2 WINEGLASSES RED WINE
1 ANCHOVY FILLET, MASHED

Fry the garlic in the oil until golden. Add capers, sage and rosemary and cook for a minute or two. Pour in the red wine and bring to the boil. When slightly reduced, stir in the an~ chovy and use to baste any barbecued game from rabbit, or pigeon to pheasant. It is also excellent with roast pork. When the meat is cooked, spoon any remaining sauce over it and serve hot.

· FIORI FRITTI ·
Courgette flower fritters (6)

Freshly picked courgette flowers are a delicacy usually available only to people fortunate enough to have their own vegetable gardens. In Tuscany, however, the huge orange and green blossoms are available through~ out the summer in most markets.

(continued on next page)

16 ~18 COURGETTE (ZUCCHINI) FLOWERS
SMALL HANDFUL FRESH HERBS (PARSLEY
AND/OR THYME) FINELY CHOPPED
3¾ OZ / 96 G PLAIN·WHITE FLOUR
½ PT / 300 ML COLD WATER
SALT & PEPPER
OIL FOR DEEP FRYING

Gently wash & dry
the flowers. Trim
off stems. In a bowl
slowly sift the
flour into the water,
beating well with a
wooden spoon until the
mixture is like a smooth
pancake batter. Mix in the herbs.
Heat the oil in a deep pan and
when very hot, dip the blossoms
quickly into the batter & then into
the oil. When they are golden
brown drain on a kitchen towel &
sprinkle with salt and pepper.
Serve immediately while still hot.
In Tuscany this method is used to
cook many different flowers and
leaves, such as clematis and borage.

· FIORI con RIPIENO ·
Stuffed zucchini flowers (6)

For a more filling
version of the frit-
ters the flowers
can be filled with
a savoury stuffing.

6 OZ / 175 G GRATED
PARMESAN
2 OZ / 60 G HAM OR BACON
CHOPPED
1 CLOVE GARLIC, CRUSHED
2 TBSP PARSLEY, FINELY CHOPPED
3 OZ / 75 G FINE BREADCRUMBS
SALT & FRESHLY GROUND BLACK PEPPER
1 BEATEN EGG
2 TBSP MILK

Mix all the ingredients together.
Spoon the mixture carefully into the
flowers, tucking over the petal tops
so it won't escape, then follow the
previous recipe for simple flower
fritters. Serve hot.

For July, in Siena, by the willow tree, I give you barrels of white Tuscan wine...

(SAN GIMIGNANO FOLKLORE)

And that most Tuscan of Tuscan white wines ~ Vernaccia di San Gimignano is as much a part of San Gimignano as its towers. Reputedly favoured by Dante it is now sold in shops & cantinas all over the town. Some vineyards, such as Fattoria di Cusano, Raccianello & Pietrafitta, are open to the public. Enrico Teruzzi's Ponte a Rondolino vineyard serves one of the best vernaccias at its own excellent trattoria just outside town.

RISOTTO alla VERNACCIA
· Risotto with white wine (6) ·

Of the several risotto recipes in this book, this is the plainest & most delicate & therefore the most easy to make badly. The rice must be Italian Arborio rice for the proper outer creaminess & inner firmness & both the stock & the wine must be of good quality. For preference use Vernaccia, a vigorous tasting white wine, but if it is not available,

use a similarly strong flavoured white wine. Be lavish, the risotto should taste of wine, not water.

1 MEDIUM ONION, FINELY CHOPPED
1½ OZ / 40 G BUTTER
12 OZ / 350 G ITALIAN ARBORIO RICE
1½ PTS / 900 ML CHICKEN STOCK (APPROX)
6 FL OZ / 175 ML VERNACCIA (OR MORE)

Melt the butter in a medium-sized pan. Saute the onion until a pale brown and then add the rice, stirring until glistening & semi-transparent. Meanwhile heat the stock in a saucepan. Turn up the heat under the rice and pour in the wine, when it has almost disappeared add about ½ pt / 300 ml hot stock and, when absorbed, add a similar amount. Continue to add more stock (or wine for a stronger flavour) a spoonful at a time as it is absorbed by the rice (the rice will become noticeably flat on top when it needs more liquid). It should take about 20~30 minutes to cook. Stir frequently while adding liquid & just before serving stir in some butter & several tablespoons of grated pecorino or parmesan cheese.

· LOCANDA · DELL' AMOROSA ·

The best Sienese food is served not in Siena but half an hour's drive away near the old town of Sinalunga. A long straight line of spiky black cypresses leads up a hill to a brick archway, the entrance to the Locanda dell'Amorosa, the 'lover's' inn. It is less a hotel and restaurant than a small village,

the heart of a busy farm estate or 'fattoria' producing its own Chianti colli Senesi (chianti from the Sienese hills) as well as olive oil, homemade marmelades, jams and honeys.

In Siena's Museo Civico there is a fresco showing the farm as it was in 1300, but it could hardly have been a more beautiful or magical place then than it is now. The res-taurant, built into the old stables, looks out on a peaceful central courtyard of the 1400s where roses climb over mellow pink bricks. The menu changes to suit each season and is skilfully supervised by the shy and dedicated Guiseppe Vacarini, who is also one of the best sommeliers in Italy. The owner, Carlo Citterio, whose fam-ily has lived and worked at

l'Amorosa
for generations,
is completely enam~
oured of his home, as are
all his staff. It shows.
It is possible to arrive at
l'Amorosa, tired and har~
assed, with half of Tuscany's
considerable insect popul~
ation stuck to your car's
windshield and to leave
there (though unwillingly)
two hours later appetite
satisfied and spirits res~
tored completely.

·LOCANDA dell'AMOROSA·

The food at the Locanda dell' Amorosa can be as simple as a plate of fresh raw porcini mushrooms sliced paper thin and marinated in local oil and garden herbs, or rabbit simmered slowly in wine with the subtle taste of wild fennel seeds. In season there is the elegance of grilled quail and pheasant from the Sienese hills, or more traditional and substantial recipes like these two, excellent for cold days in late autumn when the first frost is on the ground.

· STRISCE con CECI ·
Ribbon noodles & chickpea soup (4)

STRISCE are wide ribbon noodles ideal for this thick soup that is more like noodles with a chickpea sauce.

14 OZ/400 G DRIED CHICK PEAS
  (SOAKED FOR 10 HRS, WATER DISCARDED)
4 OZ/100 G CARROTS, FINELY CHOPPED
1 SMALL ONION, FINELY CHOPPED
1 STICK CELERY, FINELY CHOPPED
4 TBSP OLIVE OIL
3 CLOVES GARLIC, PEELED
1 SPRIG ROSEMARY OR 2 TSP CHOPPED
  DRIED ROSEMARY
5 BLACK PEPPERCORNS
SALT
STRISCE OR MACCHERONI FOR 4~5
  (PASTA RECIPE PAGE 76)
  OR 250 G COMMERCIAL PASTA

Put the chickpeas in a deep saucepan with the garlic and pepper. Add enough water to cover plus one inch. Cover and cook slowly on a low heat for 3 hours. When tender remove the chickpeas, saving the liquid, and put all but 6 tablespoons of the chickpeas through a food processor or vegetable mill with the garlic. Heat the oil in a large saucepan and saute the carrots, onion, celery and rosemary until softened. Put everything, including the remaining chickpea liquid, into a saucepan & cook for another 30 minutes. Add salt to taste & the pasta & cook until just tender. Serve hot with grated parmesan.

· BOLLITO in SALSA ·
di DRAGONCELLO
Boiled beef & tarragon sauce (4)

Except for the Siena area tarragon is not commonly used in Tuscany. When it does appear it's often raw, rather than cooked in the French method. At the Locanda dell'Amorosa fresh tarragon for this recipe is grown in their old walled herb garden on a hill overlooking the surrounding vineyards.

· SAUCE ·
3 OZ/80 G FRESH BREADCRUMBS
1 OZ/20 G FRESH TARRAGON
1 TBSP WHITE WINE VINEGAR
5 TBSP OLIVE OIL
3 CLOVES GARLIC
SALT

· BOLLITO ·
14 OZ/400 G FATTY BEEF BRISKET,
  RUMP OR CHUCK STEAK
14 OZ/400 G BONED SHOULDER OF
  VEAL OR BEEF IN ONE PIECE
1 CARROT
1 SMALL ONION
1 CELERY STICK
1 TBSP CHOPPED PARSLEY
1 TSP SEA SALT

Put 3 litres of water into a deep saucepan with the vegetables, salt & parsley & bring to the boil. Add the meat & simmer slowly for 3 hours. Skim off any scum that rises to the surface. In the meantime make the sauce. Soak the breadcrumbs in vinegar for 15 minutes & squeeze out. Crush the tarragon & garlic to a paste in a mortar & rub through a sieve with the breadcrumbs. Mix well & slowly beat in the olive oil to obtain a thick smooth sauce. Salt to taste. When the beef is cooked slice it thinly, pour several ladles of broth over it & serve it with the tarragon sauce on the side.

· P A S T A ·

Commercial pasta bears little resemblance to the homemade variety, apart from a similar shape. Where pasta 'asciutta' (dry pasta available in packets) is only a vehicle for its sauce, homemade pasta is good enough to be an end in itself. The main difference is that the homemade varieties are made with fresh eggs and obviously worked by hand instead of machine. But many things can affect the quality of even an expert cook's pasta. Onelia, the pasta cook at the Locanda dell'Amorosa, cannot achieve the same degree of tenderness when making pasta dough at l'Amorosa as she can using the same technique in the Chianti district. One reason is the difference in water. Another is that many of the eggs in Chianti have very large yolks which absorb more flour. And as every good pasta cook knows, the more flour used, the firmer the dough and the firmer the dough, the better the pasta. Unfortunately for the novice, it is more difficult to work a very stiff dough.

· RAVIOLI con SPINACI ·
— Ravioli stuffed with — spinach & ricotta (6)

Although pasta is not as much a speciality in Tuscany as it is in Emilia~Romagna, it is still very popular. This recipe is one of the best Tuscan ways of serving fresh pasta, but the same ingredients for the dough may also be used to produce tagliatelle or pappardelle.

PASTA INGREDIENTS:
11~13 oz /300~375 g PLAIN
    UNBLEACHED FLOUR
3 EGGS
PINCH OF SALT

STUFFING:
2 ½ LB /1.2 KG FRESH SPINACH
    (OR NETTLES) WASHED WELL
½ TSP SALT
½ TSP NUTMEG
2 EGG YOLKS
12 OZ /350 G RICOTTA CHEESE

1 First make the stuffing. Wash the spinach and put it into a saucepan with just the water that clings to the leaves. Add the salt. Cover and cook for 15~20 minutes, until tender. Drain, squeeze out moisture and chop very finely. Mix together with the other ingredients & salt to taste.

2 To make the pasta sift the flour with the salt on to a wooden table. Make a well in the middle of the flour and pour in the yolks, beaten lightly together with a fork. With your hand start stirring in flour from inside the well until the eggs are no longer liquid, and continue to work in until the eggs have absorbed as much flour as possible without losing pliability.

3 Wash your hands, clean the work surface of flour & knead the dough for about 10 minutes until it is a shiny flexible ball. Fold it over and turn it continuously as you knead it. Leave, covered, for about 10 minutes.

4 At this point you can use a pasta machine to do the final rolling out. Otherwise divide dough in two to make it easier to handle. Always keep unused dough covered. Rub some oil into a long thin rolling pin (24~30 in/60~75 cm long and 2 in/5 cm diameter is a good size) & then dust with flour. On a floured surface begin to roll the dough out as quickly as possible into a regular oval shape. Roll it smoothly away from you & turn it after each roll. As it gets thinner, occasionally wrap the sheet of pasta around a rolling pin and stretch towards you. When paper thin, fold loosely, cover & repeat the process with the other half.

5 Lay one sheet on a floured surface, cut into an even rectangular shape & place small teaspoonfuls of spinach filling approximately 1½ in/4 cm apart in straight rows. Between rows brush water, lay the other sheet of dough on top & with the side of the hand press firmly down between rows to seal. Cut into squares with a pastry cutter and place on greaseproof paper. Cover.

(Continued on following page)

(Continued from preceding page)

6 Boil 8 pints/4.5 litres of water with 1 tbsp oil & a tsp of salt. Add the pasta and about 5 minutes after the water has returned to the boil remove the ravioli, which should be cooked al dente. Serve immediately with butter and grated cheese or with butter in which you have fried 6~8 leaves of sage.

RAVIOLI GNUDI
Naked Ravioli (6)

There is another type of so-called 'ravioli' that is particularly popular in Tuscany although almost unavailable in any restaurants there. It is a bit like the stuffing without the pasta and in fact is called 'Ravioli gnudi' in Arezzo to indicate 'naked' ravioli. It is a great delicacy, good enough to eat with just freshly chopped tomatoes and a sprinkling of parmesan on top.

1½ LB/675 G FRESH SPINACH, COOKED AS PREVIOUS RECIPE & FINELY CHOPPED
9 OZ/250 G RICOTTA CHEESE
4½ OZ/130 G PLAIN FLOUR
3 EGG YOLKS
5 OZ/150 G FRESHLY GRATED PECORINO OR PARMESAN
½ TSP NUTMEG
½ SMALL ONION, FINELY CHOPPED
2 OZ/50 G BUTTER
SALT

Melt the butter in a large saucepan. Cook the onion in it until golden. Add the spinach and salt and saute for about 5 minutes. Cool slightly and then in a large bowl mix together thoroughly with the ricotta and flour. Add the yolks, nutmeg and pecorino and work together well. Salt to taste. Chill well for easier handling and then form into oval pellets about 1 in/2.5 cm long by ½ in/1 cm across. Boil 8 pints/4.5 litres salted water and cook the ravioli a few at a time. They should be ready about 3 or 4 minutes after the water has returned to the boil. Remove and keep warm until ready to eat. In the unlikely occurrence of leftovers, roll them in egg yolk and breadcrumbs the next day and deep fry until crunchy and brown.

Arezzo is a prosperous, rather austere provincial town, the centre of a rich farming zone. It is internationally famous for the stunning frescoes there by Piero della Francesco but locally more famous for Mario de Filippis' friendly little trattoria, Buca di San Francesco. There you can sit in the frescoed cellar of a sixteenth-century palace and eat specialities such as zuppa di fagioli (bean soup), homemade tagliolini, ricotta with acacia honey, and chicken from the nearby Valdarno cooked 'in porchetta'. Porchetta is a whole roast piglet usually sold from stalls by travelling vendors throughout Tuscany and Umbria. Chicken cooked in the same way is stuffed with quantities of leafy wild fennel, sage leaves and garlic.

SFORMATO di VERDURE
—— con FEGATINI ——
• Spinach souffle with •
chicken livers (4)

Buca di San Francesco is one of a group of restaurants 'del Buon Ricordo' (good memory), established to keep alive the traditions of regional cooking in Italy. Each one has a dish, like this one, particularly typical of the area, called the 'Piatto del Buon Ricordo', and a regional menu that the restaurant's owner will recommend on request. This recipe uses spinach for the sformato, but is equally good made with nettles or swiss chard.

• SFORMATO •

2 lB 2 oz / 1 KG	SPINACH
3 FL oz / 75 ML	THICK BECHAMEL
3 EGG WHITES, BEATEN STIFFLY	
1 EGG YOLK, BEATEN	
1/4 – 1/2 TSP	NUTMEG
2 1/2 TBSP	PARMESAN
2 OZ / 50G	BUTTER
4 OZ / 100 G	FINE, DRY BREADCRUMBS
SALT & FRESHLY GROUND PEPPER	

· SAUCE ·

1 LB/450 G CHICKEN LIVERS, TRIMMED OF FAT & WASHED
1 SMALL ONION, FINELY CHOPPED
4~6 TBSP OLIVE OIL
2 WINEGLASSES WHITE WINE
9~10 SAGE LEAVES, CHOPPED

Wash the spinach in several
changes of cold water. Cook in
a covered saucepan for 15 min~
utes. Cool, chop and put through
a coarse sieve. Melt the butter
in a frying pan & gently saute
the spinach for about 10 min~
utes. Remove from heat & stir in
the bechamel, egg yolk, nutmeg,
parmesan, salt and pepper. Fold
in the egg whites and pour into
a deep baking dish, buttered &
dusted with breadcrumbs. Place
in a bain marie & bake in an
oven preheated to 400°F/200°C/
Gas Mark 6 for 20 minutes, or
until golden on top.

In the meantime saute the
onion in olive oil over a medium
heat. When just golden, turn
up the heat & add chicken livers
and sage. Cook for a few minutes,
until the liver has turned pale.
Remove from pan & keep hot.
Add the wine and boil briskly
until reduced by half, stirring
in the bits from the pan. Return
the livers to the pan, stir quickly,
add salt & pepper & remove
from heat. Turn the sformato
out onto a dish (it should now
have a crunchy golden crust) &
pour the livers into the middle.
Serve immediately.

· GINESTRATA ·
Chicken and wine cordial (4)

In the spring in Tuscany the
perfume of wild broom, gin~
estra, is overpowering and
the roads are lined with huge
bushes covered in the brilliant
yellow blossoms. These flowers
give their name to a famous
Tuscan soup that was once en~
dowed with miraculous powers.
It could supposedly increase
potency, cure disease and im~
prove the powers of the brain
(essential after too much Chianti
the night before). Although it
was & is a recipe particularly
associated with the Chianti
region where the ginestra
blooms most profusely, they
make a similar soup at the Buca
di San Francesco called 'cordiale'.
It lays equal claims to renew
vigour & health in just one bowlful.

4 EGGS
2 OZ/50 G BUTTER
1 WINEGLASS OF MARSALA OR VIN SANTO
3/4 PINT/½ LITRE GOOD HOME MADE CHICKEN STOCK
½ TSP CINNAMON
PINCH OF SAFFRON
PINCH OF NUTMEG
JUICE OF ½ LEMON
SUGAR

Beat the eggs and while mix~
ing steadily, slowly add
marsala, chicken stock, cinn~
amon & saffron. Heat gently
and add butter cut in small
pieces. Continue to mix and
when it begins to thicken
remove from heat and pour
into pretty cups. Stir in lemon
juice and sprinkle with sugar
and nutmeg.

· FOCACCIA ·
Savoury flat bread (4~6)

This dimpled salty bread is popular not only in Tuscany and its origins would probably be hotly contested by every baker in Italy. It is particularly good with crispy pieces of bacon or onion worked into the dough.

8~10 OZ/225~275 G RISEN BREAD DOUGH
(SEE RECIPE PAGE 65)

COARSE SEA SALT

OLIVE OIL

Pour a thin layer of oil into a large flat baking sheet. Roll the dough out to ½in/1cm thickness and place on the baking sheet. Every 2½in/6cm make a dimple by pressing your finger well down into the dough. Pour 4~5 tbsp of oil over and sprinkle on lots of salt. Bake for 20~25 minutes until deep golden & crusty in an oven preheated to 200°C/400°F/Gas Mark 6. Serve warm.

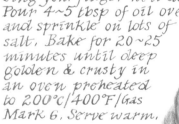

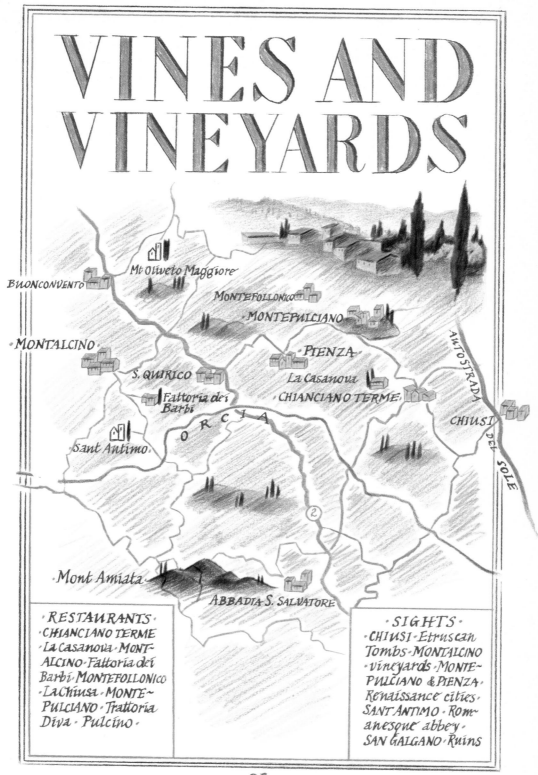

VINES AND VINEYARDS

Mt Oliveto Maggiore

BUONCONVENTO

MONTEFOLLONICO

MONTEPULCIANO

MONTALCINO

PIENZA

S. QUIRICO

La Casanova

CHIANCIANO TERME

Fattoria dei Barbi

ORCIA

AUTOSTRADA

CHIUSI

DEL SOLE

Sant Antimo

Mont Amiata

ABBADIA S. SALVATORE

·RESTAURANTS·
·CHIANCIANO TERME
·La Casanova·MONT-
ALCINO·Fattoria dei
Barbi·MONTEFOLLONICO
·LaChiusa·MONTE~
PULCIANO·Trattoria
Diva·Pulcino·

·SIGHTS·
·CHIUSI·Etruscan
Tombs·MONTALCINO
·vineyards·MONTE~
PULCIANO & PIENZA·
Renaissance cities·
SANT ANTIMO·Rom-
anesque abbey·
SAN GALGANO·Ruins

· INTRODUCTION ·

The area between Montalcino and Montepulciano, south of Siena, is notable not only for the beauty of its countryside and fine Renaissance towns but also for the quality of its wines. Vino Nobile di Montepulciano, an elegant Chianti-style wine, has had its praises sung by poets for centuries. In the seventeenth century the poet-physician Francesco Redi wrote 'Montepulciano d'ogni vino e re' ~ Montepulciano of all wines is King. If modern vino nobile is less the king than one of the crown princes of traditional Tuscan wines, it is still worthy of its title. One of the best vino nobiles comes from the little estate of Poderi Boscarelli, lying on the south-eastern slopes of the hill that is crowned by the lovely city of Montepulciano.

Together with its neighbour Pienza, Montepulciano is a model of fifteenth-century town planning. Walk up the main street, the Corso, on a windy spring day and panoramic views of distant vineyards are glimpsed around the corners of impressive baroque palaces. Small balconied piazzas are conveniently designed to open up these views off each of the cobbled streets that climb steeply to the Piazza Grande, the wide and splendid central square that is the highest point in Montepulciano, as well as the focus of the annual music and mime festival every August.

Nine miles to the west of Montepulciano lies Pienza, the ideal city of Piccolomini (Pope Pius II 1458~64), who virtually created the city out of his birthplace, Corsignano. In 1459 he commissioned the Florentine architect Bernardo Rossellino to rebuild the town and make it, and its cathedral, 'the finest in all Italy'. He almost succeeded. Although Piccolomini died before his dream could be realized, he left behind him a beautiful miniature city, complete enough to inspire the director Franco Zeffirelli to use it as the setting for his film of Romeo and Juliet.

Pienza is on the road leading to Montalcino, home of one of the costliest and most prestigious red wines in Italy, Brunello di Montalcino. It has become so in a relatively short time, largely due to the efforts of the Biondi~Santi family. From 1865, when the family first won a citation for a 'Brunello', they have been steadily improving its quality until today it has achieved almost legendary status as a wine whose flavour can outlive some of the longest aged wines in the world. A bottle of Biondi-Santis' Brunello takes years, even decades, to come to full maturity, and if the end result is superb, the cost is prohibitive. Fortunately there are other vineyards producing Brunello at more accessible costs. One of the pleasantest ways to pass a warm autumn afternoon is at Montalcino's elegant little open-air 'Caffè Fiaschetteria Italiana' sampling and discussing vintage Brunellos with the local experts. Or drive through olive and vine-clad hills of matchless beauty to one of the vineyards open to visitors. The Fattoria dei Barbi is one which has the added advantage of its own excellent trattoria serving local recipes and products from the estate.

The food in the area can vary from Sienese-inspired cuisine at the country restaurant La Chiusa (that also sells olive oil pressed in its own antique 'frantoio' or oil press) to the more robust home-cooking of ribollita and grilled meats at the Fattoria Pulcino near Monte-pulciano's main gate. There is frequent use of local herbs like tarragon and of the giant porcini mushrooms (BOLETUS EDULIS) picked wild from the slopes of nearby Mont Amiata, an extinct volcano. And the beautiful Ristorante La Casanova near Chian-ciano Terme has fresh lake fish and imag-inative game dishes in season.

· TRATTORIA · DIVA ·

PICI DOUGH OF JUST FLOUR AND WATER ROLLED WITH 4 FOOT LONG ROLLING PIN AND THEN DIPPED IN CORN FLOUR

ADA MAKING 'PICI' ON SATURDAY MORNING AT DIVA RESTAURANT IN MONTEPULCIANO WHERE THE LOCAL FARMERS BRING ALL THEIR FRESH PRODUCE.

SLICED IN INCH WIDE STRIPS TO ROLL WITH FINGERS IN YELLOW CORN FLOUR

AMAZINGLY LONG AND WIGGLY LIKE THE ROADS UP AND DOWN MONTEPULCIANO.

The Trattoria Diva, named after the owner's wife, is a small jolly family~run trattoria near the main gate in Monte~pulciano. The specialities are simple unpretentious dishes, always accompanied by an excellent selection of local wines from the owner's next door wine enoteca.

· PICI ·
Tuscan eggless pasta (6)

Pici is/are an amazingly time~consuming, completely hand~rolled pasta with no eggs, originally made only by and for the very poor in the area around Montepulciano. They consist of just flour, salt and water. The following is a very approximate recipe.

12 OZ / 350 G PLAIN FLOUR, SIFTED
PINCH SALT
SEVERAL TBSP WATER

Knead all the ingredients together to form a stretchy pasta dough. Leave covered for 20 minutes. Roll out until the dough is ¼ in /5mm thick and cut into strips of ½ in/1 cm wide. Then work and twist each piece by hand into extremely long and wiggly spaghetti. Keep each string of pasta covered until ready to use. Cook in boiling water in the usual way.

· SALSA di SALSICCIE ·
Sausage sauce (6)

If you can be bothered to make pici, they are an excellent and chewy vehicle for this traditional sauce which comes from the foothills of Mont Amiata. And near Chiusi south of Montepulciano pici are eaten tossed in a sauce of 'caviar' from pike caught in the nearby lake.

12 OZ/350 G SPICY ITALIAN SAUSAGE, SKINNED AND CRUMBLED IN PIECES
14 OZ / 400 G RIPE TOMATOES, PEELED AND MASHED WITH A FORK
8 OZ/240G FRESH BOLETUS EDULIS OR
1OZ/25G DRIED 'FUNGHI' MUSHROOMS SOAKED IN TEPID WATER 30 MINS
1 LARGE ONION, FINELY CHOPPED
2 TBSP OLIVE OIL
RED WINE (OPTIONAL)

Heat the oil in a shallow flame~proof casserole. Cook the onions in it, and when starting to turn transparent, add the sausages and the mushrooms (squeezed out and sliced if dried), Cook, stirring occasionally, for about ten minutes and then add the tomatoes, salt and pepper to taste and a generous splash of red wine if you like. Cook for another 30 minutes on a low heat. Serve over the cooked, drained pici ~ or any other pasta.

· PICI con CONIGLIO ·
Pasta with rabbit sauce (4)

This, one of the most traditional sauces to serve with pici, can also be used as a sauce with more readily available pastas such as spaghetti or penne.

1 OZ / 25 G PANCETTA OR BACON, FINELY CHOPPED
1 LARGE RABBIT, CUT IN PIECES, WITH GIBLETS
1 SMALL ONION, FINELY CHOPPED
1 CARROT, FINELY CHOPPED
2~3 SPRIGS FRESH THYME
1 LB 2 OZ / 500 G TOMATOES, PEELED, SEEDED AND CHOPPED
½ BOTTLE CHIANTI
3 TBSP OLIVE OIL
SALT
PEPPER

Sauté the pancetta, onion and carrot until softened in the oil. Add the rabbit pieces (except the giblets) and brown on all sides. Then add the wine and when nearly evap~ orated the tomatoes and the thyme. Cover and simmer gently until the rabbit is tender ~ about 1~1½ hours. After about half an hour, add the giblets, finely chopped,

and a few tablespoons of warm water or beef stock to ensure that the sauce stays quite liquid. About 10 minutes before the end of cooking remove the rabbit and keep hot. Add the pici and cook through. Or, if using dried pasta, cook the pasta until softened but still firm in boiling water and then add to the sauce. Serve the pasta as a first course with the rabbit to follow, served with spinach and olive oil.

✳ FUNGHI SECCHI ~
(Boletus edulis / Porcini / Ceps)
These huge mushrooms are widely available throughout Tuscany in the late spring & autumn, both in markets & growing wild in woodland clearings (especially on the slopes of Mont Amiata). Their rich flavour is used to enhance everything from peasant stews & simple pasta sauces to elegant veal dishes. Where fresh porcini are not available it is still possible to capture some of their fragrance using dried funghi, 'funghi secchi' (available in packets from many speciality stores).

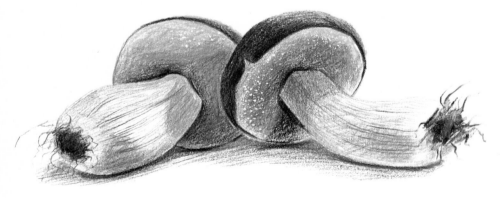

89

· FATTORIA · DEI · BARBI ·

In the restaurant of the Fattoria dei Barbi near Montalcino there is an English cook from Bournemouth who makes one of the best bean soups in Tuscany. Even the Tuscans will admit this, which shows how good it must be. It helps that she has been in the country for 20 years, is married to a Tuscan and, even more importantly, has a Tuscan mother~in~law. And it also helps to have the Fattoria products to cook with, herb~flavoured ricotta, fresh pecorino, olive oil, peppery prosciutto, pork steaks for the grill and the famous Barbi/Columbini Brunello wine. It is a good place to go on a hot summer's day, to sit at a check~cloth covered table in the middle of a vineyard and hear the history of Brunello and to follow this with a visit to the beaut~ iful old wine cellars, where you may also taste some of the wines.

· ZUPPA di FAGIOLI ·
Tuscan bean soup (6)

This bean soup, a version of the famous 'ribollita' (meaning re~ boiled), may well have an even longer history than Brunello wine, & is best made the day be~ fore.

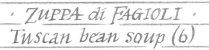

2 LB 2 OZ /1 KG FRESH CANNELINI (SMALL HARICOT) BEANS OR 14½ OZ/ 420 G DRIED ONES, SOAKED OVERNIGHT

3~4 RIPE TOMATOES, PEELED, SEEDED AND MASHED

2 STICKS CELERY, FINELY CHOPPED

2 CARROTS, FINELY CHOPPED

2 LEEKS, FINELY CHOPPED

11 OZ /300 G CAVOLO NERO (TUSCAN BLACK CABBAGE) OR YOU CAN SUBSTITUTE SWISS CHARD, SPINACH BEET OR ANY DARK GREEN CABBAGE

(Continued)

7 OZ/200 G SAVOY CABBAGE (SAUTED
    SEPARATELY & KEPT FOR TOPPING)
2 CLOVES GARLIC, CRUSHED
2 SPRIGS FRESH THYME
6~8 TBSP OLIVE OIL
STOCK
SALT & PEPPER
6 PIECES HARD STALE BREAD

Boil the beans in plenty of water until slightly softened. Cover, leave for an hour & drain. Sieve 3/4 into an equal amount of fresh water & reserve the rest. Put the oil in a large saucepan & cook the carrots, celery & leeks. When soft add the tomatoes, garlic & thyme. After 5 minutes add the cabbage, salt & pepper. Cook about 10 minutes & add the bean puree & the bean water. Cook slowly for an hour, adding tepid water if the soup becomes too solid, although it should be fairly thick. About 5~10 minutes before end of cooking, stir in the whole beans to heat through & ladle some of the hot soup over the bread in each bowl. Serve with cooked cabbage on top, a bowl of sliced red or spring onions and a jug of good green olive oil.

RISOTTO PRIMAVERA
· Spring Risotto (6) ·

This is a very festive looking risotto.

1 LB 2 OZ /500 G ITALIAN ARBORIO RICE
11 OZ/300 G GREENISH TOMATOES,
    DICED
12 OZ/350 G SMALL COURGETTES
    (ZUCCHINI), DICED
7 OZ /200 G GREEN PEPPER OR
    ASPARAGUS, DICED
4 OZ /100 G CARROT, DICED
1 ONION OR LEEK, CHOPPED
BEEF STOCK
5 OZ/150 G BUTTER
2 TBSP OLIVE OIL
SALT & PEPPER

Cook the onion in oil in a saucepan & when beginning to brown, add all the vegetables except the tomatoes. Cook 10 minutes over moderate heat & add tomatoes, salt & pepper. Cook for 15 minutes & then pour in the rice & a little hot stock. Continue adding tablespoons of hot stock every few minutes as the rice absorbs the liquid. It should take 20~30 minutes for the rice to cook to the 'al dente' stage. Then stir in butter & serve.

Tuscany is justifiably famous for the quality of its meat & fresh vegetable dishes, but less well~known (outside Italy) for the variety of ways in which wild herbs are used for any~thing from pasta filling to souffles or sformati, a Tuscan cross between a souffle and a vegetable mold. These two rec~ipes come from an old lady encountered picking a basket of nettles near Montepulciano.

SFORMATO di ORTICA
· Souffle of Nettles ·
— or spinach (4) —

2 LB 2 OZ /1 KG TENDER SPRING
NETTLE LEAVES (OR SPINACH)
4 EGGS, BEATEN
4 OZ /100 G PARMESAN CHEESE,
GRATED
PINCH GRATED NUTMEG
4 OZ /100 G BUTTER
CLOVE GARLIC, CRUSHED
SALT
PEPPER

Wash the nettles under running water for at least half an hour. Boil (save water for soup) for 10~15 minutes until tender, drain well and chop. Melt the butter in a medium~sized pan and saute the nettles, garlic and salt for 5 minutes. Add pepper and nutmeg and put through a food processor or vegetable mill. Stir in the eggs and cheese and pour into a buttered souffle dish. Place in a bain marie or roasting tin with water about ½ in/1cm deep and bake in an oven pre~heated to 400°F/200°C/Gas 6 for about 30 minutes or until it has risen and is golden brown. Serve immediately.

MINESTRA di PISCIALETTO
· Tuscan Dandelion ·
— greens soup (4) —

Translated literally, piscialetto means pissbed, a Tuscan ref~erence to the colour of the dandelion flowers and its proximity to passing dogs. Elsewhere, however, it is trad~itionally regarded as having medicinal properties for humans.

9 OZ /250 G TINY DANDELION
LEAVES
2 CLOVES GARLIC, CRUSHED
1 3/4 PT/ 1 LTR WATER OR STOCK
LEEK, FINELY CHOPPED
STICK CELERY, FINELY CHOPPED
OLIVE OIL
SALT
BLACK PEPPER

Saute the onion, garlic and celery in oil in a medium~sized pan. When softened, add the dandelion leaves (keep a few for garnishing the soup), washed well and chopped. Cook for 5 minutes and then add water or stock, salt and pepper. Cook for half an hour and then put through a food processor or vegetable mill. It can then be re~heated and served over toasted bread.

BORAGINE

SANT ANTIMO
· Wild Herbs ·

One of the loveliest & most peaceful sights in Tuscany is the Benedictine abbey of Sant Antimo. Set in a golden green valley south of Montalcino, this French~Romanesque church was founded, according to tradition, by Charlemagne sometime in the ninth century. Legend has it that at the same time Charlemagne also introduced tarragon or 'dragoncello' as a cooking herb in the region between Montalcino and Siena. Tarragon, essentially a French herb, is rarely used anywhere else in Tuscany but is found growing abundantly near Sant Antimo, as is the

94

more common wild borage. The
young tender leaves and vivid
blue flowers of borage can
be cooked as fritters
(like the zucchini
flower fritters on
page 70), tossed in
salads with other wild
greens such as dandelions
or sauted gently in oil
and added to beaten
eggs to make a borage
frittata. Tuscan frittatas,
although similar in some
ways to French omelettes,
differ in that they are
cooked slowly until firm
over a low heat and are
then usually grilled
quickly to set the top
side. They are often
served as a light
evening meal with a
selection of antipasti,
but also make an
interesting alternative to
sandwiches when served
cold on a picnic.

DRAGONCELLO

· PAN CO' SANTI ·
— Saint's bread —

Just outside Montepulciano is the farm estate and trattoria PULCINO, selling its own Vino Nobile as well as sausages, home cured hams, sweet breads and cakes made from old local recipes by aunts, uncles and other relatives of the owner. One of these recipes is for Pan co' Santi (bread with saints), an ancient sweet bread that is traditionally eaten on All Soul's Day. It can be adapted from most bread recipes (or use the recipe page 65). To make it knead 17oz/510g of risen bread dough with the following ingredients:

2 TBSP MELTED HONEY
2 OZ/60G WALNUTS, TOASTED & CHOPPED
2 OZ/60G DRIED FIGS OR PEARS, FINELY CHOPPED
2 OZ/60G DATES, CHOPPED
1 TSP ROSEMARY, CHOPPED
2 OZ/60 G PINENUTS,
GENEROUS HANDFUL RAISINS
3 TBSP OLIVE OIL

When well amalgamated shape into an oval & leave to rise for 30~40 minutes. Brush the top with beaten egg and bake the loaf in an oven preheated to 400°F/200°C/Gas 6.

THE ETRUSCAN MAREMMA

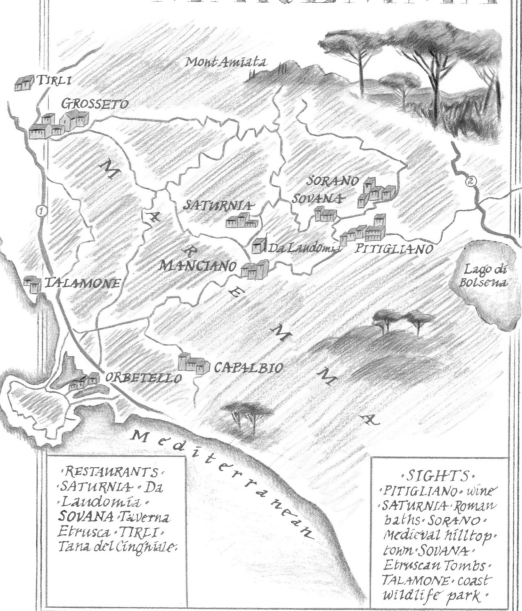

TIRLI

GROSSETO

Mont Amiata

MAREMMA

SATURNIA

SORANO
SOVANA

Da Laudomia · PITIGLIANO

MANCIANO

TALAMONE

Lago di Bolsena

ORBETELLO · CAPALBIO

Mediterranean

· RESTAURANTS ·
· SATURNIA · Da
· Laudomia ·
SOVANA · Taverna
Etrusca · TIRLI ·
Tana del Cinghiale ·

· SIGHTS ·
· PITIGLIANO · wine
· SATURNIA · Roman
baths · SORANO ·
Medieval hilltop ·
town · SOVANA ·
Etruscan Tombs ·
TALAMONE · coast
wildlife park ·

97

· INTRODUCTION ·

Driving through the wide meadows and gently rolling low hills that are the Tuscan Maremma today, it is almost impossible to believe that less than a hundred years ago much of this now fertile countryside was malaria~ridden marshland. During Etruscan times the area northeast of the principal city of Grosseto was a navigable gulf. By the middle ages this had become a freshwater lake, which in turn became a swamp, causing widespread disease and famine. Many unsuccessful efforts were made to reclaim the land but it was not until the early years of this century that the Maremma was effectively rid of the malaria that had wiped out whole towns. In the 1950s a systematic government programme of agricultural incentives and repopulation was begun and the area's past prosperity virtually restored. Today the Etruscan-red soil produces abundant flowers, vegetables, grains and grapes.

The word 'Maremma' means coastal plain and, apart from the modern resorts along the coast, the area was probably more densely populated in Etruscan times, 2000 years ago, than it is now. Certainly evidence of these earliest settlers of Tuscany is everywhere. They left behind their name for the country, 'Tuscia', as well as many of their tombs and burial sites. At the lonely semi~abandoned village of Sovana the single~story medieval houses seem less inhabited than the Etruscan necropolis set in a cool birch gulley a mile away. Five miles to the south~east, Sovana's gloomy & forbidding neighbour, Pitigliano, grows out of a magnificent rocky mountain~top whose base is riddled with caves that were once Etruscan and Roman tombs but now serve as cellars for the excellent Pitigliano white wine. The three deep ravines around the town formed a natural moat when this town was the seat of the Roman Orsini barons during the thirteenth century.

The Etruscans were not the only settlers to leave their mark on the land. During the mid~1500s, when Orbetello was the capital of the Spanish Garrison States, pirates from the Barbary coast were a constant hazard along the coast and close to the sea are the crumbling remains of a few towers from which watch was kept for the invaders. Despite these precautions however, one night in April 1543, the beautiful young daughter of a local family, the Marsilis, was kidnapped by Barbarossa's pirates and survived to become the favourite wife of Sultan Solimani. And at Orbetello many of the present~day inhabitants still retain the swarthy good looks of Moorish forbears.

Much of the Maremman coast has been ruined by expensive resort developments but fortunately some of the original terrain is protected by the Monti dell' Uccellina, the Maremman Nature Reserve. In this long stretch of wood & scrubland wildlife flourishes and the huge umbrella pines, so typical of the area, shade miles of white deserted beaches. It is possible to see hare, deer and porcupines, and most unexpectedly, herds of long~horn cattle & wild horses rounded up by 'butteri', the cowboys of the Maremma. At the medieval town of Capalbio these cowboys have their own riders fair in October.

Capalbio is the main centre of horse breeding in southern Tuscany and also an excellent place to sample wild game prepared in appetizing local recipes. But throughout the Maremma game is readily available. During the autumn hunting season small family restaurants, Da Laudomia near Saturnia and the Taverna Etrusca in Sovana, serve hearty toe~warming dishes that make use not only of the plentiful wild boar and roebuck but also of fresh local herbs, tomatoes and wild mushrooms. Garlic is used here far more than in the rest of Tuscany, perhaps because it is a cheap way of adding flavour to a simple dish. The Maremman people do not easily forget that their region has only very recently become agriculturally rich after centuries of much hardship.

For centuries the Tuscans, some of the world's most avid hunters, shot anything that moved: wild boar, deer, pheasant, thrushes, porcupines and even hedgehogs. And then it usually reappeared on the table. Now there is an increasing reluctance to wipe out songbirds. There is much less reluctance, however, to halt the hunting of wild boar, or cinghiale, which, being large and quite fierce, provides more sport than a songbird. All over Tuscany you can buy delicious hams and sausages made from this tasty meat, particularly in the Maremma where the broom~covered hills provide excellent cinghiale cover. The recipes below come from the cook at the Tana del Cinghiale, a remote hunting lodge at the tiny village of Tirli in the Maremman hills.

CINGHIALE alle MELE
Wild boar with apples (6)

Wild boar, unless very young and tender, needs to be marinated, but before that it should have been hung for a few days. Ask your butcher or game dealer, he should know its history.

2½ LB/1·2 KG WILD BOAR ~ THE RIB MEAT FOR PREFERENCE
3~4 LARGE COOKING APPLES, PEELED, CORED & SLICED
1 ONION, CHOPPED
2 GLASSES RED WINE
SMALL PIECE CHILI PEPPER
CARROT, CHOPPED
CELERY STICK, CHOPPED
SALT
FRESH ROSEMARY
FRESH THYME
OLIVE OIL
ABOUT 1¾ PT/ 1 LTR BEEF STOCK

MARINADE

1 ¾ PT / 1 LTR RED WINE
¼ PT / 150 ML VINEGAR
3 ¼ PT / 1.75 LTR WATER
5~6 BAY LEAVES
½ TSP CINNAMON
6 WHOLE PEPPERCORNS
4 LEAVES FRESH MINT
2 OZ / 50 G SEA SALT
3~4 SPRIGS FRESH ROSEMARY
3~4 SPRIGS FRESH THYME

Combine all the ingredients for the marinade. Cut the meat into chunks and completely cover in the marinade. Add more wine if the meat is not covered. Leave for three days in a refrigerator and stir often. If it begins to give an unpleas~ ant smell, change the liquid~ this is not a 'cucina povera' dish. After three days rinse well in warm water. Heat the oil in a heat~proof casserole and add the onion, carrot, celery, chili and herbs. When soft add the meat, salt and pepper, and brown well. Pour in the red wine and when slightly

evaporated lower the heat and add a cup of beef stock. Cover and cook gently for 2~3 hours, until tender, adding stock as necessary to prevent it drying out. Half an hour before the end of cooking, pack the apples over the meat. Recover and finish cooking. Serve over toasted bread or deep fried polenta (see page 49).

LEPRE in DOLCE e FORTE
Hare in strong sweet sauce (6)

This classic way of cooking both boar and hare requires a strong wild meat. The quan~ tities are for the more readily available hare. The dish has a strange, exotic taste and is much better made the day before it is required. Be sure of your guests' capabilities before serving it ~ it is definitely not nouvelle cuisine.

1 LARGE HARE, CLEANED
2 OZ / 50 G PANCETTA, FINELY
    CHOPPED
3 SPRIGS THYME
GOOD BEEF OR CHICKEN STOCK
OLIVE OIL
11 OZ / 300 G TOMATOES
2 TBSP CHOPPED PARSLEY
LARGE WINEGLASS WHITE WINE
2 CRUMBLED BAY LEAVES

MARINADE

1 PT / ½ LTR WHITE WINE
WINEGLASS OF WHITE
    WINE VINEGAR
ONION STUCK WITH 4 CLOVES
CELERY STICK, SLICED
CARROT, SLICED
CLOVE GARLIC, CRUSHED
3 JUNIPER BERRIES
6 PEPPERCORNS
(continued...)

PECORINO MAREMMANO
£12.00 L'ETTO

GGI CINGHIALE

SALSA AGRODOLCE

2 TBSP GRANULATED SUGAR

2 TBSP WATER

2 TBSP RED WINE VINEGAR

2 OZ/50 G BITTER COOKING
    CHOCOLATE

1½ OZ/40 G RAISINS, SOAKED

2½ OZ/60 G PINENUTS

2 TBSP MIXED CANDIED LEMON
    AND ORANGE PEEL

Combine all the ingredients for the marinade. Cut the hare in pieces, wash well and cover with the marinade for 24 hours, stirring often. Drain, wash and dry the hare. Heat a little oil in a flame proof casserole, add the thyme, parsley, bay leaves & finely chopped pancetta & soften. Then add the hare & saute well. Add salt, pour in a glass of wine & when it has evaporated add the tomatoes. Cover & cook slowly over a low heat for at least 2 hours, adding hot stock as needed to stop the stew drying out. About half an hour before the hare has finished cooking, melt the sugar with water over low heat until slightly brown. Add the chocolate melted in the vinegar, and after a few minutes the raisins, pinenuts & peel. Mix well & take from the heat. Remove hare from the liquid, & sieve or liquid-ize the remaining juices. Return meat & sauce to the casserole & slowly add the agrodolce. Heat through for 10 minutes & serve with a crisp borage salad.

CIPOLLE alla GROSSETANA
· Stuffed onions ·
Grosseto style (4)

This recipe has hundreds of variations in the Maremma. Some cooks substitute half a finely chopped chili pepper for the nutmeg & cinnamon, some add ½ oz/15 g dried mushrooms, soaked, squeezed out & chopped. Whatever variation you use, these onions make a good lunch for a cold winter's day.

4 LARGE OR 8 SMALL WHITE ONIONS

4 OZ/125 G LEAN BEEF, GROUND
    OR MINCED

BUTTER

OLIVE OIL

SALT & PEPPER

¼ TSP NUTMEG

4 OZ/125 G GROUND SPICY SAUSAGE

1 EGG

1 WINE GLASS DRY WHITE WINE

4 TBSP GRATED PECORINO OR
    PARMESAN CHEESE *

¼ TSP CINNAMON

Peel the onions and boil until slightly softened in salted water (about 10 minutes). Trim enough off one end so the onions will stand upright. Remove a little of the other end & most of the inside, leaving just a shell. Chop the remaining onion finely & saute in butter with the beef and sausage until brown. Stir in the spices and wine. When the wine has nearly evaporated, turn off the heat and leave to cool. Then mix the sauce with egg and cheese and stuff the onion shells with this. Bake at a moderate heat, 350°F/180°C/Gas 4, in an oiled baking dish for about 25 minutes until brown, moistening with water or stock if the onions seem to be burning.

* It is also good to serve this dish with several tablespoons of bechamel sauce instead of cheese.

103

DA LAUDOMIA

One hundred years ago Da Laudomia was a small posting inn (called Locanda Butelli after the present owner's grandparents) where tired travellers stopped to eat, change horses and buy anything from trousers to home-made sweets. The store and the horses have gone, but Da Laudomia remains much the same (despite the change of name) and the present patronne, Clara Detti, can tell you more about the history & the

practice of Maremman cooking than can be found
in any book on the subject

·ACQUACOTTA·

Tomato and bread soup (4)

Signora Detti believes that Acquacotta (literally 'cooked water')
began when itinerant carbonari
or charcoal~burners worked
through the winters in the
Maremma. They were so poor
that they lived in igloos of twigs
built around their ever~burning
charcoal fires, and over each of
these fires hung a pot of
simmering water. Any food
that could be scrounged or
exchanged for charcoal was put
in this pot ~ usually garlic,
stale bread and onions, but as
times got better, tomatoes,
celery and an egg or two went
in. From these humble
beginnings Acquacotta has
evolved into this slightly
more sophisticated version
without losing its original
simplicity. There are an
almost infinite number of
variations to this soup, one
of the best is the addition
of several dried
mushrooms
and one
spicy
grilled
sausage per
person at the
beginning of
(continued ...)

(continued from previous page)
cooking. But whatever variation
you follow, this soup always
tastes best if eaten when you
are tired and hungry.

2~3 LARGE ONIONS, FINELY CHOPPED
1 LB 10 OZ/750 G TOMATOES, PEELED
    AND DESEEDED(OR A MIXTURE
    OF 11 OZ/300 G SWEET RED PEPPERS
    AND 1 LB/450 G TOMATOES)
5~6 STICKS CELERY, DICED
    (INCLUDING THE LEAVES)
4 TBSP GOOD OLIVE OIL
1 3/4 PT/1 LTR BOILING SALTED WATER
4 EGGS
8 PIECES STALE BREAD, TOASTED(OR
    FRIED IN OLIVE OIL. IF YOU ARE
    NOT TOO WEIGHT CONSCIOUS)
SALT & PEPPER

Heat the olive oil in a medium
saucepan and cook the onion &
celery over a low heat until
just beginning to brown. Add
the tomatoes, salt and pepper
and cook for 20 minutes. Pour
in the boiling water and leave
to simmer. Meanwhile toast (or
fry) the bread and put on the
bottom of a fireproof soup
tureen. When the soup tastes
good (after about 30 minutes)
put the tureen over a low heat
and pour the soup over the
bread. Then break each egg
separately into the soup,
spacing them well apart and
taking care that the yolks do
not break. (For safety's sake
you can break the eggs into a
cup first.) Serve the soup as
soon as the eggs have set,
with plenty of freshly grated
parmesan or pecorino cheese
sprinkled over.

· MAIALE con LATTE ·
Pork with milk (4)

As this dish is served at Da
Laudomia, the sauce at the
end has a slightly curdled
appearance. If this offends
you, sieve the cooked sauce
and reheat gently before
serving it.

2 LB 2 OZ/1 KG LOIN OF PORK, BONED
4 OZ/100 KG BUTTER
1 LARGE TOMATO, PEELED, SEEDED
    AND FINELY CHOPPED
3 LEEKS, FINELY CHOPPED
1 STICK CELERY, DICED WITH LEAVES
2 LARGE SPRIGS FRESH THYME
1 3/4 PT/1 LTR MILK
SALT & PEPPER
FLOUR
CLOVE GARLIC, CRUSHED

Melt the butter in a casserole
large enough to hold all the
ingredients. Put in the celery,
leeks, garlic and tomatoes. Cook
over a low heat until the celery
and leeks have softened. Mean~
while snip the thyme over the
pork, roll the meat up with
the thyme inside, tie it with
string and rub salt & pepper
well into the skin. Roll tightly
in the flour and brown over a
low heat in the casserole with
the vegetables. While it is
browning, heat the milk almost
to boiling and pour over the
meat. Cover & cook for about 2
hours, or until the meat is
tender, in an oven preheated to
350°F/180°C/Mark 4. Check
occasionally to see the milk
does not burn. If the meat seems
to be drying out, add a few tbsps
of water. To serve, slice the meat
thickly & pour the sauce over it,
after scraping all the meat from
the casserole & stirring it in.

At Mario and Nadia Lupi's bar on the cliffs of Sorano, they make Gli Sfratti, a honey~filled sweet, at Christmas.

· GLI SFRATTI ·

Sweet walnut rolls (2 dozen)

This delicious sweet is extremely ancient in origin. As far as it can be traced, the Etruscans enjoyed it as much as the 'Gioca' playing customers in the Lupis' bar.

FOR THE PASTRY

4 oz/110 G GRANULATED SUGAR
4 oz/110 G COLD BUTTER, CUT IN
    SMALL PIECES
9 oz/250 G PLAIN FLOUR
1 EGG, BEATEN
PINCH OF BICARBONATE OF SODA
2 TBSP MILK (APPROXIMATE)
GRATED PEEL OF ½ LEMON

FOR THE FILLING

9 oz/250 G HONEY
9 oz/250 G WALNUTS, CHOPPED
    VERY FINELY
1 oz/25 G FINE BREADCRUMBS
GRATED PEEL OF ½ LEMON

First make the stuffing. Cook the honey over a low heat for 20 minutes. Add the walnuts and continue cooking for a further 10 minutes. Stir in the bread~crumbs and lemon peel very thoroughly and put the mixture in the refrigerator to cool. Meanwhile make the pastry. Sift the flour and bicarbonate together together onto a pastryboard or worksurface. Mix in the sugar, make a well in the middle & into this put the egg, lemon peel and butter. Rub this in and knead it to form a stiff dough, adding a little milk if necessary to keep it pliable. Put aside and chill for about 30 minutes. Then roll the dough out very thinly and trim to a width of 2 in/5 cm. Spread with a thin layer of the filling mixture. Roll the dough up carefully to form a long finger. Trim to fit onto a greased baking sheet and brush all over with beaten egg yolk. Bake in an oven preheated to 400°F/200°C/Gas 6 for 15 minutes until golden. Cool on a wire rack and serve sliced into 'fingers' or rounds.

LETTO L 2000

LETTO L 1200

PECORINO
NOSTRALE

PECORINO DI LATTE INTERO
L'AMATORE

CASEIFICIO
AMADORI

TUTTA PECORA

PECORINO SENESE

PURA
PECORA
FRESCO

TORTINO di POMODORI
Hot tomato pie (4)

This simple recipe from Tuscany's south bears a strong resemblance to the Basque dish 'piperade' without the ham. It is best cooked in the dish it will be served in and then carried, still sizzling, straight to the table.

6 EGGS, BEATEN
4 RIPE TOMATOES, PEELED, SEEDED AND CHOPPED
¼ ~ ½ HOT CHILI PEPPER, FINELY CHOPPED
1 CLOVE GARLIC, CRUSHED
4~5 FRESH BASIL LEAVES, TORN IN SMALL PIECES
½ ONION, FINELY CHOPPED
OLIVE OIL
SALT & PEPPER
GRATED PECORINO CHEESE

Cook the onion, garlic and chili pepper in oil over a low heat. When softened but not brown add the tomatoes and the basil. Cover and leave to cook just until the tomatoes look slightly mashed. Add beaten eggs, salt and pepper to taste and leave to set. When it is firm throughout but still creamy on top, sprinkle on several tablespoons of cheese and put under a hot grill until bubbling. Serve it piping hot with more basil on top and plenty of fresh crusty bread.

✳ Another simple & good 'tortino' is made by mixing 2½ tbsp flour, 7 tbsp milk, 5 tsp granulated sugar & 2 sliced apples. Fry in butter like an omelette & dust with sugar.

> ...My dear abbot, 'twixt cakes and soups
> so much cheese have you my body imbued
> that should I continue my stay with you
> I would Paulo cease to be and a form
> of cheese would I assume.
> (ATTRIBUTED TO PAULO UCCELLO WHEN HE WAS WORKING ON A
> FRESCO FOR THE ABBOT OF SAN MINIATO)

It seems likely that Uccello's surfeit was of pecorino, the pungent cheese made of sheeps milk whose origins date back to Roman times. It is still the most popular and widely available cheese in Tuscany. Some people would say too popular. There are over 100 different varieties but when trying them be open~minded. Creamy yellow Maremman pecorino is excellent & may seem more appetizing, but equally good are the small Siena cheeses with hard red rinds, & the mold covered pecorino that has absorbed different flavours from the leaves in which it has been wrapped to mature. All pecorino cheeses change character with age, varying from a Gouda~like consistency when young or 'fresco' to a pungent crumbly Parmesan texture when mature.

OLIO all'ARRABIATA
'Enraged' oil

If you are unsure of your own or your friends' liking for hot chili pepper, fill a small stoppered bottle ¾ full of olive oil and into it put a couple of whole chili peppers (slightly bruised). Left for several days, the chili will 'enrage' the oil enough to satisfy any hot~ blooded person. Serve as a condiment at the table so every~ one can add a few drops, or not to their own taste. This is a particularly good idea when serving Fettunta (page 29) or any of the robust Tuscan soups like Pappa al Pomodoro.

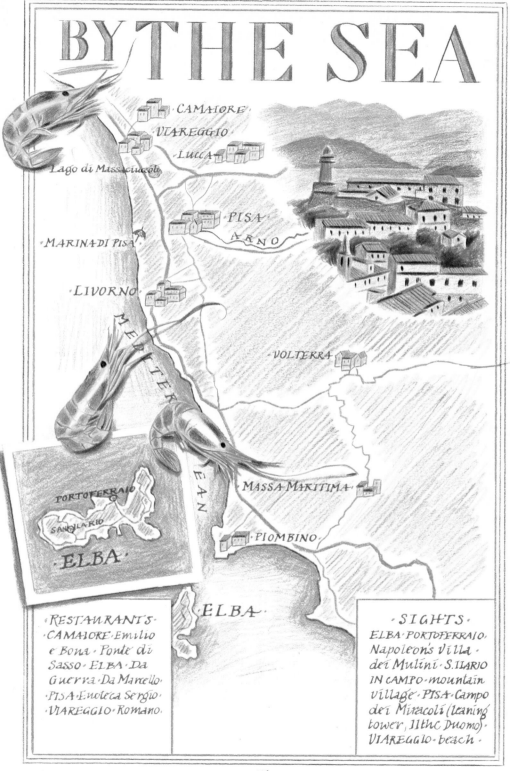

BY THE SEA

CAMAIORE
VIAREGGIO
LUCCA
Lago di Massaciucoli
PISA
ARNO
MARINA DI PISA
LIVORNO
MEDITER
VOLTERRA
MASSA MARITIMA
PORTOFERRAIO
SAN ILARIO
ELBA
PIOMBINO
ELBA

·RESTAURANTS·
·CAMAIORE·Emilio
e Bona · Ponte di
Sasso · ELBA · Da
Guerra · Da Marcello ·
PISA · Enoteca Sergio ·
VIAREGGIO · Romano.

· SIGHTS ·
ELBA·PORTOFERRAIO·
Napoleon's villa ·
dei Mulini · S.ILARIO
IN CAMPO·mountain
village · PISA·Campo
dei Miracoli (leaning
tower, 11thc Duomo) ·
VIAREGGIO · beach

· INTRODUCTION ·

An hour by ferry from the Tuscan Maremma lies mountainous Elba, the largest island in the Tuscan archipelago. Its huge supply of iron ore provides much of Italy's requirement and has been mined on the island for at least 3000 years. The main port was called Portoferraio (Port Iron) as early as the eigth century and the rich palette of Elba's wines is due to the high iron content in the soil.

Possibly because of this mineral wealth, Elba has been in turn invaded & settled by the Sicilians, Etruscans, Romans, Moors, Spanish, Pisans & finally, of course, by the French under Napoleon. It is not surprising then that the island's cuisine is such a melting pot of cookery styles, each with its own distinctive Elban twist. It is possible to eat 'puttenaio', a ratatouille-like vegetable stew, in Portoferraio, or 'la sburrida', a fish soup of Spanish origin in Capoliveri, where legend has it that Cosimo de' Medici promised sixteenth-century Spanish pirates he would leave their favourite haunt unharassed if they would do the same for his town of Cosmopolia.

Not all past visitors to Elba were military ones. The tourist trade certainly existed in 1914. In a book, Napoleon's Elba, published in that year, an Englishwoman, Lydia Bushnell Smith, mentions buying '...the obligatory picture card of the island.' But it was not until later in this century that tourists began coming to Elba for its fine sandy beaches instead of its Napoleonic associations.

Livorno, the major Tuscan commercial port, is less likely to suffer change than Elba as a result of the tourist trade. The 'ideal city' created by the Medici grand dukes suffered heavy bombing during World War 2, losing in the process much of its charm along with many of its fine buildings. The sixteenth-century foreigners who knew and loved Livorno under the old English name 'Leghorn' would barely recognize it today. Still one of the greatest ports in the Mediterranean, it is now best known for its famous fish dishes 'alla Livornese', rich with tomatoes, parsley and garlic, a style of cooking whose influence can be appreciated along most of the Tuscan coast.

On the river Arno, a few miles north, lies Pisa, a thriving port when Livorno was still a small medieval fishing village. Thriving, that is, until 1284, when Pisa's navy was destroyed in battle, & its government allowed the harbour to fill with silt. Now Pisa lies miles inland, no longer a port but a university town, one of the most respected in Italy. The university's science faculty is as strong today as it was when Galileo dropped 3 metal balls from the top of the famous leaning bell tower, the Campanile, to disprove Aristotle's theories about the acceleration of falling objects. The Campanile, along with the black & white pyjama-striped Duomo, the lovely Baptistry & the vast cemetery is both the tourist & the ecclesiastical centre of the city. But the heart of Pisa must be the market area sprawling over a maze of streets north of the Arno. Here medieval buildings lean crazily over the pavements to form narrow tunnels linking piazzas. Foreign university students jostle stout Pisan housewives for freshest mullet & tiniest 'Cee', the local name for the tiny eels that are a speciality.

The poet Percy Bysse Shelley lived for years in Tuscany & wrote some of his best poems in Pisa in the 1800s. He described the region as a 'paradise of exiles', a particularly apt description of the coastal resort Viareggio. During the summer the city's famous square, the Piazza Shelley, fills with parties of English tourists, standing mournfully in front of the poet's monument. It records that in 1822 Shelley's drowned body was washed up on Viareggio's beach, a fact that doesn't deter these same mournful tourists from later dining well in one of Viareggio's excellent fish restaurants.

When the defeated Nap~oleon arrived on Elba, he immediately set about turning his island prison into a setting more suitable for an emperor~ even if a deposed one. One of the first things he did was to convert two old windmills into the lovely villa 'Palazzino dei Mulini', which still stands today, surrounded by palm trees and cypresses on top of the hill at Portoferraio.

· PUTTENAIO ·
Prostitutes' stew (4)

Napoleon's stay, short though it was, brought a decidedly French influence to the island's cooking. Evidence is this vegetable stew, derogatorily called 'Puttenaio' (prostitute's stew) which bears a distinct resemblance to the famous French ratatouille.

1 LB 6 OZ / 600 G GREEN PEPPERS
2 LARGE POTATOES
2 AUBERGINES (EGGPLANTS)
1 STICK CELERY
CARROT
LARGE ONION
1 LB 6 OZ / 600 G RIPE TOMATOES, PEELED AND SEEDED
2 ZUCCHINI (COURGETTES)
1/4 PT OLIVE OIL
SMALL HANDFUL OF FRESH HERBS SUCH AS PARSLEY, ROSEMARY, THYME OR BASIL
COARSE SEA SALT
2 CLOVES GARLIC, CRUSHED

Cut the onion into thin slices and the rest of the vegetables into rough chunks. Heat the oil in a large saucepan and cook everything except the tomatoes and the herbs for 10~15 minutes. Add the salt and tomatoes, cover and cook over a high heat for 10 minutes. Then simmer for about 1 hour. 15 minutes before the end of cooking add the fresh herbs. This is an excellent dish served hot or cold with boiled meat.

✳ If the tomatoes are not very tasty it is a good idea to add several tablespoons of a good tomato puree at the start of cooking.

· PESCI ARROSTO ·
Grilled fish (4)

There is a story that Napoleon, on one of his frequent restless walks around Porto-ferraio, stopped to admire a catch brought in by some fishermen. The emperor was known to like simple people and simple food. After a chat with the men he invited them back to dinner at the Villa Mulini. And the dinner that night was their own fish! This recipe for grilled fresh sardines comes from Signora Pierangela Piras' excellent book L'ISOLA D'ELBA IN CUCINA, but it is such a (continued ...)

(continued from previous page...)
classic way of cooking fish that it
could well have been served
that night.

FRESH SARDINES, THE NUMBER PER
  PERSON DEPENDING ON WHETHER
  THEY ARE BEING SERVED AS A
  STARTER OR A MAIN DISH
TSP SEA SALT
CLOVE GARLIC
3 TBSP OLIVE OIL
4 OZ/100 G FENNEL BULB & LEAVES,
  FINELY CHOPPED
½ HOT CHILI PEPPER
1 TBSP WHITE WINE VINEGAR

Clean, scale and thoroughly
wash the fish, Make a marinade
by crushing all the remaining

ingredients together in a mortar,
adding more oil if necessary. Put
fish in the marinade and leave
it for 30~40 minutes, turning
often. Grill the fish, turning
once only and basting frequently
with the marinade oil. If using
a grilling rack, wipe it with oil
first so the fish don't stick.

Quite understandably, these fish
taste best cooked over a wood
fire (the Tuscans use chestnut
which is particularly aromatic)
but if you must use charcoal,
try throwing fresh herbs on it
to scent both the air & the fish.

S. ILARIO
IN CAMPO

· ZUCCHINI RIPIENO ·
Stuffed zucchini/courgettes (4)

This delicious Elban method of cooking the first young spring zucchini is equally good using small aubergines (eggplants) instead. Or serve a big mixed plateful with whole zucchini flower fritters.

8 TINY ZUCCHINI
7 OZ/200 G GROUND LEAN BEEF
4 OZ/100 G CHOPPED MORTADELLA
OLIVE OIL
OIL FOR DEEP FRYING
4 EGGS, BEATEN
4 TBSP GRATED PARMESAN
2 TBSP FRESH THYME, CHOPPED
2 CLOVES GARLIC, CRUSHED
1½ CUPS (APPROX) FINE BREAD CRUMBS

Boil the whole zucchini for 2~3 minutes until just tender. Cut in half lengthwise and remove the pulp. In a frying pan heat the olive oil and cook the beef and garlic until browned and then mix with mortadella, zucchini pulp, cheese, thyme and 2 eggs. Stuff the zucchini with this mixture and tie the two halves together with thread. Dip each stuffed zucchini into beaten egg and then roll in breadcrumbs until well covered. Deep fry or bake in a hot oven preheated to 450°F/230°C/Gas 8 until crisp and brown. Remove the thread before eating.

117

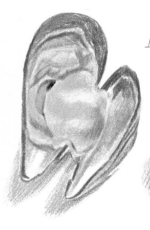

People come from all over Elba to eat at Marcello's small and cosy fish restaurant on the waterfront in the fishing village of Marciana Marina. There he serves fresh fish and regional specialities to both regular customers and discerning visitors.

SPAGHETTI alla MARINARA
Spaghetti & seafood sauce (4)

This is a loose interpretation of Marcello's delicious recipe, but it can be varied according to the season and individual taste, including crab and lobster, although that seems rather an extravagance.

1 LB/450 G THINNEST SPAGHETTI
4 OZ/100 G OCTOPUS
4 OZ/100 G CUTTLEFISH WITHOUT
   THE INKSAC
1 LB 2 OZ/500 G MUSSELS
1 LB 2 OZ/500 G ARSELLE (BABY
   CLAMS), SOAKED OVERNIGHT IN
   SALT WATER
3 TBSP FRESH CHOPPED PARSLEY
2 CLOVES GARLIC, CRUSHED
1~2 GLASSES DRY WHITE WINE
6 TBSP OLIVE OIL
SALT
1 ONION, FINELY CHOPPED

Cook half the mussels in a little water until just beginning to open. Keep half the mussels and all the clams aside. Clean the cuttlefish and octopus and chop finely. Remove the cooked mussels from their shells and chop finely. Heat the oil in a medium-sized pan and sauté the onion. When soft add the octopus, cuttlefish and chopped mussels. Cook for about 5 minutes and then add the wine. When partially evaporated, put in the garlic and parsley. After 10 minutes add the clams and mussels in their shells, adjust salt and cook for another 5~10 minutes or until they have all opened. Discard any that remain closed. Meanwhile put the spaghetti on to cook in boiling salted water. When just cooked, drain and toss with the sauce. Serve with more chopped parsley sprinkled on top.

· DA GUERRA ·

The Elbans claim it never rains in summer. Don't believe them, it can and it does. But if you, too, are unlucky, don't mourn those lost days on the beach, enjoy instead long leisurely meals, for Elban cooking has much to offer. Da Guerra in Portoferraio is a large family-run trattoria, serving excellent fish as well as other specialities.

· RISO NERO ·
Black Rice (4~6)

Riso nero was originally a Florentine dish, but it could have travelled to Elba with anyone from Cosimo de'Medici onwards. Don't be put off by its appearance ~ riso nero means black rice and black it is (made so by the cuttlefish ink-sac). But it's also a wonderful dish.

1 LB 8 OZ / 700 G SMALL CUTTLEFISH OR BABY SQUID
½ ONION, FINELY CHOPPED
3 HEAPED TBSP FINELY CHOPPED PARSLEY
2 CLOVES GARLIC, CRUSHED
1 LB 2 OZ / 500 G TOMATOES, PEELED, SEEDED AND PUT THROUGH A FOOD PROCESSOR OR VEGETABLE MILL
¼ CRUSHED CHILI PEPPER
¼ PT / 120 ML OLIVE OIL
1 LB / 450 G ITALIAN ARBORIO RICE
SEA SALT
BLACK PEPPER
½ PT / 300 ML DRY WHITE WINE

Wash the cuttlefish very well, taking care not to break the ink-sacs which should be cut off and kept aside. Chop the fish, including the tentacles, quite finely. In a deep saucepan heat the oil and cook the onion gently until soft, then add the cuttlefish. Simmer for about 10 minutes, then add the white wine. When this has evaporated put in the tomatoes, parsley, garlic, chili and salt & pepper to taste. Cook for another 15 minutes, adding water if necessary, as the sauce must be quite liquid to cook the rice. Add the rice and the 'ink' from the fish and stir well. Continue as for any other risotto: adding a little water at intervals as the rice absorbs the liquid. Once the rice is added the cooking time should be approximately 20~30 minutes. Serve hot, as a starter or light dinner.

TRIGLIA alla LIVORNESE
· Red mullet as · cooked in Livorno (4)

Livorno may not be a city that most tourists would choose to visit, but from its substantial port area come many of Tuscany's most famous fish recipes. If you encounter them far from Livorno, their heavy use of tomatoes, garlic and parsley is a clue to their origins.

12 SMALL CLEANED RED MULLETS
1 LB 2 OZ/500 G TOMATOES, PEELED, SEEDED & CHOPPED
2 CLOVES GARLIC, CRUSHED
2 SPRIGS FRESH THYME
SEA SALT
BLACK PEPPER
4 TBSP CHOPPED PARSLEY
FLOUR
OLIVE OIL FOR FRYING
½ HOT CHILI PEPPER, CRUSHED

Dust the fish liberally with flour and put in a large frying pan in which the oil has been heating. Fry for about 3~4 minutes on each side. Remove fish from pan and keep warm. Add garlic, 3 tablespoons of the parsley, thyme, and chili and cook until the garlic begins to brown. Then add tomatoes, salt and pepper and cook over a low flame for 20~30 minutes or just until the sauce begins to thicken. Return the fish to the pan, taking care not to break them and cook for a further 5 minutes. Sprinkle with remaining parsley and serve immediately.

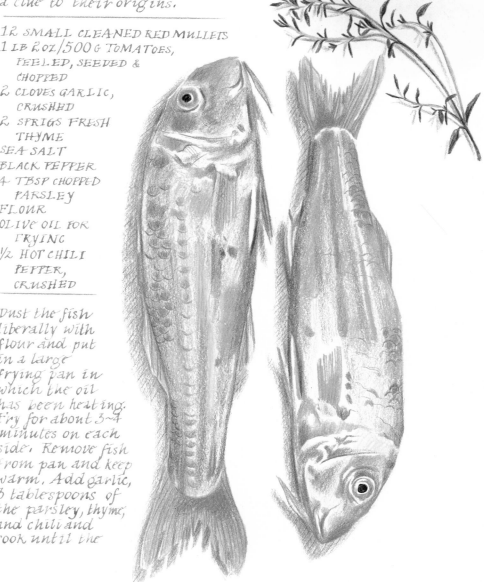

PILES OF CHEESE & SALAMI IN A PISA SHOP

One of the nicest and fastest ways to find the 'real' Pisa (not the easiest thing to do) is to wander the rabbit warren of narrow streets leading off Piazza S. Uomobuono, the main market square. Here there are vendors selling every imag~ inable, and some unimaginable, type of produce. At Tuttovo, 1 Piazza Donati, you can watch through a glass wall while they make a startling variety of pasta: everything from wild nettle ravioli to bitter chocolate tagliatelle. And there are almost as many different types and ages of Tuscan pecorino cheese at the Casa del Formaggio, where an astute enquiry may yield a free taste.

POLLO all'ARRABIATA
'Enraged' chicken (4)

This recipe is best made with the excellent free~range chickens sold at the butcher's shop in the main piazza, but is almost as good with a more ordinary bird.

1 CHICKEN, ABOUT 2½ LB / 1 KG,
   CUT IN PIECES
1 LARGE ONION, FINELY CHOPPED
½ HOT CHILI PEPPER, SLIGHTLY
   CRUSHED
2 CLOVES GARLIC, CRUSHED
4~5 TOMATOES, PEELED, SEEDED
   AND ROUGHLY CHOPPED
½ PT / 275 ML CHIANTI WINE
3 TBSP OLIVE OIL
SALT & PEPPER

Heat the oil in a large heavy saucepan and sauté the onion and garlic until golden (but not brown). Add the chicken pieces and brown well on all sides. Then add the wine, chili pepper, salt and pepper and cook over a low heat, turning frequently, until the wine is half evaporated. At this point add the tomatoes, cover and continue cooking for another 25 minutes or until the chicken is tender. Delicious when served with plain tagliatelle tossed in a little olive oil and lots of freshly chopped parsley.

✳ Other popular and delicious variations on this recipe are: the addition of 4 tsps of finely chopped capers (soaked in water to remove some of the vinegar) and 1 finely chopped anchovy fillet 10 minutes before the end of the cooking; the addition of two large finely sliced red or green peppers 15 minutes before the end of cooking; the addition of a generous handful of small green olives (previously rinsed in cold water) at the start of cooking the chicken pieces.

· CECI alla PISANA ·
Chickpea stew (4~6)

This is a hearty peasant stew that is even better cooked in advance, reheated and served in the same dish.

11 OZ/300 G DRIED CHICKPEAS
2 LARGE RIPE TOMATOES, PEELED & CHOPPED
2 TBSP FRESH CHOPPED ROSEMARY
4~6 SLICES OF BREAD
2 LARGE TINNED SARDINES, WASHED UNDER RUNNING WATER & MASHED
1 MEDIUM ONION, FINELY CHOPPED
3 CLOVES GARLIC
11 OZ/300 G BEET TOPS OR DARK GREEN CABBAGE
OLIVE OIL
COARSE SEA SALT
FRESHLY GROUND BLACK PEPPER

Cover the chickpeas with water and soak overnight in a warm place. Drain, cover with fresh water, bring to boil and cook for 1½ hours or until tender. Drain, but keep the cooking liquid. Sauté the onion, sardines and garlic in oil over medium heat in a heavy saucepan. Meanwhile briefly blanch the beet tops in some of the water used to cook the chickpeas. Remove the garlic (or not, as desired) from the onion and sardines and add the chickpeas, beet tops (with half a cup of their water), tomatoes, salt and pepper. Cook covered for about 3 hours on a low heat, adding several tablespoons of chickpea liquid if the stew seems to be drying out. Put a slice of grilled or toasted bread in each soup bowl, pour the stew over and serve with a jug of cold olive oil in which the rosemary has previously been heated for 10~15 minutes. A large bowl of bitter greens such as curly endive, chicory & dandelions makes a good accompaniment to this dish, especially if the greens are tossed with lemon juice and herb-flavoured olive oil.

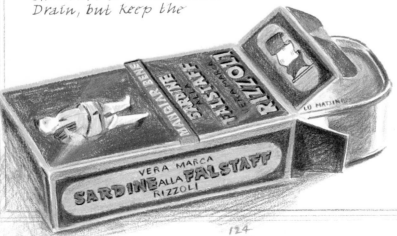

8 SMALL NEW POTATOES
7 OZ/200 G TUNA FISH (IN
OLIVE OIL)
1 MEDIUM RED ONION,
SLICED PAPER THIN
2~3 TBSP WHITE
WINE VINEGAR, TO
TASTE
HANDFUL FINELY
CHOPPED PARSLEY
1 CLOVE GARLIC,
CRUSHED
4~5 TBSP
OLIVE OIL
SALT & PEPPER

Boil the pot~
atoes in their
skins until tender
but still firm. Cut
in halves or quarters dep~
ending on their size. While
still warm season with
garlic, oil, vinegar and
onions. Break up the
tuna with a fork and add
to the potatoes. Sprinkle
with parsley and salt
and pepper to taste.

INSALATA di TONNO
• PATATE •

Tuna & potato salad (4)

The Tuscan salad of tuna
and beans is not so much
famous as infamous but
when there are fresh white
cannelloni beans available
it is still a delicious summer
dish. An alternative,
suggested by a fishmonger
in Pisa's market, is to sub~
stitute tiny new potatoes
for the beans. He uses
fresh tuna, barbecued over
a chestnut fire, but the
dish is still tasty when
made with good tinned tuna

✳ TONNO e FAGIOLI

To make the classic bean
salad, substitute 7 oz/200g
dried white beans for
potatoes. Soak the beans
overnight. Rinse and
boil in fresh water
until tender (1~1¼ hrs).
Drain and follow the
recipe above. If using
fresh cannelloni beans
boil in water for 40
minutes. This makes a
lovely summer meal when
served with chilled Pappa
al Pomodoro.

Sergio Lorenzi was not born a cook. Or perhaps he was just late in discovering his vocation. Although these days he is better with food, he worked first as a mechanic and still has a gruff straightforward manner that belies his rather more delicate touch in the kitchen. His lively and fashionable res~ taurant on the river Arno in Pisa is one of the best in the city, specializing in elegant versions of the local cuisine like 'Cee alla Pisana' (see page 140) and Trippa, spicy with nutmeg and fresh herbs. He serves (and sells) oil made from his own olives and swears it is some of the best in Tuscany for raw vegetables and salads because of the salty sea breezes that blow in from the coast.

ZUPPA del TARLATI VESCOVO

· Chicken soup ·
alla Bishop Tarlati (8~10)

Shortly after opening his own restaurant in 1976 Sergio wrote a cookbook with every~ thing in it from tips on how to organise a good kitchen, to recipes retrieved from rare sixteenth~century notes found in a Tuscan library. Among the recipes was this one from Arezzo for Zuppa del Tarlati Vescovo which Bishop Tarlati may well have brought with him from the papal court in Avignon. Its creamy richness bears a close resemblance to the French 'Soupe à la Reine'.

2 OZ/50 G BUTTER
2 OZ/50 G PLAIN WHITE FLOUR
3½ PT/2 LTRS GOOD CHICKEN STOCK
2½ LB/1.3 KG BOILING CHICKEN
1 ONION, COARSELY CHOPPED
1 STICK CELERY & LEAVES,
   COARSELY CHOPPED
½ TSP WHOLE PEPPERCORNS
3~4 CLOVES
2 BAY LEAVES
100 G DOUBLE CREAM
4 PIECES OF BREAD, CUT IN HALF
   & TOASTED OR FRIED IN OIL
SALT

In a heavy saucepan, melt the butter and mix in the flour to make a roux. Very slowly add the chicken stock, stirring well with a wooden spoon to avoid lumps. Bring slowly to a boil, still stirring. In the meantime wash the chicken and stuff with the onion, celery, peppercorns, cloves and bayleaves. Sew up the cavity to prevent anything escaping. Put the chicken in the broth already prepared and simmer for 45 minutes to an hour. Take the chicken out, remove skin and chop the breast meat finely. Pound the thigh meat into a paste in a mortar and mix thoroughly with the cream. Skim the original broth and add slowly to the mixture to obtain a smooth velvety soup. Stir in the breast meat, salt to taste, reheat and serve over the bread.

MINESTRA di PESCE
· Fish soup (4~6) ·

Sergio originally comes from Camaiore, between Lucca and Viareggio, an area that prob~ ably has more soup recipes per square mile than any~ where in Tuscany. This is one for a fish soup that unlike Cacciuco, is very simple to prepare. A speciality of the trawling fishermen of the river Serchio, it should, if
(continued...)

(continued ...)
possible, have eel in it to make
a good traditional soup.

1½ lb / 700 g SALT WATER FISH
   (ANCHOVIES, BRILL ETC)
   CLEANED & CUT INTO
   LARGE CHUNKS
11 oz / 300 g FRESH WATER FISH (EEL,
   TROUT ETC) CLEANED & CUT
   INTO LARGE CHUNKS
3 ~ 4 CLOVES GARLIC, CRUSHED
HANDFUL ROUGHLY CHOPPED
   FRESH PARSLEY
1 ONION, CHOPPED
1 STICK CELERY, CHOPPED
1 CARROT, CHOPPED
2 TOMATOES, CHOPPED
PEEL OF 1 LEMON
RIND (LEFTOVER) OF PECORINO
   OR PARMESAN CHEESE
6 TBSP OLIVE OIL
SALT & PEPPER

In 3½ pints / 1½ litres water
boil the onion, carrot, celery,
tomatoes, lemon peel and
cheese rind for about 20
minutes. In the meantime
put the oil and garlic in a
large heavy pan until the
garlic slightly browns. Add
the chopped parsley and stir
2 or 3 times, then add the
fish. Brown slightly on
both sides, then add to the
broth and continue to boil
for about 20 minutes. Ad~
just salt and pepper and
put everything through a
food processor or vegetable
mill (not too fine as the
soup should have a chunky
texture). Pour the soup into
a tureen into which you
have put 2 large slices of
bread fried in oil & rubbed
with garlic.

· SORBETTO al VINO ·
ROSSO CON PROFUMO
—— di LAMPONE ——

Red wine sorbet with
raspberries (4 ~ 6)

Like so many other excellent
ideas, the making of fresh
fruit sorbets was invented
in Tuscany, taken to France
in the sixteenth century
and made famous there.
However, it still remains a
very Italian skill. At Sergio's
a light sorbet like this one
is often served between
courses to provide a refreshing
pause, particularly between
dishes of fish and meat.

---

1 PINT / ½ LTR YOUNG RED
   WINE, PREFERABLY FIZZY
7 oz / 200 g FRESH RASPBERRIES,
   SLIGHTLY CRUSHED
5 oz / 150 g SUGAR
5 ~ 6 FRESH MINT LEAVES
   (AND MORE FOR GARNISH)

Boil the sugar, mint leaves
and wine together for 2
minutes or until the sugar
is dissolved. Add to the
raspberries and allow to sit
for at least 1 hour, stirring
occasionally. Remove the
mint and put the mixture
through a food processor.
Freeze in an ice tray in the
freezer (normal ice~making
setting) for about 3 hours,
stirring frequently until
no more ice crystals form.
Serve with more mint
leaves (dipped in
sugar & water,
then frozen)
as a
garnish.

A variation on this basic red wine sorbet is to add the finely grated peel (using only the outside skin, not the white pith) of ½ an orange or ½ a lemon just before freezing. Or, for a more del~icately coloured sorbet, use one of the new pale Tuscan rosés or spumante~style sparkling wines instead of the red wine suggested, and white seedless grapes instead of the raspberries.

· DA ROMANO ·

Walk around the rather seedy streets of Viareggio now and it is possible to chart the gradual decline over the decades of this once grand old dame of Italian coastal resorts. Her heyday was the turn of the century when most of the still remark~ ably beautiful Art Nouveau hotels and casinos were built. Then came the slightly less elegant, but still sleek 1920s and 1930s, with their ocean liner facades and Art Deco neon signs. Then, finally, the inevitable 1960's and 1970's plasticized consumerism. Viareggio today is more deserving of a place in her own outrageous spring carnival than in a polite drawing room. But if the pearls are a bit tarnished, the oysters and clams are still fresh, and it is possible to find hidden in the back~streets some of the best fish restaurants in Tuscany. One is Romano Franceschini's, where he and his wife Franca, who is the cook, serve excellent versions of local seafood specialities.

SPAGHETTI al CARTOCCIO
Spaghetti with seafood cooked in a bag (4)

This is one of Franca's special recipes. When the 'cartoccio' is opened at the table it gives off a delicious aroma that is one of the highlights of the dish.

11 OZ/300 G SPAGHETTI
20 BABY SQUID, CLEANED ✳
4 GIANT PRAWNS
10 BABY CLAMS, CLEANED
8 LARGE CLAMS, CLEANED
6 MUSSELS, CLEANED
1 RED MULLET, CLEANED & BONED
1 CLOVE GARLIC, CRUSHED
6~8 BASIL LEAVES
6 TBSP OLIVE OIL
4 RIPE TOMATOES, PEELED,
   SEEDED & FINELY CHOPPED
1/4 CHILI PEPPER, FINELY CHOPPED
2 TBSP PARSLEY, FINELY CHOPPED
SALT

Put 5 PT/3 LTR water in a large saucepan and bring to the boil. Meanwhile heat the oil in a cast~iron pan and in it cook the chili, garlic and all the fish. After 5~10 minutes, add the tomatoes, basil and parsley. Cook over a low heat for another 5~10 minutes. When the water in the big pot is boiling add salt and the spaghetti. When half cooked, drain and add to the fish. Adjust seasoning. Take a large piece of aluminum foil and fold it in half. Open it out flat and place on a large plate or serving dish. Put the fish and spaghetti on half the foil. Fold the edges of the foil together on all three sides so no juices or steam can escape. Place the dish in an oven preheated to 475°F/250°C/Gas 9 for 5 minutes or until the foil puffs up. Take immediately to the table and serve.

✳ To clean clams & mussels, scrub the shells with a stiff brush under cold running water until clean. Cut off the mussels' beards (the stringy tufts that protrude from the shells) and discard any of the shellfish that are not tightly

(continued...)

· PENNE ·

· PAPPARDELLE ·

· RAVIOLI · ROLLING · PIN ·

· RAVIOLI · STAMP ·

· RAVIOLI ·

· TORTELLI ·

· TAGLIATELLE ·

· MACCHERONI (TUSCAN) ·

· FUSILLI ·

· PICI ·

(continued from previous page...)
closed, or rather that do not close up again when lightly tapped. Continue to rinse the shellfish under running water until no more sand or grit appears.

ROMBO al FORNO con ASPARAGI
• Turbot baked with asparagus (6) •

This is another of Franca Franceschini's modern adaptations of a regional fish dish.

1 LB 12 OZ / 800 G TURBOT
6 SCAMPI
1 OZ / 20 G BUTTER
2 TBSP OIL
20 ASPARAGUS TIPS
2 WINE GLASSES FISH STOCK
SALT & PEPPER

Clean & wash the turbot. Shell the scampi & remove the black intestinal track but not the heads. Pat fish dry and flour lightly, only flouring the

white part of the turbot. Arrange the fish in
a greased baking dish with the asparagus tips, salt
& freshly ground black pepper. Dot with butter and
pour over the oil & about 2 wine glasses of
good fish stock. Bake in an oven preheated
to 400°F/200°C/Gas 6 for 20 minutes. Serve hot.

✳Make good fish stock by boiling together
the following ingredients: 4 or 5 fish heads,
½ onion, 1 bay leaf, 1 stick celery, 5 peppercorns,
1 tsp sea salt   1 clove garlic, 5 wine
                        glasses water & 5 tbsp
                        dry white wine. After
                        20 minutes, remove the
                        bay leaf & pass other
                        ingredients through
                        a food processor or mouli.

UMBRELLA CASES
OFF SEASON
-VIAREGGIO-

· THE CERRAGIOLI FAMILY ·

Drive up into the hills between Camaiore and Lucca and keep going until you run out of road. If you have taken the right road you will probably be at the village of Greppolungo. Park your car and walk to the only alimentari shop there. You will find Paulo Cerragioli and his wife selling their own excellent olive oil and, if you are lucky and have had the sense to ring beforehand, they will be ready and willing to cook you an excellent meal. They serve only a few dishes, and theirs is the real 'casalinga' ~ the home cooking that is almost impossible to find in restaurants.

LA GALLINA RIPIENA
Stuffed chicken (6)

This recipe for stuffed boiled chicken is one of the best and most typical of the Camaiore area. At Greppolungo they splash rough red wine into the chicken broth just before serving, an interesting Tuscan variation on sherry in consommé.

1 LARGE BOILING FOWL WITH
   GIBLETS
2 CARROTS
1 STICK CELERY
1 ONION
SALT
1 LEEK
OLIVE OIL

FOR THE STUFFING
2 SLICES HAM OR MORTADELLA
   SAUSAGE, CHOPPED
2 SPRIGS FRESH THYME, CHOPPED
3 SLICES BREAD, SOAKED IN MILK
6 TBSP PECORINO CHEESE, GRATED
8 OZ/225 G GROUND (MINCED) VEAL
   OR LEAN BEEF
1 ~ 2 EGGS
2 CLOVES GARLIC, CRUSHED
4 TBSP OLIVE OIL
3 TBSP PARSLEY, FINELY CHOPPED
½ ~ ¾ TSP NUTMEG

First make the stuffing. In a large frying pan gently cook the chicken giblets in the oil until they change colour. Chop finely and reserve. Add the sausage, meat and garlic to the pan and cook just until the meat starts to brown. Mix with the giblets, herbs, bread, cheese and 1 beaten egg. If this does not bind the stuffing, add another beaten egg.

Clean, wash and dry the inside of the chicken. Pack loosely with the stuffing ~ the stuffing tends to swell in cooking and you don't want an exploding chicken. Sew up both ends of the chicken so that nothing can escape. Put in a large flame~ proof casserole with the carrots, celery, onion, leek and salt and cover with water. The water should be about 1in/2.5cm over the chicken. Bring to a boil and then simmer over a low heat for about 2½ hours, until the chicken is cooked. Remove it from the pan, cut the threads, carefully lift out the stuffing, which should be quite solid, and serve both the chicken and the stuffing sliced thinly and garnished with either fresh thyme or Tuscan salsa verde (see page 75). To make a complete meal of this, remove the vegetables from the broth and boil fresh tortellini or ravioli gnudi (page 78) in it to serve as soup before the chicken.

Of course Cacciucco is a Mediterranean fish soup, originally from Livorno, as the Livornese will proudly tell you; and the cooks in Viareggio will disdainfully say that no good ever came from Livorno, and certainly not Cacciucco. Its a subject for endless, inconclusive debates. Certainly one of the best versions of cacciucco must be that served at the Ponte di Sasso restaurant outside Camaiore. A good cacciucco is a joy to behold, like fine wine first enjoy its rich colour, then its bouquet and finally the time the rich flavour remains on the tongue.

· CACCIUCCO ·
Fish soup (6)

Cacciucco is a poor man's dish, at least theoretically, so most of the fish should be cheap, salt water scaled ones ~ not salmon or sole! There should also be at least five different types of fish, preferably more. Franco, the brilliant chef at Ponte di Sasso, used twelve.

10 LB 10 OZ/5 KG ~ ½ ORDINARY
   SCALED FISH SUCH AS DOGFISH,
   NON BONY PIECES OF EEL, ½ A
   MIXTURE OF SQUID, CUTTLEFISH,
   OCTOPUS, SHRIMP, CLAMS
   AND MUSSELS
3 CLOVES GARLIC, CRUSHED
4 TBSP TOMATO PUREE
2 TBSP RED WINE VINEGAR
4 TBSP FRESH PARSLEY, CHOPPED
SMALL HOT CHILI PEPPERS (1~2)
½ BOTTLE ROBUST RED WINE (DRY)
6 PIECES WHOLEMEAL BREAD
2~3 TOMATOES, PEELED AND
   CHOPPED ROUGHLY
      COARSE SEA SALT
       BLACK PEPPER,
       FRESHLY
       GROUND
       OLIVE OIL

Clean and scale the fish, cut off and save the heads and tails for stock. Remove the beak and insides of the squid and the cuttlefish's ink sac. (Your fishmonger may do this for you if you ask, but be sure that you ask him for the heads and tails.) Put the fish heads and tails, 1 clove garlic, 2 tbsp parsley, the tom~ atoes and tomato puree in a large pan with 1 pint/600 ml of water and bring to the boil. Cover and simmer for 20 minutes.

136

Discard the fish heads and tails. Add the fish, beginning with the boniest variety (ask your fishmonger's advice), cover and simmer for 20 minutes. Rub through a sieve and continue cooking the various more tender fish, for a further 15 minutes. Meanwhile, saute the other two crushed cloves of garlic in a large pan. When just turning brown add salt,

chili pepper, pepper and remaining parsley. Put in the shellfish, squid and cuttlefish and when the water they release has evaporated, add the vinegar. Swirl around the pan and pour in the red wine. When this has almost evaporated add the extra tomatoes (if desired) and continue cooking for 15 minutes. Toast the bread, rub thoroughly with fresh garlic and put in bowls. Pour the rest of the fish, in their rich tomato sauce, over the top. Serve immediately. Cacciucco is meant to be a complete meal in a dish rather than just a first course. It should be served with plenty of crusty bread and look more like a hearty fish stew than a soup, its wide variety of fish and crustaceans only just covered by a thick binding of hot and garlicky sauce.

· POLENTA MATUFFI ·
Sausage & polenta stew (6)

This is a sturdy, old-fashioned peasant dish, redolent of cheese and spicy sausages. It should be eaten with a spoon and a minimum of good table manners, and of course plenty of equally
(continued...)

In Viareggio there is a tradition that in addition to the healthy quantity of whiting, hake, red mullet, John Dory, gurnard and crawfish, a good cacciucco should always contain one stone from the ocean. Perhaps this is because cacciucco is a dish that was eaten originally only by Tuscan fishermen. Whatever they scooped up with their nets and lines went in the cooking pot.

Although the origins of cacciucco are thus very humble, it can be made as elegant as the fish used. The only absolutely essential ingredient (apart from the stone) is the hot chili pepper.

(continued from previous page,
sturdy young red wine should be
available to wash it down.

1 LB 2 OZ/500 G FINE GRAIN CORN
   MEAL, SIFTED
6 BIG LEAN TUSCAN SAUSAGES
1/4 PT/120 ML OLIVE OIL
2 LB 2 OZ/1 KG TOMATOES, PEELED
   AND CHOPPED
3/4 OZ/15 G DRIED MUSHROOMS,
   SOAKED FOR AT LEAST 10 MINUTES
   IN WARM WATER, DRAINED
   & CHOPPED
1 SMALL CARROT, CHOPPED
1 SMALL STICK CELERY, CHOPPED
1 ONION, CHOPPED
BAY LEAF
1/2 BOTTLE RED WINE
GENEROUS QUANTITIES OF
   GRATED PECORINO OR PARMESAN
SALT & PEPPER

Heat the oil in a medium-sized
sauce pan. Saute the carrot,
onion and celery in it until
softened. Mash the sausages
with a fork, add to the pan and
brown with the vegetables. Skim
off 1/2 the fat (if there is any) and
add the red wine. When it has
almost evaporated, add the mushrooms. Brown and put in the
tomatoes and bay leaf. Simmer
gently for 20 minutes. Mean~
while bring 1 3/4 pt/1 ltr of
salted water to the boil in a
large pan. Add the corn meal
very slowly, stirring constantly
with a wooden spoon to prevent
lumps forming. Continue
cooking and stirring for 20
minutes. Then put a ladleful
of polenta into each bowl,
followed by a ladleful of sauce &
lots of cheese. Continue in
layers with each bowl until the
sauce is finished.

Scarpaccia is a zucchini pie without pastry from the region around Camaiore. At the beautiful Art Nouveau hotel Il Giardinetto in northern Tuscany they serve a delicious version called Torta di Zucchini, as well as another delicious Tuscan side dish, Panzerotti. These are golf~ball size pieces of raw bread dough that are wrapped around chunks of cooked sausage or pecorino cheese and then deep~fried to a crisp gol~den brown and sprinkled with coarse sea~salt.

SCARPACCIA
Zucchini pie (6)

The name Scarpaccia means 'old, flat battered shoe' and refers to the fact that the pie should have a sim~ilar appearance. There are two versions, a sweet one somewhat like Lucca's Torta di Verdure (page 148) and this savoury one, an ideal side dish with summer roasts and salads.

14 OZ /400G SMALLEST ZUCCHINI/ COURGETTES (WITH THEIR FLOWERS IF POSSIBLE)
3 LARGE SPRING ONIONS, FINELY CHOPPED
½ CLOVE GARLIC, CRUSHED
½ CUP MILK & WATER, MIXED
4 TBSP FLOUR, SIFTED
2 EGGS
4 TBSP GRATED PARMESAN
SALT & PEPPER
OLIVE OIL

Finely chop the zucchini. Salt them and allow to drain for 20 minutes. In the meantime, beat together the eggs, flour, milk and water to form a smooth batter. Rinse salt off the zucchini and dry with kitchen paper towels. Mix the zucchini, onions, cheese and garlic into the batter and pour into 2 greased 8in/ 20.5cm baking tins. (You can use 1 large one, but the batter should not be more than ½ in /1 cm deep.) Drizzle sev~eral tablespoons of olive oil on top and bake in an oven pre~heated to 425°F/220°C/Gas 7 until set and golden brown on top ~ about 30 minutes. Serve with more grated cheese on top if desired.

· CEE alla PISANA ·

Probably the most famous dish in Pisa
is 'Cee alla Pisana'. Cee is Tuscan
slang for 'cieche' meaning blind, and
also for the tiny baby eels ('elvers' in England)
that are caught at the mouth of the Arno
during the winter months. In Pisa the
eels (4oz/100g per person), are first
washed several times and dried very well.
Then they are put into a frying pan with
lots of very hot oil in which have been
browned 2 cloves of garlic, 3~4 sage leaves
and ½ hot chili pepper finely chopped. The
little eels, no more than 3in/7.5cm long, are
stirred rapidly for about 15 minutes until
they turn white, then mixed with 2 beaten
eggs, the juice of
a lemon and 3
tablespoons grated
parmesan. This is
stirred until just
barely set and
served still creamy,
looking rather like
spaghetti carbonara.

OLIVES & CHESTNUTS

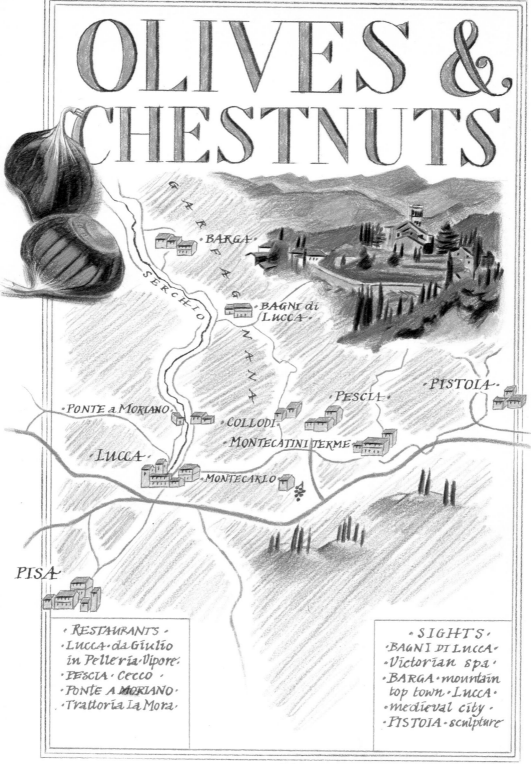

GARFAGNANA

SERCHIO

· BARGA ·

· BAGNI di LUCCA ·

· PISTOIA ·

· PESCIA ·

· PONTE a MORIANO ·

· COLLODI ·

· MONTECATINI TERME ·

· LUCCA ·

· MONTECARLO ·

PISA ·

· RESTAURANTS ·
· LUCCA · da Giulio
in Pelle ria · Vipore ·
· PESCIA · Cecco ·
· PONTE A MORIANO ·
· Trattoria La Mora ·

· SIGHTS ·
· BAGNI DI LUCCA ·
· Victorian spa ·
· BARGA · mountain
top town · LUCCA ·
· medieval city ·
· PISTOIA · sculpture

· INTRODUCTION ·

The Garfagnana and Pistoian mountains, high foot-hills of the rugged Appennines, are divided lengthwise by the river Serchio. Tiny villages, where rocks hold red roof tiles in place, cling perilously to steep hillsides, their bars and outdoor cafes dropping away to the valleys below. Because this is a relatively poor region of Tuscany, the best cooking makes good use of available local products ~ trout fresh from the rivers, porcini the size of t~bone steaks and a stunning variety of other wild mushrooms, simple flat cakes made with sweet chestnut flour and smeared with honey and creamy ricotta cheese, and everywhere near Lucca, the famous Luccan olive oil, considered the best in the world.

Perhaps because of its remoteness and its history of poverty, the wild Garfagnana region north of Lucca remains unspoilt, in fact almost undiscovered, by the tourists that have overrun the Tuscan coast. Hill towns like beautiful Barga, with steep cobbled streets and honey~coloured buildings, have sweeping views of pine forests, castles and distant snowy mountains. West of Barga, straggling along rivers a startling shade of turquoise, are towns whose streets rise almost vertically from the river bank into high mountain fields. During World War 2 many of these moun~tain villages were havens for the Italian resistance, their remoteness making them almost impossible for the government troops to control. Memories of those war years are still fresh and many stories are told in the bars of escaped prisoners hidden for months in cellars or shepherds' huts.

On the southernmost edge of the Garfagnana moun~tains lies walled Lucca, birthplace of the opera composer Giacomo Puccini, and the only city in Tuscany to resist Florence successfully. It remained an indep~endant city state until becoming part of the Grand Duchy of Tuscany in the nineteenth century and even today preserves an air of aloofness.

Lucca, with Siena, is one of the loveliest small cities in Italy. The poverty of the Garfagnana seems not to have penetrated the massive sixteenth century walls. John Ruskin, writing in the nineteenth century, claimed to have begun his study of architecture after seeing Lucca's beautifully preserved twelfth~century buildings, built '... in material so incorruptible, that after 600 years of sunshine & rain, a lancet could not now be put between their joints.' Narrow medieval streets between these buildings lead quietly to huge windy piazzas and past elaborate Romanesque churches like tiered marble wedding cakes.

From the plane tree~shaded pathway that tops the city walls living trees growing on the high tower of the Palazzo Guinigi are clearly visible, as are private and public gardens hidden from city streets by the red brick facades of palaces built during the fourteenth and fifteenth centuries~Lucca's richest period. The Palazzo Pfanner is one of the most elegant with symmetrical rows of white marble statues and lemon trees in terracotta pots, but it cannot match for splendour the summer palaces outside Lucca, built by Lucchese nobility between the sixteenth and eighteenth centuries. Three of them, Villa Imperiale at Marlia, Villa Mansi at Segromigno & Villa Torrigiani at Camigliano, lie in magnificent gardens in cool hills to the north of the city. At the Villa Imperiale, summer residence of Napoleon's sister Elisa Baciocchi, Paganini (said to have been one of her many lovers) gave his first musical performance.

It is not only Lucca's past that is attractive. Like Siena the city is famous for its sweet breads and pastries, and where better to sample them than sitting in one of the many sunny cafes, set in flowered courtyards, distracted only by the occasional (and inevitable) moped buzzing past?

· PALAZZO · PFANNER ·

144

Lucca is an elegant little city rather than a town and the pleasures to be enjoyed there are naturally rather more sophisticated than in the villages of the Garfagnana. The lovely, well~preserved turn~of~the~century shop fronts and signs are particularly pleasing. If you're exploring the city walls on a hot day, a glass of the local white wine, Montecarlo Buonamico, at the beautiful Antico Caffe della Mura, is a certain reviver. Or, in less auspicious weather, find your way to Puccini's favourite cafe, Cafe di Simo, for cups of frothy cappucino and Torta di Verdure, Lucca's great speciality.

· TORTA di VERDURE ·
Sweet spinach pie

This sweet is sold in most of Lucca's delicatessans & tastes something like a Tuscan ver~ sion of American pumpkin pie.

FOR THE PASTRY
11 oz/300G PLAIN WHITE FLOUR
3 1/4 oz/80G SUGAR
4 oz/100G BUTTER, SOFTENED
2 EGG YOLKS
PINCH SALT

FOR THE FILLING
7 oz/200 G ZUCCHINI/COURGETTES
11 oz/300 G SPINACH OR
  SWISS CHARD
3 oz/75G SUGAR
2 oz/50 G PINE NUTS
1 1/4 oz/30 G RAISINS
1 EGG, BEATEN
2 TBSP GRATED ORANGE PEEL
2 TBSP GRATED PARMESAN
1/2 TSP CINNAMON
1/2 TSP NUTMEG
PINCH SALT
1~1 1/4 oz/25~30 G BUTTER

To make the pastry, sift the flour on to a pastry board or work~ surface. Make a hole in the middle and put in the butter, sugar, salt and egg yolks. Work into a soft smooth dough with your fingertips. Cover and leave for 2 hours in a warm place.

To make the filling, first chop the zucchini and spinach finely, discarding any tough stalks. Wash and drain well, then sim~ mer in the butter until soft. Let cool and then mix well with the other ingredients.

When the dough is ready, cut off about a quarter and keep aside to make a lattice top for the pie. Roll the remainder out into a large circle and place in a greased, floured flan dish. Pour in the filling. Roll out the remaining pastry and cut into strips for the lattice top. Brush with beaten egg yolk and bake for 25~30 minutes in an oven preheated to 375°F/190°C/Gas 5 (until a toothpick put into the centre of the pie comes out dry).

· DA GIULIO IN PELLERIA ·

Lucca and olives are synonymous. In fact some gastronomes consider the delicate Luccan olive oils to be among the world's best, although there is stiff competition from i colli senesi oils ~ the green gold of the hills around Siena. When the olives are plump and ideal for eating, they are pickled with lemon, cinnamon, salt and hot chili peppers ~a particular speciality at the Ristorante Vipore, west of Lucca. Or else they are used to add bite to fatty rabbit or lamb stews, as in the recipe below.

AGNELLO CON OLIVE NERE
Lamb and black olive stew (4~6)

Variations on this recipe are served in many of the restaurants of the area, but it is particularly good at the Buca di San Antonio as well as at the little cafe Da Giulio, both in the back streets of Lucca.

You can give this dish something of the tang provided by fresh olives if you add a tablespoon of grated lemon peel during the cooking.

2 LB 2 OZ / 1 KG STEWING LAMB
14-OZ / 400 G RIPE TOMATOES, PEELD & SEEDED
30 PLUMP BLACK OLIVES (OR MORE ACCORDING TO TASTE)
6~8 TBSP OLIVE OIL
2 SPRIGS FRESH ROSEMARY
2 (GENEROUS) WINE GLASSES OF DRY WHITE WINE
2 CLOVES GARLIC, CRUSHED
SEA SALT
BLACK PEPPER

Put the oil in a big frying pan and gently cook the garlic and rosemary. When the garlic is golden add the lamb cut in bite size chunks and brown it. Add the wine and when it has almost evaporated, the tomatoes (and the lemon peel if desired). Stir, cover and cook over a low heat for 15 minutes. If using fresh olives boil them for sev~ eral minutes; if using pickled ones (tinned, bottled etc) rinse them well. Add to the lamb, cover and cook very slowly un~ til the meat is tender, about 1½ hours, adding warm water or stock if the stew seems to be drying out. For a less rich stew skim off any visible fat that rises during cooking. Serve poured over polenta or with tiny boiled potatoes to soak up the sauce.

✳ When buying olive oil, be sure to get 'cold pressed extra virgin' from the first pressing. It is the best, expensive even in Italy, but well worth the price. Olive oils are classed by their acidity level; the less acidic they are, the better and more costly. During oil~pressing time (Nov~ Feb) around Lucca you may come across a soup called 'Zuppa alla Frantoiana' or 'oil~press soup'. It is basically a form of Ribollita. Where Ribollita is usually yes~ terday's minestrone re~heated today, Zuppa alla Frantoiana has zucchini, carrots, celery, onions and cabbage cooked freshly, mixed with pre~cooked beans & ham, & served with a jug of the newly pressed olive oil.

some of 'La Cucina Povera' ~ dishes that might have otherwise disappeared, if not from Tuscan homes, at least from Tuscan restaurant menus.

TRATTORIA LA MORA

Some restaurants serve food. Others serve atmosphere ~ a taste of a place, of its people, its countryside and its history. Sauro Brunicardi's Trattoria La Mora, north of Lucca, is one of these. The wine (from his own enoteca) is excellent, the food delicious and creative, but almost more important is the warmth & generosity of Signor Brunicardi and his staff. Sauro Brunicardi is one of the small group of Italian restauranteurs who in 1980 formed 'La Linea Italia in Cucina' to preserve the traditional regional cooking of Italy, and to serve carefully researched and prepared dishes from their own areas. As a result of this fidelity to tradition, with additional ingenuity because not all traditional food is necessarily good, it is still possible to find

· GRAN FARRO ·
Grain and bean soup (4)

Gran Farro is traditional wheat soup made in Tuscany from raw spelt (hard wheat) but if unavailable you can make a similar soup using buckwheat (kasha) boiled for about an hour.

5 OZ/150 G RAW SPELT OR
   GERMAN WHEAT, BOILED
   FOR AT LEAST 3 HOURS
9 OZ/250 G DRIED OR 1 LB 6 OZ/
   600 G FRESH KIDNEY BEANS
½ ONION, SLICED THINLY
3 TBSP OLIVE OIL
STICK CELERY, DICED WITH LEAVES
CLOVE GARLIC, CRUSHED
4 OZ/100 G PROSCIUTTO OR FATTY
   HAM, FINELY CHOPPED
8 OZ/225 G TOMATOES, PEELED,
   SEEDED & FINELY SIEVED
3~4 SAGE LEAVES
1 TSP MARJORAM
½ TSP NUTMEG
SALT &
PEPPER

Boil fresh beans in water un~
til tender (about 1~1½ hrs).
If using dried beans, soak them
overnight, rinse and then boil
in fresh water for about 45
minutes. Drain and put
through a food processor or
mouli, reserving the water &
¼ of the whole beans. Heat
the oil in a deep saucepan &
add the onion, ham, celery,
garlic, sage, marjoram and
nutmeg. Saute gently and
when the onion starts to
brown, add the tomatoes,
salt and pepper to taste. Sim~
mer for about 15 minutes
until the mixture is well
blended. Add the bean puree
with a little of its own water.
Mix well before adding the
wheat. Simmer for about 40
minutes, adding more
bean water if the soup
seems to be drying out.
About 10 minutes before
the end of this time,
add the whole beans
and allow to heat
through. Serve with a jug
of olive oil to pour over.

GARMUGIA alla LUCCHESE
· Spring vegetable ·
soup as made in Lucca (6)

This is a soup made only in
the spring when the tiniest
fresh vegetables are available.
The cooking times given are
approximate ~ the vegetables
should be just barely cooked
and served while
they are still a
bright clear green.

---

4 SPRING ONIONS,
  FINELY CHOPPED
1 LB 2 OZ /500 G GROUND
  (MINCED) LEAN BEEF
4 OZ /100 G PROSCIUTTO OR BACON
7 OZ /200 G FRESH BROAD BEANS,
  SHELLED
TENDER LEAVES FROM 3 ART~
  ICHOKES, TRIMMED
    9 OZ /250 G FRESH
      PEAS, SHELLED
    2 CLOVES GARLIC
    7 OZ /200 G TENDER
      ASPARAGUS, CHOPPED
    3 ~4 CUPS BEEF STOCK
    5 TBSP OLIVE OIL
    SALT & PEPPER

Heat the oil in a deep pan. Add
the onions, garlic & ham &
when the onion starts to brown
add the beef. Saute for 5 min~
utes, then add the artichokes
and broad beans. If the mix~
ture needs moistening, add
a drop or two of oil, but if pos~
sible the vegetables should cook
in their own juices. When the
vegetables are starting to soften,
but still firm, pour in the stock.
After 5~10 minutes, add peas &
asparagus & cook until tender.
Serve over toasted bread.

· CRESPELLE ·
alla FIORENTINA
Spinach crepes

This dish is of questionable
Tuscan origin, but Beppe the
chef makes crepes with such
verve and expertise it would
be a pity to leave them out.
You can toss the pancakes if
you do not possess the asbes~
tos fingertips needed to
turn them by hand as
Beppe does.

· FOR THE BATTER ·
3½ OZ /90 G PLAIN WHITE FLOUR
3 EGGS, BEATEN
2 WINEGLASSES MILK
SALT
OIL

· FOR THE FILLING ·
14 OZ /400 G RICOTTA
1 LB 6 OZ /600 G FRESH SPINACH
1 EGG, BEATEN
½ TSP NUTMEG
SALT
FRESHLY GROUND BLACK
PEPPER

· FOR THE SAUCE ·

3 OZ/75G FLOUR PLAIN WHITE
3 OZ/75 G BUTTER
1¼ PT/3/4 LTR MILK
SALT & PEPPER
5 TBSP OF A HOMEMADE
  TOMATO SAUCE (AS A
  GARNISH) OR 3 VERY TASTY
  TOMATOES, PEELED, SEEDED
  & FINELY CHOPPED
3 TBSP GRATED PECORINO OR
  PARMESAN CHEESE

To make the filling, trim & clean spinach, remove any tough stalks and cook, covered, in a little water until tender. Drain well through a fine-mesh sieve or strainer, pressing with the back of a wooden spoon to get out all the water. Chop very finely and mix with the other ingredients.

To make the sauce, melt the butter in a pan, add the flour and once blended with the fat, cook for a few minutes over a low heat. Add the milk gradually, stirring all the time to prevent lumps forming. When all the milk has been added, raise the temperature and bring sauce to the boil. Cook for 2-3 minutes, continuing to stir. Remove from the heat and add salt and black pepper to taste.

To make the crepes, sift the flour into a basin, make a well in the middle and put in the eggs and salt. Beat in the milk gradually, using either a wooden spatula or a small sauce whisk. Stir rapidly at first, then more slowly while mixing the flour from the sides of the bowl. The batter must be quite liquid and never thick or doughy. Leave for 30 minutes. Heat a crepe pan or else a smooth frying pan with round sides and when very hot wipe with a cloth or pastry brush dipped in oil. Immediately ladle or pour in just enough batter to make a paper thin covering over the bottom of the pan - swirl the batter around the pan as you pour because it will set quickly. When bubbles form and the edges curl away from the sides of the pan, gently lift the pancake with your fingertips or a spatula and flip it over to cook the other side. Continue with the rest of the batter. Spread each pancake with some of the stuffing, roll up and put in a greased baking dish. Cover with the sauce, the tomatoes and the grated cheese. Bake in an oven preheated to 350°F/180°C/Gas4 for 15-20 minutes and then under a grill for a minute or two to make the top bubbling and golden. Serve with a crisp salad as a starter or light main course.

152

Driving to the Eremo di Calomini it is increasingly clear why it is obligatory to sound the car horn. A narrow mountain road with snake-like bends and recent worrying evidence of landslides leads slowly but persistently upwards to the final breath-taking view from this isolated monastery, that at week-ends has an open-air restaurant. It serves some of the best trout in Tuscany ~ if not the world ~ caught in the stream running beside the restaurant.

TROTA alla GARFAGNANA

Grilled trout as cooked in the Garfagnana

1 TROUT PER PERSON
COARSE SEA SALT
BLACK PEPPER
LEMON JUICE
FRESH ROSEMARY
OLIVE OIL

First prepare the fire. In Tuscany they use chestnut wood which gives a characteristic sweet taste to the fish. Failing this use a charcoal grill or the grill of your cooker. Clean, scale and rinse the trout under cold running water. Sprinkle the inside cavity with coarse sea salt, pepper and lemon juice and stuff with plenty of fresh rosemary (or if necessary use dried). Brush olive oil all over the fish & on the grill rack to prevent sticking. Cook the fish about 4~5 in/10~12.5 cm from the wood or charcoal, turning only once. The fish is cooked when the juices run out clear and the flesh is opaque, about 10 minutes for a 2 lb/450 g fish. This is very good served with a simple salad of finely sliced tomatoes, red peppers and onions.

For a more substantial meal cook small potatoes and tomatoes together as they do in the Garfagnana. Take 1~2 potatoes per person (cut in pieces if they are large) & 1 tomato, peeled & chopped for each potato. Put in a lidded flameproof casserole with 5~6 tbsp of olive oil per 6 small potatoes, 1~2 cloves of garlic, crushed, 1 carrot, 1 stick of celery and 1 large onion, all finely chopped. Add salt and black pepper to taste and cook over a low flame until the juice from the tomatoes has evaporated & potatoes are tender.

A particularly soft sweet flour is made from the chestnuts that grow so abundantly in the mountains north of the city of Pistoia. From it the local cooks make a strange, aromatic flat cake called castagnaccio. It is an acquired taste ~ difficult for non-Italians unused to sweets made with olive oil and rosemary, but certainly a taste that is very reminiscent of Tuscany.

Ricotta Puda
£4.60

CASTAGNACCIO
· Chestnut cake ·

This recipe comes from the big alimentari shop in Pistoia's permanent central market. The buxom proprietress was quite clearly amused that a foreigner should be asking for 'farina di castagna', chestnut flour, out of season (as the flour doesn't keep well it is only available from late autumn to spring, after the chestnut harvest) & also clearly concerned that it should be used properly.

1LB4OZ/550G SIFTED
   CHESTNUT FLOUR
1PT/550 ML WATER
4~5 SPRIGS ROSEMARY,
   COARSELY CHOPPED
5 TBSP OLIVE OIL
GENEROUS HANDFUL RAISINS
2½ OZ/60G PINENUTS
PINCH SALT
2 TBSP GRANULATED SUGAR

Mix chestnut flour and water carefully with wooden spoon or spatula so as not to form lumps. It should be quite a liquid batter. Add raisins, pinenuts, salt and sugar. Pour into a greased baking tray not more than 3/4 inch/2 cm deep. Sprinkle with the rosemary and drizzle the oil over the top. Bake in an oven preheated to 400°F/200°C/Gas 6 until brown and, as the Pistoian lady described it, 'cracked like dry earth' or, more accurately, about 40 minutes. It is delicious straight from the pan either hot or cold, dredged with icing sugar or smeared with honey and fresh ricotta cheese.

* PISTOIA * EARLY MORNING MARKET *

· CECCO ·

The town of Pescia is famous for its flowers, its proximity to Pinocchio's home town of Collodi and its local Asparagi giganti, although to those of us used to small tasty green stalks, these giants of the asparagus world are not so impressive.

· ZUPPA di FUNGHI ·
Wild mushroom soup (4)

This delicious and delicate soup is made at Cecco's with an amazing quantity of fresh porcini mushrooms (BOLETUS EDULIS).

Commercial mushrooms are no substitute but you can use other wild mushrooms such as morels and chanterelles or, and only if pressed, use cultivated mushrooms and add ¾ oz/15g of packaged dried porcini.

1 LB/450G SMALL CLEAN PORCINI
   (OR MORE IF YOU CAN AFFORD IT)
3~4 CUPS GOOD BEEF STOCK
CLOVE GARLIC, CRUSHED
2 TBSP PARSLEY, FINELY CHOPPED
5~6 LEAVES NEPITELLA (THIS IS
   CATMINT, IF IT IS NOT AVAILABLE
   USE ANY FRESH GARDEN MINT)
4 SLICES BREAD
OLIVE OIL
SALT & PEPPER

Heat a little olive oil in a medium-sized saucepan, cut the porcini into small pieces & sauté gently with the nepitella, adding salt and pepper to taste; When browned add the stock and then simmer for 10~15 minutes (with the dried mushrooms if using). After about 7 minutes stir in the garlic and parsley pounded together in a mortar. Toast the bread and rub with a garlic clove, freshly cut. Put the bread in bowls and pour the soup over.

POLLASTRINO al MATTONE
·Chicken under a brick (2)·

A mattone is a terracotta housebrick and the chicken in this recipe gets its characteristic crispy texture from the weight of a heavy glazed terracotta plate pressed down on it all through the cooking. You can buy traditional mattone plates in Lucca, or use any clean, heavy glazed terracotta brick.

1 SMALL CHICKEN, CUT IN HALF
   DOWN THE BREASTBONE AND
   POUNDED FAIRLY FLAT
JUICE OF 1 LEMON
CLOVE GARLIC, CRUSHED
FRESH ROSEMARY
3~4 TBSP OLIVE OIL
COARSE SEA SALT
COARSE GROUND BLACK PEPPER

Rub all the ingredients well into the chicken's skin and then put the chicken in a frying pan. Place the brick on top and fry (in plenty of olive oil) over a low heat for about 20 minutes on each side until the skin is crunchy. Or put the chicken in a marinade made of the same ingredients. Leave for several hours, turning occasionally, and then fry as above.

157

·· RESTAURANTS ··

Restaurants mentioned in
the text

· THE VALE of FLORENCE ·
BORGO ANTICO ~ Piazza Santa
Spirito, Florence
LA CARABACCIA ~ Via Palazzuolo,
Florence
LE CAVE DI MAIANO ~ Via delle
Cave 16, Maiano
CIBREO ~ Via de' Macci 118/R,
Florence
COCO LEZZONE ~ Via del Parioncino,
26r, Florence
DA GANINO ~ Piazza de' Cimatori,
4, Florence
MASHA INNOCENTI (cookery
school) ~ Via Trieste 1, Florence
SOSTANZA ~ Via del Porcellana 25,
Florence

· THE CHIANTI HILLS ·
ALBERGO LOCANDA GIOVANNI
DA VERRAZZANO ~ Greve
CASTELLO DI SPALTENNA ~ Gaiole
IL PEDINO ~ San Casciano in
Val di Pesa
TRATTORIA DEL MONTAGLIARI ~
near Panzano

· MEDIEVAL CITIES ·
BUCA DI SAN FRANCESCO ~ Via di
San Francesco 1, Arezzo
LOCANDA DELL'AMOROSA ~ Sinalunga
PONTE A RONDOLINO ~ Via Sevestro
32, San Gimignano

· VINES & VINEYARDS ·
LA CASANOVA ~ Strada della
Vittoria 10, Chianciano Terme

DIVA ~ Via Gracciano nel Corso
92, Montepulciano
FATTORIA DEI BARBI ~ 4 km
from Montalcino on the road
to Castelnuovo dell'Abate
FATTORIA LA CHIUSA ~ Via della
Madonnina 88, Montefollónico
FATTORIA PULCINO ~ Località
Fonte Castagno, Montepulciano

· THE ETRUSCAN MAREMMA ·
BAR LUPI ~ Sorano
DA LAUDOMIA ~ Poderi di
Montemerano
TANA DEL CINGHIALE ~ Tirli

· BY THE SEA ·
DA GUERRA ~ Portoferraio, Elba
RENDEZ-VOUS DA MARCELLO ~
Marciana Marina, Elba
RISTORANTE ENOTECA SERGIO ~
Lungarno Pacinotti 1, Pisa
PONTE DI SASSO ~ Località Ponte
di Sasso, Viareggio
DA ROMANO ~ Via Mazzini 122,
Viareggio

· OLIVES & CHESTNUTS ·
LA BUCA DI SANT'ANTONIO, Via
della Cervia 3, Lucca
CECCO ~ Viale Forti 84, Pescia
DA GIULIO IN PELLERIA ~ Via
San Tommaso 29, Lucca
TRATTORIA LA MORA ~ Località
Sesto di Moriano 104
VIPORE ~ Località Pieve Santo
Stefano

· INDEX ·

Recipes are indexed according
to their English names

SAUCES, SOUPS & STARTERS
Sauces, hunter's, for game   69
     rabbit, for pasta   88
     sausage, for pasta   87
     walnut, for pasta   49
Soups, bean   90
   bread & tomato   25
   chicken   126
   chicken & wine   81
   dandelion   93
   egg & tomato   105
   fish   127,136
   grain & bean   148
   onion   14,16
   spring vegetable   149
   tomato & bread   25,106
   wild mushroom   156
Starters, broad beans with
   cheese & ham   29
   chicken livers with lemon   37
   chicken livers on toast   19
   olive oil dip   58
   ricotta, grilled with herbs   29
   sage leaf rolls   35
   spinach crepes   150
   tomatoes on toast   48

· BREAD, PASTA & RICE ·
Bread, chickpea   48
   flat savoury   82
   garlic   29
   rosemary   38
   saints' (fruit)   96
   Tuscan country   65
Pasta, butterflies with peas   20
   cooked in a bag   130
   eggless   87
   naked   78
   with chickpea soup   75
   with seafood   118
   with spinach & ricotta   76
Polenta, deep fried   49

Rice, black (with squid)   120
   risotto with white wine   71
   spring risotto   91

· FISH ·
Eels with sage & garlic   140
Mixed fish stew   121
Red mullet & tomatoes   121
Sardines, grilled   115
Trout, grilled   153
Tuna & bean salad   125
   and new potato salad   125
Turbot with asparagus   132

· POULTRY, MEAT & GAME ·
Beef, in red wine   54
   boiled, with tarragon   75
Boar with apples   100
Chicken, enraged with chilis   123
   stuffed   135
   under a brick   157
   with lemon sauce   27
Duck with vin santo   32
Hare in strong sweet sauce   101
Lamb with olives   146
Pork in milk   106
   liver bruschettes   57
   meatballs   52
   roast   51
Rabbit, stuffed   56
   with olives   26
Sausages with polenta   137
Tripe, Florentine   17
Veal stew   52

· VEGETABLES ·
Artichoke omelette   18
Beans cooked in a bottle   21
   cooked like small birds   30
Borage omelette   95
Chickpea stew   124
Courgettes see Zucchini
Nettle souffle   93
Onions, stuffed   102
Potatoes & tomatoes   153

Spinach & chicken livers 80
  & ricotta 'ravioli' 78
  crepes 150
  with pine nuts 33
Tomato & basil omelette 108
  and bread salad 45
  pie 109
Vegetable stew 114
Zucchini flower fritters 69
  flowers, stuffed 70
  pie 139
  whole, stuffed 117

· DESSERTS & PASTRIES ·

Biscuits, Prato 36
  sweet almond 67
Cake, chestnut 154
  grandmother's 28
  grape 46
  Sienese spice (Panforte) 66
Pastry twists 23
Pears with pecorino 29
Raspberry & red wine sorbet 128
Sweet green pie 145
Walnut rolls 107